The
Rough
Road
Home

The

University

of North

Carolina

Press

Chapel Hill

& London

STORIES

BY

NORTH

CAROLINA

WRITERS

Edited & with an Introduction by

ROBERT GINGHER

The
Rough
Road
Home

Manufactured in the

United States of America

03 02 01 00 99

7 6 5 4 3

Library of Congress

Cataloging-in-Publication Data

The rough road home : stories by

North Carolina writers / edited and with

an introduction by Robert Gingher.

　　p.　cm.

ISBN 0-8078-2064-4 (cloth : alk. paper).—

ISBN 0-8078-4397-0 (pbk. : alk. paper)

1. Short stories, American—North Carolina.

2. North Carolina—Fiction.

I. Gingher, Robert.

PS558.N8R68 1992 92-53705

813'.01089756—dc20 CIP

Permission to reproduce

these stories can be found

on page 331 of this volume.

FOR SUSAN

Contents

Acknowledgments

In preparing this anthology I am indebted to hundreds of students who have commented on and applauded in class these and other stories by North Carolina writers. In my reading of short fiction, and especially of southern narrative, I am grateful for the influence of many teachers, particularly Louis D. Rubin, Jr., and Weldon Thornton, and the late C. Hugh Holman, Lewis Leary, and Richard Walser.

Without the invaluable resources of Fred Chappell, Lee Smith, and especially Max Steele this collection would, I believe, have been less representative and interesting – though an anthology by any one of these writer-teachers would surely vary greatly from this one. I owe debts to Weldon Thornton for his encouraging evaluation of a much longer early version of the introduction; to George Core for his incisive reading of an unrelated piece, which helped spare the reader unnecessary prose here; to Laurie White for a close, thoughtful review; to Kathy Shaer for her help with credits, and to David Perry and Sandy Eisdorfer, editor's editors; and to Susan McMullen, my faithful and attentive wife. Special thanks to producer Gary

Hawkins for his inspiring dramatic documentary (the UNC-TV production, "The Rough South") on Tim McLaurin and to Tina Secreast for insisting that I see it and meet him. Without the important contributions of other colleagues, friends, and acquaintances, I would have been less happy with the selections included here.

I am especially thankful for the blessing and patience of Susan, Sam, Rory, Bryan, Kristina, and Jeff, and for the support of my mother and father, Annette and Clair Gingher.

Introduction

It has been over forty years since the University of North Carolina Press published *North Carolina and the Short Story* and more than thirty since its *Short Stories of the Old North State*. With the dramatic rise in short story writers from North Carolina (or with strong North Carolina ties), a new collection celebrating North Carolina short story writers is clearly overdue.

The most striking current literary phenomenon is the resurgence of the American short story, with North Carolina hands-down contributing the lion's share per state. Per capita, North Carolina arguably "raises" more writers than any state in the country, or it sure feels like it (the North Carolina Writers Network, at last count, had a membership of something over twelve hundred).

A haven for writers? One thinks of the stellar teaching of Randall Jarrell at the University of North Carolina at Greensboro (then Woman's College) or of Jessie Rehder at the University of North Carolina at Chapel Hill and, not least, of William Blackburn at Duke, among whose students number

Fred Chappell, Reynolds Price, William Styron, and Anne Tyler.

Other fine writing teachers — most of the writers in this collection — have for years shaped the direction of fiction writers here and abroad. So has the University of North Carolina at Greensboro's spirited writing program, one of the finest Master of Fine Arts programs in writing in the country. We must also reckon with the enduring mark Greensboro's William Sidney Porter (O. Henry) left on the short story and Thomas Wolfe on the novel.

The Rough Road Home is a representative collection of spirited stories by North Carolina writers. All the authors have lived in North Carolina (twenty of the twenty-two still do), and most have grown up here. As writers they have found wings to fly away from home only to return imaginatively and behold it with new eyes.

Readers enjoy geographical correlatives. Unlike many of the townsfolk Thomas Wolfe caricatured in 1929, we relish knowing that our best-known writer drew from his Asheville hometown to create "Altamont" in *Look Homeward, Angel*. Or that he fabricated "Pulpit Hill" from his Chapel Hill student days at the University of North Carolina.

We like knowing that Alice Adams recreates Chapel Hill as "Hilton" in the title story of her collection *Return Trips*; that Daphne Athas recasts both Chapel Hill and Carrboro in *Entering Ephesus*; that Fred Chappell reconstructs Canton in *I Am One of You Forever*; that Allan Gurganus's fictional Falls, North Carolina, in some way springs from his native town of Rocky Mount; that Robert Morgan's *The Blue Valleys* evolves from the Blue Ridge Mountains; that Reynolds Price's fictional landscape originates in Warren County; that Donald Secreast chisels the furniture-industry town of "Boehm" from Lenoir.

But what makes a writer a "North Carolina writer" — other than the obvious matters of residence and/or fictional terrain? Beyond the complex ways territories claim their dwellers, there is no easy answer. Certainly any reader imaginatively visiting

Clyde Edgerton's Listre, North Carolina, could be interested in the small rural communities that served as its inspiration; however, that reader will likely be more interested in how Edgerton renders what Tim McLaurin calls the "eternal and internal" dimensions of Home itself and its constant foil, the Road.

Only incidentally do the directions on narrative maps run west and east, south and north. The important directions are familiar and mysterious, here and there. Our best narratives explore and elaborate upon the escape from and return to home.

Family, habit, custom, and the past are the raw, requisite materials of any wayfarer. As the clichés suggest, *familiarity breeds contempt* and *absence makes the heart grow fonder*. The voyager hears the call of the Road. It is the classic highway to the outside, and the stranger, its representative, signifies the Extraordinary. But the traveler leaves home's cloister only temporarily, ever to return and witness its glory anew. *There's no place like home*: Dorothy and Don Quixote have things to tell us.

The dramatic introduction of these themes – home and road – occurs in one of two ways: either by a journey away from home or a visitor arriving there. Each of the twenty-two stories gathered here involves in some way, usually quite directly, an outsider or a voyage. This flight-and-return pattern is in the genes, as old as blood.

It is an honorable and substantial theme in North Carolina fiction, as the titles of Thomas Wolfe's *Look Homeward, Angel* and *You Can't Go Home Again* testify. Stories show us we *can* go home again, but it's a rough road back. At journey's end we "arrive where we started/ And know the place for the first time."

Mystery, the extraordinary incident, may be dynamite for petrified custom as in stories here by Alice Adams, Maya Angelou, Elizabeth Cox, Kaye Gibbons, Allan Gurganus, Randall Kenan, Tim McLaurin, Robert Morgan, Reynolds Price,

Louis Rubin, Jr., Elizabeth Spencer, and Lee Zacharias. On the other hand, *Custom*, the ordinary, the code of durable community, may itself appraise the unfamiliar. It may challenge or even eliminate the renegade who confronts accustomed order or threatens its well-being. Protagonists of the stories by Doris Betts, Linda Beatrice Brown, Fred Chappell, and Charles Edward Eaton fit precisely into that conflict. Or the collision between mystery and custom may produce irresistible humor, as witnessed in the stories by Daphne Athas, Clyde Edgerton, Jill McCorkle, Donald Secreast, Lee Smith, and Max Steele.

There are lessons here surely older than Boccaccio, Apuleius, or even Homer. The dream of escaping custom and convention seems to be a compulsory rite of passage in human evolution. In Joyce's *A Portrait of the Artist as a Young Man* Stephen Dedalus strives to "fly by the nets" of all to which he is accustomed — family, religion, race. But only in *Ulysses* does he learn not to fly wild like Icarus but to soar prudently like his namesake. The worthy artist must look closer to home, must in some measure embrace roots and custom in order to render them authentically. Mere exit is the way of hubris or folly, of linear and isolate knowledge.

There is no Eldorado, so the right road must ever take us not beyond but back — to the here and now. The true road provides not an escape *from* reality but an escape *to* reality. The hero's success "in circuit lies." The kingdom of heaven on earth can only be witnessed by the returning traveler — Dorothy with her back to Oz or Ulysses beholding Penelope after slaying the ravening suitors. Wisdom, grace, and joy are the way that turns back in, the honest return to root and origin.

Narrative recounts wisdom gleaned in the bruising, familiar flight from the mannerly. It features broken wings, dreams, or blossoms in all the familiar human varieties. The heroic voyage — necessarily at the heart of any story worth recounting — relates separation from the familiar, encounter with mystery, and a return in which the familiar is apprehended in a profoundly new form. The stories collected here illustrate the manifold enlightening ways in which mystery, in fiction as in life, penetrates the familiar, leaving us a bit wiser, or at least more wondering.

One constitutional quality of any anthology – especially one put together in a state teeming with first-rate writers – is the impossibility of "definitive" selection. Every reader is an anthologist of sorts with particular stories in mind and heart. Add to these private "anthologies" North Carolina's profusion of writers – not to mention the delimiting business of permission rights. A one-volume collection will clearly displease the reader in search of *the* anthology. But then *The Rough Road Home* is not intended as a "best" anthology but as a useful and representative one. I hope it will be one of several anthologies to celebrate – take your pick – our "regional" writers, or some of the best writers writing today.

The
Rough
Road
Home

We shall not cease from exploration

And the end of all our exploring

Will be to arrive where we started

And know the place for the first time.

– T. S. Eliot, "Little Gidding"

   from *Four Quartets*

The dragon is by the side of the road, watching those who

pass. Beware lest he devour you. We go to the Father of Souls,

but it is necessary to pass by the dragon.

– St. Cyril of Jerusalem

   From the preface to Flannery O'Connor's

   "A Good Man Is Hard to Find"

Tell all the Truth but tell it slant –

Success in Circuit lies

Too bright for our infirm Delight

The Truth's superb surprise

As Lightning to the Children eased

With explanation kind

The Truth must dazzle gradually

Or every man be blind –

– Emily Dickinson, "1129"

The Oasis

In Palm Springs the poor are as dry as old brown leaves, blown in from the desert – wispily thin and almost invisible. Perhaps they are embarrassed at finding themselves among so much opulence (Indeed, why are they there at all? Why not somewhere else?), among such soaring, thick-trunked palms, such gleamingly white, palatial hotels.

And actually, poor people are only seen in the more or less outlying areas, the stretch of North Canyon Drive, for example, where even the stores are full of sleazy, cut-rate goods, and the pastel stucco hotels are small, one-story, and a little seedy, with small, shallow, too-bright blue pools. The poor are not seen in those stores, though, and certainly not in even the tawdriest motels; they stick to the street; for the most part they keep moving. A hunched up, rag-bound man with his swollen bundle (of what? impossible to guess) might lean against a sturdy palm tree, so much fatter and stronger than he is – but only for a moment, and he would be looking around, aware of himself as displaced. And on one of the city benches a poor woman with her plastic splintered bag looks perched there, an uneasy, watchful bird, with sharp, fierce, wary eyes.

A visibly rich person would look quite odd there too, in that nebulous, interim area, unless he or she were just hurrying through – maybe running, in smart pale jogging clothes, or briskly stepping along toward the new decorator showrooms, just springing up on the outskirts of town. In any case, rich people, except in cars, are seen in that particular area of Palm Springs as infrequently as the very poor are.

However, on a strange day in early April – so cold, such a biting wind, in a place where bad weather is almost unheard of and could be illegal – on that day a woman all wrapped in fine pale Italian wool and French silk, with fine, perfect champagne hair and an expensive color on her mouth – that woman, whose name is Clara Gibson, sits on a bench in what she knows is the wrong part of Palm Springs (she also knows that it is the wrong day for her to be there), and she wonders what on earth to do.

There are certain huge and quite insoluble problems lying always heavily on her mind (is this true of everyone? She half suspects that it is, but has wondered); these have to do with her husband and her daughter, and with an entity that she vaguely and rather sadly thinks of as herself. But at the moment she can do nothing about any of these three quite problematic people. And so she concentrates on what is immediate, the fact that she has a billfold full of credit cards and almost no cash: a ten, two ones, not even much change. And her cards are not coded for sidewalk cash withdrawal from banks because her husband, Bradley, believes that this is dangerous. Also: Today is Tuesday, and because she confused the dates (or something) she will be here alone until Thursday, when Bradley arrives. The confusion itself is suspicious, so unlike her; was she anxious to get away from her daughter, Jennifer, whom she was just visiting in San Francisco? Or, did she wish to curtail Bradley's time alone at his meetings, in Chicago? However, this is not the time for such imponderables. She must simply decide what to do for the rest of the afternoon, and where best to go for dinner – by herself, on a credit card; the hotel in which she is staying (the wrong hotel, another error) does not serve meals.

And she must decide whether or not to give her last ten dollars to the withered, dessicated woman, with such crazed, dark, terrified eyes, whom she has been watching on the bench one down from hers. A woman very possibly her own age, or maybe younger; no one could tell. But: Should she give her the money, and if so how? (It hardly matters whether Clara is left with ten or two.)

And: Why has this poor woman come to Palm Springs, of all places? Was it by mistake? Is she poor because a long time ago she made a mistaken, wrong marriage – just as Clara's own was so eminently "right"? (Marriage, for women, has often struck Clara as a sort of horse race.) But now Clara passionately wonders all these things about this woman, and she wonders too if there is a shelter for such people here. From time to time she has given money to some of the various shelter organizations in New York, where she comes from, but she has meant to do more, perhaps to go and work in one. Is there a welfare office with emergency funds available for distribution? Or have all the cuts that one reads about affected everything? Lots of MX missiles, no relief. Is there a free clinic, in case the woman is sick?

Something purple is wound among the other garments around that woman's shoulders: a remnant of a somewhat better life or a handout from someone? But it can't be warm, that purple thing, and the wind is terrible.

If Clara doesn't somehow – soon – give her the money, that woman will be gone, gone scuttering down the street like blown tumbleweed, thinks Clara, who is suddenly sensing the desert that surrounds them as an inimical force. Miles of desert, which she has never seen before, so much vaster than this small, square, green, artificial city.

Clara's plane had arrived promptly at 10:10 this morning, and after her first strange views of gray, crevassed mountains, the airport building was comfortingly small, air-conditioned (unnecessary, as things turned out, in this odd cold weather), with everything near and accessible.

The first thing she found out was that the plane from Chicago, due in at 10:30 (this reunion has been a masterpiece of timing, Clara had thought) would not arrive until 11:04. An easy wait; Clara even welcomed the time, during which she could redo her face (Brad, a surgeon, is a perfectionist in such matters), and reassemble her thoughts about and reactions to their daughter. What to tell Brad and what to relegate to her own private, silent scrutiny.

Should it be upsetting that a daughter in her early thirties earns more money than her father does at almost twice her age, her father the successful surgeon? (Clara has even secretly thought that surgeons quite possibly charge too much: Is it right, really, for operations to impoverish people? not to mention rumors that some operations are not even necessary?) In any case, Jennifer, a corporation lawyer, is a very rich, very young person. And she is unhappy, and the cause of her discomfort is nothing as simple as not being married – the supposedly classic complaint among young women of her age. Jennifer does not want to get married, yet, although she goes out a great deal with young men. What she seems to want, really, is even more money than she has, and more *things*. She has friends of her own age and education who are earning more money than she is, even, who own more boats and condominiums. This is all very distressing to her mother; the very unfamiliarity of such problems and attitudes is upsetting (plus the hated word Yuppie, which would seem to apply). Resolutely, as she sat there in the waiting room, Clara, with her perfectly made up face, decided that she would simply say to Brad, "Well, Jennifer's fine. She looks marvelous, she's going out a lot but nothing serious. And she's earning scads of money." (Scads? A word she has not used nor surely heard for many years, not since the days when she seemed to understand so much more than she seems to now.)

Brad, though, was not among the passengers from Chicago who poured through the gate in their inappropriate warm-weather vacation clothes, swinging tennis rackets, sacks of golf clubs.

Clara sat down to think. Out of habit, then, and out of some small nagging suspicion, she checked her small pocket notebook – and indeed it was she who had arrived on the wrong day, Tuesday. Brad would come, presumably, on Thursday.

Just next to her yellow plastic bench was a glassed-in gift shop where she could see a shelf of toy animals, one of which she remarked on as especially appealing: a silky brown dog about the size of some miniature breed. Now, as Clara watched, a woman in a fancy pink pants suit came up to exclaim, to stroke the head of the toy. A man, her companion, did the same, and then another group came over to pet and to exclaim over the adorable small false dog.

Clara found this small tableau unaccountably disturbing, and on a sudden wave of decisiveness she got up and went out to the curb where the taxis and hotel limousines assembled. She asked the snappily uniformed man about transportation to the Maxwell. Oh yes, he assured her; a limousine. And then, "You know there're two Maxwells?"

No, Clara did not know that.

His agile eyes appraised her hair, her careful face, her clothes. "Well, I'm sure you'd be going to the Maxwell Plaza," he concluded, and he ushered her into a long white stretch Mercedes, in which she was driven for several miles of broad palm-lined streets to a huge but wonderfully low-key hotel, sand-colored – the desert motif continued in cactus plantings, a green display of succulents.

At the desk, though, in that largest and most subdued of lobbies, Clara was gently, firmly informed that she (they) had no reservation. And, "Could Mrs. Gibson possibly have booked into the Maxwell Oasis by mistake?" This of course was the Maxwell *Plaza*.

Well, indeed it was possible that Clara had made that mistake. However, should anyone, especially her husband, *Doctor* Gibson, call or otherwise try to get in touch with her here, at the Plaza, would they kindly direct him to the Oasis, which is (probably) where Clara would be?

The Maxwell Oasis is out on North Canyon Drive, not far from the bench on which Clara was to sit and to observe the windblown man and the fierce-eyed, purple-swathed bag lady.

The Oasis is small, a pink stucco, peeling, one-story building, with a small blue oblong pool. All shrouded with seedy bougainvillea. And it was there, indeed, that Clara by some chance or mischance had made a reservation. But for Thursday, not Tuesday, not today; however, luckily, they still had a room available.

In the lower level bar of the Maxwell Plaza, though, the desert has been lavishly romanticized: behind the huge, deep, dark leather armchairs are glassed-in displays of permanently flowering cactus, interesting brown shapes of rocks, and bright polished skulls (not too many skulls, just a tasteful few).

Clara, after her meditative, observant afternoon on the bench, decided that it would make some sort of sense to come to this hotel for a drink and dinner. But just now (so out of character for her) she is engaged in telling a series of quite egregious lies to some people who are perfectly all right, probably, but who have insisted that she join them for a drink. A couple: just plain rich, aging people from Seattle, who assume that a woman alone must be lonely.

"Of course I've always loved the desert," has been Clara's first lie. The desert on closer acquaintance could become acutely terrifying is what she truly thinks.

She has also given them a curious version of her daughter, Jennifer, describing her as a social worker in East Oakland,

" – not much money but she's *very* happy." And she has been gratified to hear her companions, "Oh, isn't that nice! So many young people these days are so – so materialistic. What is it they call them? Yuppies!" Beaming at Clara, who is not the mother of a Yuppie.

The only excuse that Clara can make for her own preposterousness is that their joining her was almost forcible. She was enjoying her drink alone and her private thoughts. She was recalling what happened earlier that very afternoon, when, just as she was reaching into her purse for the ten-dollar bill which, yes, she would give to the bag lady (who fortunately seemed to have dozed off on her bench) Clara remembered the hundred secreted (always, on Brad's instructions) in the lining of her bag. And so, tiptoeing (feeling foolish, tiptoes on a sidewalk) Clara slipped both bills down into the red plastic bag, out of sight.

She had been imagining, thinking of the woman's discovery of the money – surely she would be pleased? She needed it for something? – at the very moment these Seattle tourists came and practically sat on top of her.

Clara had been thinking of how Brad would have objected. But what will that woman do with it, he would have wondered. Suppose she has a drinking problem? Clara recognizes that she herself does not much care what the woman does with her money; she simply wanted to make the gift of it. It will do no harm, she believes – although pitifully little good, so little to assuage the thick, heavy terribleness of that life, of most lives.

And then she heard, "Well, you can't sit there drinking all by yourself? You must let us join you."

Aside from their ill-timed intrusiveness, these people are annoying to Clara because (she has to face this) in certain clear ways they so strongly resemble herself and Brad. The woman's hair is the same improbably fragile pale wine color, her clothes Italian/French. And the man's clothes are just like Brad's, doctor-banker-lawyer clothes (Nixon-Reagan clothes). The couple effect is markedly similar.

And so, partly to differentiate herself from these honest, upright, upper-middle-class citizens, Clara continues to lie.

"No, my husband isn't coming along on this trip," she tells them. "I like to get away by myself." And she smiles, a bright, independent-woman smile. "My life in New York seems impossible sometimes."

As she thinks, Well, that is at least partially true. And, conceivably, Brad too has confused the dates, and will not show up for some time – another week? I could be here by myself for quite a while, Clara thinks, though she knows this to be unlikely. But I could go somewhere else?

No, she says to the couple from Seattle, she is not going to have dinner in this hotel. She has to meet someone.

Actually Clara on the way here noticed a big, flashy delicatessen, a place that assuredly will take her credit cards. But, a place where a bag lady might possibly go? A bag lady with a little recent cash? Very likely not; still, the very possibility is more interesting than that of dinner with this couple.

Clara stands up, and the gentleman too rises. "Well," says Clara, "I've certainly enjoyed talking to you."

Which she very much hopes will be her last lie for quite some time, even if that will take a certain rearrangement of her life.

M A Y A   A N G E L O U

The Reunion

Nobody could have told me that she'd be out with a black man; out, like going out. But there she was in 1958, sitting up in the Blue Palm Café, when I played the Sunday matinee with Cal Callen's band.

Here's how it was. After we got on the stage, the place was packed, first Cal led us into "D. B. Blues." Of course I know just like everybody else that Cal's got a thing for Lester Young. Maybe because Cal plays the tenor sax, or maybe because he's about as red as Lester Young, or maybe just cause Lester is the Prez. Anybody that's played with Cal knows that the kickoff tune is gotta be "D. B. Blues." So I was ready. We romped.

I'd played with some of those guys, but never all together, but we took off on that tune like we were headed for Birdland in New York City. The audience liked it. Applauded as much as black audiences ever applaud. Black folks act like they are sure that with a little bit of study they could do whatever you're doing on the stage as well as you do it. If not better. So they clap for your luck. Lucky for you that they're not up there to show you where it's really at.

9

Anyway, after the applause, Cal started to introduce the band. That's his style. Everybody knows that too. After he's through introducing everybody, he's not going to say anything else till the next set, it doesn't matter how many times we play. So he's got a little comedy worked into the introduction patter. He started with Olly, the trumpet man. . . . "And here we have a real Chicagoan . . . by way of Atlanta, Georgia . . . bringing soul to Soulville . . . Mr. Olly Martin."

He went on. I looked out into the audience. People sitting, not listening, or better, listening with one side of their ears and talking with both sides of their mouths. Some couples were making a little love . . . and some whites were there trying hard to act natural . . . like they come to the South Side of Chicago every day or maybe like they live there . . . then I saw her. Saw Miss Beth Ann Baker, sitting up with her blond self with a big black man . . . pretty black man. What? White girls, when they look alike, can look so much alike, I thought maybe it wasn't Beth. I looked again. It was her. I remember too well the turn of her cheek. The sliding way her jaw goes up to her hair. That was her. I might have missed a few notes, I might have in fact missed the whole interlude music.

What was she doing in Chicago? On the South Side. And with a black man? Beth Ann Baker of the Baker Cotton Gin. Miss Cotton Queen Baker of Georgia . . .

Then I heard Cal get round to me. He saved me for the last. Mainly cause I'm female and he can get a little rise out of the audience if he says, as he did say, "And our piano man is a lady. And what a lady. A cooker and a looker. Ladies and Gentlemen, I'd like to introduce to you Miss Philomena Jenkins. Folks call her Meanie." I noticed some applause, but mainly I was watching Beth. She heard my name and she looked right into my eyes. Her blue ones got as big as my black ones. She recognized me, in fact in a second we tipped eyelids at each other. Not winking. Just squinting, to see better. There was something that I couldn't recognize. Something I'd never seen in all those years in Baker, Georgia. Not panic, and it wasn't fear. Whatever was in that face seemed familiar, but before I could really read it, Cal announced our next number. "Round 'bout Midnight."

That used to be my song, for so many reasons. In Baker, the only time I could practice jazz, in the church, was round 'bout midnight. When the best chord changes came to me it was generally round 'bout midnight. When my first lover held me in his arms, it was round 'bout midnight. Usually when it's time to play that tune I dig right in it. But this time, I was too busy thinking about Beth and her family . . . and what she was doing in Chicago, on the South Side, escorted by the grooviest looking cat I'd seen in a long time. I was really trying to figure it out, then Cal's saxophone pushed its way into my figurings. Forced me to remember "Round 'bout Midnight." Reminded me of the years of loneliness, the doing-without days, the C.M.E. church, and the old ladies with hands like men and round 'bout midnight dreams of crossing over Jordan. Then I took thirty-two bars. My fingers found the places between the keys where the blues and the truth lay hiding. I dug out the story of a woman without a man, and a man without hope. I tried to wedge myself in and lay down in the groove between B-flat and B-natural. I must of gotten close to it, because the audience brought me out with their clapping. Even Cal said, "Yeah baby, that's it." I nodded to him then to the audience and looked around for Beth.

How did she like them apples? What did she think of little Philomena that used to shake the farts out of her sheets, wash her dirty drawers, pick up after her slovenly mama? What did she think now? Did she know that I was still aching from the hurt Georgia put on me? But Beth was gone. So was her boyfriend.

I had lived with my parents until I was thirteen in the servants' quarters. A house behind the Baker main house. Daddy was the butler, my mother was the cook, and I went to a segregated school on the other side of town where the other kids called me the Baker Nigger. Momma's nimble fingers were never able to sew away the truth of Beth's hand-me-down and thrown away clothing. I had a lot to say to Beth, and she was gone.

That was a bring-down. I guess what I wanted was to rub her face in "See now, you thought all I would ever be was you and your mama's flunky." And "See now, how folks, even you, pay to listen to me" and "See now, I'm saying something nobody else can say. Not the way I say it, anyway." But her table was empty.

We did the rest of the set. Some of my favorite tunes, "Sophisticated Lady," "Misty," and "Cool Blues." I admit that I never got back into the groove until we did "When Your Lover Has Gone."

After the closing tune, "Lester Leaps In," which Cal set at a tempo like he was trying to catch the last train to Mobile, was over, the audience gave us their usual thank-you, and we were off for a twenty-minute intermission.

Some of the guys went out to turn on and a couple went to tables where they had ladies waiting for them. But I went to the back of the dark smoky bar where even the occasional sunlight from the front door made no difference. My blood was still fluttering in my fingertips, throbbing. If she was listed in the phone directory I would call her. Hello Miss Beth . . . this is Philomena . . . who was your maid, whose whole family worked for you. Or could I say, Hello Beth. Is this Beth? Well, this is Miss Jenkins. I saw you yesterday at the Blue Palm Café. I used to know your parents. In fact your mother said my mother was a gem, and my father was a treasure. I used to laugh 'cause your mother drank so much whiskey, but my Momma said, "Judge not, that ye be not judged." Then I found out your father had three children down in our part of town and they all looked just like you, only prettier. Oh Beth, now . . . now . . . shouldn't have a chip . . . mustn't be bitter . . . She of course would hang up.

Just imagining what I would have said to her cheered me up. I ordered a drink from the bartender and settled back into my reverie. . . . Hello Beth . . . this is a friend from Baker. What were you doing with that black man Sunday? . . .

"Philomena? Remember me?" She stood before me absorbing the light. The drawl was still there. The soft accent rich white girls practice in Georgia to show that they had breeding. I couldn't think of anything to say. Did I remember her? There was no way I could answer the question.

"I asked Willard to wait for me in the car. I wanted to talk to you."

I sipped my drink and looked in the mirror over the bar and wondered what she really wanted. Her reflection wasn't threatening at all.

"I told him that we grew up . . . in the same town."

I was relieved that she hadn't said we grew up together. By the time I was ten, I knew growing up meant going to work. She smiled and I held my drink.

"I'm engaged to Willard and very happy."

I'm proud of my face. It didn't jump up and walk the bar.

She gave a practiced nod to the bartender and ordered a drink. "He teaches high school here on the South Side." Her drink came and she lifted the glass and our eyes met in the mirror. "I met him two years ago in Canada. We are very happy."

Why the hell was she telling me her fairy story? We weren't kin. So she had a black man. Did she think like most whites in mixed marriages that she had done the whole race a favor?

"My parents . . ." her voice became small, whispery. "My parents don't understand. They think I'm with Willard just to spite them. They . . . When's the last time you went home, Mena?" She didn't wait for my answer.

"They hate him. So much, they say they will disown me." Disbelief made her voice strong again. "They said I could never set foot in Baker again." She tried to catch my eyes in the mirror but I looked down at my drink. "I know there's a lot wrong with Baker, but it's my home." The drawl was turning into a whine. "Mother said, now mind you, she has never laid eyes on Willard, she said, if she had dreamed when I was a baby that I would grow up to marry a nig . . . a black man, she'd have choked me to death on her breast. That's a cruel thing for a mother to say. I told her so."

She bent forward and I shifted to see her expression, but her profile was hidden by the blond hair. "He doesn't understand, and me either. He didn't grow up in the South." I thought, no matter where he grew up, he wasn't white and rich and spoiled. "I just wanted to talk to somebody who knew me. Knew Baker. You know, a person can get lonely. . . . I don't see any of my friends, anymore. Do you understand, Mena? My parents gave me everything."

Well, they owned everything.

"Willard is the first thing I ever got for myself. And I'm not going to give him up."

We faced each other for the first time. She sounded like her mother and looked like a ten-year-old just before a tantrum.

"He's mine. He belongs to me."

The musicians were tuning up on the bandstand. I drained my glass and stood.

"Mena, I really enjoyed seeing you again, and talking about old times. I live in New York, but I come to Chicago every other weekend. Say, will you come to our wedding? We haven't set the date yet. Please come. It's going to be here . . . in a black church . . . somewhere."

"Good-bye Beth. Tell your parents I said to go to hell and take you with them, just for company."

I sat down at the piano. She still had everything. Her mother would understand the stubbornness and send her off to Paris or the Moon. Her father couldn't deny that black skin was beautiful. She had money and a wonderful-looking man to play with. If she stopped wanting him she could always walk away. She'd still be white.

The band was halfway into the "D. B. Blues" release before I thought, she had the money, but I had the music. She and her parents had had the power to hurt me when I was young, but look, the stuff in me lifted me up high above them. No matter how bad times became, I would always be the song struggling to be heard.

The piano keys were slippery with tears. I know, I sure as hell wasn't crying for myself.

Hugh

I first met Hugh Cox in Wilson Library, there being no Davis-Royall then, when he came up to me and said he'd heard my reading at a Bull's Head Bookshop Tea where Muriel Mebane introduced my first novel, *The Smell of the Dark*, and a woman had come up afterward and warned me not to be like Virginia Woolf and kill myself. I'd told her defensively: "I identify with Carson McCullers, *The Heart is a Lonely Hunter*," being spooked by the thought that long noses might mean propensity to suicide.

Hugh was writing one story a week in the Wilson reference room. We joked about the creaking oaken chairs which looked like upside-down behinds, protuberances to fit crevices. He'd just sold stories to *Harper's*, *The Atlantic*, and to *Collier's*. He said he always knew when I was in the library — he heard me creaking. I invited him to my house. I was sponging off my family till I finished my second novel. He was starting a novel, he said.

In our living room a week later he told me about the misprint on page 39 of my book. Where it was supposed to be

"She stroked her thin elbows," they had put a "g" after the "thin." "She stroked her 'thing'" he quoted with his Georgia accent, plopping the syllable out of his mouth like a tobacco wad into a can.

I'd never thought of writers as jokers. To me writing meant Truth of Life, but from that moment I knew I was going to introduce him to Lake who'd been my friend for a year. She was a *sensitif*, poet and aristocrat who'd had TB like Keats, Katherine Mansfield and Hans Castorp, and been in a sanitarium and had her dishes scalded. She lived in a cinderblock hut named Hiroshima in a field opposite Moody's Gas Station at the fork in Carrboro. I knew he'd be fascinated with her and vice versa.

Lake, Hugh and I had already been out in life, Lake in Chicago, Hugh in Trinidad in the army as a meteorologist on the Green Project deploying troops from the ETO to the Pacific War Zone, and me in New York typing for the Office of War Information. Our return to Chapel Hill had coincided with the GI Bill – Hugh was on it – and the town was exciting, bursting with intellectually serious veterans, real men, older than the beer-frat types before the war. But for us it was retread. We'd been here before, studied here, and now we were back, living cheap, trying to finish our novels while we waited for one thing: to get to Europe.

Whenever Lake didn't want people to visit, she strung red or yellow yarn across the door like a spider web. But it was all clear today, so we knocked and waited. When she came to the door, my advance hype had so intimidated Hugh, who was shy really, that he couldn't think of anything to say. We stood there nervously and then went in. He still couldn't think of anything to say.

"Diagram yourself," I told him.

He was shocked. She was too.

"Diagraph," he corrected.

It was the We of Me Era. We were into identity. Hugh said I'd gotten my first novel out of Muriel Mebane's garbage can. So much for its being autobiographical. I retorted his name was really "Harold Huguenot Cox" which was true, he just called himself Hugh because he hated Harold Huguenot, especially Harold, but that if it were me, I'd call myself "Hugue Not." Lake said it sounded like an oversized tie that you couldn't untie. That clinched their friendship so Hugh told how he and his sister Harriet had once got so mixed up that she'd gone to a psychiatrist and he'd gone with her and she was so scared that when the psychiatrist asked her her name she answered: "I'm Harold and I think I'm growing a beard. So," he added: "I'm going to transpose my names around and go by the name Cox."

"Do you think I look like Alfred E. Neumann?" he used to ask us. We told him we didn't think so, he didn't have crossed eyes, and his ears weren't all that big. But he identified all the same and often those days talked about Alfred E. Neumann. He pretended to be proud of his wrists. He took to stroking his arms saying, "Don't I have magnificent forearms?" And: "Don't you hate fat wrists? My wrists are elegant because of these hollows below my wrist bones." They were. He was a weight lifter and swimmer.

That winter was so cold that in our badly heated houses our fingers froze on the typewriter keys. We conned offices out of the churches, Hugh in the Presbyterian, Lake in the Baptist and me in the Episcopal, but Lake didn't want the Baptist, so she got the basement of the Chapel of the Cross while I was in the choir-robe room on the second floor where I had to ward off presences emanating out of the robes hanging on hooks. Late afternoons we would find each other in town. Lake was the only one with a car, so it was easy to track her down. We smelled each other out. Hugh said he always knew where Lake and I were because of the smell of kerosene.

One late afternoon at Ptomaine Tommy's we huddled over our coffee.

"What's the best first line of any novel you've ever read?" Hugh asked, holding his hands tight around the mug to warm them.

"Last night I dreamed I went to Manderlay again," I said.

"It happened that green and crazy summer," said Lake.

These were too easy to guess.

"I remember that my heart finally broke in Naples," Hugh said, making our future subsume our past in one fervent twitch. John Horne Burns hadn't killed himself yet, but Lake and I knew the answer, and Europe was a promise that was already sad.

Hugh said how lonesome writing was. The word "lonesome" echoed through the knives and forks and across the dishes like an echo across the universe. He could make the word "lonesome" sound awesome and endless, like *Om* in the Marabar caves.

In March of 1950 Lake and I decided on impulse to drive to the coast. As we headed out of town, we spotted Hugh walking on the gravel sidewalk near Muriel Mebane's house. I opened the window and screamed, "Hey, Hugh, get in."

"Where are you going?" he said when he'd slammed the door shut.

"To the ocean," said Lake.

It was only when we'd descended Strowd's Hill and passed the drive-in movie in the field where Eastgate is now — there was no Durham Boulevard — that he believed us.

"You're kidding." But he said it like the banker, Buddenbrooks. He had a test on Monday and had left his books and notes open on a reading table in Wilson. He was the one who usually got to play the outrageous roles. Once he told my mother I'd gone up in Elaine Lou Nowinsky's airplane one hot day — Elaine Lou Nowinsky was a sculptor we knew — and how Elaine Lou Nowinsky was drunk and had to make three passes at Horace Williams Airfield before she could beat the updraft and get the plane down to the ground — it felt like hanging in the sky in a pail. And my mother believed him, and ever after considered him an ill-willed liar, not a gloriously inspired fiction writer. Once later when Muriel Mebane (she'd just had her third success with *Cheer in the Evening*) was saying from the podium of State College how ignorant graduate students were — "Imagine! they've never heard of Eudora Welty?" — Hugh asked "Who?" from the panel table, and she leaned forward to the audience to explain, catching herself too late. She blushed to the roots of her honey-blonde hair. All in the timing, said Hugh.

On the outskirts of Durham he asked, "When did you know you were going to the beach?"

"Only a half-hour ago. Before we saw you. It was an inspiration," I stuttered. I was intimidated, halfway apologetic, afraid he'd decide to be mad. But Lake laughed and aimed him a look from her brown eyes as lethal as the shot from the hip. Under his frog mask there was an itch.

Past Raleigh near Goldsboro he shifted emotional gear without betraying the exact moment. We were halted at a railroad crossing in the heat of the afternoon, waiting for a long, rusty freight train to clack by.

"Someday I'm going to hop a freight," I said, "and eat from a can in a hobo jungle." *On the Road* had not yet been published, but we had the tradition from Steinbeck.

"Let's do it now," said Hugh, and shouting to Lake, "We'll meet you in Morehead City!" was out of the car in a flash, me after him running toward the tracks.

"Last one to Atlantic Beach's a dirty rotten egg!" I shouted back to her.

The train was inching and shrieking, cinders flying up, slow as a snail, heat smelling of tar, but I knew I would swing on, so I jumped past Hugh at the moment he stopped. I grabbed onto the corroded handle and pulled myself on, but he wasn't moving, I was, while he, stock still, retreated into the distance. So I jumped off.

"My God! I thought you two were going through with it and I'd have to drive the rest of the way alone," swore Lake as we hurled ourselves laughing back into the car. I was disappointed, but the point had been made. We had passed into myth-making. We were turning our lives into fiction.

Just before Kinston he told me, "You should have worn your red shoes." Whenever I wore my red shoes, Hugh and Lake invented me as a trashy waitress who ended up murdered by the roadside. It was the shoes they saw, brighter than innocence or blood, but empty. I actually did have a job as a waitress part-time at the Rendez-vous Room, the snack bar in the bottom of Graham Memorial, then the Student Union, which was where the Lab Theater is now. Since we were poor, living on the razor's edge, we grabbed what jobs we could. My novel was ballooning endlessly, I told everybody I slung hash. There was a barbershop down there too, with a 31-year-old barber who loved country music and fell in love with me because I heated up Campbell's soup in a special contraption for him. I learned country music songs as compensation for not requiting it.

"We have two toothbrushes," said Hugh, getting into the spirit. He was no longer worried about his test next Monday.

"No money for hotels either," Lake said.

I sang "When Moses was in Egypt-land" and "You are my Sunshine" wanting them to sing with me, but neither of them was any good at music. I switched to a theme from Beethoven's Seventh. Hugh listened rapt because in the second grade he'd been forbidden to sing. The teacher divided the class into the nightingales and the crows and he was a crow and ever afterward had an obsessive love of music. We stopped by the roadside and with Lake's jackknife opened two cans of what we pronounced Vye Anus Sausage.

"We can sleep in churches," I said.

We worked in churches. We had faith in churches as asylum from *Les Misérables*, and asylum was a word not just for the insane, but drifters, outlaws, incognito kings, vagrants, writers, criminals on the lam, unwed mothers and all glamorous outcasts.

The tobacco and cotton fields, freshly plowed, flattened out and a church stood on the horizon. It had that dark and weathered look of old naked wood. The air smelled like shore and we could sense the salt horizon beyond the pecan groves. We stopped the car, walked past a mangy umbrella tree and went in. The air was musty. The floor was bare. We lay down on the pews to try them out, but they were very hard.

"We need an Episcopal Church, they have cushions," I said.

"Look! A cockroach!" Hugh whispered. It was really a spider, but we saw cockroaches swarming in Protestant churches and decided to try our luck at the next one.

By New Bern dusk merged into darkness and we came to a church whose windows, ablaze with light, replicated Rosie the Riveter's eyes and the shape of her false eyelashes. Its mouth was wide open, and claps and gospel singing exploded out. We went in, and stood behind the black congregation. It was before Civil Rights and they stomped and sang pretending not to notice our color and our presence.

There was a black woman preacher down from the North, and when she got to the top of her versicle and response, she came to a dead stop and said in a thrilling voice to Hugh, "Are you washed in the blood of the Lamb?" and when he didn't answer, asked, "What's your name, honey? Come on down here and say."

He answered but didn't go down, but instead gave her a grin that slayed her. The audience didn't move.

"I see a light above your head!" she cried.

The hair stood up on my arms because this was the second time somebody had seen a nimbus surrounding Hugh. There was a woman who we heard was a Hungarian countess named Baroness Orczy (or something that sounded like that curious romancer of the Pimpernel), who hung around Graham Memorial in refined gauze dresses and gold spectacles, knitting at lectures, who had seen a light emanating from both Hugh's and Lake's foreheads. (Later we found out she was the widow of Edward MacDowell, the composer, and she invited us to the famous MacDowell Colony for Artists.)

"And where you from, honey?" the woman preacher asked,

turning to Lake. Lake said her name and "Chicago, Illinois," and the preacher-woman said, "I see a light above your head too."

It was my turn, and when I answered my name and Chapel Hill, North Carolina, the preacher-woman said, "We're glad to welcome you all to church tonight."

"Now tell me one thing," she sang. "I see some pillow, wet with tears. Is that your pillow, honey?" she asked Hugh. He smiled, embarrassed, and shook his head. She asked Lake if it were her pillow, and when she shook her head, turned to me: "Oh honey, is that your pillow, wet with tears?" I said "No," but she rolled her eyes up and proclaimed to the three of us and the congregation: "Don't you be 'shamed of crying tears into no pillow, for I see that pillow wet with tears, and the Lord sees that pillow with tears, and the Lord knows them tears, and the Lord knows them tears on that pillow tonight. And you don't have to cry no more. No, Lord. You remember that!"

"No, Lord," the congregation said.

At the Inland Waterway there was an empty coast guard boat moored to a dock. It was pitch black. We parked beneath the shoulder of the bridge, and the dogwood blossoms jittered in the cold black breeze shaking and jerking incandescent eyes in the light of the bridge lamps, peculiar, religious eyes the shape of the cross.

We decided to sleep on the boat. We each chose a separate deck, and when we had disappeared from each other's view, our presences grew enormous. Waves lapped the hull bottom, a series of knocks which spoke some message. The vibration was punctuated by bullfrog grunts. Now and then something rustled in the underbrush. The boards were hard, the spring dew clammy, and suddenly a giant stood at the corner of the galley, stroking its arms and shivering, making the sound of suffocated laughter.

"We can't sleep here!" whispered Hugh. "It's too cold."

Hugh 23 〰〰

On the other side of the galley came Lake's echo, a sharp laugh.

So we drove the rest of the way to Atlantic Beach. Nothing was open and no lights. We drove to the edge of sand dunes whose bald heads sprouted silhouettes of grasses, like the last creatures on earth. We waded upwards in the freezing velvet, deep footsteps to the top where the great blank of the ocean roared beneath us in the darkness.

"This is the Atlantic Ocean," I said, testing the word in its ultimate banality. But Lake and Hugh would not condescend, moved away upon separate paths toward the sound of the horizon. The sand's cold consistency was of Elysium, the land of Shades, and the waves pushed their phosphorescent syllables onto it, so Lake and I took off our shoes and socks, wading into it to read the meaning through the soles of our feet. It caused an ache from our ankles to our knees. The shells shone, but our feet were too numb to feel them cutting. Hugh had stripped to jockey shorts and run into the surf and swum out of sight. When he returned, his shorts were phosphorescent with small sea organisms.

"Your halo has slipped," Lake said.

He looked inside his jockey shorts and was delighted.

Later we found a telephone booth lying on its side without its telephone, rooted, perhaps, out of some defunct casino and discarded on the waves to wash up here, a trundle bed for the one most likely to understand the message.

We were euphoric. Which one of us would sleep in it?

Hugh tried it first. It was uncomfortable, he said. Lake tried it, but she said it smelled of seaweed and deceased clams. It was claustrophobic. Was it a farce to mock our endeavor? I tried it too, trying to stay in it longer than the others. It shielded the wind, but was harder than the church pews or the coast guard boat, so I got up and lay against the velvet sand and fell asleep in the cold wind.

The next morning we bought some coffee and lit a fire of

grasses and driftwood in a hole in the sand and fried bacon. And the sun warmed us up despite the strong spring wind. Hugh, crouching next to the fire, told how he had gone insane in Trinidad.

He described the water and how he had looked across it and into the jungle and his brains had leaked out into the jungle and disappeared into bird cries and waves which then came licking back to his feet. "But when I leaned down and tried to get a handful of the water, they sucked away again."

"There, in Trinidad," he said in his quiet, mesmerizing voice, "suddenly terrible memories of the mainland of my life rose up before me coming in and going out, coming in, going out."

As he remembered, we knew we were no longer real. Hugh's insanity was musical, and he had masterminded our disappearance into the dark waters, into the jungle, with those same cadences Carson McCullers spoke in her green and crazy summer.

We didn't talk for hours, not even in the car driving back. It was long after we passed Goldsboro, where we did not recognize the train tracks of that other life, the one before we had kidnapped him, when he said, "Let's each one of us write this trip from our own point of view. Then we'll read each one and see what happened."

But we never did. Hugh finished his novel and it won the Landhurst Award for that year and he was asked to ride with Muriel Mebane on the Christmas float, throwing candy to fraternity students along Franklin Street.

"You know what's the best thing about winning that award?" he said, blowing the steam off his coffee in Ptomaine Tommy's, where Continental Travel is now – for other than mocking his success he didn't change.

"What?" we asked.

"I'll never be lonely again."

We were sitting one warm March day on the wall across

from the Post Office when he made a discovery. "Do you realize that the rose blossoms out of the thorn?" We were amazed
at such a paradox and it took us weeks to perceive the lit-
eral truth. But Europe was opening up. In May Hugh left for
France, and soon after, Lake left too.

~~~~~~~~~~~~~~~~~~~~~~

This Is the Only Time I'll Tell It

Maybe we should never have given Zelene the baby.

Except for me, everybody else on those rocky farms had more babies than they could feed.

Tom Jamison could have fed his – he'll never get that excuse from me – that man was always crazy. After his wife died he got drunker and crazier, and it was nothing but accident that Zelene Bolick was walking past his house and heard that baby scream and keep screaming. She beat on the locked front door, she called, and finally ran on the wraparound porch to a kitchen window in time to see him sticking the baby headfirst down a bucket. How Zelene got inside she never said much about. That woman must have exploded through the glass. As usual, she wore half a blanket for a shawl; I guess she wrapped up her head and drove straight through the panes.

Tom, maybe thinking the whole wall would come next, let go the baby's feet and ran out the back door while Zelene yanked the baby's face out of the water and blew breath through the mouth. That picture — her with a scatter of bleeding cuts and her blanket shining with broken glass bits while she matched her big lungs to those little ones — well? It affected us. The baby, a girl, was nine months old.

When she brought back breath and screams, Zelene opened her clothes and fixed that naked baby flat against her naked breasts and buttoned her tight inside and started running to the crossroads with the blanket wadded to her front. The lump was still glittering with glass when Zelene ran yelling into my store. Blood on her forearms had stained down to the elbow points and dripped off.

While we waited for the Sheriff, she laid the bare baby girl on my counter by the cash register. "Give her your coat," said Zelene, breathing hard.

I wished that wooden surface was softer when I saw the bruises. Would you drive off a sparrow with a log? I just can't tell you.

The Jamison baby cried through my red wool coat. "He's bringing the county nurse," I told Zelene.

"O.K.," she said, stepping back to shake a few bits of glass to my oiled floor. "I'm going back and kill him." Before I could move, she lifted the biggest ax off my shelf and was gone.

She didn't find Tom Jamison, of course. Nobody did for six months, and then in another state. By the time he was safe in prison the baby was better, her arm bones grown back shut; and we Presbyterians had voted her to Zelene and told the State what we called a *righteous* lie about next-of-kin. There's nobody can lie like a Presbyterian if he thinks good sense requires it. My wife's people, Baptists, are a lot more soft-headed; one of them would have read his Commandments wrong and weakened someday.

But we had 37 lifetime Presbyterian mouths gone flat against their teeth till Judgement Day, and 20 of them — not counting mine – had been heard to declare it was a shame Zelene had not drove home her ax.

Before the Jamison baby, see, Zelene had been pitiable herself. She was 38, and built like a salt block. Even the widowers needing a good worker in the house never thought of courting her. I don't believe her broad mouth was ever put to another human mouth until that day in Tom Jamison's kitchen; I don't think more than a washrag had ever touched her chest before. She owned an old cabin her daddy had left, two cows, some chickens, hogs, a garden to can from, one hound dog so dumb it split one ear and then two on the same barbwire fence. She had lived up the road so long alone that she went by touch and not talk. I know I often shouted the weather at her in the store – her nods and pointing made me nervous. She would pinch, too, if you took down sugar when she wanted tea.

But Zelene was a Presbyterian – God, yes.

Yes *sir*, I ought to say. On foot to church and prayer meeting, snow or not. Coming through the rain with her wide face wet, and leaving empty a whole back bench or two around her goaty smell. Bringing, not money for the plate, but one of those oak stave baskets she wove, full of squash, beans, or wild fox grapes, for the preacher's table. The basket stayed with the food; I thought he must have dozens getting brittle in his loft.

She brought her own cow on a chain to be bred; she birthed the calves alone and slaughtered a hog in November and cured her own hams. Everything at Zelene's moved through the circles; what seeds she planted she had dried and saved; the cow's turds went straight to her garden rows; she never wrung a rooster's neck until the young cock had whopped him once. I sold her everything on trade. She put good handles on those baskets; I've carried stones in some of mine.

Zelene couldn't read – my wife brought that up at the special church meeting. Two of the elders rolled their eyes away from that Baptist flaw and toward me till I had to stand up, fast and brag on the memorized Scripture any of our members knew by now. Somebody else said school buses would stop for anyone's children waiting by the road.

Before the health nurse brought the baby back, our whole church cleaned out Tom Jamison's house of whatever Zelene could use, even the mantel clock my wife would have liked to own. We carried the stuff a long way uphill to her front yard. Zelene came out wearing a blue dress I didn't know she owned, her mother's maybe. We formed a wheel of people near her woodpile for a baptism with cold water dipped out of the Bolick spring. The preacher bent, whispered to her, waited, poured a cupped handful on the head which now belonged to Silver Bolick. The people were expecting some choice more Biblical. My wife said the name would have better suited a cow.

All of us shook Zelene's big crusty hand. My wife told her Silver would never remember all of that early pain. A blessing.

Zelene shook her cropped brown hair. "The pain went *in* her."

Her fierce voice surprised us, she spoke so little.

"I wouldn't ever tell that little girl a thing about it," said my wife, avoiding the baptized name.

Nodding, Zelene only ran one finger down the thin arm that crazy man had broken, saying in silence that the mark was made, made deep, that water meant for drowning had gone inside this child, that no grown body — at any size — would ever be fully dry of that knowledge.

Oh, yes, Zelene, a Presbyterian.

Listen. It's true. Count them by hundreds; terrible things are true. It's all I can take eating Christmas dinner with my wife's stribbly kinfolk. They live on *should be*; I live on *is*. Open your Bible; which Testament is longer? There's not a single good argument against Jesus picking His time back in Egypt, when the Jews really needed Him. Forty years His ancestors wandered to Canaan; He never needed but 33 to set up the whole system. If you were planning all along to walk on the water, why not to Noah?

First time I ever scattered a dandelion seedhead, I knew how much life was planned to be wasted. Right away, Abel was blown on the wind?

I slid my fingers once on the baby's damp hair. "Let's go home," I said to my wife.

You can't make Ruby see anything. She jumps from Genesis 1 to Luke 2 in a breath, and all the heathen before and since those times pass through her mind in some kind of blur, without counting. I see their one-by-one breakable faces, so much like mine. Waking many a night, I have laid furious in my own bed, certain I could have run the whole thing with some speed and a lot more kindness. But you have to be Presbyterian to feel that bitter in the dark.

My wife Ruby sleeps sweetly through the nights like a Christian and prays over sins too small for a man like Adam or me to notice.

All that was back in the thirties. Ruby, who still thought she could pray out a child of our own, let that one go to Zelene with a smile. We have been waiting ever since.

I kept a close weekly eye on Silver Bolick, carried as she was through all weathers to church. When she could walk, I would keep her outdoors during services. We wrote and drew in that packed, hard dirt with sticks, while the high singing voices at our backs bounced through "By and By," and cut by tenor and soprano the Depression down to size.

Sometimes, at the courthouse, I put down a little on Zelene's land taxes. Sometimes for her I turned back the scales at my store. I told her people in town had paid cash for the baskets my mules were then eating from. Ruby wanted to carry the woman and child her own butter and pound cake; she is never going to live in these hills like a native.

All of us natives took on our voted jobs. Some, during church hours, forked more hay into her barn; others would lift Zelene's hens and add eggs. My job was to watch Tom Jamison, keep track of where the State sent him next, when he would come up for parole and how to keep him from winning.

One time the guards found a knife in his mattress; I am not going to tell you how I did that.

When she was six, Silver stood behind the organ and said to the whole congregation the Children's Catechism. Thirty-one pages. Not a lip in the house failed to move through the words while she answered those questions, then to mouth prayers one syllable behind her voice. "Give me neither poverty nor riches," she said in this wire-thin voice of hers, "feed me with the food that is needful to me; lest I be full and deny Thee, and say, Who is Jehovah?"

All of us shared the recital except Shank Evans; that was his Sunday to cull out Zelene's two sickly piglets and replace them as near matched as possible. By August, Silver was half through the harder Westminster. That year, she got off the school bus at my crossroads and swept my clear floor every day till her shoes were paid for.

Slowly, I learned what her life with Zelene was like. Kerosene lamps blown out early, though by now the electric tower stood in her own pasture. Each egg-shell saved to be fed to the chickens, each chicken bone sucked dry and crushed and sent back mixed with their feed. When the straw ticks went flat, they were emptied on the clear stable floor, what had been shoveled out steamed down their cornrows; every brown corncob started the morning fires. Wheel in a wheel. The girl could learn worse, I thought.

As she grew tall and got long in her limbs, I would try to tell which had been broken. You couldn't see it.

One time she told me her daddy had frozen to death just before she was born. Who would have guessed our Zelene could have thought of that? I passed it on. During cold winters, we took to recalling him for Silver. It was a night like this. So was the ice in the creek that day.

The talk molded Zelene's blunt face to a widow's. With her hair streaking now, with her head thrown back, she had gotten her beauty long past any practical use to her, at a time when our other women were pinching inward.

How to explain this. Well, have you ever walked up on a feeding deer and had your breath stolen? Knowing the deer had no slight intent of beauty, he was just eating grass? Like that.

With Silver, the good looks came early. She could give feed sacks a shape. Where Mabel Jamison's hair had been sparse and pale, Silver's was full as a wheatfield and the edge curled under like a soft hem. Behind that swirl of yellow hair she had a brain you could almost hear humming; I would listen anytime she hugged me. She could outwrite and outspell the low-country children. Nobody else read the Psalms as well. Once when she did parts of Isaiah, I had to go outside and stand by myself in the heated air. She was reading from the late chapters, what they call the Rhapsodies. "The voice said, Cry. And he said, What shall I cry? All flesh is grass." I stayed out there until everyone else had, on her voice alone, mounted up with wings as the eagles.

Did she remember, through some mended crack in a full-sized bone, anything at all? Was there a spot in her trained from the very first to know, some part that ticked far away to the words she read? I could see nothing hurt or frightened in her, and her voice warmed up that whirlwind.

Then she was seventeen, and in my store trading rag dolls for cornmeal, when the man came in.

He looked at her. He was my age. He took a cold wet bottle from the drink box and paid for it in coins.

They did not look alike — let's settle that now.

"How you doing, Coley?" he said to me.

Even the voice sounded different. Last time I heard, he had fought with a prisoner and that fighting canceled his appeal.

"I don't know you," I said, and started Silver to the door. My hand was pushing on her back where the hair touched.

"Jamison," he said. He touched himself on the chest as easily? Well? I have seen flies set themselves down harder than that. He said, "I'm looking for Zelene Bolick. She still live up the road?"

Broke out, I thought, although they've got a lot of Baptists in State Government these days.

Naturally, Silver turned to see him better. I thought he searched her over for the marks that might have been there.

"She's home," said Silver, but I shook my head at her. My telephone was in the very back of the store. Once I thought that was better; you could call in while the thieves were still scraping back the screen.

How she did stare at him! Maybe her bones were looking. Maybe below her ribs there moved a memory of water. What if she raised against this man the arm that knew his hand had broken it? Well?

I kept my axes still on the very shelf. It was so light, the one I chose, that I felt a whole crowd of us had lifted it high, and swung. She did not scream until after he burst to the blade.

Babies should not be beaten; I do not care Who made this world.

~~~~~~~~~~~~~~~~~~~~~~~~~

1940 — Winter

It looked like there were no more doors gonna open for her and no more ways to turn it round. He had brought her to the shining light of love returned. For the only time in her life he had brought her to that secret spot, that place where her soul was balanced and the angels hummed, and now that she had lost it, all she had left was the desire not to feel. What did she do to end up with nothin'? What had she ever done but answer the call? She carried her anger like a sack of fire, and it burned with a toxic fury that left her exhausted and drained after each dream.

Lean and dark, a young black leopard was chasing her, running her down, pinning her to the ground and taking her with his sleek body. Taking her to the summit of her pleasure, and then she would wake up suddenly and be laid low by the desire, the grief and the shame. The desire for him, the grief that she had it still, and the shame that she had been truly touched by him again; that she loved it, and that she would still do almost anything to have him back.

Her smile was strange these days. Had she seen herself in

the mirror she might have been warned by the fever-splayed eyes shot through with fire. She often found her mind wandering around in New Orleans. She remembered the Dambella, the great source of life and then she decided. She'd remember enough. She'd remember enough or she would be damned. Probably both, she thought, smiling with her mouth. There was less and less of Florice living behind her eyes. She remembered the Petro loa who were wicked and terrible and trafficked in sacrifices. So. Finally.

A Friday winter afternoon. Florice locked herself in. She would be theirs for ten days. Carefully, just so. There would be no mistake. The gods would know exactly who it was. She worked late. Without eating, without needing to use the bathroom. This was something she could do about it. Something she could say. Without saying it, without standing on a street corner, throwing her head back and wailing that somehow, somehow it wasn't meant to be this way and there had been a mistake. Her mouth was slightly open. She had left herself. Slipping into a dark corner. Slipping on a thread. Getting thinner and thinner and disappearing into a howl. But for now she saw only this, only that she must do something about this pain. And someone would find it, and her, and someone would finally know that it wasn't fair that she had suffered and she could scream in relief, finally, silently, and forever. She was looking for her scissors. She began to turn out kitchen drawers, frantic with the decision to finish this thing. She took her long hair down from its wound braids. It fell onto her shoulders. Heavy. Black. One long lock. Cut off and wound around in her favorite style.

The house was very cold in the December night, but there were no chill bumps on her arms and she left the back door open and went out without her coat. Wind blew in and ruffled some scraps of blue cotton on the kitchen table, pieces of rope and a few strands of hair. Anyone passing would have heard someone nailing briefly and then silence. The screen was banging against the house and she pulled it closed quickly just as the winter light broke into morning.

SATURDAY

The pain was welcome. At least you could blame your agony on it and not say to anybody that you wanted to die because your sanctuary from the storm, your warming place, your seed fire had left you and you would never be all the way alive again. You could hold on to the pain and not call it hatred. You could say you were sick and maybe you had the flu. She dragged to work and dragged home, and wondered how long it would be before she had to give in and lie down and let them take her.

SUNDAY

Had been a hard day. There was church. And then all that to-do afterwards about choir practice and who would sing the solo. Rochetta Gilbert had followed her to the ladies' room and stood in there doing something to her hair while Florice closed herself off and tried to vomit.

MONDAY

In the bustle of Christmas excitement on campus, they didn't notice her frequent swallows, and how many times she had excused herself from the dining room. Alice was very busy with the Christmas week menus and by the end of the day, her own head was splitting. Another nail in. There was a big rat out there near the trash can this morning. She must get Mr. Newell at the school to see to some poison.

TUESDAY

Got to work early. Nobody witnessed the fall, up the steps to the Kirkfield union. She was still able to do most of her work, but the smell of food was getting harder and harder to bear. That afternoon she dropped the cake bowl and spilled batter all over the floor. Her arm suddenly lost all its strength and jerked forward. Alice concerned but patient.

WEDNESDAY

The Robert dream came. She laughed aloud when the cramps started. Like it was her period, they ran from her side down her leg. Alice wanted to know why she wore those ugly shoes to work, and were her feet painin' her. The walk home was slowly and carefully executed. She stopped once beside a large bush. Nothing would come up from her slightly bloated stomach.

THURSDAY

She went out to the tree that faced north at 3:00 A.M. First nail in the womb. She'd cause her own labor pains, she thought, and twisted her mouth. So she'd never have a baby; she'd have a doll. She'd have a doll. It would have his eyes, be his color. She started to laugh bitterly. Somebody would tell him she was a witch and he would feel right that he had left. The air was pre-dawn, chilling. She had to kneel suddenly with pain. The pain was running into her bones, the pain was running into her tears, turning her tears to ice.

FRIDAY

Woke to vomit in her bed. Called in sick. There were only two more. Two more nails. Alice came by. Bless her. She had the flu. Alice knew that. Why did she come why did she always come. Put too much cover on her. Changed sheets. Washed.

SATURDAY

There was a reason. To put on a coat. There was a reason yesterday. Case someone saw her. Too hot all the time. Turn the heat down. Her hair was too dry. Gonna look like steel wire. Stand up. Her eyes rolled. Back and forth like a drunkard back and forth. Get fired drunk. The hammer was under the bed. Somewhere. There was only one nail left. Down. Down the stairs. Hold on tight. Open the damn door one more time and get cool at least. House was very dark. She wanted lights. Afraid. Must not sleep in the dark room. Not tonight.

SUNDAY

Ninth day. Wire it up and spit it out. Wire it up and spit it out. Why did she need to find it? Why wasn't it under the bed where she left it? Attic. Trunk. Only there has to be an end now. They said so back home. The old lady at the river who danced all night. No wire. No wire. Push these things over. So heavy these clothes. Under. Old Christmas decorations. Wire. Saliva on her chin. No dignity, Florice. No dignity left. He left you with no. Wire it up and spit it out. Under the stomach. Around the back. And tight. So long. It was too hot out here and under the place of pleasure until the blue was covered. It would be good. To dig. Be cool. Garden is mine. Die in it. Die there.

Alice knew this wasn't the flu. She was used to being patient and letting Florice talk at her own pace, but she had known for a long time that the thing with Robert Brown was dangerous. Because Florice had put it all there, everything Theodore had denied. Every feeling she ever had, all the love and all the selfishness. All the goodness and all the lust. All the joy for just bein' on the earth alive and all the fury at having joy denied. And somewhere, something had to give. And Alice knew in her very bones that Florice was going to have to pay for this one. She couldn't stand the silence any longer. They were going to have this one out, one way or another.

Florice was in the herb garden. It was, at the most, 40° outside. She stared straight ahead as if she heard nothing, and kept digging in her herbs around the section where the skull cap grew in the summer.

Alice spoke out of her dismay, gently. "An' what you out here diggin' for? Ain't nothin' gonna grow in this weather. Com'on gurl, we go into the house now. Up with you. Com'on gurl." There was only the sound of the passing cars. Florice was very silent. She would go into the pain and into the darkness and the end of it. Her stomach had been upset for so long that she was very thin. Alice noticed how much smaller her arms had become as she helped pull the nightgown down. She winced, noticing the bones outlined in Florice's back. "You get in bed for some rest and we have a nice mashed potato and you eat it for sure, right? That be good for your stomach and you eat it for sure, right? We got to feed you some." December evening was coming down at 5:30 in the afternoon and the windows rattled in the wind just a little. Alice turned on a light. "We got to get some fight back in you, gurl." She mumbled to herself on the way downstairs. "Lord, Lord what you gone and done gurl, what you gone and done?"

Florice opened her eyes briefly. They rested on a small china box Robert had given her in the flush of their affair. Then she closed her eyes again and the pain swept her past her memory.

Alice shivered, thinking about Florice's illness; knowing Florice as well as she did, she had her own ideas about the nature of this illness. Something was rotten somewhere, or she wasn't from "de islands," something unholy was sho goin' on heah, she thought. She could feel it. She could see it in the unnatural face of her friend. Love for Florice held her in the house, frightened as she was. Alice had always said she would never touch roots, never. She shook her head and peeled a potato, found some pipsissewa and made hot tea, hands shaking. And she was so good, too good to lose her soul over loving some man. Lord, Lord. She shook her head back and forth and began to pray under her breath as the potato boiled.

The garbage can was always in the backyard next to the big tree. It was a strange tree, full of knots and grew somehow mostly on one side, its branches reaching out toward the north rather than the south; the south side had a big gash in it where some children had ridden a branch off and Florice had worried about the tree, and doctored on it with black tar. Alice lifted the garbage can lid and slammed it closed. "Sho is cold, for true," she mumbled to herself, and was about to go back into the house when her eye caught a blue scrap of something on the rounded corner of the tree. Alice frowned and took two tentative steps forward. "Oh, my Lord, my Lord Jesus, have mercy on us all, his chillun," and she caught herself on the tree just before she fell forward all the way. Her hand landed on a doll, nailed firmly to the tree, and on Florice's hair which was blowing fiercely in the wind, on the doll's head. The doll's face was turned toward the tree. There were nine nails in it. Alice clawed at the ugly thing, desperately afraid, angry, and in agony for her dear love of a friend. All she knew at that moment was that she had to get those nails out, and as she tore at it, she began to repeat phrases she had known all her life. "The Lord is my shepherd," she began, "the Lord is my shepherd. Sweet Jesus, sweet Jesus, come by heah, come by heah." There was no mistaking it was Florice. An exaggerated copy. Cocoa colored. Long legged. Nine nails. One in the heart, two in the legs, and at least four in the abdomen and pelvic area; and a wire around the waist pulling it in so tight that the doll was almost all wire in the middle.

As she pulled at the doll, she heard a scream that tore at her own body, and the thing finally came off in her hands. Somehow, holding the image at arm's length, she found the kitchen.

Florice was moaning upstairs. The floor creaked every time she'd toss violently in bed. Alice's hands shook so much she was having trouble untying and twisting the wire. She kept repeating "Lead us not into temptation, but deliver us from evil." It fell to the floor finally. "Deliver us from evil, but deliver us from evil," she had begun to stammer and then she smelled the burning potato and leaped to the stove to turn it off. Something would have to be done fast. If ah could just remember them spells, she thought, how to uncross evil, how to do it. She was climbing the stairs as fast as she could, but she had never been so weak and frightened, and her mind was racing, racing toward graveyard dust, and incenses, and she remembered the old ones putting a dime under somebody's tongue.

Florice was leaning over the wastebasket. She had tried for the toilet, but her legs were too weak now. She was sweating heavily, her gown as wet as if she had bathed in it. The pain had taken over her eyes completely and she was far away in her own hell. This is the time, Alice thought, it's now or we done lost her. She was standing at the bedroom door looking at the back of Florice's head. The doll's head flashed into Alice's mind. She brought her breath in sharply. The thick head of hair she was staring at that had been cut just enough to cover the head of a doll, was matted and had lost its luster. Alice smelled vomit and a musky odor she had never noticed about Florice. "What chu figur to do, just die? What chu believe, gurl, that the Lord promised you just what chu wanted?" Alice's voice was loud and angry. "That you come here for getting what chu want? What you think, the Lord gon keep you from trouble 'cause you Rebecca Florice? The Lord give you all them gifts for a reason. Not to be workin' wid no devils!" Alice's mouth tightened. Her teeth touched. She stayed in the doorway. Florice was almost on the floor, crouched, holding on to the bed. She rocked herself back and forth and made little pained noises. "If you gon die for true, you gon die and I can't save you. But if you gon die, you sho do talk some good talk, and that's it. What kind of talk you been talkin'? You been tellin' me to hold on, hold on, believe this, believe that. You sho do talk purty, Miss Florice. I recollect the Master say 'the world would hate you if He changed yo' name,' that's what I recollect."

Florice's shoulders began to shake and she covered her eyes with her hands. It was the crack in the door. Alice walked around the bed quickly and put her arms around her friend and rocked and rocked and rocked. "Now ain't you got a right to the tree of life, huh?" she said softly. "No matter what that man's gone and done." And then she began to sing. "Ain't you got a right to the tree of life, ain't you got a right to the tree of life? Tell my mother, ain't you got a right? Tell my Father, ain't you got a right, ain't you got a right to the tree of life?" She would hold her through the night until the crying was done.

Florice slept as if in a coma. Alice unwound her large arms from around her and set out to do what her memory had told her was needed. She took the pieces of the doll she had dropped in the kitchen and piled them up on the table, carefully looking to see that she had all the hair. Then she went into the parlor and looked through any drawers she saw for white candles. There ought to be plenty, all the formal dinners Florice had had in that house for college girls practicing to be ladies. She found two long candles and placed them in silver candle holders, one on each side of the still recognizable doll. She was reluctant to touch the doll at all, but she would have to take it all apart. She quickly undid Florice's stitches and piled up what was left between the candles. Now she must find the Bible. Time was going fast. It was always by the bed, but maybe there was an extra one in the parlor. She lit the candles and began to pray quickly but intensely, asking God to heal Florice and to make the awful deed powerless. She asked that this "doll" be returned to dust as harmless and she read Florice's favorite passage, St. Paul's letter on charity.

There wasn't much time. She must bury the pieces of the doll in a neutral place. The vacant lot behind the library would do. Florice had always loved the chinaberry tree for its brilliant orange berries so Alice had planted one for her near the dining hall where they spent so many hours together. It was Monday morning, students would be leaving for their holiday soon, but at 7:00, only those hardy souls working morning shift would be up. She saw nobody as she pulled up the softest, youngest root and cut a large piece off. Her hands were steady now. She patted the root back in the ground and thought, It must be 7:15. The fish market opens at 7:30. Alice pulled into her coat tightly and turned the collar up, wrapping her scarf around her head and neck, starting out to walk the two miles to town. She bought a half-pound of mussels, and because she was worried that Florice would wake up and find her gone, was glad to see the bus that would take her most of the way back to campus.

She was still sleeping. But tossing, calling names of people Alice didn't know, snatches of prayers and strange Creole chants. She was feverish. Alice hurried down to the kitchen, almost stumbling on the last step. She washed the chinaberry root and cleaned the mussel shells, throwing the living part away. Then she boiled the shells and root, until she was satisfied the brew tasted vile enough.

Every three hours she would wake Florice as much as she could. And every three hours she would pour the brew down her and hold her head, Florice retching, and vomiting up what Alice was afraid to look at. The first time she had looked. After that for the entire day and a half while the vomiting went on, she hid her eyes. The stuff was horrible, streaked with black, and it looked alive with something, something Alice didn't want to remember.

It was Tuesday night. Alice had not been home since Sunday afternoon. In the early hours of Wednesday morning, Florice's fever broke. She awoke, as if from a long dream. There was such a deep silence in her, she felt startled almost as if she had been returned from some unknown place, another realm, another reality, and had been put here, a traveler in a strange place, but at peace within her strangeness. Her mouth was chapped and tasted bitter with some foreign taste she didn't recognize. She felt light, light as talcum powder floating on the surface of her bed. It took a while for her eyes to see in the dark night. There was a starchy odor, someone had changed her sheets, and the pillowslips smelled of the sun. For a little while she lay there in such profound peace and relief that it wasn't necessary to remember why she was there. That there was no pain was the overwhelming truth of the moment. And then she began to remember and cry silently, covering her face in revulsion for what she had done, and in horror at what she had willed. There was in her heart the most crushing of all sadnesses, that at having let herself down. She kept whispering "sorry . . . sorry . . ." and used the back of her hand to wipe her face. Gradually she felt someone's presence in the dark room. It spread out and over her like a sweet electricity and though she knew herself to be alone, she was not by herself. The energy surrounded her, lifted her with its Light and set her down in a place of wonder far away from her scream with no bottom. And, while she continued to weep, she knew that somewhere in her deep grief joy was still alive, and as Alice would say, "all is well for true, Florice, all is well. It stands so."

The bagworm moths are best known for the cases the larvae spin around themselves. They carry them wherever they go, and enlarge them as they grow. The adult bagworm is wingless and never feeds but only serves in her reproductive function to help the species survive. The burnet moths manufacture a poison which circulates in their blood, helping them to survive the attack of many hostile organisms.

Broken Blossoms

At first it is strangely colored stones and oddly shaped leaves and bird nests and cicada husks, and perhaps that ought to end it, when one is seven or eight years old, and attracted to the gathering of things by the eye's joy and by a reverence for something which the natural world – then so shadowy mysterious – has seemed to cast aside. Whatever it later turns into will be only pleasure in collecting for the sake of collecting, in pigeonholing, in aligning things in rows, in piecing out objectives.

In my own case this dark latter urge struck me hard when I was eleven and manifested itself as stamp collecting. The stamp album from that time has long been lost, or maybe I traded it away when I was a teenager. I should like to see it now, though I would redden with shame if I had to display if before a true philatelist. I remember the color, a matte chocolate-maroon, and the gold lettering across the front, STAMPS OF MANY COUNTRIES, and my name too in gold letters in the lower righthand corner. The situation in which I most vividly recall it is lying cater-cornered on the coffee table which served me as a desk (I sat crosslegged on the floor) under the bronze-painted table lamp with its dusty yellow shade. Lying there unopened, a big square book which spoke my own name to me vehemently again and again.

Inside, what a mess! The stamps were to attach to the album pages with little gummed cellophane hinges, this requiring some minimal amount of manual dexterity which I did not have and never acquired. The stamps themselves were supposed to be stuck to the smaller flap of the hinge, while the large flap was pressed tight against the page. Often as not I got the flaps reversed. And for some reason, spit was disallowed as a dampening agent; a saucer of lukewarm water was to be used, temperature tested with the back of the wrist. I eschewed any such frivolous precision and laid stamp, hinge, and all on my tongue and mashed the gluey bit of paper onto the page with the heel of my hand. A typical finished-out page would look something like a miniature crazy quilt, each scrap of color at any angle to another, each solidly stuck there forever or clinging tenuously like a butterfly to a leaf.

Yet I regarded such a filled page with a prideful tenderness. I had collected the stamps; I had affixed them; I had already in my life accomplished something. Sometimes I would open the book to one such page and stare at it until I was overwhelmed, and then I would spring to my feet and twirl about in a circle, quite overcome with happiness, with the feeling that a bright and shining future lay in store and here gave a sweet hint of itself. Or I would stare at it long and pensively, in melancholy reverie dreaming a blurred and half-imagined history of the world.

But the true and fatal attraction in hoarding stamps — it is difficult to name it collecting — was the lure of instant wealth and global fame. It seemed quite improbable that I should not discover a rare stamp equal in worth to the fable British Guiana or one with a magnificent printing error like the twenty-five cent airmail stamp with the upside-down airplane. I did not deceive myself that the odds were against me, but I was simply secure in the belief that I would beat the odds. For, look here, I had already filled in five pages of this huge book, cheating only a little by sticking seven or eight stamps in or near the spaces where they did not belong.

So that even if I had been able to afford the expensive sets of stamps I saw advertised in boys' magazines — mint sets of new Nicaraguan issues, or Swiss first-day covers — it is doubtful I would have been much interested. For me it was those big envelopes given away as introductory enticements, thick wads of ordinary canceled stamps, rose two-pence British, and French and Italian airmail, and even three-cent Jeffersons. When one of these envelopes arrived, my father handing it over with a half-amused smile, I would tear it open and pour under the bronze table lamp this useless clutter of paper and claw through it feverishly. There would of course be nothing I hadn't seen and rejected some scores of times before. But that was merely the preliminary examination. After I had stirred about in this heap until my initial fervor had worn off, I would go downstairs to the bathroom medicine chest and borrow my mother's tweezers, take up each stamp, look at it on both sides, and hold it against the light. Not that I knew what I was looking for. Watermarks I had read about and had seen sketches of in the magazines, but I never glimpsed one in a stamp and didn't know how to search. There were ribbed lines running horizontally through many stamps, but I didn't believe that these could be watermarks because they were simply not exciting. I thought that if I could just once find a watermark of any sort I would be well on my way to making my famous and inevitable discovery because I would have been able to recognize one of the ingredients of rarity . . . But at the end I would have to look down sadly upon them and toss them by handfuls into the wastebasket.

Of how my parents regarded this outlandish enthusiasm I can form only a vague idea. My father, though educated, was a farmer, and a practical man. I think that he may have been mildly concerned about my interest, for at this time he would occasionally bring me toys of a different sort, miniature farms with barns and silos and brightly painted toy tractors. My mother, fastidious and vocal as always, would complain about the disorder and about the absence of her tweezers. But their objections could not have been serious, I reasoned, for after all they had given me the album and the first bulky envelopes of stamps for my birthday. And anyway, once I had made my discovery, once my name appeared in all the newspapers, once the renowned dealers began to telephone with their unheard-of offers, I would be vindicated a hundredfold. And it wasn't only the money and the world-wide recognition – I would have proved to them that my imagination was healthy and brilliantly practical and would make its way in the world. Then my activities, which were not limited to stamp collecting but included chemistry experiments and poetry writing, would have to be reckoned with seriously.

Meanwhile my schoolwork had to be kept up, and more importantly, the work of the farm had to go on. Ours was no large farm, comprised not more than a hundred acres; but I am convinced that a plot of ground fifty feet square will work a man to his grave if he lets it. I don't remember that I shirked my share or even much resented it, but I do remember that even as I pitched hay or shelled corn or fed the animals my mind was still occupied by my stamps and by the tinsel future. This caused me to go about with a dreamy unintelligent expression on my face, occasioning some scolding and a great deal of raillery.

After my father, chief among my cheerful tormentors was Harmon Cody. Mr. Cody was a spare sandy-haired man with unyielding green eyes who lived down the narrow dirt road about half a mile from our farmhouse. The arrangement by which he worked on our farm is obscure to me, for he worked neither entirely for shares nor for salary but for some intermediate combination. He took other jobs too, mostly part-time farm work or repair work; but what was obscure showed in the way he and my father treated each other personally. He rose to suggestions with such ready deference and spoke in such re-spectful tones that anyone unacquainted must have supposed his position was that of an ordinary sharecropper. But his po-sition was independent, and my father never talked to him in any manner suggesting dependence, and such hint of inequali-ty as there was came all on his side.

Mr. Cody's attitude toward me was another matter. It was clear to him that I was a new kind of animal upon this earth, and he would gaze on me with unabashed wonder as I drifted empty-eyed from one chore to another, so abstracted some-times as actually to stumble over something beneath my feet. He began to ply me with bland jokes. "What's the weather where you are?" he would say; or "Don't forget your hands are at the ends of your arms and your head is at the top of your neck." And when I smiled back dreamily his mouth would quiver with sheer amazement. His joking kept on and after a while became more pointed, but his motive I believe was never malice but a kind of bemused experimentation. What *will* this creature ever react to? he must have wondered. And I, only half-conscious of what went on in his mind, was mostly pleased with any attention he gave to me.

It would be hard for a boy of eleven not to be pleased with the attention of Mr. Cody. It seemed to me that he knew everything there was to know about the world out-of-doors, and that he could perform miracles of craft and repair, upon which he looked with a baleful skepticism. He would restrap and brad together an ancient mule harness, glance at what he'd done and remark, "That wouldn't hold a puppy dog from his meal dish." He held every manmade object in suspicion, and I once heard him say of a neighbor's gleaming new John Deere tractor, "Ain't no use him pretending that's going to *do*." Male Americans are born to be Boy Scouts, and a young boy regards an adult of Mr. Cody's cut as an enlarged Scout, one of the geniuses who wrote that Handbook so full of thumb-mashers and knuckle-crushers. Of mammals, birds, and insects he knew every secret: how to cure colic in newborn calves, names of birds by their nests, how to keep bees from swarming – an endless variety of information. His knowledge was so various and profound, in fact, that I early despaired of attaining to anything like it. The natural world became a gulf between us; for him so plain and easy, for me so dim and bewildering.

For all this we were good friends, because he was at last a boy at heart. This was perhaps the reason he held my father in such clear respect; Mr. Cody must have felt that my father was a respectable adult, since he had schooling and owned property and kept together a family, no matter how odd the offspring of the family might be. Mr. Cody was a bachelor and owned nothing but his house and small lot, his piecemeal old Ford, and five lugubrious hound dogs. He was a foxhunter, and many mornings he would come to work in the fields directly from some mountainside campfire, redeyed and edgy from a night of black coffee, but still energetic and industrious enough that my father and I had to strain to keep up with him. Twice he invited me to go hunting with him, but that never came about. The first time my father refused permission and Mr. Cody nodded, accepting this rejoinder as adult wisdom. The second time I myself refused, thinking of some lamp-smelling project I had underway at home, and he merely gazed at me; I had added one more lump of fuel to the fire of his astonishment.

My mother too was fond of Mr. Cody, but in a rather distant way. Her mind was full of priorities, of matters ranked in orders of importance, and Harmon Cody, being only an overgrown boy, was as useful and as amusing as Archie, our collie who was trained to cattle. That and no more; but no less, either. Mr. Cody on his side regarded my mother as he did all women: they were here in the world like starlight and moonlight, but their purpose must be finally incidental, since a man could do as well without them as with them.

Came a time when an evangelical impulse rose in Mr. Cody. He must have decided that he had learned about me all he was ever going to with his gentle jokes, and that now he must educate me before I blundered on into my teens in a numb haze without discovering how to handle the pragmatic imperatives the world of objects forces upon us all. He took me walking in the woods on Sundays, making laconic observations on bird and beast and bush. He took me troutfishing and instructed me in the use of the fly rod. He requested my help in fixing his car, whose motor he spent much time tearing down and putting back together.

But I was a sorry pupil, and once when for the hundredth time I had entangled my nylon fishing leader in the overhanging branches of a laurel, he laid down his rod and put his hands on his hips and said, "Just where in the world are you from?"

I grinned and shook my head.

"No," he said, "I mean it. Where are you *from*?"

"Well, you know," I said.

"No," he said, "I truly can't figure it out."

There was nothing for me to say to that. I indicated my line stretched across the swift little stream. "Well," I said, "I guess I better wade into the old H$_2$O and get my line loose."

"Wade into the what?"

"H$_2$O. That's the chemical formula for water."

He nodded, and I think that if then I had begun to speak Mandarin Chinese and flapped my arms and flown up to roost in the top of the near sourwood tree he would no longer have been surprised.

This incident marked a turn in our relationship. There was an order of things Mr. Cody had determined that he would never understand, and now I went into it, along with women, cats, and foreign cars. We were no less friendly, but there were no further attempts on his side to reach me, to tear away my blindness. Just as well. This happy man must at last have broken his heart if he had kept to his original resolution.

That was Mr. Cody. With my father it was a different proposition. If he was toiling to get our one horse harnessed to the plow and asked me to go to the shed and bring him a small clevis, I would trot off and return after too long a while with a broken and useless scrap of iron. His face grew scarlet and his eyes enlarged and seemed to whiten. "My God!" he would say. "A clevis, boy, a *clevis!* Don't you know what a clevis is?" And he would snatch my wrist and drag me tumbling after across the lot to the shed. He would find it and thrust it directly in my face, shaking it. "This is a clevis, dammit. How can you grow up here and not know that? What are you thinking about?"

"I don't know, sir," I would say, and I was telling the truth.

And then when we got back to the plow the horse would have stepped out of the traces, and there would be a delay of twenty minutes or so, enlivened by grunting and some fiery profanity.

Once it happened — and, remembering, I hardly believe it myself — that I lost his drinking water. He had gone off to one of the farthest corners of the farm to break ground for some new tobacco beds and had left me in the house with instructions to find him in an hour with water. I was happy to be left there with an incomprehensible book called *Industrial Chemistry* and, for a wonder, I didn't forget what I was charged with. At the appointed time I rose regretfully from my wingback chair and went into the kitchen and dropped into a Mason jar as many ice cubes as I could. Then I filled the jar with tap water and sealed it with the cap and the rubber and started out, the jar tucked under my arm. It was a gloriously hot August day and I went along the dusty road in oblivious reverie.

But when I arrived where my father was working I had no water. He had seen me coming over the top of the hill and had halted the horse at the end of a furrow to wait. His face and arms were pouring sweat and his old cotton shirt was drowned.

"Where's the water?" he asked hoarsely.

I couldn't answer because I was so completely astonished at not having it with me. I think my impulse may have been to search my pockets.

"Well, didn't you bring it?"

"I don't know where it is," I said. A sudden hopeless depression darkened me like a blanket thrown over.

"You mean you came all the way out here and forgot my drinking water?"

From his tone of voice I could tell he didn't believe it either. He was thinking perhaps that I was tricking him, that I had hidden it nearby and wanted merely to give him a turn. And I wished sorely that it could be that way because the poor man needed it desperately.

"No sir, I didn't forget."

"Where is it then?"

"I don't know."

"How can you not know? Did you drop it on the road and break it?"

"No sir, I don't think so." Certainly I must have noticed breaking a Mason jar in the middle of the road.

"What's there to think about? If you started out with a jar of water, surely to God you know what happened to it."

"I had it when I left the house. I was carrying it under my arm."

"And now you don't know where it is?"

"No sir."

"Boy, you beat anything, you know that?"

"Yes sir, I guess so." I raised and dropped my hands.

He turned and surveyed how much ground he had plowed and how much there was yet to do. When he turned back toward me, his face wore such an expression of trapped frustration that I could have wept. "By the time you got back with more, I'd be finished here," he said. "Not that I expect you *would* get back with any . . . You just sit down over there and wait and we'll go back together. I've got some things I want to say to you."

"Yes sir."

In another hour he had finished and I helped him unharness and load the plow onto the sled and then we rehitched and started back. When we came to the road he drove along more slowly and began to lecture me vehemently, but now it was too late. I had drifted down into my placeless lethargy again, like a dry leaf floating down, down into a well.

Then he stopped the sled and pointed. "Just look there," he said.

In a clump of ragweed in the ditch I saw the Mason jar, still intact and full of water, gleaming and dripping.

That wasn't what he pointed at. His trembling finger pointed at my footprints in the red dust where they struggled aimlessly from one side of the road to the other.

"Just look," he said. "You're walking like a crazy man. What in the world is the matter with you?"

I said nothing, and as the sled dragged on, cutting two stark sensible lines through my tracks, it occurred to me that they looked like writing in an unknown language, transgressing the boundaries of the copybook lines the sled made. And I thought too that here was another matter that I must study, and that by mastering it I would have one more vital clue to the future life which awaited me, incandescent with promise.

So I began to pursue my odd interests with even more energy and persistence. The evidence of my freakishness had at last impressed itself upon me, and now it seemed my duty to transform myself from ugly duckling to swan by force of will power; because the great good luck that was to come to me was already overdue, and the impatience of my parents had soon to be satisfied.

But the grand event did not happen soon. In a month school began again and school work coupled with the ordinary farm chores and the time for my personal projects dwindled, until I had only a few hours, at twilight and again after supper. This constricted schedule made me anxious and I blocked out several elaborate time-plans by which I reckoned to increase my efficiency. So many minutes would go for my chemistry experiments, so many for the writing of poetry, so many for the study of cryptography (a new interest), and so much time would be allotted to the stamps. None of these plans proved viable because that lurid vein of dreaminess in me was enlarging, encroaching now upon the same activities it fed from. My head swam with visions even in the middle of some rote chemistry experiment until the solution of potassium permanganate boiled over on the card table I had set up on the side porch. In fact, the whole idea of chemistry was proving disastrous. What stinks and ruin of glassware! What obscene noises! But the worst of it was the holes eaten in my shirts and jeans by acids. And I was learning nothing at all about the science of chemistry except that powdered magnesium gave off a magnificent quick brilliance when touched with a match. When my mother put a stop to this possibly dangerous fooling around I was more relieved than disappointed. I poured the liquids and powders into proper containers, labeled them carefully, and stored them in boxes in a corner beside the coalbin in the basement.

Cryptography too was becoming frustrating. I had been attracted to it by the reading of a Sherlock Holmes story, "The Adventure of the Dancing Men," a neat piece of work which — because I could follow the thread of its simple logic — confirmed my estimates of my own intelligence. But there was little information on this science in the school library or in the books about the house. I was of course already familiar with the Superman code, in which the alphabet runs counter to itself. I learned the typewriter code in which one row of letters as it appears on the typewriter keyboard is substituted for another and a few other elementary codes, but that was as far as I could go unaided. I did put together a number of codes of my own, but what use were they? Since I knew the keys I could read them, and I knew better than to trouble my parents' forbearance with puzzles. And anyway, I had as yet no message to send. So my cryptography dwindled away, leaving in my mind a jumbled heap of letters and symbols like a box of pi in a printer's office.

Now it was February, the harshest month of the year in the

Carolina mountains. Snows and rain continually, and the days short and overcast, and the nights long and bitterly cold. My physical energy subsided to a dull murmur and with that in abeyance my nerveless dreaminess increased even more. I was able to continue to some extent with poetry and the stamps, but now these too were infused with lethargy. Still I kept on.

I dread trying to speak about the poetry. It goes without saying that it consisted in the most awful trash thinkable. My purpose here is to try to suggest the special weirdness of that junk. It was expectably romantic to the hilt, and it was, to a degree, nature poetry. But the kind of nature it portrayed will never exist, because this poetry concerned itself with the planet Varn, thousands of light-years from Earth, and spinning in a figure-eight orbit about its double suns. I had attempted to imagine the whole thing: a landscape completely alien and observed in an entirely new spectrum of colors, and the sentient perambulatory plants which roamed this landscape and the immobile insentient animals the plants preyed upon. I imagined the dominant race of the planet Varn, a species of flying creatures something like terrestrial butterflies, whose method of communication was a music composed of tones beyond the range of human hearing, and whose habitations were enormous crystal eyries lodged in the crests of craggy mountains. For these beings I set down nature sonnets as I supposed they would have written them and love poems and battle hymns and courtly addresses to their council of rulers. I even tried to imagine what their sciences would be like, considering their different organs of perception, and I endowed them with sophisticated machinery adapted to their bodies.

The manuscript of this poetry, *The Cycle of Varn*, grew to be huge. It filled to overflowing a loose-leaf notebook, and the composition of new poems got to be a cumbersome task. Since I was improvising natural and physiognomic and cultural detail as I went along, in order to write almost any new poem in the series I had to reread almost everything I had already written. So it would take an hour or so before I could even begin to compose the long gelatinous arhythmic lines which I believed had more color and importance than anything by my model, Walt Whitman. Nothing in the world could induce me to introduce here a sample of this stuff, even if I were able. For all I know it may still exist somewhere, crammed into boxes in an attic or basement, but I am not going to search it out. All that is gone from me, the steady opiate urge to spin about myself cocoons of incomprehensibility. This poetry was after all merely the overlapping of my usual dream-state into a limited physical activity. And after some time I began to suspect it as self-indulgent.

But the ideal of the stamps stayed with me fairly constantly. I still kept my faith, though I was becoming aware that my method of procedure was mistaken for the purposes I had in mind. I procured a magnifying glass, and I stopped spending my money on the worthless bags of ordinary stamps. I began to send off for new issues of Brazilian or Mauritanian stamps, printed in two or three colors and portraying, often as not, nude girls. I would then scrutinize these stamps with the magnifying glass, comparing them minutely with the written descriptions which appeared in the philately pages of *Boy's Life*. I was searching for anomalies, for it had come to me that if I could find discrepancies between what I was looking at and the description of it, I might actually have discovered a recognizable error, and my fortune would be made. I read up on the processes of printing and engraving, having come to realize that a figure or emblem printed upside down was enormously unlikely, and that the kind of thing I was looking for would be subtle, or even mundane, in appearance.

This new procedure was expensive. We were not poor, but we were by no means wealthy; and even if we had been it was none of my father's philosophy to dole out great heaps of money to children. Where before I had bought buckets full of stamps for fifty cents, I now sent off two dollars and received eight stamps, royally mounted on cardboard and wrapped in sparkling cellophane. I have to admit to the great pleasure in first opening an envelope of these, with the colors bright and pristine, the depicted scenes exotic, the stamps oversized. But the examination of these new acquisitions could last, with the most harrowingly minute scrutiny, two or three hours at longest. After that I could only stick them in the album, and then there would be a wait of perhaps three months before I could save enough money to afford another set. Between times, I would merely languish or go over and over again the crazy pages of my album, hoping that in my earlier ignorance I had missed something important.

During this period our family life went on in its usual fashion, my parents worrying about my schoolwork and about the state of my health and of course scolding me constantly. But I took no more notice of them than of an empty wind blowing. Their anxieties of temper were to me only a piece of the weather, inevitable and ceaseless. It was still my conviction that my eventual success would straighten everything out, the past as well as the future.

Once, though, something happened that did fix my attention. I have no real notion of the background of the incident — something to do with surveying deeded boundaries for tax purposes, I think — but there appeared on the dining room table an old bulky manila envelope. It was addressed not to my father but to his father, who had been dead now some seven years. And in the corner of this envelope was a one-dollar special delivery stamp, printed in red, white, and blue, and displaying the American Eagle. I had never before seen this stamp or even heard of it. Naturally I lusted for it and my father, preoccupied, gave it to me with a minimum of haranguing. I took it, studied it with my customary thoroughness, and finally interred it in the album.

This stamp started a whole new train of thought. In various places in our house were boxes and boxes of old letters, bales of business and personal correspondence. Why it had never occurred to me to examine the stamps on these letters I could not now imagine, and I began to tremble at the prospect. I felt as someone must who has come into an unlooked-for inheritance of thousands of dollars. It was among these documents, here always right under my nose, that I would make my fateful discovery. It was to be the final delicious irony of my success that I would discover the long-sought treasure here in the house of my family among my father's own discarded belongings. I did not deceive myself that I would find it right away; but somewhere amidst all that paper it reposed waiting, like an emerald in a garbage dump.

I gave myself over to an evening of reverie, and the next afternoon I began, down there in the corner by the coalbin where we stored the things we could not bring ourselves to throw away. It was there that I had shoved my disused chemicals, and when I saw those boxes, I felt a sort of pitying contempt for the person I used to be, not at all the same person who was on the verge of enjoying riches and celebrity . . .

There were plenty of envelopes, sure enough, but I soon discovered that most of them were Christmas cards from the friends of my parents, from people whose names I might have heard vaguely or might never have heard. There must have been hundreds of these and of course each of them bore only the blue Jefferson, but I looked over each of them dutifully, sneezing and wiping my nose on my sleeve. By the time I had to come away to supper I was black with dust from fingertip to elbow and the front of my green plaid cotton shirt was smeared beyond recognition. So far in one afternoon's work I had found only Adamses and Jeffersons, but I was not discouraged. The feeling about these letters was too strong in me; I had to trust my intuition; and anyway, I had a long way to go. So at supper I received my scolding for the filthy state of my clothes with equanimity.

February became March and March April. The landscape brightened and thawed and began to warm, and still I plundered the dusty boxes and found nothing. In all the boxes in the basement there had been not one unfamiliar stamp to place in the album, much less anything resembling the great prize.

On the main floor of the house were two closets containing letters, one in the hallway and one in my parents' bedroom, but it would not be easy to search them out, with my parents spending all their house time there, and so I put these off until later and moved to the upstairs. There was one small closet at the top of the stairs and another large room which served as a storage room for all sorts of things, for we had no proper attic. The small closet I went through in less than an hour, finding nothing, but not finally discouraged, for I entertained bright hopes of the storage room.

This was a dark room about fourteen feet long with its ceiling beaded lathe, the sloping roof of the house. Illumination was one naked 50-watt bulb hanging from a cord. This room was the real Aladdin's cave, if my interests could have been different, for in here all sorts of family memorabilia had been laid up. There was a violin case, for example, and inside it on the patchy green velvet a fiddle and bow, out of tune and screechy as car brakes when I attempted to sound it. It belonged to my mother – as I later discovered – and once she had been proud of her playing and used to perform at square dances with my uncle who was a famous caller of tunes. There were the boots and hat of a First World War uniform which had belonged to my grandfather's brother. There was an old icebox of heavy oak, and a barrel butter churn made of hickory, its dasher handle worn thin at the end. There were, in fact, all sorts of beautiful and amazing objects which preserved in their essentials a history of the times of my family. But I did not know how to value any of them, my interests perverted and running counter to natural feelings. Even so, the patina of human usage upon them managed to impinge itself and I did examine them and touch their textures with some curiosity.

Once again, though, I was disappointed in my quest. There were three boxes of letters, many fewer than I had expected, but the letters bore no interesting stamps, only the Adamses and Jeffersons the glimpse of which now began to make me ill with disgust, a cold crawling sensation growing in my stomach and shuddering upward to my chest. After so much disappointment, hopelessness was at last beginning to lodge in me, and I was starting to feel a cloudy sense of shame at myself and to see that I was childish beyond the limits. I could not yet bring myself to give up the search, but I determined that when I had looked through the house that would be the end of it. I would turn my attention to another scheme. The world was full of opportunities for money and glory, not contingent on little bits of paper.

In this room there was a large trunk of heavy black metal with rusty brass moldings. It sat longwise on the floor and was locked. I knew it was against every rule for me to open this trunk, but I knew as soon as I encountered it that I was going to. Though the trunk was heavy, the lock was flimsy, a flat brass plate with a hasp and a latch. I looked in the room perfunctorily for a key, but I had already known that I could open it with a claw hammer and, hardly reflecting upon propriety, that is what I did.

When I laid the hammer beside me on the floor and, kneeling, opened the trunk lid, a strange heavy odor, camphor and mothballs and sachet and another bitter unnameable smell, washed over me instantly. It was such a dizzying sensation that I almost dropped the lid. Then I looked inside, and if the trunk had been mysterious when it was locked it was no less so when opened. Nothing within it was what I could have expected. There was, first of all, a football jersey, green with the number 14. It had to have been my father's, but he had never mentioned to me that he played football. I lifted the jersey out and laid it on the floor, uncovering a cardboard box with a cellophane panel in the top which showed inside a doll with exquisite features in an elaborate dress, a finely fashioned red crinoline skirt with a candy stripe bodice. It looked expensive and so I handled it carefully as I read the legend on the box: *Official Scarlett O'Hara Doll*. Next was a small square tin box without a lid and inside it were a number of small metal cylinders, copper-colored and about three-quarters of an inch in diameter and with one end open. I looked at these for a while, shaking the box gently to make them rattle, but I could think of no possible use for them, and I set the box down on the football jersey. This trunk was filled with all sorts of fascinating objects: medals, coins commemorating the Chicago World's Fair, dance programs with gold-thread tassels, belts and leather work, family photographs of all sorts, some of them so old as to be backed with tin plate, a number of college newspapers in some of which I found poems by my mother and pictures of my father who, I discovered, had made All-Conference tackle at Carolina Christian College. A wave of tenderness came over me as I fumbled through these things and I determined, as a boy will, that I would begin to be a better person, that I would obey my parents more readily, and that I would take hold of myself.

The trunk contained no letters, not a single paper bearing a stamp. This was the final let-down, of course, but in a way I felt relieved too, as if a misty heavy weight had been removed from my body. This was the end of it. I was never going to be rich and famous by finding a stamp. It rested in my mind with all the certainty of a gun muzzle that I had been wasting my time, staking all my daydreams on a chance so slim, fantastic, and ephemeral that only a desperate person could have conceived it and only a retarded person could have persisted in it. But now this was the end. I would not even bother to look through the other closets downstairs; I could close this chapter of my life for good and all.

I replaced gently all the things I had taken out, as nearly as I could in the order they had been. I closed the trunk and tried to snap the lock shut, but it wouldn't go. I wasn't trying to hide the evidences of my snooping; the truth was that I wanted to undo the fact that I had been prying into this personal cache of history, and this ritual replacement of objects partook of something in the nature of a magical act, the purpose being to erase the deed entirely. Impossible, but necessary to my presence of mind.

Now I had not become a different person; I still believed (though perhaps now slightly unwillingly) that my immediate future was flaming with a glorious treasure. But the collecting of stamps was a false lead; I must search out another path to my success; I must plunge more deeply and thoroughly into the waters of my dreaming reverie. Somewhere at the bottom of my preoccupation lay gleaming the key to it all.

Three days later I returned home from school, books under my arm and one shoelace untied and dragging, to find Harmon Cody sitting on our porch steps. He was smoking a cigarette, and a .22 rifle lay across his lap. When I greeted him, he grinned and waved his hand. "You better go on in the house," he said. "Your daddy's waiting to talk to you."

When I entered I found him sitting there, and it was obvious that he was waiting for me because he was dressed in his work clothes and had on the heavy brogans he never wore inside the house. He was sitting in the wingback chair and he gestured for me to sit down opposite him on the sofa.

"How was school today?" he asked, and his voice was gentle and tired.

"All right, I guess. It doesn't change much."

"That so?"

He didn't look directly at me but into a space above my head. For a long time he said nothing, and then he leaned forward, resting his elbows on his knees. "You've been poking around in the stuff in the house, haven't you?"

"Yes sir I was looking for stamps for my – "

"You took a hammer or something and broke into the trunk up in the storage room."

"Yes sir. Like I said, I was – "

"And you don't need for me even having to say anything to know that it's wrong to be busting into places that are locked."

"No sir."

"Tie your shoe," he said, still not looking at me. "If something is locked, there's a reason for it. The first reason would be, to keep people out. And there might be some other reason too."

Bent to my shoelace, I craned to see him. "I'm sorry," I said. "It was only – "

"I want you to take a little walk with Mr. Cody," he said. "I've asked him to show you something. You go with him. After that, you can come back here and change clothes and meet me in the second barn. Some of that damp hay has been heating up and we've got to move it around."

"All right," I said. I put my schoolbooks on the coffee table and went outside.

Mr. Cody rose as I came through the door and flipped his cigarette away. "Let's you and me go out in the pasture a ways," he said; and we set off, walking easily and deliberately.

It was a warm bright cheerful day, one of those days you might look about you, breathing deeply and thinking, Yes, this is springtime, this is the best time of year, this is the real beginning. The landscape glowed a clear pale green and the waters in the ground seemed almost audibly loosening underfoot. From near and far on all sides came birdsong.

Mr. Cody didn't look at me, but kept his intent green gaze on the bushes and the tops of the hills. He carried the .22 loosely in his left hand, half-twirling it by the trigger guard, the way a man walking along will play carelessly with a stick he has picked up somewhere.

There had been something so grave in my father's manner of speaking, and there was now something so studied in the way that Mr. Cody avoided talking that I asked no questions. Whatever was to happen, it was obvious that the two men attached importance to it, and I would only spoil the drama by anticipating. So I walked along silently, swinging my arms, and taking about half again as many steps as Mr. Cody. But as we came nearer and nearer to the far southeast corner of the pasture, my curiosity rose, for there was nothing here I knew of but a few easily sloping hills and grass and yellow broomsedge.

I had forgotten the apple tree. This was a little tree which stood halfway up the side of an otherwise empty hill. It was dwarfed and stunted because it had once been struck by lightning. The crown had flattened out and what was left of the trunk was twisted back until it looked as if it might fall over against the side of the hill. Half of it was missing; the whole front side from where we stood was a pith of weathered long splinters enclosed in a canal of bark so smooth and tough where it had grown over the firescar that it looked like molded wax. Part of it yet struggled toward life. The other side with its sheared-off platform of twiggy branches was blooming, was absolutely rife with blossom, pinkish-white, already freckled now with bees. It was a marvelous sight, this tree riven down half its life, one side of it shattered and barren as sand, the other side a warm fountain of flowers.

Mr. Cody halted about fifty yards from it, and I halted too. He handed me the rifle and from his shirt pocket took a cardboard prescription pill box. He opened it and removed carefully a square of white cotton batting to reveal, lying on top of another square of cotton, one of the little copper cylinders which had been among the others, in the tin box I had discovered when I broke into the trunk. "This is a blasting cap," he said. "You stay right here. Don't move."

He held the pill box before him and walked up the hill to the apple tree. When he got there he took the cylinder from the box and fitted it carefully into a crotch of the branches on the lefthand side of the tree. Then he tossed the box down and came back, and over his shoulder I could see the button of gleam among the leaves, a tiny spot of polished gold shining among the green and white.

"Here," he said, and I handed him the rifle. He took a single shell from his pants pocket and fitted it into the chamber. Then he raised the rifle and, without seeming to aim, squeezed the trigger. The apple tree jerked and quivered and a big piece of it fell to the ground and a ladder of black smoke climbed the blue air. My ears buzzed with the explosion, but I could still make out Mr. Cody's words: "You see, honey, you're going to have to take better care. Happened you hit one of those caps a lick up in your attic, you'd have been blowed to pieces. Blowed half the roof off."

And that, I suppose, is the way it happened. But when I remember it, it takes place in a different time-scale, much slower in duration. When I remember, the muzzle of the gun comes down slowly, then wavers to a rest, and the trigger is squeezed, and the graphite-colored bullet leaves the muzzle, screwing forward steadily through the dark waves of air it displaces. When the bullet reaches the burnished dynamite cap it touches it gently. Then there is an orange-white flash, jagged as in a comic strip panel, and a heavy remnant of the tree tears away agonizingly with a sound like bones breaking and the white flesh of the wood shows clear and watery. The mass of limbs plummets the damp earth and a sprinkle of pink-white petals showers up and slowly settles like snow drifting windblown.

At this moment invisible layers of clothing peel away from my body. My eyesight perceives the objects around me as more colorful, more angular, more distinctly themselves than I have ever known them. My skin receives a shock as if I had stepped from a warm bath into a freshet of icy wind. Every nerve opens its eyes. The world about suddenly rushes in upon me, a being so long closed away that it can take its proper domain in no manner but violently.

And in the same moment that someone who is myself is born again, someone who is myself also dies. From this instant I can date my awkward tumble into the world; and here now I remain, alert and half-alive.

If I could get it back, if I could return, I would undo it all. I would wrap myself in dream ever more warmly and would sink to the bottom of the stream of time, a stone uncaring, swaddled in moss. And when the Judgment Day trumpet shattered open this world, and when I had to go sit across the desk from that harassed angel who sat there making out the endless dreary forms for every person who ever lived, I would account for my life in this way:

"I slept and never woke. Even in my dreams I never harmed another, for no one else entered those dreams. I am so innocent I might never have existed."

— But now, now I could no longer say that.

~~~~~~~~~

Bargains in the Real World

Ernie wrote a letter to his wife on the computer, but the computer lost it, and as he tried to reconstruct what he had said, he found that he couldn't retrace the words. Mrs. Lamb from the next office came in to help him.

"Sometimes these things get a *virus*," said Mrs. Lamb. "Do you think your machine has a *virus*?" She spoke the word as though it had a foreign meaning.

"I don't think so." Ernie Bosch had just come back from having lunch with his son. He told Joel the divorce papers were complete and that he planned to marry Rose in the fall. Rose was the woman he had been seeing for the past year.

"What about Mom?" Joel asked.

"She'll probably marry again too."

"You mean I'll have two sets of parents?" Joel spoke with a tinge of disgust, but his body sat like a fortress, private and wordless. He shared with his father an indisputable ability to concede; and though he didn't say it, he felt renounced.

Ernie saw this, and thought of all the times he sat beside Joel and vowed to be different for him. If Ernie had to guess, he would say that his life now was due to his own ignorance about things. Ernie never blamed others for what happened, though because of that he blamed himself doubly. His life was like a dress rehearsal, he expected it not to go well.

Mrs. Lamb pushed more buttons trying to find the letter Ernie had written. She knew that Ernie and Janice were separated, but she never asked any questions about it. Ernie wondered if he himself might have a virus, or that maybe he looked sick and that was why Mrs. Lamb had mentioned it.

Ernie had just turned fifty, short and slightly overweight. He was bruised by the world, but wasn't conscious of his bruises. His clothes had a ramshackle appearance, and for that reason the world looked too big for him. His hands lay flat and large like sycamore leaves, and since his divorce, his pant legs crept up above his ankles. People worried about him. He walked around in an uncollected state of mind.

"Why, Joel's here," Mrs. Lamb said. She looked up to see Joel in the doorway. Joel hadn't said anything when he came in, but his face looked as if a brush fire had swept over it, bare and raw as burned ground.

"Lucas Wiley's gone," Joel said. Lucas was Joel's best friend. He always threatened to run away, and his parents spoke of these threats without believing them.

"What do you mean?"

"He left. That's it. That's just what I mean." Joel sounded angry with his father, and Mrs. Lamb slipped quietly into her own office. Joel still had on his coat and Ernie lifted his from the coat rack. He put it on as they walked to the car.

"I knew it when we were having lunch. I probably would've told you, but what you said made me forget until when I got back to school and everybody was scared. He left a note. Like a suicide or something, but he just went off. There was police and everybody asking questions. I didn't say what I knew, or even that I knew anything."

"Did anybody ask you?"

"No. Not police. Some people, though, said did I know. I said I didn't know where he went, and that part was true."

They had arrived at the car and Joel waited for his father to unlock his side.

"It's not locked," Ernie said, and they got in. "You should say if you know anything."

"But I don't."

"Not anything?"

"I know where he *might* be. I know he might be one of two places."

"Where's that?"

"He likes to go to a place way back in the woods, and he keeps beer there, sometimes whiskey, and he gets drunk some-times, but it doesn't take much for him to get drunk. I think he just acts like it."

Ernie wondered if Joel did this too, but it wasn't the time to ask. He started the car and asked where this place was, and where Joel thought the other place he might be was. Ernie said they would look in both places. He said Joel had to tell what he knew, because Lucas was the kind of boy who might hurt himself and maybe they could protect him from it.

Ernie Bosch was not a man of action, but he was a man of principle. He found the will to act if there was a reason and if the reason was to protect someone. He left his marriage because his wife no longer loved him and he wanted to protect her from spending a bad life with him. He made the decision to marry Rose because she needed him and said she didn't know what would happen if he wasn't around. He protected Joel in all the ways he knew, and now he would try to keep Lucas from performing something regretful. They drove five miles outside town to the edge of Barrow's Pond, and walked from there into the woods.

"He walk all this way?"

"He walks all this way all the time. His parents don't care."

The woods had the smell of rain. The ground around the pond was soggy, even with the dry spell that had come in September. Ernie tried to think of what they might encounter, and if they would find Lucas or if they would have to wait for him.

In the restaurant where they had lunch, Ernie had not minded waiting for Joel. Joel had to walk from school and usually arrived a few minutes after the hour, so Ernie sat in the queasy smell of long-cooked food and talked with the waitress whose name was Viola – though it was spelled wrong on the name tag she wore over her big left breast and said instead *Voila*.

When Joel finally came in he sat down and they ordered the cheese melts. Viola brought them cokes before they even told her to.

"What I say may surprise you," Ernie said, deciding to blurt it out. He couldn't think of what else to do. "I'm going to get married again."

Joel knew Rose, but didn't like her. "Why?" He didn't like the way she smelled, like biscuit dough.

"Well, we like each other a lot." Ernie scooted around in his chair. "I don't want anything to be different between us though." His words sounded stupid and hollow.

"Is she gonna move into your apartment?" Joel spent weekends with his Dad, and wondered now what would happen to these weekends.

"No. But her house is big, and far enough out that we can hunt dove and even deer on the land out there."

It was the beginning of summer when Ernie fell in love with Rose, though he had known her for seven years and knew her husband before he died. Rose took care of him in ways that Janice could never do, and she had a sweetness that almost never crossed him. He thought he could be around someone like that forever. It might even be easy.

"Did you tell your mother you were coming out here with me?"

"Yeah." He spoke as if Ernie had no right to ask anything about his mother.

There was a path that Joel was following, though it was not a clear one, and at times the path turned into no path at all, then it picked up again as they went on.

Ernie followed him, looking up at times to see a scattering of clouds and sky moving away in every direction. He tried to get a picture in his head of how it might be when the distance burned away and he was left standing alone. He wondered sometimes if this had already happened.

"I didn't even think of coming here until you kept asking me. I mean, I hadn't been here since summer."

They were headed toward a specific place, and though Ernie had been in these woods before, he didn't recognize anything he saw. Joel walked in front of him, a small, wiry boy with the burden of being thirteen.

They shifted through the brush and sticky branches, avoiding broken places in the ground until Ernie saw, and Joel pointed to, a shack leaning and almost fallen. Ernie opened the makeshift door carefully, because the whole structure looked as though it might collapse in moments. He didn't want to go inside, and told Joel not to.

"It's all right," Joel said. He was in a good mood now. "It's sturdier than it looks." He pushed the wall to show its sturdiness. The wall did not budge.

"He's not here." Joel spoke with disappointment, but then he saw a few school books and Lucas' bookbag in the corner and said, "Maybe he is."

"You think he heard us coming?" Ernie asked.

Joel gazed around for other evidence of Lucas. "He won't like to have somebody else in here. Even me. He told me once I couldn't come back, because I brought another person. He said I broke the code he had with me. But I didn't know he felt that way. Anyhow, he won't let me back in. I hadn't been here since summer."

Joel sat on the floor of the shed. In the corner lay a small pallet where Lucas Wiley sometimes slept. Sheets were tucked neatly around the pallet, and a crate beside it had a clock and portable radio.

"Looks real homey," Ernie said to no one.

Ernie had to admit that in this shed there existed a dark, protective peace. He wanted to sit down and stay awhile. He wanted to see what was so simply felt. The floor was made of old wood boards, pink with dust and spangled with light that fell through the cracks. The rays of dust extenuated his feeling of shadowy peace. It was not a calmness. Instead, all his senses felt heightened, as fear does sometimes, or sickness. He felt alive, adrift, afire.

"What's the matter?" Joel said. "You look funny."

"I'm just thinking," Ernie lied. "I'm just trying to think of where Lucas might be. Maybe we'll wait here for him."

"I don't know. He's gonna be mad I brought you."

"I think we should wait." Ernie spoke with the authority of a father who knows just what to do in such situations.

The floor was swept clean, with the dust of years settled on the boards, and Ernie let his hands rest in the softness of the wood. He had never felt like this before. He was afraid he might never feel this way again.

Lucas Wiley's parents were not his real parents. They owned a big house in a section of town reserved for the very rich. Joel visited Lucas there with Mrs. Wiley, a lawyer, thin, her face dimmed by a miserable spirit, and Mr. Wiley, who served on the City Council and sold real estate. Lucas' real parents died in a car wreck four years ago. The Wileys adopted him out of pity and out of their own wish for a child. They expected Lucas to be grateful, not to be the kind of trouble he was.

Ernie knew about Lucas. He had studied his case even before Joel grew to be his friend. Ernie worked at the Board of Education as a Special Assistant to the Superintendent. His promotion a few years ago was due to a speech he wrote called "The Ten Tenets of Education." And though the speech was without much imagination, it was simple and direct enough to hit the hearts of school officials. Ernie visited around the state to deliver his speech, and once it was xeroxed and sent out to superintendents in other states. Now, Ernie couldn't remember even one of the tenets which had made him so famous.

Joel hadn't said anything for several minutes, then he spoke. "Are you really gonna get married?"

"What?"

"I told Mom and she didn't know anything about it," as though this might nullify Ernie's marriage to Rose.

"No, she doesn't know. I wanted to tell her myself. I forgot to say I wanted to tell her."

"Well, she knows now. But she thinks that maybe you're just *thinking* about getting married, and that probably you won't do it at all."

Ernie wondered if Janice could be right. She was often right about such things. He would have to face her now, and the disclosure of this made him depressed. He hated to hear her reproaches. He wanted to tell Janice he was sorry, and to say that Rose was the one he loved.

The door swung open and a huge yellow dog came barreling in, stumbling and barking at finding these strangers here. The dog's head was larger than any Ernie had ever seen on a dog. Not exactly his head, but his face. His face was larger than normal.

Lucas came in behind the dog. He carried a gun and a rabbit he had shot, and a sack of food from McDonald's.

"Hey, Lucas!" Joel spoke quickly and with such friendliness that Lucas was taken off guard and didn't see, at first, Ernie behind Joel. "We thought you were gone off."

Lucas saw Ernie. "What are you here for, Mr. Bosch?" He was polite. Lucas knew how to be polite. He would try to act as though nothing was wrong.

"Everybody's worried about you," Ernie said. "They found your note."

"So what?"

"So, they don't know where you are."

"So, I'm here." He was surly now, not polite at all. "What're you going to do?"

"We're not going to do anything," Joel said. "We're just seeing where you are." It was one of those friendships, anyone could see, where one boy thinks the world of the other, and the other hardly notices the one who worships him. The dog had been shooed out, but came back now, and the shed was suddenly and irrevocably crowded. The dead rabbit lay in the corner next to the book bag and the dog went for it, growling as though it might still be alive. Lucas and Joel yelled and pounded it away from him.

"Get outa here, Galilee," Lucas yelled, and Galilee went to lie down just outside the door. "He nearly tore it to pieces." Lucas held up the bloody rabbit. "I might as well give it to him now." He threw the rabbit out the door and Galilee carried it into the woods to feast.

"You want some of this food?" They sat down in a circle and Lucas opened the white McDonald's sack. Ernie wanted to mention that he should wash his hands first, but nothing seemed appropriate in a usual way, so they each took whatever sandwich Lucas gave. They ate sharing one large drink. Ernie refused anything to drink until he had finished his sandwich, then took a few sips. He praised this place, and Lucas could tell that everything Mr. Bosch said, he meant it.

It was while they were sitting there that it happened. The sun was going down, so there was no reason for there to be so much light. But for what seemed a full minute, a light came in from an angle higher than where the sun was, and spangles of light flew all around them — moving and jerking like some old-time ballroom dance floor. And the effect was one of intense movement or a jerky movie, so that nothing for that time seemed real, except the moment.

The experience was like a dream Ernie sometimes had when there was an image the mind would light on for a longer than usual time. And maybe there even seemed to be a shimmer around one moment, or part of the dream, and when Ernie woke he remembered the shimmer though he could never describe it very well. While the light was so furious around them, they were quiet as if they had heard a voice speak, and Galilee came in and stood very still – looking, but not barking. His yellow presence sealed the experience for them. They felt balanced by his full head.

When it was over, Lucas said, "Did you hear anything?" and Ernie said he didn't, but he wouldn't have been surprised if he had. Joel didn't answer, but Lucas said he heard something and it was like a voice, but not outside his head. He said he heard it say something.

"What'd it say?" Joel asked him.

"It said, 'Bury the bones.'" Lucas looked slightly weary when he said this. Weary and puzzled. "It said, 'Bury the bones where-they-are.'" And he got up as if he might be ready to do such a thing.

"What bones?"

"I don't know."

"You don't know what that means?"

"No."

Ernie thought how strange this was, and he thought too that maybe Lucas had been drinking, but he didn't smell any liquor and if he'd been drinking Ernie would be able to smell it. "So, what do you think then?" Ernie asked.

"We have to find them," Lucas said. "We have to find the bones." He included all of them in this. He was on a mission and expected them to be on a mission too. "I think I know where they are."

"You do?" Joel was surprised.

"Yeah, because when I heard it, I saw the place in my mind. It's near the edge of the pond, on the other side."

Ernie decided to play along, though he also felt he believed Lucas completely. As they walked toward the pond, Joel said, "I heard it too."

Ernie did not believe Joel, but said nothing.

"I did," said Joel. "I heard it and know exactly where you're going." And it was not until that moment that Ernie realized that he too had a picture of where they were going, though he hadn't been on this side of the pond before. This side of the pond belonged to the Johnson's nephews and they had No Trespassing signs posted everywhere, not wanting or approving of hunting of any kind. Hunters avoided the Johnson side. Still, Ernie knew what the place looked like, but he didn't say this because he wanted to see if the picture already in his head would match up with the real thing.

Galilee tagged along, but when they moved onto the Johnson's land, he loped ahead and came upon a small clearing that was exactly what Ernie had pictured and Joel said, "That's it."

Lucas nodded. The clearing had tall, thin trees surrounding it, and in the middle they could see where a large tree had been cut down leaving a space about the size of a small room. Grass had already begun to sprout up on the forest floor.

There were bones on the ground, and Ernie, when he saw it, was amazed. "What do you know about this?" Ernie spoke as though he interrogated them.

"Nothing," Lucas said. "I only know what we just did. I only came here because of what just happened in the shed. That's all." There was nothing frantic or untrue in his voice, and Ernie turned to Joel.

"And you?"

"I never even been here before. Not to this place. I been all over everywhere else though." The bones were at his feet and Ernie lifted one of them. It felt dry and brittle.

Galilee walked around the bones, then wandered off to find a piece of clothing and brought it to them. It was a vest, the size of a woman or a young girl, and it was intact, though covered with muddy leaves and small white bugs.

"We'll have to report this," Ernie said. "It might be that somebody's died out here on the Johnson's land." He put down the bone.

"It hardly looks like a human bone though," said Lucas.

"Probably just some deer or something." Then he said, "How can we say we found it? How will we tell it?"

"Say Galilee found it. Say he came and got us and made us come here. Say he barked and went crazy till we did." Joel spoke, but Lucas didn't deny that they should say this. He didn't mind using Galilee for an excuse. They needed a reason other than the spangles of light.

"We'll have to report this," Ernie said.

Lucas took the vest and folded it in a soft wad. His eyes had the meekness of someone in love. "We need to bury the bones." He spoke with authority. "We have to."

Lucas had been adopted several months after his family was killed by a truck crashing into their car. They were coming home from a visit with his father's brother in Comer, Georgia. Lucas was ten years old. The truck driver believed everyone in the car was dead when he went to get help, but Lucas had crawled out the back window, alive. He had seen his family scattered and unrecognizable.

Once when Lucas got suspended from school, he came with his mother to the superintendent's office. They sat in Ernie's office first. Lucas tried to defend his actions, but Mrs. Wiley said, "You don't live in the real world, Lucas."

Lucas thought he knew the real world better than anyone. He had seen it. He had stood for a long while looking at his family before anyone came. "You're not my real mother," Lucas said back to her.

They dug a hole now with sharp rocks and scooped dirt with their hands. Joel and Ernie placed the few bones in the hole while Lucas made a cross with two sticks. He wrapped it with a vine to make it stay in the shape of a cross. Ernie helped build a slight mound so it would look like a grave, and Joel put some leaves and sections of moss on top. Ernie said he thought it probably was an animal of some kind, but now Lucas and Joel liked the dangerous thought that it might be a person.

"There," said Lucas. "I guess we should pray or something."

"I guess so." Joel put the last of the dirt onto the bones. "Who's gonna do it?"

Ernie didn't offer. It had been a long time since he had prayed for anything at all.

"I will," said Lucas, surprising everyone. They all bowed their heads, as Lucas shifted his feet into a sure place on the ground.

"*Oh Lord*," he began, knowing how to begin, "*there has been somebody here that you know and that we have buried and we think it is some woman. So now, if you take her up with you and if you wish this soul to come from the ground, then we will be glad to have participated in this thing. And we think something has happened, but we don't know what, or how to explain it to anyone. So, if you can tell us how to say this, then people will know that what we did was the right thing. Because we have done what was asked, and we cannot forget ever this place and how it all came to pass here. And now we hope nothing bad happens again, not to anyone we know or don't know. And when we go home, please make us heroes in the town so that people will say our names,*" and he added, "*on the radio. Amen.*"

When he was through, there was a silence. They could smell the cool odor of earth. And when they all looked up, Galilee stood with his head still bowed. He was chewing on the cross.

It was after six o'clock when they got back to town, but the sun had not set. They went straight to Sheriff Munsy's office — a hot airless room off Seventh Street. They told how they had come across bones in the woods, and buried them. Lucas held the muddy vest. Their voices were haggard and proud as they told it, and the sheriff listened along with the other two men in the office with him.

"Did you see anybody else out there?"

"No, sir."

"Well, I mean, what made you go out to the Johnson's land? It's posted, right?"

"I know. We were looking for Lucas." Ernie told most of it,

but he didn't mention the shed, or the spangled light. "Joel and I looked for him in the woods. We saw Galilee first, then we saw Lucas. He'd been hunting rabbits out there."

"You think he had anything to do with this?" Sheriff Munsy asked the question to Ernie, but looked toward Lucas.

"No, sir. We ran across the bones coming back. Just saw them there. Lucas was as surprised as anybody." Ernie's lie came as a shock to himself, as well as to Joel and Lucas.

The sheriff spoke thoughtfully. "You think those bones had been out there long?"

"Yeah," said Ernie. "Some animal, probably."

Then Joel said how he and Lucas hunted out there all the time. He said they'd seen old cow bones before.

Sheriff Munsy lifted the muddy fabric from Lucas and shook it over the trash can. "Probably not much chance of finding out anything." He looked at the three of them standing together like tired soldiers. "What made you run off like that, boy?" he said to Lucas.

Lucas smiled, but not a real smile. It was one learned more than felt.

"We couldn't make heads or tails of that note you wrote. You nearly scared us to death." Sheriff Munsy touched Lucas' shoulder. "Come on, I'll drive you home."

"No thanks, Sheriff," Ernie said. "We got Galilee outside. Anyway, I have to take Joel to his mama's. Lucas can ride with me."

"I'm gonna stay with *you* tonight," Joel said. He didn't usually spend weeknights at his dad's, so the suggestion felt like a promise.

They told the sheriff goodnight.

Mrs. Wiley held her cat to her chest when she opened the door to see Lucas, Ernie, and Joel. Her arms looked long in her wide-sleeved robe. "Where have you been?" She spoke like a ventriloquist and stepped toward Lucas. Mr. Wiley stood back from everyone, as though he couldn't be touched.

Ernie told them everything, but nothing about the shed of light. There was only one world to live in, though there were many to experience. He spoke from the world they lived in and never tried to explain the other.

He made what they had done sound heroic, but in the car Joel asked his father, "If we'd told them what happened in the shed, would they've believed it?"

"I don't think so."

"His parents sure looked surprised to see him," Joel said. "His mother looked sick."

Ernie looked off over the dark fields. He felt like a man leaving mountains that had always been familiar to him – not turning to see them again, but not able to forget their shape at his back.

Joel went into the house to get his pajamas and his school books. Janice came to the door and Ernie told her that Joel would stay with him for the night. He told her, too, that he would marry Rose in the spring.

Later, when he tucked Joel into bed, Ernie said, "If you need anything, call to me. I'll leave the door open so I can hear."

"Okay, Dad." Then he said, "Listen – "

"What."

"It's all right if you marry that Rose person. I mean, it'd be good, you know? I could come out there and hunt. We'd have fun."

"Sure," Ernie patted Joel's arm. He could feel the warmth of skin through his pajamas.

"Do you think we'll get our names in the paper?"

"Maybe."

"Will it be on the radio, like Lucas said?"

"It might." Ernie leaned to turn off the light. "Joel, do you know what Lucas wrote in that note? Did you see it?"

"Yeah. He said what his name was, I mean, his real name. It said, *My name is Luke Sanford.*" When Joel said this, he underlined in the air with his finger. "That's all it said."

Thinking of Lucas — picturing his face, then hearing his real name — was like the difference between seeing a reflection in a window and then seeing through it. So for the rest of that night, Ernie tried to understand the mad proportion of their experience. He thought of all the arbitrary forces acting together in the world, and the algebra of other worlds. Of Lucas in bed, and Joel, and the unsleeping that went on in the dark woods.

Then Ernie closed his eyes, but before he slept, he turned his head sideways, trying to bring back the shed of light, and he bargained silently for an answer. But for many nights beyond that night, Ernie wondered if it was lunacy to try and rid anybody of an old life.

CHARLES EDWARD EATON

The Case of the Missing Photographs

The experience of feeling like a punching bag is endemic to cocktail parties. People pass by, take a well-aimed jab just to show who the competition is, and leave you swinging wildly back and forth only too aware of what hit you but unable to do anything very decisive about it. Marjorie and I often come away with a sense of having been knocked about by champions or left to hang unnoticed in a corner of the social gymnasium.

Thus it can hardly be described as anything less than a "beautiful event" when someone turns the metaphor, surrounding us like a pleasant summer breeze where we are suspended, available and unthreatening, like those Chinese chimes that used to hang on old-fashioned porches. The pendent pieces of glass painted with flowers or little figures reminiscent of ideograms were at once transparent and appealingly exotic. There is nothing more congenial than equating one's feelings with such an image which can be approached, and is receptive, from all angles, responding with light-hearted music.

The day we were going to the Cowdens I was determined to maintain just such an affirmative mood. Lying in my bath, pleasantly relaxed, I initiated my usual ritual with Marjorie. Going over the list of our friends, several of whom I thought would be there, I planted in her mind the notion that we might meet someone new. We did not know the Cowdens all that well, and they must have a portfolio of at least ten or twelve people who were good prospects. Marjorie is patient with me in my bath, as though she understands what it is to be a supine male in his late thirties, subject to her intrusions from the dressing room where she carefully selects and applies just the right armor a Connecticut woman should wear in a given situation. I think, too, she rather enjoys the ritual of preparation, as if it might, indeed, exert some kind of mystical control over coming events, and as I towel off, she looks at me as if *there* were a man who should be able to ring anybody's bells. Thank God, Marjorie and I are on very musical terms with each other, and I have no qualms about being "viewed in the nude" by a woman who long ago surrounded me like a summer breeze.

When we arrived at the Cowdens, Marjorie looked and smelled as fresh as one of the peonies which bloomed along the walk, and you might say that we could have been taken for a pair of champions if you only glanced at us. The party was in the garden, the light a filtered radiance of the sort one feels has been earned by the purification of the long winter, and the voices rose like a confessional of bees. But underneath the canopy of sound, more melodious than it would ever have been indoors, the reality of the situation set in. To whom were we going to talk – Mrs. Arlington Smith who had the longest nose and the oldest house in Meadowmount, the Laynes whose minimal art matched their personalities, the Daleys who pushed the collecting of old maps, the Irvings who seemed to breathe a cloud of geographical halitosis as they expatiated on their travels? Instead we soon found ourselves talking to each other. Marjorie began to look like a damp peony dipped in some social fountain of dismay, and I rocked back and forth on my feet, reflecting that an impasse of this sort can do sad and irreparable damage to a lovely Connecticut afternoon.

Janice and Nat Cowden looked utterly punch-drunk from their efforts to bring people together, but Janice finally got wind of the fact that all was not well in our corner of the garden, and snatched a couple from under the long nose of Mrs. Arlington Smith, applying them as a tourniquet to our ebbing spirits.

It was a brilliant decision to match us with Claire and David Steadman, for we prospered the moment we accepted the transfusion of their company. I am a literary critic, writing fairly successfully for the quality journals, and Claire, it turned out, had read one of my books, which in itself is always a summer breeze. David, an Englishman, applied just the right touch of gallantry to the damp peony which gladly entrusted itself to his subtle, grooming hand. While I was allowing myself to be praised, standing in a scented wind that dried up all my nervous perspiration, I discovered that I found the praiser physically attractive as well, not so much as Marjorie, but then a man's imagination must have its harem of second bests. Claire was tall and slender, but one could have wished for a bit less plain and a bit more promontory. She had gray-green eyes and hair of a rusted strawberry color tending in the direction of gold. Though her two front teeth were slightly pushed together in the point of a V as if her face had at one time meant to be broader, freer, then had contracted and crowded the oral cavity, it was not unattractive, suggesting the quality of a child who has yet to have her teeth straightened.

When we switched partners, David let me do most of the talking, perhaps in gracious acknowledgment of how attentively I had listened to his wife. But no one seemed stanched or repressed. We were brimming cups as our mutual interests bubbled up and over — books, music, painting, theater, swimming, walking in the woods. David, who brimmed the least, nevertheless nodded frequently, looked wise, and, though he was not tall, his fresh English complexion, regular features, and imperturbable manners created a solid impression that provided weighty periods for his wife's ecstatic sentences. All of us went home happily assuaged as though four people had been making love in public. The garden had rung with our laughter, and Janice Cowden, tired as a sheared sheep, beamed gratefully at us when we left.

Claire was the first to call and invite us to dinner the following weekend. They entertained, she explained, only on Saturday, since David, an English master at Choton, was always busy with extracurricular activities during the week. Her directions were precise, and we found their house without difficulty, a charming old saltbox, huddled in a larkspurish and snapdragon sort of garden. There were two other couples, a young poet and his wife from Choton, and a doctor whose wife Claire had known in art school. Claire introduced us with just the right amount of pride in her voice as Evan and Marjorie Harrington, and managed to give us the impression that the party had been built around us.

As it grew cooler, we went inside for dinner, finding the tasteful interior one would expect from Claire, country-house Connecticut without any corny, pseudo-colonial effects, though we were surprised to find that they occupied only the first floor. Claire alluded to the fact when there was a loud scuffling above by saying that "our mice have big feet," but I noticed that her wit had an element of strain in it.

This was the first indication that she was not as much at ease in her own environment as she might have been. She served a delicious but complicated curry which was later to have such disastrous effect on our digestions that we were ready to answer Ruskin's famous question, "What do you have to say to India?," entirely in the negative.

It was pleasantly obvious, however, that Claire felt particularly drawn to me since she arranged for us to sit together both during and after dinner, and I had the foolish, though not ungratifying, feeling that she looked to me for some almost extrasensory communication not afforded by the others. Though everyone else called me Ev, she always addressed me as Evan, but the formal approach did not always harmonize with her ardent, almost hectic desire to get her thoughts across. Consequently, she tended to enter a serious conversation without preliminaries, rather as one might split a melon.

Noticing that I was glancing through a book on modern painting, she came over, put down her coffee, and observed, "I think Vlaminck was right when he said Picasso was the perverter of modern art, don't you?"

"Well, perhaps," I hedged. "If you mean he was obsessively devoted to change."

"*Après* Picasso, *le déluge*," she persisted. "Nothing but a runaway river of change. Nothing but fads and fashions. Abstract Expressionism, Pop Art, Op Art, Minimal Art. The works." She picked up another book which had a painting of a large, unsavory hot dog and bun on the cover and handed it to me.

"What about the Blue and Rose periods?" I asked lamely, returning the book to the coffee table. "Paintings like *Femmes au Bar* and *Les Saltimbanques*?"

"They were done by another man. Vlaminck wasn't talking about them."

And that was that. No compromises. No concessions. Only the high, thin laughter that floated around us when I looked too troubled. I sensed that in some way I was not satisfying her, but, for the life of me, I could not discover what was lacking. When she turned to talk to her other guests there was an aura of psychological excitation about her which made me feel vaguely guilty as if I caused her to react in a manner that was not altogether good for her.

But the evening, nevertheless, was a "beautiful event" as far as we were concerned, and we let only a respectable three weeks pass so as not to seem pushing before we returned their invitation. Marjorie keeps a sharp lookout for what she calls "the drama of the garden," and tries not to invite anyone over between the acts. For the Steadmans, the jeweled scepters of the phlox were in bloom and, in another part of the garden, the mounds of pink and red rambler roses seemed to cover the barrows of ancient kings. Our house is also old, but we have made less effort than the Steadmans to remain true to the period, mixing old and new, preferring to let it live its life in the present century as well. Hoping to make them feel at home, we invited their poet friend and his wife from Choton, inarticulate as we found them to be, and Maisie Freemantle, an English artist in her sixties, who looked rather like a cocker spaniel fed all year on plum pudding.

We did not give them the tour of house and garden we sometimes inflict on champions for want of a better way of getting the occasion off the ground, but Claire visited each flower bed like a butterfly until Maisie, entirely unaware of the floppy canine image she aroused, stood in her way before a final one as if to say you have seen all the flowers in the world except the rarest: "Smell me. Admire me. You don't know what you've been missing." But Claire soon sought me out, turning Maisie over to David, and, taciturn though he was, I saw him occasionally open and shut his mouth like a pair of shears as if even he were tempted to cut the stem of her garrulity.

Again I noticed this ectoplasm of nervous irritability which surrounded Claire whenever she came to grips with me. I pass for good-looking and have some reputation in the literary world but I have never thought of myself as either a lady-killer or a Sainte-Beuve. But was I, without meaning to be, some kind of eidolon to Claire? Was it that I had the qualities she associated only with artists and yet had a comfortable and agreeable background, a combination that might annoy a strict moralist such as I deemed her to be?

Several times while we were having cocktails, when I flirted a little or took her less than seriously, she made me feel I sat too casually on the rock of my insouciance, a happy, sunny, but wayward toad who overlooked the lily pond where the mysterious, disklike leaves of her thought let down roots into the opaque water. No one wants to be thought of as an ornamental toad, no matter how gleaming and glistening with life, and I suppose I went out of my way to illustrate that frogs were the equal of lily pads. But none of this helped. I began to sense that the first, fine, careless rapture was over and that she wanted to take me down a peg or two.

During dinner this became awkwardly evident when, unable to keep the conversation light after compliments on Marjorie's excellent food went around the group, Claire introduced the notion of genius and asked whether an artist ever really *knew* when he was one. Various theories were proposed more or less idly by the rest of us who were at the moment more devoted to the first half of that maxim "Dine with the rich, and talk with the wise," when Claire turned abruptly to me and asked, "Evan, do you think you are a genius?"

With my mouth full of deviled crab, I laughed and said, "Of course, can't you see what a big head I've got. Geniuses always have big heads. Look at Churchill, Paderevski."

"Maybe some of it was hair in Paderevski's case," Claire went on with dogged seriousness.

Maisie, uneasy that this curious conversation might redound to my advantage after all, swallowed an enormous mouthful of food in one gulp.

"Talk about big heads. Have you ever seen one larger than mine?" she asked, and put her hands to her cowl of brown hair as if it were a great rock of genius.

Ignoring her, Claire stumbled on, addressing me as though no one else were there. "So you *really* do think so?"

"Think what?" I said, slightly annoyed by now.

"That you are a genius."

The poet dropped his fork, and Marjorie broke in with her warmest smile, "Evan has no doubt whatsoever about his abilities, but he doesn't overrate them either. I find it restful. So few people have the courage to be realistic about themselves. Have some more aspic, Claire, dear?"

"Thank you, Marjorie, my love," I said with a wink. "All that's necessary to have a happy life is to delude one other person. Whom have you deluded, Claire?" I continued, turning to her without a trace of apparent rancor, congratulating myself on how beautifully Marjorie and I worked together.

"Me, of course," David answered as he watched a deep blush spread over Claire's face like a contagion from her hair. "I agree with Marjorie though. I respect self-confidence. Do you remember E. M. Forster saying somewhere that he admired most the people who acted as if they were immortal and society eternal?"

Good old silent, watchful Dave, I thought. He had saved the day, diffusing the tension into something literary and general. He was my man from that moment on.

"You're so right, Mr. Steadman," said Maisie among whose many roles was the ultimate one of peacemaker. "We can all be geniuses in that way, can't we?"

Suddenly, as if someone had just slain the dragon, we found ourselves admiring Marjorie's Bavarian cream molded into a white castlelike tower, and Maisie was able to go home thinking that she had made the party.

But, in spite of Claire's penchant for recognition scenes which dress the drabbest ego in the motley of bruised self-esteem, we saw a lot of the Steadmans and were determined to like them. I became more adept in sidestepping the conflict between Claire and myself, whatever it was, and, if the going got rough, Marjorie would advance like Salome and distract us with the beautiful veils of her wit and grace, and David was our philosopher.

Nevertheless, when Christmas came along with its round of parties, the Harringtons and the Steadmans were exposed to each other in circumstances that could not always be so delicately maneuvered. Maisie Freemantle went into her yearly deep mourning at the approach of the birth of Our Savior as if no man, mortal or immortal, should be given that much attention, and Marjorie and I joked about the "Christmas syndrome" when we noticed Claire growing paler and more staccato as the social pace quickened.

Someone had told us that she had a very beautiful sister who was the family favorite. Another suggested that she had brooded over the fact that she could not have children. In a psychologically oriented world, these little facts about each other seep out and seem to explain our actions as well perhaps, and as superficially, as the ancient humors did. We began to feel a little sorry for Claire, and, if she were not going to provide a summer breeze for us, our kindness and understanding might help to keep some of the winter chill from her heart.

This attitude still prevailed when we saw her on Christmas Eve at the Weavers, a charming couple who always try to give their parties an original twist. That evening it was to be the passing of a Christmas Box from which each couple would take a slip of folded paper, and whoever had the winning number would win a series of photographs of one person in the family. The prize had been donated by Jacques Rimbaud, a rather unsavory character and sometime photographer whose wife Maureen (née Rafferty) ostensibly ran an art gallery but actually specialized in acting out episodes from Krafft-Ebing.

I who never win anything drew the winning number, and I suppose there were others who thought "Them that has, gets," but everyone was perfectly agreeable about it. Only Claire spoke out in a loud voice, "Well, I hope you are going to let Marjorie have *her* picture taken."

Perhaps it was the word *let* that did it, but I had a nice Christmasy desire to slap her.

This time Marjorie was considerably quicker than I. "Claire, dear," she said, "you make it sound as if Ev keeps me in a dark room."

"Darkroom," one of the more potted guests snickered. "Isn't that where all the developments take place?"

Claire let the rest of the group move back to the punch bowl, and said again, "You *are* going to let her have her picture taken, aren't you?"

I could not think of any answer that did not have a four-letter word in it. But Marjorie once more came forward. "I think it's a family affair, don't you, Claire, dear? But since you insist, I think you ought to know I have already decided it is Evan's turn. He has a new book coming out in the spring."

Claire blushed like the little girl who peed in class, her eyes misted over, and I could have sworn she did not herself entirely know why she had persisted. I got a little drunk that night because I, too, did not know why I aroused such infantile animosity in someone I basically admired. It was as though somewhere in the darkness of the soul Claire and I were children together, and I had been given something for Christmas which she wanted and of which I was unaware. No doubt for some people Christmas, in this sense, is the only day of the year.

After the holidays, there was no direct confrontation between Claire and myself, partly because the ties that bind were no longer so blessed, and we had begun gently to loosen them. Even so, whenever we did run into the Steadmans, Claire made some reference to "those photographs." If Marjorie had swerved one inch from her persistent marital decorum, I think Claire would have been all over her with protectiveness and solicitude. One sensed that her desire to ferret out some difficulty between us was overwhelming and that it had taken this bizarre outlet.

Meanwhile, posed as we were off and on before the camera of her obsession, we did nothing at all about the photographs themselves, admitting that we had developed a slight complex. We felt as though some bad luck would be hidden in a photograph which had become such a strange idol to someone we had so much wanted to like. It seemed to shuttle us foolishly back and forth between appearance and reality that we could be judged by the mere taking of a picture. If either of us decided to have the photograph taken, we would be yielding to Claire, who would read something into an act which was totally superficial in its implications for us.

Another disturbing aspect of the whole thing was that if this sort of febrile mythmaking could go on in the mind of a friend, what caricatures of ourselves must exist in the thoughts of casual acquaintances. It suggested to us in our less sanguine moods that people simply projected others as they went along, posing them as subjects of a private pathology. Claire wanted a mug shot of me, and was determined to have it at the cost of a more pleasant "reality" I had been trying to present to her.

Nevertheless, at the end of February, when we received an invitation to an exhibition of Claire's paintings in the tiny gallery of the local bookstore, we accepted. It was one of those bleak winter days when the radiant Connecticut I so much love shows the sorrows of her soul, and the vivid colors of the paintings with their welcome warmth seemed like so many heaters of various sizes embedded in the walls. But the little room itself turned out to be crowded and stuffy, the paintings, at second glance, were considerably less than first-rate, and one had the uneasy feeling that that was where the work would always remain. Mostly of beautiful young women, conceived, one felt, in too precious an idealism, they revealed a certain interesting documentation of longing. I could not help thinking of Claire's sister.

Maisie Freemantle, dressed in a purple dress which made her bosom look stuffed with a bushel of mashed plums, was the first one to vocalize her feelings.

Pushing heavily against me, plums and all, she whispered loudly, "Aren't they awful? Hasn't she got a nerve giving herself an exhibition?"

The poet from Choton, thin and pale as a paper straw, was poking himself nearsightedly into a strawberry-colored painting as though stirring a soda. Suddenly I was touched with the pathos of it all. This was Claire's collection of friends, about each of whom no doubt she suppurated some "photograph," better or worse than the subject warranted. They were the real exhibit in all their weird vitality and variety, most of them totally unwilling to be developed in the darkroom of her temperament.

Astringent, fastidious Claire was beaded with sweat, her high laughter puffing out of her like steam, and she looked martyred with bewilderment. Not a single painting was sold, and the nonexistent profits were consumed at the large punch bowl. I knew I had to make a special effort and that, in this case, it would not be the "truth that set us free."

As we were leaving, I kissed her, tasting the cosmetic flavor of her damp cheek, and said, "Claire, what a handsome showing of pictures. We do want to come and see them again. Congratulations!"

She looked at me as though she thought I were lying, and closed abruptly that hiatus of cordiality and good manners, sincere in its insincerity, in which we reveal and discover those representations which mediate between the world as it is and we would like it to be.

"What about those photographs? Have you had them taken yet?" she asked, her face whitening. I was too confused by the harsh geography of the closing gap to do anything but smile, bow, and back away with my receding half of a friendship.

So the photographs that meant so much to Claire never got taken. I half-heartedly tried to persuade Marjorie to call Jacques Rimbaud and make an appointment with him to come over, but she said again she loathed the man and that he would merely use the sitting as an excuse to visually undress her. He did not pursue the matter either, and I had every reason to believe that the fact that I worked at home would have inconvenienced his philandering instincts. We agreed, however, that we would not let Claire know one way or the other. We felt we owed ourselves at least the vengeance of keeping the photographs forever in the files of missing persons.

Why didn't it end there? Why do human beings keep toying with each other past the point of reason and civilized endurance? Loneliness provides part of the answer, but I think one must look elsewhere into some basic lust for human encounter, some fascination with what's difficult in the face of the absurdities of human coexistence. Claire could not let go of us, and we would not let go of her as long as the unknown still had any potent charge left in it.

Maisie Freemantle's birthday came up in April, "the cruelest month." Maisie claimed to have known T. S. Eliot, and one of the local wags said that he had no doubt penned that line after encountering her on her birthday. Next to Christmas, it was the hardest day of the year for her to get through, and Claire decided to cheer her up with a "surprise" dinner party of some of her closer friends. We accepted but, the situation being what it was, Marjorie warned me to watch the drinks and steer clear of "the darkroom," the expression we had come to use about anything relating to my difficulties with Claire. I agreed and tried to put on the suit of *bienaise* I had first worn to the Steadmans', now stiffened, it seemed to me, beyond all style or comfort.

Maisie was to arrive late, but we found already assembled the Weavers, the poet from Choton, to whom Maisie had taken quite a shine since he said almost nothing and all of it complimentary of her, his wife, and the usual odd couple who would presumably provide the spice for the occasion.

By that evening, however, Maisie had worked herself into one of her moods, claiming that a storm which had passed through the evening before had upset her "vibrations." Maisie's perceptions extended to the ends of the earth, and a volcanic eruption in Japan produced a tremor in her. Consequently, she was not amused by the surprise party, for she had hoped to come over to the Steadmans', drown the knowledge of the passing years in alcohol, and "cozy off," as she would say of an evening which presented an unbroken aspect of adulation and acquiescence.

Downing a drink, she said to me, "Why didn't she say this was going to be a party for me? I would have worn something else. I don't like surprises. I think they are aggressive. They mean to throw you off balance. How did she know it was my birthday anyway?"

I couldn't resist saying, "Why, Maisie, she probably looked you up in *Who's Who.*"

She blanched as if I had produced a birth certificate and promptly called for another drink. I mentioned to Marjorie that Maisie was seriously in need of some expert "cherishing," and managed to escape and spend a silent, restful cocktail hour with the poet from Choton.

It turned out that I needed it. Claire had gone all-out for the occasion, and was an incandescent bundle of nerves, particularly after she sensed Maisie's ingratitude. The dinner was delicious but promised for me a long and fiery trip down the alimentary canal. It was topped off by one of Claire's spectaculars, which consisted of little clay flowerpots filled with chocolate ice cream like earth into which at the last minute she inserted an iris from the florist. It represented such a striving for effect I felt like eating the iris as I am told Einstein did in the case of an orchid a fancy hostess had put on his service plate. Maisie, overcome in spite of herself, wiped hers clean and stuck it in between her bosoms where it seemed to take root in the richest of soils.

After dinner I sat on the love seat with a generous glass of brandy as compensation for the fact I had only two drinks, hoping that the poet's wife would settle down with me for some discreet politicking in behalf of her husband's career. But Claire, the grand effort of the dinner over, beat her to the draw. I stiffened perceptibly, and we sat there looking out into the room like two people in a daguerreotype, capable of only the most mechanical small talk.

But it was destined momentarily to be a modern color photograph after all, for Claire soon began touching up our study in black and white with little caustic personal remarks. I instructed my diencephalon to hold its fire, but I am afraid it listened to the brandy instead, and the moment perhaps both of us needed arrived like a late, paltry, but nevertheless irresistible impulse from a Greek drama.

"Oh, Evan," Claire said, her face as feverish as Phaedra's. "You never did tell me whether Marjorie had those photographs taken."

"No, I never did," I said impassively, but my brain stem, having folded the gracious umbrella of its cortex, throbbed with mayhem.

"But you did let her have them taken, didn't you?" she continued, giving me her self-righteous Pallas Athena look which I so much loathed.

"God damn it, Claire," I said with a relief that had a curiously vital sensation in it. "Why don't you mind your own business? You've been hounding me about those photographs for months. What's your angle?" I had at long last torn up the likeness of myself I had tried to maintain and given her the pieces.

Claire promptly burst into tears and left the room as if I had assaulted her. Barbaric little flakes of a relationship I had apparently exploded seemed to float down around me like fallout.

Too late now to do any good, the poet's wife came over to me, and I think I may have been fairly rude to her as well. David, who never rushed, did so this time to see to Claire, and Maisie gargled some foolish remark to the effect that Claire too must still be feeling the proximity of that awful storm, so hard on "us sensitives."

I knew I should have held on, but I simply couldn't. I wanted to pour corrosive developing fluid all over Claire as well as myself – See, this is what you are, Claire. This is what I am. Two can play at this game of photographs.

A rueful David reappeared after a while, looking like "a verray, parfit gentil knyght" who nevertheless had a serious woman-problem on his hands. Maisie, warm-hearted at her best, rose to the occasion, said all the appropriate things as she gathered up her birthday loot, let me nuzzle her iris in its very special place, and managed to make David think the party had been a success.

But that evening closed the darkroom forever, or so it seemed. Our friendship with the Steadmans had lasted less than a year, and, since it had every possible affinity to insure its viability, the loss was all the more regretted. The incident was gossiped about in Meadowmount for a while, and then nobody cared. In August we heard that David had given up his job at Choton and that they were living in New York where Claire could pursue her art studies. Later we were told they had gone to live in England, then Europe, and finally we lost track of them altogether.

Perhaps three or four years later, on a beautiful day in July, Marjorie and I went to a large cocktail party at Grandview, a club thickly sown with the seed of champions. We were in a lucid, confident mood, and our skill at giving as well as taking the briskly delivered social punch was better than usual. But since I can never be a wholehearted competitor, I withdrew after a while to smoke a cigarette and enjoy a moment of psychic distance so necessary to anyone who feels that most of his life is spent shadowboxing with elusive ideas and images. Marjorie, beautiful as a marigold in yellow silk, relaxed and released from having delivered her share of uppercuts, was dutifully embrocating Maisie, who looked bruised and loose all over, a punching bag gone to seed. As I was on the point of joining them to add my adhesive touch, I felt a gentle tap on my shoulder, turned and saw Claire Steadman, not looking a day older in a lovely green dress, but somehow more muted and insubstantial, like an image that had blown in from outer space.

One hoped to see David moving slowly though the crowd but sensed with desolating certainty that he was now inoperative in Claire's life. Perhaps it was this intuition that contributed to her insubstantiality – the look of a woman without a man, as if she mattered less to others because she mattered less to herself. It was horrifying, as I was later to think, that dear, kindhearted David had been the most expendable of any of us, so soon to have become a hardened, crusted memory, like a suit of armor from which the meat of a man had been extracted.

Though Claire kissed me lightly on the cheek, and I responded with earthier vigor, something was missing. I realized that it was the cloud of intense nervous excitement that had always surrounded us. There was nothing obsessive in the air, but there was nothing else milling around either — no suffocating martyrdoms, no tortured mythologies. She told us she was now living in Philadelphia and working at the Museum, coming back to Meadowmount for occasional weekends.

I kept waiting for the question, which now seemed age-old, "Evan, what about those photographs?," but it never came. In the slow, suffering chemistry of her emotions, Claire had finally "developed" me. It was probably not the image I wanted to give her and certainly not the one she offered me, but it was a photograph we could both accept. Marjorie and Maisie came up to be kissed and to receive Claire's final version of their likenesses, and we talked together like perfectly normal human beings for half an hour.

None of us gave in to our latent feelings that it was "too late" in the cohesive sense of nows and tomorrows bound together. What might have been in its full, generous entirety would remain forever in the files of missing persons. But it was still time in that Claire had come back if only for a moment to meet us in that hiatus of representations where we suspend the opposing cliffs of personalities like the terrible, frozen music of avalanches which might crush beyond all recognition those fragile surrogates with which we mainly communicate with each other.

When Marjorie and I left Grandview without a noticeable bruise upon us, still looking like champions, Claire was already oddly mystical, even recessive, but it was, no doubt, all for the best that we had not stood too long under opposite eaves, neighborly though they appeared on the surface. The unknown constantly recharges itself, incubating its challenges and rebuffs, and Claire and I, perhaps, were not meant to endure together its struggles and depredations more than once. In retrospect, the mood for everybody concerned had been sensible and civilized: "Let's leave it at that." But when we remember, as we frequently do, how Claire "came back," a visitant to an enigma, Marjorie and I feel our hearts, like the futurists they insist on being, respond to their old fond dream of summer breezes and Chinese chimes.

Washing Dishes

The dog was a tan fice – cowlicked, thin pointed sticks
for legs, a pointed little face with powerful whiskers, one ear
flopped and one straight.

He was lying on the back steps of Mattie Rigsbee's brick
ranch one summer Saturday morning when she opened the
door to throw out a pan of table scraps for the birds. She
placed her foot on the step beside him. She was wearing the
leather shoes she'd cut slits in for her corns. The dog didn't
move. Holding the bowl, Mattie stepped on out into the yard
and tried to see if it was a him or her so she could decide
whether or not it *would* have been possible to keep it if she
were younger and more able. If it insisted on staying she'd have
to call the dogcatcher because she was too old to look after a
dog – with everything else she had to do to keep up the house
and yard. She was, after all, seventy-eight, lived alone, and was
– as she kept having to explain – slowing down. Yet her neighbor, Alora Swanson, was fond of saying, "Yeah, she cuts her
own grass, and keeps that place looking better than I would, or
could." Alora liked to tell about how Mattie fell in the kitchen

and fractured her hip when she was seventy-six and then worked around the house for two weeks before finally, after a sleepless night, consenting to go to the doctor — who had to put a pin in. And during those two weeks Mattie picked butterbeans at least four or five times. After the pin was in, Alora would say: "Mattie, I told you it was broke. I told her it was broke," she would say, looking around. "I said, 'Mattie, it could be broke. You better go to the doctor.' But she wouldn't go. You know Mattie."

The dog, lying on the steps with Mattie bending over trying to see if it was a male, looked sick. It had no spunk — wouldn't even get up so she could see if it was a male or not.

"Well, bless your little heart," said Mattie. "Where in the world did you come from?" The tip of the dog's tail moved once. "Are you hungry, Punkie? You look kind of skinny." The dog snapped at a fly. "I guess I'll have to fix you up a little something to eat."

The dog sat up slowly.

"Well, I'll declare," said Mattie, "you *are* a male."

Back inside, Mattie put the bird bowl in its place by the sink, bent over and pulled out the cast-iron frying pan which she declared was getting too heavy for her. She then warmed some beef stew and water, poured it into a small bowl over two opened biscuits cooked that morning, and started outside with it. Maybe he's gone, she thought. She wanted him to be gone so she wouldn't have to put up with him until she called the dogcatcher. She would have run him off if he hadn't been so skinny and lacking in spunk.

The dog had not left. Mattie put the bowl down a few feet away so he would have to walk and she could tell if he'd been hit by a car. He stood, walked over to the bowl, and with large gulps ate all the food. He looked up at Mattie when he finished.

"You ain't been hit," said Mattie.

When Robert, Mattie's forty-three-year-old unmarried son who ran the Convenient Food Mart in Bethel, fifteen miles away, came that afternoon – he usually dropped by on Saturdays – he said, "Mama, what in the world do you think? Of course he ain't going nowhere after you *feed* him." Robert and Mattie were in the kitchen.

"Well, he was so skinny."

"He's skinny because he's got worms. Look at his eyes." Robert, thirty pounds overweight and graying at his temples, ate from a bowl holding a big piece of apple pie and three scoops of vanilla ice cream.

"I know how to tell worms," said Mattie.

"He's got worms." His mother was going to stand right there and not believe the dog had worms when anybody could look at the dog's eyes and tell he had worms. Why couldn't she just relax and say, "Okay, he's got worms"?

She was standing at the counter, dipping a scoop of ice cream for herself, wearing the brown button-up sweater, unbuttoned, with the hole in the elbow, that she'd been wearing every day, summer or winter, until at least mid-morning for . . . Robert knew for ten years at least. "I don't know if he has or not," she said.

"Okay, Mama." Robert had recently read an article in *Parade* magazine which explained how grown children could avoid misunderstandings with their parents. It said to give up trying to change them. So he decided to give up on the worm argument even though he knew he was right.

"I couldn't just chase him off," said Mattie, "as skinny as he is."

Robert, holding pie and ice cream in his spoon over the bowl, looked at her. "But now you're going to call the dog-catcher?"

"You know I can't keep a dog."

"Why not?" Robert wished she could get a little company, companionship of some sort. Something to care for. An animal maybe, a parakeet. He spooned the pie and ice cream into his mouth.

Mattie turned to look at her son. "With all I got to do around this place? Besides, I'm slowing down."

"All you'd have to do is feed him," said Robert, pie crust on his lower lip.

"Use your napkin. You know it takes more than feeding to keep a dog. I got as much business keeping a dog as I got walking across Egypt. I don't even know why I'm talking about it."

Monday morning, Mattie called Bill Yeats and asked him to come get her chair bottoms. She wanted the bottoms of her four kitchen-table chairs and her den-rocker bottom re-covered with some kind of oil cloth. They were looking so dingy and she needed something she could just wipe off without worrying about it.

Bill said he'd come after lunch. Mattie told him to come around eleven-thirty and she'd have a little bite for him to eat. There was that chicken in the refrigerator. He said okay.

She decided she needed a couple of short boards — so she could place them across the open bottoms of the two chairs she used most often — her kitchen chair and the den rocker. If she put it off she might forget and fall through a chair. She had some boards in the garage. She walked out the back door. She limped slightly from the hip fracture, but, as usual, walked with purpose, her brown sweater hiked up in the rear.

The dog was in the back of the garage. Mattie had refused to name him because of her plans to call the dogcatcher. He got up and walked toward her. Looked like he had gained a little weight over the last day or two, but still he didn't have much spunk. He'd been eating regular for two days now and he did not have worms. Robert jumped to conclusions.

Mattie found two short boards in the back of the garage, started back to the house, stopped and said to the dog, "Listen, I'm going to have to call the dogcatcher. I don't have time for a dog. Shouldn't have kept you this long."

She brought the two boards into the house, then decided she might as well go ahead and take the chair bottoms out and put the boards across two kitchen chairs. Bill would be there before long. She could have everything ready when he came. They would have a little more time to sit and talk. It was just four screws per chair. Bill would be impressed. She'd put on the chicken and then do it. After it cooked, she could give the neck meat to the dog — with some gravy and a biscuit or two. She ought'n to spoil him though, she thought.

She spooned grease into the frying pan, cut up and washed the chicken, salted and peppered it, rolled it in flour, and placed it in the frying pan, piece by piece. Then she got her screwdriver, carried each of the kitchen-table chairs past the kitchen counter over to the couch in the den, dragged over the rocker from in front of the TV, sat down on the couch, turned each of the kitchen chairs upside down, unscrewed the screws, and took the bottoms out. The rocker was a little more difficult. It was heavy for one thing. She turned it onto its side and unscrewed the screws, which were larger than the others, and tighter.

When Bill came, she had the bottoms leaning against the wall by the back door. The chairs were in their places and the boards from the garage were across two kitchen chairs.

"Sit down at the end of the table there; dinner's about ready," said Mattie.

"This is mighty nice of you, Mrs. Rigsbee." Bill pulled out his chair. "You took the bottoms out already?"

"Oh yes. They're over there by the door."

Bill looked. "I declare Mrs. Rigsbee. You beat all."

"Well, I try to do what I can."

"Something sure smells good. You didn't have to go to all this trouble."

"No trouble. I cook three meals a day. Except for once in a

while I'll warm up leftovers — just can't go like I used to. It slips up on you. You'll find out."

"I'm already finding out — I'll tell you." Bill adjusted the board he was sitting on, looked down at it.

"Well," said Mattie, standing at the stove, fork in hand, turning to look at Bill, "I'm lucky to have been able to keep going so long. I thank the Good Lord every day."

"Yeah, well, you sure keep going. That's for sure. Mmmmm, that smells mighty good."

"Well, it's not much. Alora brought me some corn last Friday and it was too much for one fixing, so I had some left and these potatoes are from Sunday. I picked the tomatoes this morning. I got eight plants. 'Lucky Boys.' But Finner and Alora are mighty good about keeping me stocked with other stuff. No better neighbors in the world. They let me pick all the string beans I want. Alora even helps me; but she ain't careful. She'll pick them too young or too old or with black spots. I took Pearl some. My sister. Told her I was sorry about their condition — but that I'd had help picking them."

"Yeah, Finner and Alora are fine people. That your little dog out there?"

"Lord have mercy, I'm going to have to call the dogcatcher. He just took up. I can't keep a dog." She stirred the potatoes. "This is going to have to warm just a little more."

"He's a right nice little dog."

"He's got possibilities, but I just can't keep up this place and a dog to boot. You want him?"

"Oh no. I got two bird dogs."

Mattie put bowls of food on the table. "Now I want you to eat all you want."

"Good gracious, Mrs. Rigsbee."

"Bow your head and let's say the blessing."

Bill left with the chair bottoms at 12:35. Mattie stacked the dishes beside the sink. She had gotten into the habit of not washing her dishes right away after lunch. She waited until "All My Children" was over at two. Nobody knew.

If anybody ever found out that she both watched that program and didn't clean up right after she ate, she didn't know what she would do.

But after all, things did happen in the real world just like they happened on that program. It *was* all fiction, but anybody who read the paper nowadays knew things like that were happening all the time. And that woman who played the old lady was such a good actress, and Erica, Erica was good, too — such a good character, good actress. People almost exactly like her actually existed all over the place nowadays.

And why shouldn't she sit down for an hour a day after dinner and do something for herself. Why, Alora sat around the house all day watching soap operas and then went so far as to talk to people about them. Alora's watching so much television was one reason that when she went on her daily walk she carried that pistol in her hand under a Kleenex.

Mattie poured gravy over the dog's food and took it out to him. He was standing, waiting. Why, he's already learned to tell time, she thought. I'm going to call the dogcatcher right now.

She put the bowl on the steps and watched him. She had only a few minutes before "All My Children." The dog ate all the food and licked the bowl.

"You're getting a little more frisky, ain't you?" she said. "Well, I ain't able to keep a dog. I'm going in and call the dog-catcher right now." She picked up the bowl, went back inside, looked at the clock on the mantel. It was exactly four minutes until one. "My goodness," she said. She would have time to get through to the dogcatcher — and make it brief. She called from the phone on the counter between the kitchen and den.

A woman answered. Mattie explained about the dog and gave her street address. The woman said the dogcatcher might be by that afternoon, or it could be tomorrow. Mattie hung up and glanced at the clock. It was one o'clock on the dot. She walked into the den, bent over and clicked the TV on. She slowly walked backward, still bending over, toward the rocker. Her left hand reached behind her to find the chair arm. Ah, the commercial – New Blue Cheer – was still on. She had started sitting down when a mental picture flashed in her head: *the chair without the bottom.* But her leg muscles had already gone lax. She was on the way down. Gravity was doing its job. She continued on past the customary stopping place, her eyes fastened to the New Blue Cheer box on the TV screen, her mind screaming no, wondering what bones she might break, wondering how long she was going to keep going down, down, down.

When she jolted to a stop the backs of her thighs and a spot just below her shoulders were pinched together tightly. Her arms were over her head. Her bottom was one inch from the floor. Nothing hurt except the backs of her legs, and that seemed to be only from the pressure. How *could* she have forgotten? she thought.

She was amazed that her right arm which she normally couldn't lift very high was so high over her head. And not hurting much. She tried to get her arms down but couldn't. She was wedged tightly. What was she going to do? She looked at Erica on the TV screen.

In a straight line were Mattie's eyes, her knees, and Erica's face.

Nothing seemed broken. But her arms were going to go dead to sleep if she didn't hurry and get them down. She needed to pull herself *up* somehow. What in the world? What a ridiculous fix. That dog. If I hadn't been feeding him, she thought, and calling the dogcatcher, this wouldn't have happened. Lord have mercy – what if Alora comes in the back door and sees me watching this program? What in the world will I say? Well, I'll just say I was sitting down to watch the news when I fell through, and so of course I couldn't get up to turn off that silly soap opera. That's what I'll tell her.

Then she will see my dishes stacked over there.

I've *got* to get up. She will know I came over here to sit down before I did my dishes. I've got to . . .

Mattie's predicament suddenly seemed serious. What if . . . Alora might not come. Robert might not come. For sure *he* wouldn't come before Saturday.

Mattie had known all along there was some reason Robert ought to come more than once a week. Well, this proved it. Maybe now he would start coming once in a while to see if she was all right, hadn't had a heart attack, or a stroke, or hadn't . . . for heaven's sake, fallen through a chair. Well, this was the . . . the most ridiculous fix she had ever heard of. If there were some way to get that dog to bark or somehow go get somebody. How in the world could she get that dog to do something?

She needed to get out before that program was over so that, for one thing, if the doorbell rang she could turn the TV off. And if somebody saw her dirty dishes she didn't know how in the world she could explain that.

What if she *died* one day during the hour her dishes were dirty.

She would have to change her routine.

She was looking at the TV. There was a boy who got a girl pregnant. He did it as sure as day and was lying like nobody's business.

Who might come? It was Monday. Bill said he'd bring the chair bottoms back by Thursday. No later than Thursday, he said. Alora or Finner would come over before then, wouldn't they? But what if for some reason they didn't?

She tried to move. Her right arm moved forward and then back. The chair rocked slightly. Well, she was going to have to turn the chair over – or something – to get out, that's all there was to it. Her arm moved back and forth. Then her head, in time with her arm. The chair rocked. Erica was having a conversation with somebody in somebody's foyer. Phillip's. Wasn't his name Phillip?

The phone rang. She couldn't quite see it – over on the

kitchen bar. It rang again. She strained to get up somehow; then she gave up. It rang again. Who could it be? Probably Alora. Or Pearl, her sister. It rang again . . . and again. Her rocking stopped. Then the only noise she could hear was the television and the clock ticking on the mantel above her head.

Lamar Benfield had been a dogcatcher for four days. He usually held a job for three, four months, then got tired of it and stopped. But he always saved enough money to keep going until he found another job. And he had a nice shop behind his mobile home – did odd jobs, didn't need an awful lot of money since he was still single.

Lamar liked his new job. He fancied himself as good with animals and had been looking for a job which called for travel and working outside. It was almost dark as he turned into the driveway of a brick ranch house. He had four dogs in back and had decided to get this last one so that his load for tomorrow would be light enough for him to take the afternoon off and change the points and plugs on his pickup.

He rang the front doorbell, adjusted his ball cap, shifted his weight, and looked around for a dog. So far he hadn't been bitten. This he attributed to his way with dogs. He heard something inside. Sounded like a child. Well, at least somebody was home. Was somebody saying come in? He tried the door. It was locked.

He walked around to the backyard, looked for a dog. There: a fice on the back steps. He wondered if that was the dog he was supposed to pick up. The back door was open. He looked in through the screen, glanced down at the dog. Dog's a little tired or something, he thought. He looked back inside. "Anybody home?"

"Come in. Please come in."

He opened the door and stepped into the den. The room was dark except for the TV and someone sitting . . . Damn, she didn't have no neck at all. That was the littlest person he'd ever . . . Wait a minute. What in the world was . . . ?

It spoke: "I'm stuck in this chair."

His eyes adjusted. She was stuck way down in the frame of a rocking chair. "God Almighty. How long you been like that?" he asked.

"Since the news came on — after lunch. Can you help me get out of here?"

"Well, yes ma'am. I can maybe pull you out."

"Turn on that light. And turn off that television."

The light was bright.

"My Lord," said Mattie, looking up at the dogcatcher. "I'm glad you're here. I was thinking I might have to stay like this all night. Please excuse the mess."

Lamar glanced around. "What mess?"

"Well, I fell through here before I had a chance to do the dishes."

"All right with me. Let's see. Give me your hands and let's see if I can pull you up."

"I don't know."

"Great day, your hands are cold."

Lamar held Mattie's hands and pulled upward. The chair rolled forward on the rockers and then lifted into the air with her still in it. "That ain't going to work," he said, and set her back down.

"Maybe if you can . . ." Mattie couldn't think of a thing to say.

"Let me just look for a minute." Lamar pulled the chair out a little ways and got down on his hands and knees and crawled around the chair. "Hummm," he said, "looks like you're pretty stuck."

"I know it."

"Might have to cut you out."

"Oh no, not this chair. We'll have to figure something else out."

"Well, let's see, as long as, ah . . ."

"Maybe you could turn me over on the side and just push

me on through like I was started. Think that would work? I don't want to have to cut this chair."

"Well, I could try. Let's see." Lamar tilted the chair and gently started it to the floor.

"I don't weigh but one ten," said Mattie. "I used to weigh between one thirty and one forty. That's what I weighed all my life until I started falling off."

"You ain't fell off too much."

Mattie lay on the floor, on her side, in the chair.

"You mean," said Lamar, "you want me to just kinda push you on through?"

"Have you got any better ideas?"

"No, I don't guess so. Except cutting you out. Let me see if I can pull your legs up straight. I'll have to pull your legs up straight before I can push you on through."

The dogs in the truck started barking. The fice barked back.

"You are the dogcatcher, aren't you?"

"Yes, ma'am."

"Is that the little fice barking?"

"I think so."

"I never heard him bark."

"Is he the one I come after?"

"He's the one." Mattie gasped, "Oh, that hurt."

"I don't think this is going to work."

"Listen, with all that noise I'm afraid Alora might – Alora's my neighbor – I'm afraid she might come over; I want to ask you if you'd do something for me."

"Okay. Here, let me set you back up." Lamar set Mattie back up.

"Would you wash my dishes?"

"Wash your dishes?"

"It's just a few. If you don't mind. I'll pay you something. I'm just afraid that . . . Would you do it?"

"Now?"

"Yes – if you would."

"Okay." Lamar started to the sink. He stopped and looked back at Mattie. "Would you feel better if I sort of started you rocking or something?"

"No, that's all right. The soap and stuff is all under the sink. Just run some warm water in that far sink and wash them and rinse them and put them in the other sink. The wash rag and drying towel are behind the cabinet door there under the sink."

"I let my dishes sit," said Lamar. "Change the water every three or four days."

Lamar washed the dishes. The dogs were still barking. It was dark outside.

The back floodlights came on at Finner and Alora's. The back of their house faced the back of Mattie's. Finner opened the door and looked out. "What the hell is all that?" he said.

Alora spoke from the kitchen. "Where's all them dogs?"

"In a truck it looks like."

Alora came up behind him. "What in the world? What's going on out there?"

"I reckon it's the dogcatcher. Mattie said she was going to call him, you know."

"You want to walk over there?" asked Alora.

"Naw. I've seen a dogcatcher before."

Lamar finished drying the last dish.

"How about pulling me over there so I can tell you where to put them," said Mattie.

Lamar walked over, took hold of the arms to the rocker and slid Mattie from the den into the kitchen.

"See that cabinet right there?" said Mattie. "No, the one beside it. That's right. The dishes go on the bottom shelf in there. The glasses right above. That's right. Now, put those pans under the sink. Okay. Now just drop the knives and forks in that drawer; no, the one beside it. Okay. Now would you just sort of wipe up there around the sink?"

Lamar cleaned up, then hung the dish rag and towel behind the cabinet door beneath the sink.

"I thank you," said Mattie.

"You're welcome, but we got to get you out of that chair. I think I ought to cut through the back bottom there with a saw or take it apart somehow."

"I don't want you to have to cut it."

"Well, let me see if there's some way I can . . . I could saw it right at the back here and it could be fixed back so you'd never know – glue it and brace it on the inside."

"Well, the saw's hanging in the back of the garage," said Mattie. "I don't know what else to do. Cut the light on there by the door."

Lamar got the saw from the garage, came back, and carefully cut through the bottom back of the chair. He turned Mattie onto her side, and then with Mattie lying on the kitchen floor holding onto the lower ridge of a bottom cabinet door, Lamar pried the rocker apart and pulled it from around her.

Mattie lay on the floor on her side with her knees under her chin. She tried to straighten out.

"Let me help you up," said Lamar. He placed his hands under her arms and lifted her. Mattie remained bent.

"Set me on the couch," she said.

Lamar shuffled with her over to the couch and set her down.

"My Lord," she said. "What a predicament. I have never in my life. What do I owe you?"

"Not a thing. I've just got to get the dog and get going."

"Well, let me feed him." Mattie stood very slowly. She was bent. Lamar reached for her. She kept one hand on the arm of the couch.

"I can make it; just a little stiff. If I take my time I'll

straighten out. My Lord. Wait a minute. Let me kind of shake my arms a minute here."

Severely humped, so that she had to look up toward her eyebrows to see straight ahead, Mattie walked slowly by Lamar, into the kitchen, and opened the refrigerator door. She got out a plate of chicken and a bowl of congealed gravy. With a fork she raked the meat off a chicken leg and thigh into a small pan. She spooned on gravy, then poured it all over two open biscuits in the dog's bowl. Bent over, holding the bowl, she walked to Lamar. "Would you feed him that before you take him?" she said.

Lamar took the bowl. "I guess so. If I got time. I got to get on back."

"He's hungry. He ain't eat since one."

Lamar started out the back door.

"Let it cool a little before you put it down," said Mattie.

Lamar fed the dog, then took him away.

That night, after a long hot bath, Mattie noticed that her back, arm, and leg muscles felt weak — she knew they would be sore in the morning.

She sat at her piano in the living room. On top of the piano was a picture of Paul, her husband, who had died five years earlier; a picture of Robert; one of Elaine, now thirty-eight, un-married, a twelfth-grade English teacher — gifted and talented; and a picture of the entire family together. The piano was a black studio Wurlitzer — one she and Paul had bought for Robert and Elaine. Robert had taken lessons for two years and quit. Elaine had taken for four. But she, Mattie, played just about every night, sitting on the bench stuffed with old hymn-books, thumbing through the Broadman Hymnal until she found one of the fifteen or twenty hymns she played well. She could read hymns in the easier keys, playing partly by ear.

She played "What a Friend We Have in Jesus," "Blessed Assurance," and "Send the Light." No damage to her arms from the chair accident, she decided. Then she played "To a

Wild Rose," not a hymn. She had listened as Elaine learned it years ago and liked it so much she learned it herself, and now played it almost every night.

As she walked to her bedroom, more stiffly than normal, she thought about the little dog. "I'm too old to keep a dog," she said.

Trudy Woodlief

Of Trudy's bold appearance and Lottie and Betty's first sally into the Woodlief home

"I had no close friends at all, male or female, until 1937 when Trudy Woodlief moved her family to Milk Farm Road. She and I became good friends despite the fact that I was seventeen and she was twenty-eight with several children.

My mother first told me about Trudy, who had blown into the store and more or less announced that she intended to have credit. Though it battered Porter's nerves to deny poor women credit, deny her he did, and thus Trudy left the store in a rage. People we knew didn't fall into fast rages. They simmered, as with Sade, or wormed around trouble, as with my mother. Rarely did I witness a tantrum or open fight of any public nature. Maybe it had something to do with the heat and our desire not to stir up the temperature. But Trudy apparently swung her arms and stomped and what-have-you, thus early on making a wild name for herself. My mother said she was afraid the incident took years off of Porter's life. He was exceptionally gentle.

My mother finished describing Trudy to me and recruited me to walk down the hill with her to stick our head in the door. As usual, we were not to go empty-handed so we put some canned peaches and tomatoes together with a good portion of a wonderful ham. Such lean ham was a great rarity, and of even greater rarity was the fact that my mother had baked it herself.

We walked down the hill and up to the house. We could see through the screen door all the way to the three yardbabies and two older girls in the back, all already dirty, yet rolling about in even more dirt. Trudy was in the front room, wearing a very chewed-up-looking robe, with one leg high up on a bureau, smoking a cigarette and shaving her legs with lotion and a straight razor. I was thrilled, yet scared to go inside and probably would not have had my mother not urged me through the door.

We knocked on the door and Trudy slunk over and invited us in, not at all modest in her robe. She had that washed-out, cheapy sort of look that some men can call pretty. My mother was examining everything as hard as she could, Trudy as well as the house.

Towards the food, Trudy acted as if she was more or less bored with people bringing her baked hams. She told me I could put everything on the kitchen table, which I did, but only after stacking plate upon plate. When I went back into the living room my mother was asking Trudy a thousand questions of every nature. Trudy, however, was hovered over her legs and only answered my mother if it was convenient with her smoking. I was amazed that she could even attempt to do so much at once, keeping a cigarette in her mouth talking, shaving with a straight razor, yelling at her children through the door.

She managed to answer my mother to say she'd come from

Baton Rouge. And as soon as she said this my mother shot me a look to say, *Oh my goodness! What will we do with somebody from Louisiana!* Louisiana had always been the place that no matter how miserable your life was you could always say, At least I'm not from Louisiana. We always had the impression that people in Louisiana were practicing tropical voodoo, marrying their sisters, and voting for Huey Long all day. Overall, it seemed like a very frightening place to be from.

My mother asked her if everything she'd heard about Louisiana and voodoo was true. *You know, hair balls driving grown men crazy and things of that nature.*

Trudy thought about it and then told us that right before they left Louisiana her grandfather had died and she had made her oldest daughter lean over in the coffin, pick up the dead man's hand, and press it to a strawberry scar on her neck. She said everybody at the wake went Wooo! when it faded.

We also learned that Trudy and her husband, Tommy, had picked up and hauled northward and gotten wind of work in Gordon Randolph's orchards, and so they came and were given the nicest house they'd ever had. She was thrilled with their windowscreens, and thus far things were going lovely, with the one exception that Porter wouldn't extend her credit.

My mother defended Porter, who had fallen on hard times to the point that the cash register people repossessed his cash register, leaving Porter reduced to making change out of his wife's muffin tin. She explained to Trudy that Porter was in no shape to operate on credit. We expected Trudy to say she understood and she'd have to get by the best she could. But she didn't. She said, Fine! Damn him then! And then she threw her other leg up on the bureau and proceeded to smear lotion on it.

She said, Listen, I've still got this leg to go and then feed people. How about y'all get ready and go on?

Though my mother was shaken by Trudy asking us to leave in such a point-blank manner, she had her mind enough to say, *Fine, but let me collect my pan if you don't mind.*

Trudy organized her cigarettes and razor blade and walked towards the kitchen with my mother and I following behind, my mother whispering in my ear all through the long house. *Maybe that's how they get rid of company in Louisiana. Maybe they just ask people to leave!*

When we reached the kitchen we saw all five children taking turns looking under the lid of our pan, pretending to choke, gagging themselves, and making wild faces at my mother. Trudy slapped a few fingers out of mouths and lifted the lid herself. Then she looked my mother square forward and said, They hate ham. They'd rather eat dirt than a ham. Too bad it's not a hen.

In, oh, seconds my mother and I were halfway up to the hill to our house, pulling the ham, the peaches, and tomatoes in the same wagon that had borne it downhill before.

I said, I don't suppose she'll be invited to play cards? I don't suppose they'll be asked to taffy pulls?

No! Phooey!

She yanked the wagon on home barely in time for my father to come home and remark at this odd supper of ham and peaches and cold tomatoes. My mother started to cry. *I've never known a meal to be so persecuted!* Then she excused herself and thus I excused myself and walked out behind her.

A further account of the Woodlief family, including Lottie's first compassion for them all, with the one exception of the husband

"I've always enjoyed the company of more unusual people than most, simply listening to them and looking at them, so thus I felt drawn without control back to the Woodlief household. My mother, though, told me in no uncertain terms to conquer the urge to go down the hill.

Even though she hadn't talked to Trudy but that one time, she liked her less and less every day. She told Sade and Amanda and all the rest several times exactly how high Trudy had her leg up on the bureau. Everybody, particularly those over-weight, was stunned. These were the kind of women who liked to believe that God has very definite ideas about who should be fat and who should be thin. So, when they featured Trudy, so lean, with her leg up to her shoulders, shaving, they felt doomed.

I waited and kept my distance from the Woodliefs, according to my mother's wishes. The Woodliefs kept a great deal to themselves as well. But then after about eight or nine or so months, the children fell into a sheer stealing frenzy, stealing anything they could lift to carry, even down to laundry off the line. Women were very embarrassed over having to go down the hill and ask the children to hand back socks and petticoats. I heard one woman say she would've much rather sent her husband to bring things home, but she was frankly afraid Trudy would drag him bodily into the house and corrupt his affections for her.

Trudy's husband, Tommy, stole in a very brazen manner as well, stealing first dogs and then copper, stripping it and then hoarding it in back of his house in broad daylight. My mother had predicted he would do something like this. We'd passed him several times walking, and she whispered to me that Tommy was of an undesirable element.

He's got criminal blood. He looks like he'd love to go right now and rob a bank.

How do you know?

I can tell.

You can't tell anything. You simply can't give anybody the benefit of the doubt.

Why do I have to? Where is it written that I have to give somebody with criminal blood the benefit of the doubt?

Before John Carroll could think through the copper problem, Tommy loaded it up and sold it and off he went. He just took his foot in his hand and left his wife six months along with twins, with already enough kids to bait a trotline.

This threw my mother into an awkward spot. When news of Tommy Woodlief abandoning his family reached the rummy table, she stopped us in the midst of collecting pennies for a fresh deck to announce her change in attitude. *No matter how filthy this young woman keeps her house and children, no matter how rude she is and how mean her children are, certainly no woman deserves to be fooled up with twins and left stranded.*

Everybody, especially Sade, yelled, Whew! What a bum!

My mother promised them that by the end of the day she'd think of the best way to help. She believed Trudy would be peculiar about community aid, although little did she know that, the second time Tommy left, Trudy walked all the way to town to push for Dependent Children checks. My mother developed the same stern face as she had thinking up the Wassermann solution, the same look as when she yanked the crying, newly poor Amanda Bethune up from her table and restored her self-regard, and certainly the same look as when she explained betting to women so they could have a little thrill on Saturday afternoon. Mr. Roosevelt's programs were very helpful, but I'm sure he never realized how much women like my mother were doing to help him pick up after Mr. Hoover.

Later that afternoon, as though my mother's thinking so hard on Trudy's situation had pulled her to the store, she appeared, smoking and swayback, and she proceeded straight to the counter to hound Porter again about credit. We weren't used to seeing women smoke, pregnant or otherwise.

Trudy said to Porter, I'm asking again for credit.

Porter said more than likely for the sixth time that week that he had pulled in all his accounts and couldn't set up any new ones. He said he couldn't make any exceptions, that he and Celia had to make a living, and he started rambling, overexplaining himself. And then Trudy slammed the flat of her hand on the counter and shouted out loud, Fine! Damn! Then she called the children in from playing in the dust outside. They appeared splinter barefoot and more or less clambered over each other coming through the door. Then they broke apart and shot out and slipped behind various counters like pool balls, extending themselves credit.

Porter was a very fragile man and had difficulty handling anything out of the range of normal, so thus he was robbed of fruity chews and all-day suckers and sheer pocketfuls of ten-for-a-pennies. Celia was braver in this regard and got up from the card table and encouraged the children to unload themselves.

None of this fazed Trudy, who had come back to the living room section of the store and walked around the card table, wishing somebody would make over her and the recent news of her carrying twins. She had previously told us that the X-ray man at the pre-mother clinic had noticed two babies, though the sex, he had said, was a mystery.

Sade noticed Trudy's longing and put her hand down and said, Well, how does it feel to be having twins?

Trudy said, You get more accomplished than having them one at a time. She said this as though she was talking about having one tooth extracted at a time as opposed to a whole mouthful.

My mother said, *Well, I hope you like boys then, because that's exactly what you're carrying. I took note of you walking from the rear and you seemed very squared off.*

Amanda and Sade had read girls, so Trudy was asked to walk again to break the tie. Trudy turned with her hands on what must have been a hurtfully lower back and proceeded from one end of the store to the other one. Everybody looked with an eye towards sizing up sex.

When Trudy got to the door, she turned around and asked what they thought.

Then they all agreed and swore to Trudy that she was carrying a lapful of boys.

Trudy said, Good. She said, Boys' is all the names I've got.

Then she rounded up her children and started out. Amanda

interrupted her leaving to ask what she planned to name the babies.

She told us, Bernard and Barnard, these names going so naturally together.

That fairly took our breath. My mother asked her if that wouldn't get confusing, which it would.

Trudy said, No. She said she intended to call them Pee Wee and Buddy. Then she told us all to have a nice afternoon, and she organized her children out the door and walked the side of the road towards home.

We all got up a nickel or two and my mother trotted me out following Trudy and the children with a little sack of candy. After I caught up and handed over the bag, which they snatched, the children sat down on the ditchbank and fell into the sack. They ate it instantly and threw the bag in the ditch. Trudy picked it up and looked in it, threw it back down and pinched the oldest girl for not saving her any. I thought this was unusual for a mother to care so about candy, but Trudy had birthed first at thirteen and thus understandably mourned sweets.

When I got back to the rummy table, my mother had decided what to do about the Woodliefs. She told the women they'd donate money for Trudy's groceries, giving it directly to Porter and calling it credit. That way everybody would be pleased. We'd be helping, Porter would get his money, and Trudy's gang could eat without paying without stealing.

When Trudy returned and slammed her hand on the counter, Porter said he could let her have a particular amount, whatever it was, fifty cents, a dollar each week, no more no less.

She said in a curt manner, Damn! Ain't that swell?

But Trudy shopped that day and bought as much Cream of Wheat and Post Toasties as anyone had ever seen walk out of the store at once, thus inspiring in us all a great deal of hope for the Woodliefs.

Hope was dashed, though, the following week when my mother, in trying to get up a little community one-act something, approached the oldest Woodlief girl, Florence, about taking a small part, no talking or singing, just standing there. Everyone was eager to involve Florence, as she was so pretty and appeared so thoughtful. But Florence was of her own mind, and told my mother she didn't care to act in some goddamn homemade play. My mother's color left her. Goddamn simply rolled from the child. But Florence took the part finally for a nickel, a carpetbag full of dress-up clothes, and a generous bit of raw sugarcane.

ALLAN GURGANUS

It Had Wings

Find a little yellow side-street house. Put an older woman in it. Dress her in that tatty favorite robe, pull her slippers up before the sink, have her doing dishes, gazing nowhere – at her own backyard – gazing everywhere. Something falls outside, loud. One damp thwunk into new grass. A meteor? She herself (retired from selling formal clothes at Wanamaker's, she herself – a widow and the mother of three scattered sons, she herself alone at home a lot these days) goes onto tiptoe, leans across a sinkful of suds, sees – out near her picnic table, something nude, white, overly-long. It keeps shivering. Both wings seem damaged.

"No way," she says. It appears human. Yes, it is a male one. It's face up and, you can tell, it is extremely male (uncircumcised). This old woman, pushing eighty, a history of aches, uses, fun, now presses one damp hand across her eyes. Blaming strain, the luster of new cataracts, she looks again. Still, it rests there on a bright air mattress of its own wings. Outer feathers are tough quills, broad at bottom as rowboat oars. The whole left wing bends far under. It looks hurt.

The widow, sighing, takes up her blue-willow mug of heated milk. Shaking her head, muttering, she carries it out back. She moves so slow because: arthritis. It criticizes every step. It asks about the mug she holds, Do you really need this?

She stoops, creaky, beside what can only be a young angel, unconscious. Quickly, she checks overhead, ready for what? — some TV news crew in a helicopter? She sees only a sky of the usual size, a Tuesday sky stretched between weekends. She allows herself to touch this thing's white forehead. She gets a mild electric shock. Then, odd, her tickled finger joints stop aching. They've hurt so long. A practical person, she quickly cures her other hand. The angel grunts but sounds pleased. His temperature's a hundred and fifty, easy — but for him this seems somehow normal. "Poor thing," she says, and — careful — pulls his heavy curly head onto her lap. The head hums like a phone knocked off its cradle. She scans for neighbors, hoping they'll come out, wishing they wouldn't, both.

"Look, will warm milk help?" She pours some down him. Her wrist brushes angel skin. Which pulls the way an ice tray begs whatever touches it. A thirty-year pain leaves her, enters him. Even her liver spots are lightening. He grunts with pleasure, soaking up all of it. Bold, she presses her worst hip deep into crackling feathers. The hip has been half-numb since a silly fall last February. All stiffness leaves her. He goes, "Unhh." Her griefs seem to fatten him like vitamins. Bolder, she whispers private woes: the Medicare cuts, the sons too casual by half, the daughters-in-law not bad but not so great. Those woes seem ended. "Nobody'll believe. Still, tell me some of it." She tilts nearer. Both his eyes stay shut, but his voice, like clicks from a million crickets pooled, goes, "We're just another army. We all look alike — we didn't before. It's not what you expect. We miss this other. Don't count on the next. Notice things here. We are just another army."

"Oh," she says.

Nodding, she feels limber now, sure as any girl of twenty. Admiring her unspeckled hands, she helps him rise. Wings serve as handles. Kneeling on damp ground, she watches him staggering toward her barbecue pit. Awkward for an athlete, really awkward for an angel, the poor thing climbs up there, wobbly. Standing, he is handsome, but as a vase is handsome. When he turns this way, she sees his eyes. They're silver, each reflects her: a speck, pink on green, green grass.

She now fears he plans to take her up, as thanks. She presses both palms flat to dirt, says, "The house is finally paid off. – Not just yet," and smiles.

Suddenly he's infinitely infinitely more so. Silvery. Raw. Gleaming like a sunny monument, a clock. Each wing puffs, independent. Feathers sort and shuffle like three hundred packs of playing cards. Out flings either arm; knees dip low. Then up and off he shoves, one solemn grunt. Machete swipes cross her backyard, breezes cool her upturned face. Six feet overhead, he falters, whips in makeshift circles, manages to hold aloft, then go shrub-high, gutter-high. He avoids a messy tangle of phone lines now rocking from the wind of him. "Go, go," the widow, grinning, points the way, "Do. Yeah, good." He signals back at her, open-mouthed and left down here. First a glinting man-shaped kite, next an oblong of aluminum in sun. Now a new moon shrunk to decent star, one fleck, fleck's memory: usual Tuesday sky.

She kneels, panting, happier and frisky. She is hungry but must first rush over and tell Lydia next door. Then she pictures Lydia's worry lines bunching. Lydia will maybe phone the missing sons. "Come right home. Your mom's inventing . . . company."

Maybe other angels have dropped into other Elm Street backyards? Behind fences, did neighbors help earlier hurt ones? Folks keep so much of the best stuff quiet, don't they?

Palms on knees, she stands, wirier. This retired saleswoman was the formal-gowns adviser to ten mayors' wives. She spent sixty years of nine-to-five on her feet. Scuffing indoors, now staring down at terry slippers, she decides, "Got to wash these next week." Can a person who's just sighted her first angel already be mulling about laundry? Yes. The world is like that.

From her sink, she sees her own blue-willow mug out there in the grass. It rests in muddy ruts where the falling body struck so hard. A neighbor's collie keeps barking. (It saw!) Okay. This happened. "So," she says. And plunges hands into dishwater, still warm. Heat usually helps her achy joints feel agile. But fingers don't even hurt now. Her bad hip doesn't pinch one bit. And yet, sad, they all will. By suppertime, they will again remind her what usual suffering means. To her nimble underwater hands, the widow, staring straight ahead, announces, "I helped. He flew off stronger. I really egged him on. Like *any*body would have, really. Still, it was me. I'm not just somebody in a house. I'm not just somebody alone in a house. I'm not just somebody else alone in a house."

Feeling more herself, she finishes the breakfast dishes. In time for lunch. This old woman should be famous for all she has been through — today's angel, her years in sales, the sons and friends — she should be famous for her life. She knows things, she has seen so much. She's not famous.

Still, the lady keeps gazing past her kitchen café curtains, she keeps studying her small tidy yard. An anchor fence, the picnic table, a barbecue pit, new Bermuda grass. Hands braced in her sink's cool edge, she tips nearer a bright window.

She seems to be expecting something, expecting something decent. Her kitchen clock is ticking. That dog still barks to calm itself. And she keeps staring out: nowhere, everywhere. Spots on her hands are darkening again. And yet, she whispers. "I'm right here, ready. Ready for more."

Can you guess why this old woman's chin is lifted? Why does she breathe as if to show exactly how it's done? Why should both her shoulders, usually bent, brace so square just now?

She is guarding the world.
Only, nobody knows.

RANDALL KENAN

~~~~~~~~~~~~~~~~~~~

The Virtue
Called Vanity

Is this all? Is this the way it will all end? he says. Will it all end here and like this?

The television flickers a rainbow of light, while the announcer grins a broad cosmetic grin, his teeth horse-big and white, his hair a sculptured hunk of plastic. "And now for the final question . . ."

"Oh, this is so depressing . . ."

"Come on, Guy. It's just a game show."

"'Just a game show'? 'Just a game show'? Neva, I'm not just referring to the goddamn television show, I'm talking about the whole goddamn business. This whole damn depressing god-awful life we've gotten ourselves into."

She begins to feel more than slightly annoyed. At one point she had convinced herself that she had a crush on him. A crush? Well, he's cute in his way, but . . . right now she only wants to watch her favorite game show. Where's the harm in that? She is aware of how silly it is, how tacky and pointless. But she enjoys it just the same. And she is old enough – by God is she old enough (seventy-five this year) – to decide for herself what the hell she wants to watch, when she wants to watch it and with whom for that matter.

"This fucking capitalistic system rots the mind is what it does. Marshall McLuhan wrote that – "

"Guy, I don't care what McLuhan wrote, right now. It's just 'Jeopardy.'"

"Just 'Jeopardy,' huh? You don't see the connection between 'Jeopardy,' 'Eyewitness News' and the plight of starving children in Laos, do you? Well, let me tell you – "

"Guy, you either let me finish watching my program or I'm just going home."

On a good day he reminds her of a black Sidney Greenstreet from *The Maltese Falcon* ("I'm a man who likes to talk to a man who likes to talk"). But today is not a good day. He rolls his wheelchair back sharply in a motion he has perfected to physically register disgust, resignation and moral superiority. "Fine!"

"Good."

She loathes having to put up with Guy's volcanic tirades, but since her television is busted she has no other way of seeing her shows. Guy's apartment is right down the hall, and the television in the common room tends to be monopolized by the Generals – as people in the community have taken to calling the four retired vets (none of them generals) who spend their entire days in the common room, playing poker, watching television and bullshitting about liberating France.

The returning champion has managed to add another $6,500 to her winnings, giving her a total of $26,500, and she will return tomorrow to defend her title. The credits begin to zip up the screen. Geneva slaps her knees purposefully, feeling lighthearted, thinking of what on earth the woman could do with $26,500. "Well."

Guy sits staring at the set, his mouth set in a possum-like curl as though he were constipated. He probably is.

"Well." Geneva says again, testing whether this will be one of the Three Degrees of Guy's petulant funks: a mild one which will be totally forgotten within five more minutes and telling bawdy jokes; a semi-serious one which will result in a brief lecture and demand an apology and be followed by a few hours of tension and chilliness; or a real hurricano of attitude, a quiet storm of not speaking for two days to a week and a hail of snide quips to other members of the community, which will blow over one day — a day of his choosing — never to be acknowledged, discussed or apologized for.

"Well." She tries to decipher his stony face. Oh, Guy. Dangerously overweight, a fat, red-boned man who seems stuffed into his wheelchair, a baked potato in need of splitting and buttering. She finds it hard to reconcile his amazing life story with this silliness. Oh, Guy. He's lived so hard, is so full of stories, of his many careers and adventures — a train porter, a truck driver, a carnival clown, a merchant marine, a minister, a devout Marxist. Oh, Guy. He could be kind; he could be gentle; he could be a pain in the ass. He knew such soothing words of love and peace and after Clarence's death he had been a great source of comfort. But on other days . . .

"Well." Geneva doesn't feel like playing Guy's game and decides to leave. She looks around the one bedroom apartment, so like all the others, more like a hotel room, really, than an apartment, with the high stuccoed ceilings, the peach wallpaper, the blank curtains and wall-to-wall carpet — just like her own, except for the pictures of Guy's late wife and nephews; his bookshelf full of economics and sociology textbooks; and an eerie skull on a desk cluttered to overflowing with papers and papers and more books, and maps — for the autobiography that Guy keeps talking about and planning to write, but Geneva knows, he has given up on. Only a lone IV tree standing in the middle of the room signifies that this room is not in a resort.

In a sphinxish pose Guy stares at the television, as the theme song for "The Jeffersons" begins.

"Well, I'm going." She waits for an answer, irritated that an eighty-three-year-old man could be so childish. Considering she might yell at him but refraining due to feelings of pity and fondness and an understanding that it will do absolutely no good. She stands. Perhaps he will make some sign of reconciliation? This once? He sits and stares.

"See you later, Guy."

She closes the door as Louise Jefferson begins making a great fuss over some strategic triviality. Outside the door she involuntarily rolls her eyes. Guy. So erudite. So bitter. Walking down the empty hall with the salmon carpet, the happy-happy prints of kittens and lions and chimpanzees, and the fiercely red EXIT signs constantly winking, she senses, in the cavity beneath her chest, a tiny prick of pity. But she clutches it by the neck like a poisonous snake, oh, no, honey, much too expensive. She knows not to placate it, to coddle it. Rather than go home, she has learned, better to take a walk.

Stepping off the elevator on the first floor, she is greeted by Mrs. Thomas, who clings onto the arms of a nurse like a scared monkey. "Betty," Mrs. Thomas croaks her words in a nails-on-chalkboard voice and reaches up to touch Geneva's face. "Betty." Mrs. Thomas mistakes all black women for Betty, her old housekeeper. The nurse holds Mrs. Thomas's hand. "Now, now, Mrs. Thomas, this is Mrs. Hudson." She steps back to allow Geneva off the elevator. The nurse, dark and big, reminds Geneva of her mother about the face. Geneva has tried to befriend her, but the woman always, politely, kindly, but firmly, insists on a professional distance.

In the recreation room, to the right of the main lobby — with palm trees at each entrance, sturdy wicker chairs, an expanse of Persian-patterned carpet full of ziggurats and squarish curlicues — Geneva can hear the Generals' loud guffawing

and thinks she will skip the eight-o'clock bingo game tonight; the movie tonight is *The Lady from Shanghai* ("Come here,
Lover"), but she's seen it six times; and since her television is
broken she does not know exactly what she will do. Read?
Sleep?

At the door she meets Mr. and Mrs. John and Mr. and Mrs.
Peters, just back from tennis. "Hi, Neva. Having a good day?"
Mr. John's smile, enhanced by his Dayglo false teeth, sets
Geneva's own teeth on edge. Mr. and Mrs. John are the perfect retirement couple, the administration's dream. When new
people arrive at Hillcrest, Mr. Zaco, the director, goes out of
his way to introduce them to the Johns: the very picture of
health in old age, affability in the face of looming infirmity,
social grace in the face of the anciently antisocial, the senile,
the incontinent, the deaf, the dumb and the blind; looking as
if they were born at sixty-five, happy, adjusted, carefree, living
advertisements of how You too, yes You, can "thrive in the
Autumn of your life" and finally enjoy the benefits of long
years of work and worry, can leave behind the worry of bills,
housekeeping, medical attention, companionship – provided,
of course, that you meet Hillcrest's "selective entrance require-
ment," which boils down to being able to afford the "fees."
Jesus help us, Geneva prays, grinning back at the twig-frail
white man whose face is covered with liver spots and whose
hairline recedes well into the middle of his head. There have to
be Mr. and Mrs. Johns in a Hillcrest; and when they deterio-
rate, there will be newer, fresher, brighter Mr. and Mrs. Johns,
always laughing. Geneva's pity has evolved into anger.

Yet out the majestic doors – they spring open electronical-
ly like at the grocery store – the air smells sweet, despite the
rumors about New Jersey air. Sweet and fresh. Flowers assault
the eyes: azalea, roses, periwinkle, the dogwoods. The grounds
of Hillcrest had won Geneva over in the first place, two years
ago. The formal gardens kept up with granite benches at the
ends of meandering lanes. The walks with discreetly placed
rails. Here the community doesn't seem so much like a pot-

pourri of varicose veins, slipped discs and impossible digestion. Instead these were the grounds of Tara, and she like that brazen hussy, except black and sensible. True, the landscape is disrupted by Mrs. Kuscinski, whose back is bowed like a fiddlehead and whose wig keeps falling to the ground; and Mr. DiLorenzo, with his deaf-man shouts; and blind Mr. Yerby and his tap-tappity-tap cane. But it's clean. It's tranquil. It's a place to belong.

Nor does Geneva feel bad about belonging here, for she has convinced herself she belongs in a Hillcrest. Hasn't she? Back when Clarence got so ill she could not think, she could not sleep, she could not eat; when she sat up at night feeling a cancerous knot in her belly, gnawing; when she was so tired, so very tired. Worry was not the word. Surviving. Enduring. Preoccupied with dosages and doctors and appointments, overwhelmed by the sheer logistics of getting from point A to point Q and back again to C before having to deal with F . . . People don't know. No time. No time for misery, only time for cleaning up blood and vomit and comforting moans of pain. Back when they had amputated the left leg, Bernice said: Hillcrest, and Geneva said, Hillcrest? and Bernice said what else, Mama? and Geneva cried. That was the last time she cried. She did not even cry when they amputated his right leg or when the left kidney had to go or when he finally, mercifully died, thank Jesus. Geneva said to Bernice then, Maybe I should leave now, I don't really need to be here, and Bernice said, Why? Why? Why. And Bernice had never argued so forcibly before, so intelligently, all the many reasons to stay. So she stayed. She belonged.

People say they can smell "death" in these places. How arrogant. How ignorant. What they smell is their own fear of shit, fear of being left alone, fear of no more orgasms and desire for orgasms and running around drinking in life; what they smell is their fear of having to eventually come to Hillcrest. She is stronger than all that. She knows Bernice is right.

And some days Geneva can call up within her a profound

empathy and sit and talk and help distract her fellow residents from the long and tedious hours of waiting, thinking she too will one day be halt or bedridden. On those days she is happy to be at Hillcrest and can imagine herself no place else. On other days she has perfected a way of blotting everyone and everything out, censoring all the reminders of her present widowhood, blanketing herself in the fantasy that this is all an illusion and that one day soon she will step out of it, return with Clarence to her home in Ironwood and resume her life as she left it. And there are days she neither hates nor loves nor denies nor fantasizes, days in which she just wants to get from six in the morning when she woke to ten at night when she beds down. Accepting the indifferent facts. One moment to the next.

Her walk has refreshed her and she no longer gives a damn about foul-mouthed, acid Guy. She will go home, to her apartment on the second floor, fix her own dinner in the painfully tiny kitchenette – chicken tonight, with carrots and greens – and flip through *Ebony* and begin the new Judith Krantz novel. Yes. So when she turns around the looming sight of the Hillcrest manse, red-bricked and penal, does not invoke dread as it sometimes does, and the thought of the smell of disinfectant and poorly covered-up piss and shit and vomit, and the sight of women her own age drooling and babbling retardedly will not depress her. Will not drive her to pity.

Besides, there is the trip to Atlantic City to look forward to; and the trip to Montreal in August; and the trip to Tucson to see her daughter Bernice; and the trip to San Diego to see her spacey, "New Age" daughter Benitha; and maybe even a brief trip to see that hateful, too-busy-to-visit Bertha in New York – she *does* love to travel . . .

Upon entering her apartment she leans on the back of the door and admires, through the open window, the gardenscape she has just left; the sun, now so low as to cast long, deep shadows from the sofa and chairs, creates a too-perfect portrait, almost sappy, like a scene out of technicolor Douglas Sirk.

She thinks: this is right. She could be back home, struggling, forced to make own ends meet, being subject to mugging, fighting subways, stalking grocery stores instead of having food delivered, a phone call away, not having superb medical care just downstairs. She knew a woman in Ironwood, older than she, Mrs. Clay, who could not afford Hillcrest. Mrs. Clay has a pitiable life. The difference between her life and Geneva's are like water and land. Dawn and dusk.

She picks up a letter she received the day before yesterday from her grandson Caleb, Bernice's boy.

Gram —
Fred and I just took out three couples and got $375! ($125 per couple!) American! This sailboat is great. You ought to come see it. Now we'll be able to do nothing for over a month down here. Isn't that crazy! We can just kick back and drink rum and have a good ole time. I'm learning to scuba dive, Gram. You'd love it down here. The water is so clear you can see the bottom. And blue! And so salty you can float without really trying. And when you're underwater it's like being in a magic kingdom or something. Really. Like something out of a movie. That's how I feel. You should come down here, Gram. You'd love it. You don't need to be in an Old Folks Home. You can still shake a leg. I don't care what mama says. Remember that party in Tucson last year when she got so mad cause you were dancing with Fred and me at one o'clock. Forget her, Gram. Come to Antigua. Forget about all those old fogies. You're not an old woman. Come to Antigua. Even if it's just to visit. I miss you.

Write soon.
Love,

Images of TV commercials scamper around her brain — ("Come back to fresh fruit"). Silly, good, loving boy. A little irresponsible. Should be in college like his mother says, but . . . An old woman. What in the world was she at seventy-five, if not an old woman? Mature? Well-aged? That's what Bernice had called her, an old woman, the last time she made the mistake of mentioning that she had considered leaving Hillcrest. But where are you going to go, Mama, she said. Really, it doesn't make sense. Daddy left you in good shape, so you can afford it. You're being well taken care of. You have to be realistic, Mama, really. You're an old woman now, you have to think of these things.

Geneva fears Bernice more than death, which she does not fear.

She puts on a blues record, Koko Taylor's *Earthshaker*, and sits in front of the mirror, combing her silver-rinsed hair. She remembers a line from her favorite movie, *Lion in Winter*, with Katherine Hepburn, her favorite actress, who looks into a mirror and says: "How beautiful you make me. What might Solomon have sung had he seen this?" That's what I say, "Well – there'll be other Christmases."

Cause I'm a woman, Koko sings, *W-o-m-a-n*. Geneva sings too, staring at her image: her skin, rich shades of Colombian coffee, the lines as if etched by hand, about the mouth, around the cheek, back from the lips; the darker flesh under the eyes; the graceful dome of her forehead. All leads her to feel the girl and the woman she had once been were incomplete, mere sketches, as if she is now what she was always meant to be, an Ashanti queen, a timeless dark bronze of mature feminine beauty, even the wrinkles, just right, even the sagging flesh sagging purposefully, sweet and succulent, not dried out, look at me, *I'm a ball of fire, I'm a rushing wind* and in this tiny space of her bedroom, before a mirror, before a table of sensually shaped perfume bottles, spherical jars of creams, phallic lotions, lipstick tubes, eyeliner pencils, brushes, compacts, puffs, and pills, she creates a miniature universe, *I can change old to new, I can cut stone with a pen*, open only to her, in which she rules and in which she is most beautiful indeed. *I'm a love maker, I'm an earthshaker.* She cocks her head back and smiles with the invincible smile of the best celluloid stars, assured, a bit coquettish, a bit sly, a great deal sexy. *I can hold a bolt of light-ning in the palm of my hand.* Here is beauty. She has seen the few older black models with their shiny coiffures and matronly presences. But she is more, oh yes, indeed. She can compete with any young tart. *Shake hands with the devil, make him roll in the sand.* Her beauty transcends sex and tawdry desire, cause *I'm going down yonder, beyond the sun, I'm gonna do something for you ain't never been done* . . .

She stands up from her mirror-mirror on the wall and does a little jig, *You can still shake a leg, Gram,* and glides into the kitchenette to prepare her chicken and carrots, puffed up with fancy and self-regard, so looking forward to reading a novel replete with men and settings for which she is more than a match.

"Thank you so much for your help, Mrs. Hudson. That mailing should bring in some funds."

Reverend Lang is the sort of man Geneva always had a weakness for. Not that Clarence was an ugly man. Far from it. She could see him down at Birdland now, his hair slickened back, his hands free and hot, looking nothing like an accoun-tant — but this man has those Sidney Poitier looks, darkly smooth, a thin nose, tall. He has a real preacher's voice, like the ones she heard growing up in Tims Creek.

"It's always my pleasure, Reverend."

She had joined St. Luke's Missionary Baptist Church with Clarence not long after they moved to Hillcrest. The Interde-nominational Chapel at the community — built-in like a vend-ing machine — did not satisfy them and St. Luke's was not too far away, walking distance on a good day. And the congrega-tion of black folk gave them another sense of community, deeper and more familiar than the integrated and country-clubbish Hillcrest. Here the rhythms and words and customs and after-service dinners felt more like home.

That's what keeps Geneva coming to St. Luke's now, a sense

of continuity, an opportunity to be among young members of her people, a chance to wear fine new clothing like the splendid sky-blue dress she is wearing now and the new shoes she bought at Bamburgers, an excuse to have her hair done every other week (expensive though it is), – and a reason to be close to Reverend Lang.

Though she would never ever dare, could never think about, telling anyone, she dreamt of having an affair with the forty-one-year-old pastor, of one day correctly interpreting a smile, recognizing a lingering handshake, a gentle touch as an invitation to dinner, to go to the movies, to kiss him about the neck and mouth adoringly. In quieter moments she even imagines the things he would do with his tongue (Geneva! He's a Holy man – So what?), she wonders how large his testicles are, what his brown buttocks look like unclothed (Blasphemous! – Human, child). Silly old woman, she'd think. But in her sweet secret she is head high, not young and vixenish, no, she is as she is, glowing silver and deep caramel, her beauty imperial, ageless in her finely molded cheeks, and the young man bedazzled by her grace and substance. How could a young woman command such adoration?

"See you on Sunday," she says tipping out of the sanctuary, her smile, she is certain, thrilling him a bit. Her smile certainly thrilled her. And she is out into the irrepressible New Jersey spring of Montclair, its white and white-trimmed buildings seeming in their way natural formations, the way they sculpt the light. Their lawns, imperiously green, like carpets rolled out to the world. The small-town sense of drug stores and boys on bicycles, sunshine in their cheeks, lips made of candy. Feeling just right. We were right to come here, she muses, as if she had not mused this muse a hundred times before, as if she never once had to struggle to convince and re-convince herself.

She strolls, wondering how she could have been depressed, ever considered moving away, and then of perhaps asking Reverend Lang to dinner. But he's married, Geneva. Doesn't matter. Silly old woman. And she chuckles to herself, swinging her purse, a girl of nine newly aware of the world. How long can I make this satisfaction last?

As if in fulfillment of a premonition she espies three young men leaning on a car just ahead of her. She can hear loud music from where they stand. Salsa, she thinks they call it. *Me gusta bailar contigo.* They look Latin. She is not afraid, but she smothers a sense of discomfort. Briefly, she considers walking around the block and then dismisses the thought. No, needless. But she stops girlishly swinging her purse, and picks up her step.

The music, jaggedly thumping, brassy, hysterical, *Me gusta, me gusta,* is so loud she has an urge to turn as she passes and inform the boys that they are disturbing the peace of good Christian peoples. *Baile, baile, conmigo.* But she religiously avoids eye contact and when she is just inches past them, she hears, "Excuse me. Excuse me. Miss?" *Señorita, con la camisa roja.*

Her impulse is to stop, then to keep going, then to stop — but what if she's dropped something, I'd look foolish to ignore them. *Ah, señorita, señorita.* Besides it's broad open daylight. They aren't going to — but then again — finally curiosity wins out. *Con la camisa roja . . .*

The three boys, with their spiky hair, red bandannas, torn jeans, earrings, acne and ink-black eyes look temptingly lusty, long legs, muscley arms — but in a threatening way. That kind of boy will make you do no good. One boy leans on the car, one sits on the hood and one stands free of it, his arms crossed like Sitting Bull. *Oye, señorita, oye.*

"Lady," the one perched on the hood speaks, his accent more Harlem than San Juan. "Lady, I don't mean no harm or nothing." He has a look of embarrassment about him, yet easily overcome by braggadocio. "But I just want to tell you." *Venga, chica, venga.* The boy jumps off the hood to his feet, and Geneva is so taken aback she does not flinch. The boy, cat-like, his spine in an obscene incline, looks her up and down, his admiring gaze caressing her body illicitly. "Now I ain't trying to be fresh or nothing. But you looking gooood!" And with that *gooood* his hand arcs to his side like a pendulum, *venga, aquí, chica, venga,* and his standing friend slaps the upward-turned palm in agreement and they all chime in, "Yeah!" with appreciative, harmless winks, their heads curving snake-wise, their eyes telling Geneva they speak the truth. *Venga, venga, venga.*

She stands regal as a tree, and begins to smirk and she thinks it's a silly smirk, more like a mother's than a siren's, a teak-and-bone Mae West, the way she feels. "Why, thank you, boys" she says. "Thank you. That's the nicest thing anyone's said to me all day." *Señorita, Señorita, baile conmigo.* All week, all month, all year. Lord, it feels like all my life. *Ah, venga aquí.*

She exchanges winks with them and continues down the June-bright street, basking in spring and flowers and — now, where are the little girls playing hopscotch and the healthy men washing cars? Such nice boys. Just think of that. And I must ask Guy about that cheerful music. Salsa is it? Wonderful music. *Oye, chica.* Reminds me of —

A hand pushes Geneva to the side and she loses her balance and falls, landing on her knee, tearing her hose and scraping the skin. More angry than frightened, she looks up and sees him, black, young, running like a cheetah. He turns down an alley.

"Motherfucker!" A voice from behind her. Pounding feet. She turns around. Two boys. Black. Chasing. She grips her pocketbook. She scrambles to her feet. Nearly falls. Stands against the building. Watching. Waiting. Thinking the men are after her. "Cocksucker! I'll kill you." One is big and bull-looking. One is fat and puffing and sweating. They're after the other one. The one that knocked her down. The two turn the corner like greyhounds. Geneva pokes her head around the corner. Sheepishly. Like a heroine in a horror movie. Expecting a hand to grab her by the throat.

The two overtake the one. The fat one kicks the boy in the stomach. "Motherfucker." The bullish one kicks him in the face. "Don't fuck with me, man. Don't fuck with me." They both kick him. "Fuck you, man, fuck you," the boy on the ground says. He holds his side. He pulls out a knife. The bullish one kicks it out of his hand. The fat one pulls something out of his pocket with much effort. Geneva thinks she hears a *snick* as she sees the bluish dagger flick out. The fat boy crouches over. She sees the sweat dripping off his face. "Eat shit you sorry son of a bitch." The metal disappears into the boy's belly. The boy screams. The metal disappears into his rib cage. "Fuck!" Again the metal disappears. The standing bull taps the fat boy on his shoulder and motions. The boys run. Winged. Breakneck and smooth. Down the alley. Wrongfully graceful. They sail around the corner. Birds into the night, Geneva thinks. But it's day, a warm spring day.

Geneva is an ice cube; numb, frosty. But her heartbeat is a tom-tom drum. Wild African pounding. She is her heartbeat. Someone could hear her beating. Loud. Crazy. But she is not her heartbeat. She is not her body. She is an ice cube. She is cold. A heart beat. An ice cube. A cold heartbeat. *Thu-Thumb-Thu-Thumb.*

Like a movie, she thinks, like one of those hellified thrillers she loves so much, but it's not a movie, Geneva. She wants desperately to scream, but can find no voice. She had a voice just a moment ago, but where is it now? The boys are still on the cars down the block; *Oye, oye, oye*; another child on a bicycle, Montclair cycling along, unperturbed, unaware. Didn't you hear, Montclair? Can't you see?

Geneva calls out, bellows out, yelling for the boys to call for help, and begins walking cautiously toward the boy, a little afraid, but what else can she do? She saw it; she was there. He writhes on the pavement, a mass of anonymous sweat and hair and wet cloth and moans.

"Oh shit. Oh shit. It hurts. Shit." Pain riding waves of sound.

A great wind rises up within her, powerful, stoking a furnace of empathy and purpose. His face, his lips, already swollen. His mouth bloody, vivid. He looks so tired. Some mother's child. Oh, Lord, My Lord. She kneels and sits on the ground behind him and pulls his head onto her lap, and prays, Let him live, Lord. "Eulice?" he asks. She softly says, "Sshussh, don't try to talk." "It hurts, Eulice." His body begins to convulse with sobs and the sobs seem to cause him more pain. He winces. "O Eulice." Geneva tries to hold him tighter, almost singing now, "Sshush, help's coming, help's coming," understanding, but not fully thinking: This could be Caleb. This could be my child. It's some mother's child, somewhere, wondering where's my child, this child, sweet, poor child, and she seems to be singing while rocking, "It's gonna be all right, all right, it's going to be all right, hold on."

Geneva calls out. But people are already standing about, gazing. Geneva only sees their legs, multi-colored trees of fabric, roots of leather, does not really hear their bewildered queries, their carnival curiosity. This poor boy. She hears a man standing before them telling them to stand back, to give them some air — just like in the movies, she thinks, thinking it's a silly thought, again, but true, but still not the movies, not TV.

From afar she can hear the siren, and she fails to connect it to the now-shivering boy in her arms, who says, "I'm cold."

Get a blanket, she says, and does not say, for she is still rocking and singing "It's going to be all right, don't worry, it's going to be all right" which she continues to say, wanting to say something else, something better, something to stop the blood, something healing, but she cannot think of anything better, so she says, "It's going to be all right, Son, all right," over and over.

When the ambulance comes she doesn't want to let go of this boy. She is connected to this boy as if to a lover and when she begins to pull away he grabs her blouse. "No, don't let go," he says, and after rituals with stethoscopes and pin lights, the paramedics place him on the stretcher while not separating the two, a grotesque pietà, as if they are joined in an act of sacred sexual congress, inseparable and bound. Without asking, she crouches next to him within the swaying ambulance; she feels the momentum of the small bus of an automobile, hears the funky whoop-de-whoop on the top, smells the antiseptic and alcohol and plastic and starched sheets. "You're not going to leave?" he says, squinting at her and then closing his eyes. She won't.

When the whoop-de-whoop stops and the doors open, everything becomes a whirl and frenetic confusion. Now she feels extraneous, not needed, pained in separating from the boy, who is wheeled down a corridor and through doors that swing rhythmically after he is gone. The pain is in no way akin to what she felt when Clarence died. This feels sharper, as if she has herself been stabbed. Geneva is not Geneva. She is some other woman in some other strange continuum. Eulice? *Señorita con la camisa roja!?* She looks at her dress, now splattered and smeared and smudged, rivuletted and drooled upon: an abstract in sky-blue and maroon.

She sits. She stands. She asks the nurse at the desk about . . . about . . . I don't know his name. The boy who came in. Stabbed. I was with him. I saw – oh. Okay. I'll wait.

She has not been in a hospital since Clarence died. Yet this is nothing like those Hillcrest-orchestrated comings and goings. The appointments. The respectful doctors. The more-comfortable waiting rooms with upholstered benches and chairs, instead of hard plastic seats without armrests. She has never been in the emergency room, seen so many dejected women, bandaged eyes, crying babies, wandering men absently smoking in corners. Who is Eulice? Will she ever know? She sits. She stands. She sits.

A young Indian man, bespectacled and bearded, comes through the doors and says something to the nurse at the desk. She points to Geneva. How long has it been?

"Are you the woman who came in with the stab wound victim?" His accent, thick and lilting, his manner somewhat distracted.

Geneva nods. "Is he all right?"

"I think he will be. According to the X ray his right lung was punctured – "

"Oh God! – "

"But that's not as critical as it sounds. He's stabilized. I don't think any other organs were damaged. But, of course, we'll have to see. But I suspect he'll pull through. Are you related?"

"No."

"But you witnessed the stabbing?"

"Yes."

The doctor takes her behind the swinging doors to a policeman. He is a sunbeam-headed youth looking for all the world like that blond motorcycle patroller on "CHiPs," but seeming rather early-worn and impatient. With a pencil he takes down Geneva's story, in a battered black book, and in the telling her eyes begin to well up with tears, but her voice does not break. When she finishes she says, "I have a grandboy about his age, you know. His name is Caleb."

The officer just stares for about thirty seconds, giving no sign of comprehending, as if half expecting her to explain. He checks his notes. He reads Geneva's story back to her and asks for her name and address. When she tells him he pauses, and a look comes over his face like the man who ponders a deep truth. "Oh, that's the rest home, isn't it?"

"A retirement community."

Geneva feels tired, she wants someone to take her home, but she will not ask this man. This cold man. Doesn't he know? But how could he know that a live wire has been touched to her temples and set her dancing like a marionette through the streets, crackling and sizzling, singing Sweet, sweet Jesus, take me over Jordan, O wretched Earth? That she has been flung out of sleep like a baby from a crib, crying, hollering, never to know that innocent peace again? What life has she known? What petty things her days have been made of she now sees, as if the lights in the moviehouse have been turned up and she has walked out into the naked sun; her cellophane and styrofoam days, assembled like ticky-tacky from schedules of television and walks and meals and card games and sightseeing tours on air-conditioned buses and solid, boring hotel rooms, one just like the next? How could this snide and impertinent child know that she, a seventy-five-year-old widow and mother, had heard, through the gurgling sobs and body-wrenching gasps of that sad child, the Archangel Michael whisper, Come out the wilderness and into the Kingdom of Life, O ye wretched, ye wicked, ye vain, had heard the Preacher cry, *The wind will not sow, and the clouds shall not reap, vanity of vanities, all is vanity?* He cannot know. He will not.

Surprisingly he does ask her if she is all right and if she'd like to be taken home. No, she says, it's not far. I'll walk.

"What is his name?" she asks after standing to leave.

He flips fussily through his little notebook. "Ah . . . Carl. Carl . . . ah . . . Rogers. Carl Rogers."

But she can't fix the name to the experience, and the boy continues in her mind to be an unnameable, a force of life, an emotion. As she walks to the door she catches her image in a mirror and sees afresh what a pitiful sight she will be walking down the street, and how people will look at her as if she were a gurgling mad woman. Perhaps she should let the officer of the law take her home? She walks on. She is tired, but she walks on. Thinking of how the people at the community will cast their eyes on her and their faces will stretch in bewildered terror and they will rush to her and ask, My God, Neva, what happened? and she will tell them of the boys on the car, *venga, venga, chica,* and of being knocked down and of the chase and of the stabbing and of how she, Geneva Cross Hudson, cradled that boy unto life and they will look into her eyes, looking for further answers, but they will never ever truly comprehend, never ever truly peer into her, ever see the new covenant etched upon her soul. *Senooriitaaaaa . . .*

She stands in a sea of boxes and suitcases. The movers will come to put them in storage. A taxi will arrive soon. Mr.

Zaco has already made his little speech, unconvincingly, of how he will miss her, how the staff and all her fellow residents will regret her passin – leaving. And if she should change her mind . . .

She has said all her good-byes, but she must say a final farewell to Guy. He sits in his wheelchair in the midst of the Generals, watching television. His face as consternated as ever. A Yoruba statue of the eternal fretter. This was the hardest decision, that she will leave him. When she told him he gave her the Third Funk, perhaps hoping it would change her mind. He came out of it in a fury of lectures, discourses on the horrors of the "outside world," of what a safe haven Hillcrest truly was – You have to commit yourself to something in life, you know. – I'm not a child, Guy. I was married for forty-five years, raised three children, and worked on one job for thirty years. I don't need you to tell me about commitment. He never said he'd miss her, or that he would surely die without her – had he done so she might, might have stayed. But he didn't, and he would surely die, one day, with or without her.

"Goodbye, Guy."

"Don't say Goodbye. You'll be back. Wait and see."

"Where you going, Neva?" One of the Generals looked up.

"Antigua."

"For good?"

"Who knows."

"She'll be back. Wait and see."

I'm out of here, she thought. Just as Caleb would say. I'm out of here. She feels an old and familiar clutching in her belly as she gets into the taxi. I am a foolish, vain old woman. A foolish and vain old woman, that's what they'll say. An old woman who wants to run her life like a TV movie, with a happy ending. Happy endings. Movies. Bullshit. She is old enough – by God, is she old enough, seventy-six this December – to know the truth. This is not a happy ending, and it's certainly not a beginning. Ain't going to be easy. Where will she end up?

Bernice yelled at her and said straight out she could not live in Tucson; Bertha had no room and won't even discuss it; Benitha has said "come." Or perhaps she'll go back to Ironwood and live with Mrs. Clay; perhaps she'd stay in Antigua; or perhaps her age will finally catch up with her, her legs fail, her eyesight desert her, and perhaps one fine morning a taxi will bring her back down the cobbled drive to this ineffable place, or to a place very like it. And on that day she will be ready, if not glad, to rest.

She is scared to death when the door slams shut with the finality of the grave and the car starts down the drive. She will not look back. She is too frightened. But she is a ball of fire. To hell with Bernice and Guy and Mr. Zaco and the Johns and all the rest of them. She is a rushing wind. She's going down yonder behind the sun. She's going to do something ain't never been done.

Man Watcher

What's my sign? *Slippery when wet.* Do I want to see your etchings? *No.* Have you seen me somewhere before? *Maybe, since I've been somewhere before.* What's my line? Well I've got quite a few, all depends on what I'm trying (or not trying) to catch. It's not so hard to pick up a man, matter of fact it's one of the easiest things I've ever done. A good man? Well, that's something entirely different. Believe you me, I know. My step-sister, Lorraine, is always saying *like, I don't know where you're coming from,* like if I say I've got a migraine headache, she says *"like, I don't know where you're coming from,* I have the kind of migraine that *blinds* you. The doctor says I might have the very worst kind of migraine known to man. My migraines are so horrendous I've been invited to go to Duke University for them to study me." You get the picture. *Like I don't know.* Lorraine knows a lot about everything and she has experienced the world in a way nobody can come close to touching. Still, when it comes to sizing up men, I've got her beat. I sit back and size them up while she jumps in and winds up making a mess of her life. When she opens her mouth in that long horsey way of hers, I just say *like, I don't know where you're coming from.*

I've thought of publishing a book about it all, all the different types of the species. You know it would sort of be like Audubon's bird book. I'd call it *Male Homo sapiens: What you need to know to identify different breeds.* Natural habitats, diet, mating rituals. I'd show everything from chic condos to jail cells; from raw bloody beef to couscous and sprouts; from a missionary position (showers following) to an oily tarp spread out behind a Dempsey dumpster. I'd break it all down so even the inexperienced can gain something. Of course there are a few questions that I haven't quite worked out, yet, like why is it considered *tough* for a man (usually a big city macho type) to grab himself and utter nasty things (such as an invitation to be fallated) to another man. Is there something hidden there like in those seek-and-find pictures? And why don't men have partitions between urinals? Is there a history of liking to watch or something? Does it all go back to the Greeks and Romans where a little homosexual activity was perfectly in order, like a good solid burp at the end of a meal? I'm still working on a lot of topics as you can see, but quite a bit of my research is already mapped out.

You know, you got your real *fun* guys that you love to date but you wouldn't want to marry – (he'd be addicted to something and out of work about the time you hatch the first kid). Then you got the kind who might do all right in a job and lead a relatively clean life, but they bore you to tears (I'm talking the kind that gets into little closet organizers and everything zipped up in plastic). And you've got the kind you ought to leave alone – period (I'm talking worthless pigs and middle-aged crazed sleezos). That's where Lorraine screwed up (on both accounts) and I've told her so on many occasions. Her husband, Tim, likes to drink beer and scrunch the cans on the side of his head. He likes to chew tobacco while drinking beer and talk about what he and the boys *done and seen* while *hunting up some good fat quail and some Bambi.* He wears army fatigues and drinks some more beer and talks about needing to get some sex (he actually uses all the slang terms for a woman's anatomy). He drinks still more beer and talks about needing to take a leak.

"Well just be sure you put it back," I said not long ago and Lorraine and her mother (my evil stepmother) gave me a long dirty look. My name is Lucinda, after my real mother's mother (I go by Luci) but every now and then I refer to myself as Cinda and bare my size six and a half foot just so they have to take a good look at themselves: mean ugly stepmother and self-centered stepsister, both with big snowshoe type feet.

"Take a leak. Put it back. That's a good one now," Tim said and shuffled through his magazines until he found one of his choosing for a little bathroom time, *Soldiers of Fortune* or *American Killer*, something like that. Lorraine and Mama,Too as she *used* to beg me to call her when Daddy was still alive, were still staring. They have accused me of turning my back on my family and our natural ways because I lived in Washington, D.C., for a year where I worked as a secretary in some very dull and very official office where there were a lot of very dull and very official men. I was there when there were rumors that this Senator who wanted to be president (there are LOADS of men who fit into this particular homosapien profile) had a mistress. This fellow always wins the election with the help of people like my step-brother-in-law who believe that there should be a gun in every home and school cafeterias eternally stocked with that delicious vegetable, the Catsup. What I still don't understand is who in the hell would go with that type? I'm an expert on these things and oftentimes am led by curiosity, but I have my standards. I mean if you were the *wife* at least you'd live in a nice house in Georgetown or Alexandria, the fella wouldn't utter a peep if you dropped a few thou. But just to *go* with him, good God. Lorraine's friend Ruth Sawyer has dated a man for fifteen years with nothing to show for it. Stupid, I say. I left D.C. (which was fine with me) when Daddy got so sick. I was allergic to those cherry trees the whole country raves about in the spring. Still though, if I ever even refer to the Smith-sonian, Lorraine and Mama, Too roll their eyes and smirk at each other.

"You'd be lucky to get a man like Tim," my stepmother had said.

"Like I don't know," I told her. "There are very few men in his category."

"That's right." Lorraine nodded her head as she flipped through her husband's pile of arsenal magazines to find one of her beauty ones. Tim's breed happens to travel in camouflage clothes, but they like their women to sport loud and gaudy feathers and makeup. But of course she had enough sense to know that I was not being serious so she turned quickly, eyes narrowing. "What do you mean, his category?"

"Not many men who read about the defense of the great white race while taking a leak," I said.

"Har de har har," Lorraine said. She has not changed a bit since they came into our lives not long after my mother died of liver disease. Mama, Too worked in the office of the funeral parlor which was convenient. I called her a "widower watcher" then and I still do. My daddy was not such a great man but even he was too good for Mama, Too.

Before Lorraine met Tim, she dated the man who I file in the middle-aged crazed sleezo slot. You know the type, someone who is into *hair* (especially chest) anyway he can get it: rugs, Monoxidil, transplants. That poor grotesquerie would've had some grafted on his chest if he could've afford-ed the procedure. He'd have loved enough hair on his head to perm and chest hair long enough to preen. You know the type of man I mean, the type that hangs out in the Holiday Inn lounge like a vulture sucking on some old alcoholic drink, his old wrinkled eyes getting red and slitty as he watches young meat file through the doorway. He likes chains and medallions and doesn't believe in shirt buttons.

"You're some kind of bad off aren't you, Lorraine?" I asked one night after her MAN left, his body clad in enough polyester to start a fire that would rival that of a rubber tire company. "I bet he couldn't get it up with a crane." My daddy was dying of lung cancer even as I was speaking though we hadn't gotten him diagnosed yet, and he let out with a laugh that set off a series of coughs that could have brought the house down.

"Don't you have any respect?" Mama, Too asked and I turned on her. I said, "Look, I am over thirty years old and my stepsister there is pushing forty. It isn't like he can send me to my room and keep me from going to the prom. Besides," I added and pointed to him. "He wasn't respecting me when he and Mama were out cutting up all over town, pickling their livers and getting emphysema while I was babysitting every night of the week to pay for my own week at Girl Scout Camp which I ended up hating with a passion anyway because it was run just like a military unit."

What I didn't tell her though (what I've never told anyone) is that going to Girl Scout camp gave me my first taste of self-sufficiency. It had *nothing* to do with the actual camp, but was in my getting ready for it. I found stability in my little toiletries case: my own little personal bottles of shampoo and lotion. *My* toothbrush and *my* toothpaste. These smallest personal items represent independence, a sensation you need forever. Otherwise, you're sunk. I liked having everything in miniature, rationed and hidden in my bag. For that week (the only way I made it though their bells and schedules) I was able to pull myself inward, to turn and flip until I was as compact as one of those little plastic rain bonnets. It was the key to survival and it had nothing to do with the woods (though I'll admit the birds were nice) or building a fire (I had a lighter). It had nothing to do with what leaves you could eat (I had enough Slim Jims along to eat three a day). It was my spirit that I had found. Of course I lost it the very next week once I was back home and doing as I pleased when I pleased, but I couldn't forget the freedom, the power my little sack of *essentials* had brought me.

"You could have benefitted from the military," Mama, Too

said after I'd run down my career in the Girl Scouts. She was ready to spout on her late great husband Hoover Mills and his shining military career. I told her his name sounded like an underwear or vacuum cleaner company.

"I have said it before," I told her. "And I'll say it again. I would never have a man of the church and I would never have a man of the military. I don't want anybody telling me what to do or inspecting me." I emphasized this and looked at Mama, Too.

"Who's to say they'd have *you*?" Lorraine said.

"I could have that old piece of crap who just left here if I wanted him," I told her and my daddy erupted in another phlegm fair, coughing and spewing and laughing.

"We are in love," Lorraine informed me and to this day I remind her of saying that. I remind her when Tim is standing close-by so I can watch her writhe in anger. I remind her whenever we ride by the Holiday Inn. I'll say, "Here to my left is the Holiday Inn, natural habitat of Lorraine's former lover, the middle-aged crazed sleezo of the Cootie phylum, complete with synthetic nest and transplanted feathers." Now whenever I say anything about Tim, the Soldier of UNfortune, she responds that same way, "I love him." I miss not having my daddy there to choke out some good belly laughs. Those attacks always bought me enough time for my comeback.

"It's easy to fall in love," I always say. "Easy as rolling off a log, or if I were Mama, Too's boyfriend (a new one, just that fast!) easy as rolling off a hog."

"I know your soul is in the devil's hand," Lorraine says. "You wouldn't know love if it bit you."

"Oh yes I would and oh yes it has," I say. "It's easy to fall in love. What's hard is *living* with it. And if you can't live with it, you're better off without it." I wanted to add that Mama, Too had done a fine job killing off love but I let it ride.

I've never gotten into all that love/hate rigmarole like some women do. If I want lots of drama, I'll turn on my TV set. Any time of day you can turn on the tube and hear women talking about things they need to keep to themselves. I hear it when I go to the spa. There we'll be, bitching about cellulite and sweating it out in a sauna, and somebody will start. She'll talk about how her eye has been wandering of late, how her husband bores her, how he just doesn't turn her on, nothing, zippo. "What do you do for a wandering eye?"

"See the ophthalmologist?" I ask. "Go down to the livery stable and get yourself some blinders?"

"Oh, be serious, Luci," they say. "You DO like men, don't you?" It's amazing how whenever a woman is asked this question, other women get real uncomfortable while waiting for the answer. They check to make sure that no private parts are exposed for the wandering eye of a Lesbian which I am not. Still, I let them sweat it.

"I like men the same way I like people," I say. "Some I do and some I don't."

"You know what we mean," they say and they all lean forward, more skin than swimsuits showing in this hot cedar box. It's like a giggle fest in that sauna anytime you go. Something about the heat makes everybody start talking sex and fantasy. I tell them that they need some hobbies, get a needlepoint kit, bake a loaf of bread. The truth of it all is that I'm ahead of my time. I have already figured out what I need to live a happy healthy life and I'm no longer out there on the prowl. If my life takes a swing and I meet Mr. Right and settle into a life of prosperity then so be it and if I don't then so be it. I'm in lover's purgatory. I've seen hell and I'm content to sit here in all my glorious neutrality. One woman who was all spread out in a tight chartreuse suit said that she had a stranger fantasy. She said (in front of seven of us) that she thought about meeting a man in a dark alley and just going at it, not a word spoken. Well, after she told that not a word was spoken for several minutes and then I got to feeling kind of mad about it all and I said that I just didn't think she ought to go touching a penis without knowing where it had been. "For health reasons," I added but by then there were six near naked women mopping up the floor with laughter and that seventh woman (Ms. Stranger in Chartreuse) shaking her head back and forth like *I* was stupid.

I was desperately seeking once upon a time. I was unhappily married to a man who wanted me to be somebody I wasn't and was forever making suggestions like that I get my ears pinned, that I gain some weight, that I frost my hair, learn to speak Spanish, get a job that paid better, pluck off all my eyebrows, let the hair on my legs grow and take up the piano so that I could play in the background while he read the paper. Now where was my little sack of security then? I was buying the Jumbo sizes of Suave shampoo so I could afford the frostings and the Spanish tapes and the row machine. My essentials were too big to hide from the world. I once knew a girl who went to lunch from her secretarial job and never came back. I knew another girl who woke up on her wedding day with bad vibes and just hopped a jet and left her parents with a big church wedding mess. I admired them both tremendously. I once told Lorraine she should take lessons from such a woman and she and Mama, Too did their usual eye rolling. It wouldn't surprise me if one day their eyeballs just roll on out like I've heard those of a pekinese will do if you slap it hard on the back of the head.

Before I was married, I was a rock singer. I named my band The Psychedelic Psyches, you know after the chick Cupid liked. I saw us as soulful musicians, acting out some of our better songs with interpretive dance numbers. My parents called us The Psychedelic Psychos which I did not appreciate. There were four of us in the band: I sang and played the drums; Lynn West, a tall thin brooding poet type, played the uke; Grace Williams, who was known for her peppy personality, could rip an accordion to shreds; my friend Margaret played the xylophone and had a collection of cow bells she could do wonderful things with. We were just getting hot on a local level when some jealous nothing type of a girl (someone like Lorraine) started calling us The Psychedelic Sapphos and spreading rumors about what we did in my GM Pacer which we called "the band wagon."

"Oh ignore it," I told them but Lynn and Grace quit. They said they just couldn't have a connection like that, not when Lynn was pre-engaged to a boy at Vanderbilt and Grace was supposed to inherit her family's pickle business in Mt. Olive, North Carolina. "Good Lord," I said and flipped my hair. It was as long as Cher's and I was just as skinny if not more so. "It's a new generation." But their response told me that men and pickles came first. Drugs came first for Margaret and we tried singing a few times just the two of us, but she'd get really strung out and just go wild with a cow bell. Margaret referred to our singing engagements as *gigs*. All she talked about was gigs, gigs, gigs. She'd call me on the phone in the middle of the night to ask about a gig. Nobody wanted us and I knew that. The only real *gig* we'd ever had anyway was doing little spontaneous standups in a coffee shop downtown. Nobody wanted to hear "Blowing in the Wind" sung to a cow bell from India. Margaret liked to pass her time by doing LSD and I passed mine by searching for the perfect male, dissecting specimen after specimen only to find his weaknesses and toss him aside. I thought of myself as the female version of Dion's "The Wanderer." Or maybe I was "The Traveling Woman." It was wanderlust and lustwander; it got even worse after my mother died and my dad took up with Mama, Too.

I was taking pictures of being naked in a bed long before John and Yoko, *Imagine* ha ha. I met my husband at a Halloween party and married him the next week. He looked much better when his face was painted up like a martian and I guess I kept convincing myself that there would come a night when he looked that way again. My husband believed in unemployment and a working wife and all those other things I've mentioned. Lorraine said that I should've made my marriage work, should have gone into therapy instead of running off to D.C. I've told Lorraine that I could've kept that husband, could've made a go of that life-style. All I had to do was become a drug

addict and hallucinate that everything was hunky-dory. I probably would've wound up like my friend Margaret, getting so
high you'd have to scrape her off the ceiling. Finally she got
scraped off a sidewalk. I was there when it happened. She
said she was so high the only way down was to jump and I
was too busy talking to this matty-haired man to notice she
meant business. He was wearing some of those suede German
sandals that make people's feet look so wide; you know the
kind, they're real expensive but they make you look like you
don't have a pot to pee in and couldn't care less about your appearance. I had just asked him what made him buy those shoes,
what image was he trying to fit (even then I was researching)
when all of a sudden there were screams and people running to
the window, the fire escape. There were sirens, a woman thinking she can fly like Peter Pan. You've heard it before. That
man with the matted hair expected me to go home with him
afterwards. Not long after that happened I met my future husband and decided to get married. I was convinced that I had
snapped to, but my snapping to was like a dream inside of a
dream, a hallway of doors where with every slam I woke up all
over again. I had barely begun to snap to.

That night while staring down to where Margaret was under a sheet with a little cowbell clutched in her hand, the matty
haired fellow breathing down my neck, I knew there was something powerful I needed to commit to memory but all I was
coming up with was things like *lay off the stuff, don't play on fire
escapes, don't let yourself become so lonely.* But like a lot of people
(like Lorraine) I translated that last one as needing somebody
which leads me back to what I've already told, a marriage made
in hell and me now in lover's limbo. What I know now when I
think of Margaret there, is that if you can't make it in life all
by yourself (and by that I mean without benefit of people and
substances and gigs of whatever sort you might crave) then
you simply can't make it. That's the whole ball of wax. If it
happens that you meet a person who walks right in and doesn't

change a hair on your head, then your pie is *a la mode*. I've found in my research that this type of male is most often the kind you can't squeeze into a category. His lines are blurred and intertwined. He's a little bit of a lot of things, and a lot of what counts. His feathers are like none you've ever seen. I'll hold out til I drop dead if I have to and all the while I'm holding out I'll pursue my projects, my crafts, my academic studies on why some women go the route they do. Why does someone like Lorraine who could educate herself and do better, settle, and why can't Mama, Too who has already killed off two men (that I know of) give it up and take up cross stitch? To think that a man can fill up whatever space you have is just stupid if you ask me. He can't do it any better than a box of Twinkies or a gallon of liquor and to ask it of him is unfair.

So what's my line? What's my response? These days I'm not really playing. These days I'm constructing a little diorama of my apartment kitchen and in it I have a little clay figure who looks just like me and is working on a diorama of her apartment kitchen. I have always loved the concept of infinity; it makes me feel good. There is something about the large and small of the world, the connections and movement between the two that keeps me in balance. And if ever I need to feel even better about my life, I take the "Sound of Music" test which assures me that my emotions are in working order. I have never once heard the Mother Superior sing "Climb Every Mountain" or watched the Von Trapps fleeing through the mountains at the end, without getting a lump in my throat. It is a testament to life, to survival. I could watch that movie again and again. When we all rented it not too long ago, Lorraine said that the nuns depressed her. I assured her that the feeling would be mutual if the nuns ever met her.

And speaking of religious orders, right now I'm having a nice big argument with Mama, Too over what the rules for priesthood ought to be. I say (just to see what *she* will say) that celibacy means *no* sexual interaction at all, which includes people of the same sex as well as with yourself and by yourself. "Well, how do you propose that?" she asked. "You gonna wire them up so if they touch themselves it'll set off bells?"

"No," I tell her. "A solemn vow to God is good enough for me."

"What do you know of God?" she asks and I'm about to tell her when her date walks in with a fifth of bourbon and a big slab of raw red beef.

"Why Marty," I say to this old saggy cowboy. "I never noticed how hairy you are." He grins great big and hunkers down at the kitchen table. It's sad how easily some birds are bagged. He has molted down to a patchy skinned bone. Mama, Too will have him henpecked in no time.

I guess in a way I'm waiting for the rarest breed of all, my sights set so high I have to squint to keep the sky in focus. I concentrate on migration habits. I keep in mind that owls fly silently at night. Some people (like Lorraine) might say I'm on a snipe hunt. But, call me an optimist. I'm sitting here in a pile of ashes, waiting for the Phoenix to take shape and rise.

T I M M c L A U R I N

~~~~~~~~~~~~~~~~~~~~~~~~~~~~~

Below the Last Lock

PART ONE

The river was not yet visible in the thick darkness prior to dawn, only the moon on the water like the world turned upside down. For a quarter hour Roy Breece had been in the tree stand waiting. He watched the moon sail the water, saw Venus blink on and off as she moved through leafless branches in her climb up the eastern sky. The sun was rolling up. Roy could see his hands now, his .243 rifle cradled in his lap. As high clouds gleamed pink, Venus began to grow dimmer. The world was silent, he was far enough into the woods that even the sparse Saturday traffic from the highway was muted. The first bird twittered, one single, pure warble, and that call was answered. Within minutes the world was awake, doves began their sad cooing, a large fish broke the river surface. Roy could see into the tree limbs now, and a squirrel was climbing down a tree trunk to the ground to feed. The deer would be moving now, and if that big buck was coming, he would come in the half light before the sun crested the horizon.

Roy had not moved a muscle in several minutes. The seat in his deer stand was padded, he had placed both feet on limbs wide apart, back erect. He always wore enough clothing that he stayed warm. Deer didn't live long enough to grow ten points by being stupid. Plenty of dumb hunters twisted and squirmed in their stands trying to get comfortable, blew breath into their cold hands, and to the ear of wildlife sounded like blowing trumpets.

A faint rustle of leaves, then silence, another few steps. Roy tensed his hands on his rifle and peered into the forest below him. More steps. Sounded like a deer, a large one. A man would make much more noise.

The buck stepped from a reed thicket into the open bank. He turned his head from side to side and searched, his nostrils flared. Roy judged the distance to be forty yards. A few saplings grew between them, but if the buck would move on down to the sandbar, nothing would stand between them but air.

The buck walked onto the sandbar, searched both ways on the river, then slowly lowered his head to drink. He was the one all right, that rack itself like a tree. Roy had spent hours scouting him during the off season, learning his trails, where he slept and came to drink. Only when he lowered his head to the water did Roy lift his rifle and peer into the sight. The buck was suddenly magnified four-fold. Roy clicked off the trigger safety, planted the cross hairs low down just back of the buck's shoulders, then squeezed off the round.

Thunder in the forest — the shot was true enough that the buck did not even wheel. His front legs buckled, he dropped flat to his belly and his muzzle and eyes sank into the water. In the great silence following the gun, Roy clicked on the safety before even taking his eye from the scope.

Despite the massive blood loss, at the wildlife checkpoint the buck still weighed in at eleven pounds above the county record. The rack was a perfect ten points. Roy gutted the deer and buried the offal. Noon had passed, his belly gnawed with hunger. Roy studied his watch and decided to swing by Mary's Place for just one hour. She made the best hamburgers in Cumberland County, and a beer would sure taste good. A lot of the fellows would be there by now, too, and Roy wasn't ashamed to admit to himself he wanted to show off. The guys sometimes kidded him about how well he prepared for and planned everything he did, but didn't it pay off? He'd started ten years ago as a bricklayer's helper, and now he employed a five man crew. At twenty-eight years of age, he owned his own house, loved his wife, had a three-year-old son, and hoped it was a daughter that was due to pop out in two weeks. Lying here in the bed of his truck was the carcass of the county record deer. Who would laugh last?

Mary's Place was a squat, frame building painted white and decorated with neon beer signs. The dirt parking lot was scattered with a dozen trucks and cars. A cluster of people stood at the tailgate of one of the trucks, mostly men, a few women in tight jeans and layers of makeup. Roy knew them all by name. He'd grown up in this community, had worked for or now employed nearly everyone who came to this bar. Roy parked and got out of his truck and walked over to the group. They were looking at a young buck with a four point rack. The truck belonged to Claude Phillips, a loud-mouthed guy about Roy's age. Roy had gone to school with him, had hired Claude twice and twice ended up letting him go. The deer hadn't been gutted yet. Roy saw where the first bullet had struck the buck in the lower back, probably severing his spine. Another close range shot in the head had killed him.

"He made it bout a hundred yards," Roy heard Claude say. "Strong sucker, pulling himself forward with just his front legs."

Roy figured Claude would haul the deer around a couple of days, then throw it into a road ditch.

"Bossman," Roy heard Claude shout. "You like my little trophy?"

"He's a pretty one, all right," Roy answered.

Roy saw that Claude was studying his hunting clothes, the skinning knife still suspended from his belt.

"You look like you might have been doing a little hunting yourself today," Claude said. "Have any luck?"

Everyone looked at Roy. He wished he hadn't stopped by now. Billy Peters, Roy's cousin on his mother's side, looked at Roy's truck and saw the canvas covering the deer.

"Looks like you got something back there, Roy," Billy said.

Roy shrugged one shoulder.

"Hey, Claude," Billy said, "bet ya a beer on the spot that what's under that canvas is bigger than this fawn you murdered."

Several people laughed. Billy worked for Roy, was dependable and loyal and hardworking.

Claude eyed Roy's truck, the ample sheet of canvas. He smiled, but his smile was fake. "What you got, Bossman?"

"Bout the same as you," Roy answered.

"Two beers," Billy chimed in. "Two beers, shots of liquor, your choice, that Roy's got a bigger deer under that canvas than you've got."

"You're on," Claude answered. "Show us your kill, Bossman."

Roy led a parade of people to the rear of his truck. When he pulled the canvas back, a collected gasp, then a round of whistles erupted. Roy couldn't help but grin.

"County record by eleven pounds. Call Sam down at the station if you think I'm lying. I been scouting him since last summer."

Billy slapped Roy's back. "I wish I'd bet a case now. I know this man. He don't underbid a job or waste bricks. Come opening day, he goes out and takes the county deer record."

"Heart shot," Roy heard someone say. "That buck didn't know what hit him."

Roy grinned while listening to the praise. He glanced at Claude who was still smiling, but his eyes drawn narrow.

"Yeah, the Bossman's tough," Claude said. "But when you

own the company, you can afford the time off to stalk the woods. Me, I gotta work for a living and hunt when I got a few extra hours."

Roy recalled how Claude was bad for laying out Mondays. He had often smelled whiskey on his breath following lunch break.

"Shit," Billy said. "Yours was probably a road kill, Claude. Let's go in. I got some free beer to drink."

"I cover my bets," Claude snapped. He reached into his back pocket and pulled out a pint bottle of Kessler's. He unscrewed the cap, then took a long draw. He held the bottle out to Roy.

"Have a drink, Daniel Boone."

Roy shook his head. "Naw. I stay away from the hard stuff." He remembered too well his father's fondness for whiskey and the hardships that his father's drinking had brought the family when he was growing up.

"Hell, Bossman, my whiskey ain't good enough for you? I can't afford Jack Daniels."

Claude shook the bottle. Roy exhaled and took it and turned the bottom up. The whiskey burned going down and felt like fire in his empty stomach. He handed the bottle back and Claude sucked on it again. He left two fingers in the bottom.

"Finish it."

Roy recognized the duel, but he took the bottle and drained it.

While driving home, Roy concentrated on the center line. He was way over his usual limit of four beers. The whiskey had done it — two more shots inside the bar, then round after round of beer — never did eat a hamburger. The last hour had been sort of a blur. He remembered Claude finally bringing up the subject about him getting fired, but before an argument started, Billy cold-cocked the guy. They slugged it out for a minute before Billy brought him down. The two of them had been wanting to fight all afternoon, anyway. Roy left then, weaving between tables and out the door to his truck.

He rolled down the window and hung his head out in the freezing air. Damn deer still had to be hung up to cool out. Madge would be mad. Though he was drunker than he'd been in years, he still wanted another beer. He drove slowly the last mile, taking deep breaths and trying to clear his head.

Roy stopped outside the living room window and studied Madge sitting in the Easy Boy. She wore the calico frock with the peasant neck that he liked, her thick brown hair rounding both sides of her neck. She was singing a song to Marty, the three-year-old straddling her knees. The large book was perched atop the fullness of her belly, round and taut as a melon after eight months of pregnancy. She was beautiful, her skin holding the luster of a pearl; the boy was handsome, carried Roy's mouth and chin, Madge's blue eyes. From the backyard, he could hear his black labrador, Jock, barking. He was probably hungry.

Madge looked up at the sound of the door, smiled, but her smile was tight. The boy squealed and grinned at him but clung to her.

"Hey," Roy said, glancing at the clock. He leaned his rifle against the door jam. Then he slowly removed his coat and hat and placed them on the rack.

"I was starting to worry," she said. "I called Ruth, but she didn't know where you were."

"I'm sorry, babe. I got a buck early, then decided to stop by Mary's for a beer. I ended up staying a lot longer than I wanted to."

"I saved your supper."

"I ain't too hungry." Roy tried to steer a straight path to the kitchen. He looked in the fridge, but there was no beer. "Damn," he muttered, wishing he had stopped for more. A good fight was on HBO later that night and he would want some beer. He looked in the dog feed sack. Half full. In the cabinet was a single can of cat food. He slid it behind a box of saltines. Then he took another sobering breath.

"We're out of cat food, and the cat is hollering," Roy said, walking past his family. He began putting on his coat. "I'll run out and get some and be right back."

Madge looked at him with eyes that were clear and knowing. "You don't need any more beer, honey."

"Who said anything about beer? The damn cat is hungry." Roy opened the door, then turned back to her. "We need anything else?"

Madge stood slowly, cradling Marty in her arms. "Roy, please don't go out again," she said softly. "You're drinking and shouldn't be on the road."

"And let the cat starve?"

"I'll fix the cat something. I'd rather you be with us."

Roy stared at her, and for a moment hated lying. She was so damn pretty standing there hugging the boy, ready to burst with his second child. But as suddenly, he turned angry. Shit, all he wanted was a couple more damn beers. Sit down and watch a good fight. Any man that laid bricks fifty hours a week deserved a couple of beers.

Roy looked outside at the darkness, then back at Madge. He stepped inside. "Well, hell," he said, grasping the knob and slamming the door violently.

The impact jolted the rifle, causing it to begin sliding down the wall. Roy stepped forward to grab it, but in his drunkenness he kicked the stock and the weapon fell toward the center of the room. Roy grabbed for the barrel but missed, the gun came down hard against the arm of an oak rocking chair.

The cartridge discharged with a roar. A bullet stinging as a wasp splatted into the center of the boy's chest and threw up fingers of blood that dotted the ceiling and wall. The lead punched through his little body, then buried deep to the right of Madge's heart. A huge, ringing silence followed the blast, the boy instantly sagged in her arms. Madge's eyes opened wide with astonishment. She took two steps toward Roy, one arm raised pitifully. He caught her as she fell, tucked the boy under his left arm, bent slightly to wrap his free arm around her buttocks, and lifted. Somehow he opened the door and began running for the light on his neighbor's porch. The boy felt loose like one of his teddys, his blood draining down Roy's trouser leg. Madge's arms were clasped around his neck, but her grip got weaker and weaker while he kicked at Sam's door and screamed.

Roy watched the ambulance man pump hard against Marty's still chest. At the hospital, he threw up on the floor. His mother held to his arm and sobbed into her scarf. The doctor walked slowly into the room, holding the tiny girl they had cut from Madge just minutes before her heart quit. The child was blond and blue-eyed, with Roy's mouth, Madge's eyes, her brother's pug nose. Roy turned in horror and ran outside. At the funeral the preacher talked of God's will, of how we were often not meant to understand the goodness in all of his plan. Roy walked away from his words and began a two month drunk that ended when he was carted off to Butner to the mental hospital, twenty pounds thinner and vomiting blood.

PART TWO

Roy stared through the curtainless window of his room into the gray courtyard. His room was bare except for a bed and dresser and the chair in which he sat. The first of the year had passed and snow had fallen last week, but most of it had melted now, or turned to slush. The sky was cold and blue. Roy waited to watch the black man bring out the kitchen garbage. Always the same time, give or take a few minutes, he carried out a large can full of breakfast scraps and placed it behind a trash dumpster. Probably carried it home with him to feed to hogs. The can was always heaped to overfull with leftover gobs of grits and egg whites and scraps of toast that spilled on the ground.

The rats lived in burrows under the dumpster. In seconds their heads appeared, black eyes gleaming, their noses twitched at the smell of new food. They massed at the edge of the dumpster, about a dozen in cluster, nervously turning in circles, snapping at one another, starting and stopping and acting as if in debate. Then, as if on one particular squeal of command, they ran for the garbage can, tails lifted an inch off the ice, quick, short steps, heads nearly skimming the ground. They were upon the spilled food in seconds, grabbing and snapping and swallowing. Two of the larger rats climbed the sides of the grimy can.

Roy always saw the hawk's shadow first. He could not see the bird of prey's perch — probably a tree limb where he had a clear view of the courtyard — but the shadow was his calling card. The rats saw the shadow too, and froze, hunkered even lower to the ground and waited. The hawk swooped in, talons splayed, his wings shaped in a V, and skewered one rat. He never missed.

The other rats scattered. Jaws packed with food, they raced for the shelter of the dumpster. Their unlucky brother squealed and struggled for a few seconds as the red-tailed hawk consolidated his grip. In a few moments the rat went limp, the hawk flapped his wings and rose until only his shadow remained, winged to his perch where Roy saw in his mind the bird slowly ripping his prey.

Days in and out, one rat died in sacrifice for the spoils of food, his brethren to digest their meal in the dark, warm earth tunnels. The hawk seemed to target one rat from his perch: he might be sitting on top of the can or on the ground, but he was the chosen one — he died.

Roy heard footsteps behind him, the soft patter of gum soles.

"Mr. Breece, it time for your 'pointment," the attendant said.

Roy turned slowly to face the man. He knew the attendant would wait until he got up and walked with him to the woman's office, and if he refused, another man would be called and they would take his arms and drag him there. Roy stood and walked out the door. He'd been there three times already, and hadn't said a dozen words. She just rambled on like she was reading from a book.

The psychiatrist's office was filled with a large, stacked bookcase, a desk and two stuffed chairs. Her Duke University diploma hung on the wall. Roy took his chair and stared at the floor. The psychiatrist looked to be only months out of school, wore glasses and loose sweaters, but probably looked good at home in tight jeans and a T-shirt and a beer in her hand. She opened Roy's chart and scribbled something.

"Roy, is there anything you'd like to talk about today in particular? Why don't you tell me what you've been thinking about since last week."

Roy stretched out his legs. He thought about the rats he'd seen devoured each morning. He looked up sharply for the first time into the doctor's face.

"The rules don't matter."

The doctor, startled, leaned forward on her desk. "What do you mean, Roy?"

"What I said. There ain't no rules. I understand that now."

"Well," the doctor answered, "there are rules. People don't always follow the rules, but plenty of them exist."

Roy combed his fingers through his hair. His scalp was oily. "I used to believe in the rules. Used to play by them. If I knew the rule, I wouldn't break it."

The doctor looked at Roy's chart, then back at him. She opened her mouth, paused, then spoke. "Do you think you broke a rule, Roy? Are you talking about the accident?"

Roy shut his eyes tight. "One time. One Goddamn time, and my whole world explodes."

Roy snorted in through his nose to stop his tears. "I never drink liquor. One damn time I drink too much. I always unloaded my rifle as soon as I came out of the woods. Why in the hell I set it by that door loaded, I'll never understand."

"Roy, that was an accident. A terrible accident. But you're not to blame." The doctor placed her hands palm down against the desk. "Fate. God – I'm not a theologian, but events happen sometimes that seem senseless and tragic and without meaning."

Roy shook his head violently. "They are senseless and without meaning. Shouldn't be any rules because they don't hold up. All we can do is hunker down and hope the shit don't fall on us – that we ain't the one picked. He don't respect the rule followers. Fuck up one time and you're out."

The doctor adjusted her glasses. "Who is 'he,' Roy?"

"You know who 'he' is. He's a son of a bitch."

The snow melted away for good in early March. The first blush of spring began in the courtyard, green onions first, then spears of daffodil leaves. Each morning he watched the drama of hawk and rat. Occasionally now Roy walked in the courtyard in long circles. One afternoon after his walk, Roy used the pay telephone for the first time.

"I do believe you're crazy now," Billy said and grinned. He took a seat on Roy's bed, then reached into his coat and pulled out a small cardboard box. From another pocket, he pulled out a small steel-jawed muskrat trap.

"One Pet World pedigreed rat. One spring loaded varmint trap. Man speaks to me for the first time in two months and asks me to bring him a damn rat and a trap."

Roy took the box and lifted the lid. He stared at a medium sized white rat with black markings. He closed the box and slid it under his bed. He took the trap and put it under his pillow. He looked at Billy and nodded.

"I owe you."

"You don't owe me nothing. A man in the nuthouse says he wants a pet rat and a trap, I bring it." Billy leaned forward and slapped Roy's arm. "You bout ready to come home, ain't you?"

"I been thinking about it."

"You look good. Hell of a lot better than when I brought you here. You were on some kind'a drunk."

"Wouldn't you have been?"

Billy's smile died. He exhaled slowly. "Yeah. Probably. I'm sorry Roy."

"You ain't got no reason to be sorry."

Billy slowly rolled up his shirt sleeves. He began talking while staring at his arm. "I saw your mama and the baby yesterday. That's a beautiful child, Roy."

"I don't want to hear about her, Billy."

Billy looked Roy in the eyes. "Man, she's your baby. You're all she's got, Roy."

"She's got mama. Mama can raise her."

"Your mama is old. She needs her daddy."

Roy stood from his chair and walked to the window. He gripped the sill and stared outside.

The next morning Roy watched the rats again, saw the hawk swoop in and skewer the chosen one. The morning was bright, the daffodils in bloom. A dogwood tree blazed with blossoms. Roy sat by the window nearly all day until midafternoon when the black man came and left with his can of scraps. He moved from the window then and took the cardboard box from under the bed. The rat had nibbled a piece of biscuit. Roy took the rat in his hand and studied it for a moment.

"Sorry man. My time's coming. I'll get mine, you can bet."

Roy circled the rat's neck with his thumb and index finger and squeezed. The rat gapped his mouth open and struggled. Within a minute, the rat ceased to fight. His pink eyes glazed over and closed halfway. Roy held his grip another minute until he was sure the rat was dead. Then he slipped the rat and the rat trap into his coat pocket and walked to the nurses' station to sign himself out to the courtyard.

Roy walked his usual circles for several minutes. He

scanned the trees for the hawk, but saw only robins and other song birds. When he was sure no one was paying him any attention, he let his circle carry him behind the dumpster. Quickly, he kneeled and emptied his pocket. He set the trap and carefully placed it on the ground. Using his heel, he pushed the holding stake into the soft ground. With care not to touch the trigger, he laid the dead rat in the center of the steel jaws. Roy brushed a little dirt over the chain. He stood, studied his work for a moment, then once again scanned the trees. No hawk. He turned and walked straight inside.

Roy sat by the window the rest of the afternoon. He got drowsy and twice slapped his face to wake up. The sun was barely above the western horizon when Roy was jerked bolt up in his chair by the flash of wings.

The hawk hit the rat with both feet. The force drove the rat against the trigger, springing the jaws. They closed with a snap, meshing rat and hawk talons. The stunned hawk flapped his wings and tried to take flight, but was snatched back to earth by the short chain. The bird spread his wings to keep balance and lashed at the trap with his beak. As dusk fell, the hawk's efforts grew weaker. He panted, occasionally emitting shrill cries. Finally he was swallowed by the night.

Roy awoke with a start, a shaft of sunlight coming through his window. He bolted from bed and hurried to the window. At least a dozen rats covered the hawk's carcass. Not much remained but a mass of bones and feathers.

Roy sat straight up in his chair in the psychiatrist's office, arms folded defiantly. The doctor looked at him while tapping a pencil eraser against the desk top.

"You got to be the one making the rules," Roy repeated. "I understand that now. If you're the one making the rules, you make rules you like."

"But you can't make all the rules, Roy. Other people make rules, too, and you have to follow them."

Roy unfolded his arms and leaned forward. "Control. That's

what you gotta have. I lost my control for a while, but I know how to get it back now. You got to make the rules before the other guy does. I'll be all right now. I'm ready to get out of here."

The doctor looked down at Roy's folder for several moments. "You know you've been free to leave any time. Roy, I'm glad you feel well now."

"I've got to get final control over my life. That's all. I understand where the trigger is now."

Roy stood from his chair. The doctor smiled at him, but her smile was not reflected in her eyes.

PART THREE

The canoe cut the smooth river water with hardly a sound, Roy handling his paddle with the experience of three days afloat. Jock sat high in the bow, barked occasionally and snapped at bugs. Midmorning had passed, the April air heavy with vapor and pregnant with the fragrance of honeysuckle. The sun was yet upon the water, the shady depths reflected a bank lined with mixed stands of black oak and sweetgum.

Roy cut to the inside of a long curve in the river. Ahead, he saw nearly a mile of straight, shining water. Jock raised on his front feet, his ears pitched forward while his nose twitched.

"What you see, boy?" Roy asked, drawing a wag from the animal's tail. It was then Roy heard the low rumble. His first thought was that a thunderstorm was brewing, but that was unlikely this early in the spring. Could be the drone of traffic where 64 crosses the river, he wondered next, but according to his map, the bridge was several miles distant. He paddled slower, the sound growing louder in volume like an advancing train.

Roy laid his paddle in the canoe and stood carefully, balancing his weight on slightly bent knees. He lifted his binoculars and turned the focus knob until the far curve of the river came into view. Then he backed up and refocused on something protruding from shore.

What the hell? Concrete walls. Some kind of little hut on the bank. He moved to the middle of the river. The water looked strange, the smooth sheen of reflection broken momentarily, only to reappear. After several seconds, he realized he looked at a waterfall that cracked more than half the river. Roy sat back down and pulled his map from a plastic sack. He studied carefully the area beyond the last road they passed.

"Hell yeah," he mumbled when he noted the tiny black marker. "A lock and dam. Why they need a dam on water this slow?" He wished he had taken time to purchase a topographical map.

The roar of falling water grew louder. A sign riveted to a red buoy warned boats to stay to the right bank. Jock barked at the bell shape of the buoy, Roy angered by the unexpected obstacle. He wondered if the operator would put such a small craft through, how long they would be delayed, if the lock was even in operation. He swore softly as they swung out of the faster current into slower water close to shore. He didn't need complications this last day on the river, when everything seemed almost normal the past three days. Not after the hell of the last six months.

The river had made things right. Here on the water, under the clouds of early spring, he had taken charge again. The water flowed east as steadily as the passage of time. He could ride that passage, leap ahead with several hard pulls on his paddle, or let the canoe drift broadside, moving slower than downed leaves that skittered across the surface. He could throw a stick and command Jock to retrieve it, could stop when he wanted to and open a can of beans and franks, throw out a fishing line or simply sit and listen to the sounds of birds. Slowly, he felt he had become a man again, a man in control of his fate. A strange peace had taken over his mind.

Last night, huddled near the fire, he had handled the pistol for the first time. A .38 long barrel, the chamber full of wad cutters: he liked the way the cylinder clicked each time a shell locked in place. The gun was heavily oiled and blued, the handle made from handcrafted walnut. A man's weapon. Here, swallowed by the song of crickets, he felt control again, far separated from preachers speaking of the unblaming will of God. When the trip ended, when the tremor was out of his hands and he was docked in Trenton, he planned to rent a room in the Hilton that overlooked the water. He would buy a fifth of Wild Turkey and drink it slowly while watching the twilight settle over the river. Then he would take out the big gun.

Roy kept the canoe within a few yards of shore as the roar of the falls grew louder. He scanned the dam with his binoculars. The brown river water slid heavily over the concrete lip where it dashed itself to spray and vapor on rocks twenty feet below. Soon he was only a hundred yards in front of the concrete gate that opened into the lock. If he was lucky, they would be lowered on an elevator of water. If not, they were in store for a hell of a portage. Roy took his air horn from the pack at his feet and let go a long blast. Jock yelped at the shrill sound. When they were nearly upon the lock, a man appeared above them on a metal walkway. He lifted one hand.

"Hello," Roy shouted above the din. "Reckon you could put us through that thing?"

The man nodded. He cupped his hands around his mouth. "Back up some and let me open the gate."

Roy pulled at the paddle and retreated several yards. He held the canoe steady by holding to a willow bough. The man went into the small office and shortly a humming sound began, the twin gates shuddered at first, then slowly opened to reveal a chamber as wide and long as three city buses. When the gates were fully open, the man left the office and instructed Roy to hold to a metal ladder as the water lowered. Jock trembled and barked, and Roy commanded him to sit. But the water emptied from the chamber so smoothly, Roy only knew they were being lowered by the fact that he had to keep reaching for a lower rung. Soon, the front gate opened, revealing the last twenty mile stretch of river to the sea.

Outside the chamber, the roar of the water coming over the dam was loud like thunder. The current was strong, the water from above boiling under and erupting to the surface in a fury of white bubbles and foam that churned the surface for fifty feet. Roy kept the canoe close to shore until he had passed the worst. Jock huddled low in the bow, snapping at fingers of vapor. Roy looked over his shoulder and waved once at the lock operator who watched from his perch.

Roy was startled at the change in the river. Gone was the coffee-colored water and muddy banks of the upper channel. The water here was dark and translucent like tea, the shore and sandbars made of coarse white sand. The hardwoods that had shaded his travel were rapidly thinning and replaced by thick strands of cypress and water oak. The change assured him more that his run was nearly over.

Roy ate a quick lunch of Vienna sausage and saltine crackers, throwing one of the wieners to Jock who begged with wet, brown eyes. He drank nearly a pint of water from his canteen, then resolved to paddle the rest of the day until they were off the river. He felt good, almost lightheaded. He could wield his paddle and the canoe would move and the hell with anything else right now.

Roy had rowed steady for more than two hours when he began to feel that something wasn't right. The canoe just wasn't tracking as it had upstream, didn't zip across the water like it had yesterday or the day before. Whenever he paused rowing, the canoe lost speed quickly as if she was dragging dead weight. Roy looked at the sides of the canoe and saw no branch hung up. The canoe wasn't leaking. He glanced at his watch. Three P.M. He wondered why he hadn't already passed the bridge that carried 64 over the river. According to his map, the road wasn't far below the lock and dam. He knew he'd have to pass the bridge soon if he was to make Trenton by night. By God, he was going to make Trenton.

Roy stopped rowing and scanned the bank. The slow track of the canoe stopped, the boat skirted to one side and began to drift backwards. What the hell? The current was flowing west, back toward the dam. He knew he hadn't turned around. Roy glanced at the sun and where it should be in the sky. Why is the Goddamn river flowing backwards? Then the answer struck him. That was why they built the dam. The river this close to the ocean was controlled by the tides. The tide was rising and water was being forced upriver where it backed up against the dam. Roy noticed that tree trunks were dark to a line nearly three feet above where the water stood now. High tide was still several hours away.

Damn. Everything has gone so well and now this, Roy thought. I'm exhausting myself rowing against the fucking tide.

Roy set his jaw and stabbed the river with his oar. "I'll be damned if you'll whip me," he shouted. "Not now." The canoe inched forward against the rising tide.

Roy fought the current for another three hours until his arm and back muscles were knotted and sore. He had finally sighted the bridge when a large sandbar appeared on the right side of the river. He turned and drove the bow of the canoe high on the white sand, his chest heaving down air.

Jock bounded out of the canoe and lifted his leg on a washed-up styrofoam bait bucket. Roy stood in the canoe, his knees popping, then stepped into the shallow water. He walked several yards up on the sandbar, then flopped against the ground. The sand was damp and moisture slowly soaked through the seat of his trousers. He picked up a handful of the sand and slung it toward the water. "Goddamn tide," he mumbled. Roy glanced at the sun now beginning to slide toward the western horizon. He estimated that in the past five hours he probably hadn't traveled five miles. If the current didn't turn soon, he hadn't a chance of making Trenton. He cursed, his face turned toward the sky.

Roy was startled by Jock's wet muzzle against the side of his face. He pushed the dog back and turned to see a stick in his mouth. "Get back," he grumbled, then wiped his jaw. The dog stood patiently wagging his tail. Roy took the stick from his mouth and slung it far into the river. Jock did not hesitate a second before plunging in. He caught up with the stick quickly on the swift current, then turned and fought his way back to the sandbar. Roy knew he would go after the stick a dozen times if he threw it.

Roy studied the low sun, then the contours of the sandbar. The smooth, clean sand indicated that the high tide covered the bar by at least a foot. Beyond the sandbar was marshland studded with thickets of cattail and wild blueberry. The trash from old fishing campfires littered the bank: beer cans and wood ashes and junk.

You ain't kicking my ass, river, Roy thought. I can't make Trenton before dark. I'll stop at the bridge, take what I need and hitchhike in.

Roy whistled for Jock and pointed at his spot in the bow. The dog whined, but took his position. Roy pointed the canoe downriver. He leaned over and placed his hands on both sides of the stern, then began running as he pushed the canoe toward deep water. The toes of his sneakers dug into the soft sand, the river rose to his knees.

Roy's first thought as he fell was that he had stepped off a shoal into deep water. As he pitched to one side, he almost lost his grip on the canoe, but managed to hold on with one hand. His upper torso pitched forward under water, his headlong plunge stopped suddenly by a searing pain in his lower back and right leg.

Roy pulled the canoe close to him, hung his arms and head over the side and passed out from the pain. When he opened his eyes again and pushed Jock back from his face, the water had risen to his neck, the sun was low in the sky and doves were beginning to coo. He looked wildly about. Instinctively, he struggled against his bond, a searing pain in his hip causing nausea and dizziness to roll up from his gut and into his head.

Roy steadied himself against the canoe, then reached into the murky water. His left leg pointed straight forward, the right one was buried to his groin. He ducked his head under the water, scraped at mud around his thigh, his fingers reached what felt like narrow slats of wood. Gently, he felt around his wounded leg, felt sharp splinters thrust into his flesh, a wide rusted iron band ran along the inside of his thigh. Whatever he had busted through rounded to both sides as if he straddled the back of a very wide horse.

Roy realized he had stepped through the hull of a wrecked skiff, years ago washed upside down upon the sandbar. His hip was broken, his leg held fast between the keel band and aged, treated wood. With no leverage, fighting intense pain, he saw little possibility of pulling free. The water lapped at his throat. He ducked his head under again and jerked at his leg, but the murkiness and daggers of pain made him lose all sense of direction. He surfaced gasping for air. Roy craned his head around and studied the sandbar. The tide would crest a couple of feet over his head.

Blind panic made him jerk upwards violently. He screamed as the pain made white sparks dance before his eyes. He shouted for help, but knew no one would notice him from the bridge. Jock fidgeted in the canoe yelping in confusion.

Roy's pain cleared his mind quicker than icewater, his panic replaced by rage. Soon, he was going to drown in a manner totally out of his control. Someone would find his body, a preacher would stand over his casket and say it had been God's will, that now Roy Breece had found peace. Roy opened his mouth to curse just as he noticed a length of rubber hose lying half buried in the sand.

"I ain't whipped yet, damn it all," he mumbled.

The hose lay at the edge of the bank only fifteen feet from

Roy. Roy looked at Jock. "Fetch boy, fetch," he said. The dog's ears perked up, overjoyed that his master acted normal again. He trembled as he waited for another command. "Fetch boy," Roy repeated. He steadied the canoe with one arm and made a throwing motion with the other toward where the hose lay.

Jock leaped from the canoe and started toward the sandbar. Upon the sand, he ran in circles, sniffing for Roy's scent on any of the sticks and debris. Twice he stepped on the hose as Roy yelled for him to "fetch it here." Finally the dog picked up a stick and, half swimming, half running, brought it to Roy.

"No boy, no," Roy said. He twisted the dog's head toward the hose. "Fetch that. Fetch the hose." He made another throwing motion that sent Jock splashing toward land.

Roy had to send the dog back twice more before he seized the hose between his jaws. "Yes, Jock. Fetch it here. Fetch." Roy shouted. The dog leaned back and struggled to pull the buried end from the sand. He came bounding to his master, the ends of the hose trailing behind him in the water.

The river was almost to Roy's chin. He studied the hose nearly ten feet long, one end containing a brass coupling, the other cut off clean. He swished it back and forth in the water, blew through to clear out the sand. He clamped the hose under his arm, then pulled the canoe backwards and tied the bow rope tightly to his belt. He reached inside for a gallon milk jug filled with water. He drank deeply from the jug, then poured the rest out and screwed the top on tight. His extra shoes were stowed under the seat. Roy grabbed one and removed the lace. Jock watched from the shallow water close to shore.

Roy slipped the cut end of the hose through the handle of the jug, extending it a foot beyond. Using the shoe lace, he bound the jug and hose tightly together. He held to the brass end of the hose and let the jug glide with the current until the hose was extended. The jug bobbed on the water, the end of the hose thrust upwards like a ship's mast. Roy put the coupling in his mouth, closing his lips tightly. He pinched his nose shut and leaned forward until his face was under water. He could breathe!

Jock danced upon the sand until he could stand it no longer. He leaped into the current and swam toward the floating jug. Roy screamed for him to stop, but the dog continued and grabbed the end of the hose between his jaws. He turned with it toward Roy, causing water to spill into the airline.

Roy ordered him back to shore, and once again cleared the pipe and floated it upstream. The water was nearly to his bottom lip. The sun was behind the trees now, dusk matting out the shadows. Roy was amazed at how clearly his mind worked, as if he had taken some exotic drug that extended his senses far beyond normal range. He watched Jock paw at the water, his eyes bright and eager to please.

"Stay boy, stay," he ordered. Roy pulled at the canoe until he was holding the stern. From a plastic sack he took his .38. He pulled back the hammer until it clicked twice. He clamped the hose under his chin, then pitched his shoe several yards up-river.

"Fetch boy," he shouted. "Fetch the shoe."

Even held with two hands, the gun was heavy, but Roy gripped it until the sights were fixed on the back of Jock's head. He noticed how rough the grip felt in palms long soaked with water. His friend had nearly reached the shoe when Roy squeezed off the round.

He saw a flash of blue, felt the pistol jerk toward the sky as the roar of powder numbed his ears. The dog pitched forward in the water, most of the top and back of his head blown away. He turned slowly in the current, legs splayed out and trembling, before slipping underneath. Roy stuffed the pistol under his belt. He tried to focus on the notes of a mourning dove, tried to breathe slowly and deeply. He touched his shirt pocket to make sure his small, waterproof pen light was still there. A full moon gleamed in the eastern sky when the water topped his ears and eyes.

Breathe slowly. Innnn. Ouuuut. Innnn. Ouuuut. Don't panic. Just breathe slow and easy. Keep your mouth closed right around the pipe.

The water seemed especially chill to Roy as it slowly topped his scalp. Twilight faded, and he was in a world of darkness, of muffled sounds, the river coursing around his body like a constant wind. He could hear his heart beating in his ears, rapid but regular and strong. He breathed in long hisses, fighting to push and pull air through the long hose. To reduce his panic he counted each breath, no longer aware of the pain in his leg.

Just breathe slowly. Don't think about it. A few hours and the tide will start down. Innnn. Ouuuuuut.

Something bumped into Roy's back. He jerked as a large fish slid by. Water leaked into his mouth, momentarily gagging him. He swallowed the water, but had missed a breath and now had to suck longer and harder on the pipe. His panic rose and for a moment he thought of once more trying to wrench free his leg and burst upwards to the moonlit surface. Roy raised one hand above his head until it surfaced into the cooling night air.

And you'll drown trying, he told himself. Drown and he'll have taken everything from you. Even your choice of death. Roy saw lights dance before his eyes as the lack of oxygen lightened his brain. When he looked up, he could see the moon shimmer high above in the sky.

If I ain't careful, I'll pass out and still damn drown, he thought. He concentrated on several long breaths.

Innnn. Ouuuut. Roy cried, his tears instantly swept away by the river. His sinuses ached so he momentarily removed his fingers from his nose and blew out clear snot. He was one with darkness, only aware of his heartbeat, his long, tortured breaths. But he hated himself even more now for again losing the upper hand, and hated God more, and hate would keep him breathing until he was able to finish his life his way.

The universe became softer, quieter, dimly lit by moon glow as if he floated in some diffused portion of space where existence was only the sound of a heartbeat and labored breathing. He became drowsy, so he concentrated on those sounds, rolled the taste of copper over his tongue, counted each breath. Again, he felt something bump his back. The fish swam around him. Seconds later, another fish bumped him, then another. In the dim washed light, he saw objects moving past, silvery shapes that undulated through the water. Roy wondered if he was hallucinating. He felt for his pen light and turned it on. The bright, round beam punched into the darkness.

Stripers. Dozens of them were swimming upriver. The fish migrated each spring into the rivers and creeks to lay their eggs and the first huge school was passing him, fat, pregnant females pushing against the current to that spot where they would spawn. Roy clicked off his light and remembered days when he had fished the river for stripers and shad, the schools so thick he snagged some with a grapple hook. More and more fish bumped him in the darkness. Their silvery scales caught the moonlight, causing each fish to resemble a pale ghost.

Roy stared in amazement. Hundreds of the fish moved by him now. He clicked on his light again and saw many of the striped bass were already spewing eggs. The eggs streamed behind them like strings of bubbles, catching and casting their own reflected light. He felt movement against his leg and turned the light there. The female was laying eggs, the mass sticking to him as it might to a submerged log or stump. The water flowing around Roy was thick with eggs. Some stuck to his shirt, to his arms, to the skin of his face. Fish passed him by the hundreds, the river rank with roe. In his light beam Roy saw smaller, predatory fish sucking in eggs, but for each egg eaten, a thousand more were laid. Wave after wave of the long silvery fish passed. Roy stared in wonder at the spawning of so much life.

The universe was now a world of reflected moonlight, the fish like passing comets, the eggs thousands of life-supporting planets. He felt as if he stared into the night sky at distant galaxies, nebulae, to the far boundaries of the cosmos. The eggs whirled in the current like a blizzard, millions of potential lives flushed from the womb into the currents of fate. The females swam against the current, released their eggs, some eaten within seconds, thousands more to float on the ebb and rise of tide and hatch. Some would grow into adult fish and go to sea, only to return to this same river and spill their own young. The cycle would go on and on and on. Roy shut his eyes hard. The fish bumped him, engulfed him and coated him with clouds of roe. He concentrated on his breathing in and out and in.

The wind on Roy's face brought him around slowly. Beyond his tightly shut eyes he became aware of light, of bird songs, the breeze tickled the small hairs on the back of his neck. He wondered if he was hallucinating and hesitated before opening his eyes. The light made him squint and blink before he saw water lapping around the legs of his jeans. He sat hunched forward, the hose still clinched tightly in his mouth. His skin and clothes were coated with fish eggs. The canoe trailed behind him, drawn seaward by the ebbing tide. He lifted his head; his neck muscles burned like fire. Another fire burned below the horizon in the east. Roy took the hose from his mouth and breathed deeply of cool, morning air.

Now Roy could see clearly the boat hull. His leg throbbed with every heartbeat, but the pain only made him more awake and aware. Roy studied the wood, the iron keel band running around the inside of his thigh. He took the pistol from his belt and cradled it carefully in both hands.

Doves called from the brush: a woodpecker hammered against a dead tree. The river surface was flat as glass and stilled by low tide. Roy listened for a moment to the grind of morning traffic crossing the bridge a half mile downstream.

The angle had to be perfect. Roy rolled the cylinder several times, wiped moisture from the barrel, aimed carefully and squeezed the trigger. The first shot punched out a hole two inches in diameter in the hull, splintered the grain, rushed into flight the woodpecker, several doves, a pair of mallards hiding beneath a willow limb. Two more shots rent the keel band, curled downward the ragged edges, another slug to the right of his leg shattered the hull just inches behind his buttock. Roy felt the pressure release, his leg slipped upwards several inches. Hot pain began slowly as his circulation returned, but he smiled as he slid further back upon the hull, dragging his leg from the vise.

Roy lay upon his back in the mud and straightened both legs. His muscles burned, joints ached. He felt splinters of bone grind in his hip, but was relieved that none had pierced his skin. He pushed himself sitting, fired the last shot above the water, then threw the pistol toward the spot where Jock went down. Downriver, he spied a small fishing boat coming his way.

Roy half dragged himself, half rolled until he lay on his back in the middle of his canoe, one leg over each side, his head resting against his pack. He shoved with his good leg until the canoe slid to deep water and began to float. The wind swung the canoe in slow, wide circles, the sun in the branches warmed his face. The birds resumed singing, their tune oddly familiar like a lullaby. Roy cocked his head toward the song and began to hum.

~~~~~~~~~~~~~~~~~~~~~

Murals

There was a crowd at the post office when he arrived. Gardner had never seen that many people gather at the door at opening time, except on the first of the month when Social Security checks came. There were two or three men in the crowd he recognized, Joe from the hardware store where he had bought the steel brush, and Mr. Clark the tax assessor who also sat on the board of County Commissioners. It was Mr. Clark who had written the letter to the regional office in Columbus asking, or at least agreeing, to have the murals painted in the post office lobby.

"Hurry up in there," someone shouted, and banged on the outside door.

"The war will be over before they open the damn doors," someone else muttered, and there was laughter.

A door rattled inside and Old Joyner, the postmaster, who always wore an eyeshade and garters on his sleeves, unlocked the outer door and the crowd of men pushed past him. Gardner was afraid they would knock over his scaffold as they pressed around the window. He had to stand watching, for there was not room for him to put his ladder up.

Old Joyner unlocked the inner door and let himself into the cage where stamps were sold and the mail sorted.

"What can I do for you gentlemen?" he said.

"We want registration forms," Mr. Clark said.

"Yeah, we want to sign up," another man said.

"Which registration form?" Old Joyner said. He assumed the serious air he always did when people tried to rush him.

"Don't act so dumb," Joe said. "You know damn well what we're here for."

"Some minds I can read," Joyner said. "Some I can't."

"Are you going to give us the forms, or ain't you?" Joe said.

"You applying for the Civil Service exam?" Joyner said.

For the first time Gardner saw that Joyner really didn't know what they were talking about. He lived by himself in a big old house at the edge of town and everybody knew he didn't have a radio or telephone and didn't read newspapers. His life was spent standing in the stamp window glowering at people foolish enough to bother him about letters and packages. When he was at home he worked in his garden.

"We want to register," Mr. Clark said.

"You're dumber than you look, Joyner," Joe said.

"I only have about a dozen forms," Joyner said, "If it's the draft registration form you want."

"Welcome to the Twentieth Century, Joyner."

"Hand them over old boy."

The papers were grabbed from Joyner's hand even before he could count or sort them. Some were torn. Two or three men were left without forms.

"You order some more, Joyner," they said.

"You can go over to Homer," Joyner said. "They might have some more there."

The last three men hurried out arguing about whose car to take to Homer.

"You can get gas at Leland's," one said.

"Better get gas while you can," his companion said.

When they were gone the post office was as deserted as it usually was in the early morning. Old Joyner stood looking through the bars as though he was still waking up. The bags of mail from the depot wouldn't arrive until eight-thirty. After that he'd have to spend an hour or two with Ralph the rural mail carrier sorting into pigeon holes and tying up bundles for the rural route. The first hour of the day was usually Joyner's time for dusting off his desk and counting stamps into the drawers. He claimed Gardner's work on the mural created more dust in the post office, and he resented Gardner's presence in general, disturbing his early quiet hour.

Gardner put down his paint box and got the ladder from the corner of the lobby.

"You here?" Joyner said.

"What do you think? It's Monday morning and time for work," Gardner said.

"Nobody else seems to think so."

"Things will quiet down," Gardner said, carrying his paint box up the ladder and pushing the canvas on the platform up against the wall under the spot where he would be working.

"You ain't going to join?" Joyner said.

"Not till I finish the job. I've got a contract."

"The Government will cancel your contract," Joyner said. The postmaster always thought of the most discouraging thing to say. He had a talent for it. He had complained about the mural from the beginning, about the dust and scaffold in the lobby.

Gardner had meant to work on the combine today. Since he was in art school in Chicago, indeed, since he started drawing in high school, he had taken pride in his human figures, huge men in overalls hurling shovels, women in plain dresses that flowed over their bodies revealing attractive shapes. He was good also with animals and the curves of the landscape. But he was late developing a touch with machinery. Either his drawings looked like meticulous designs for a factory, or, if he tried to be expressive, they looked wrenched and arthritic as a child's fantasy of a machine half tractor and half rhinoceros. Machines were much of the power of Rivera's murals. Most of Gardner's friends had no trouble executing something futuristic, or celebrating with cars and cottonmills, assembly lines and bulldozers, the energy of the industrial sublime.

But Gardner had dedicated himself to the goal of learning. He would never be a really good muralist if he couldn't do machinery. His plan was to stick with simplicity, bold direct lines like a Rockwell Kent, say. Draw machinery as if he were designing a woodcut using the fewest lines. Over the weekend he had made several drawings for the combine, each one bolder and plainer than the one before. At first he had thought of the combine as a kind of steamboat of the prairie, with its paddlewheel slapping through the wheat. Gardner was pleased with the comparison until he thought about it more, about the gamblers and ladies in fine dresses on a steamboat, and saw the parallel was only superficial. He kept drawing the combine from different angles, once with horses pulling it, once with a caterpillar. But the version he liked best was a view of the combine almost from underneath, with the paddlewheel against the sky, turning like a windmill. The wheat reached like hands and flames through the turning blades.

Men and women would be advancing around the combine as though pulling themselves up out of the earth. "Get up and Go," he privately called the mural. His boss from Columbus had not seen the new designs, but Gardner was sure he would approve them. Johnson liked epic struggles in his murals, men and women fighting with, and along with, nature for a decent community, for dignity.

"Picasso turns people into flounders," Johnson liked to say, "Two eyes on one side of their face and thin as paper. Our job is to draw the future, draw people as they are and can be.

There's no need for art to rub people's faces in ashes. Their faces are rubbed in crap everyday anyway."

By the time the stores opened around nine Gardner was up on the scaffold trying to draw in the combine. It was harder to work from his new designs than he had thought. He had never been good at transferring designs, not as good as he should be. Any technician can transfer, he told himself. But he knew that was no excuse. He rubbed out what he had started and began again, working free hand, from memory. The top blade of the paddlewheel went almost to the ceiling. He wanted to put a cloud up there, a white bulging cloud of lightness and assurance. But the cloud would have to be put slightly to the side.

Working close to the ceiling was fine in winter. The heat collected up there and he didn't mind the smells of sweeping compound and ink and newsprint from the back of the post office. The summer was when mural work was terrible. At his last job in Kentucky the heat and humidity had gathered around the ceiling and could not be dispelled. The smell of sweaty bodies, including his own, hung there, and sweat dripped in his eyes. The electric lamp made it even hotter. He had looked forward to the winter, and to this new job, his first on his own. The post office here was small but had a long high wall above the postmaster's window.

People gathered on the street as though it was a holiday. He could not see the street from the scaffold, but he could see the sidewalk where clusters of men formed and dissolved. He could hear some of the talk, bits of the conversation.

"If they bomb here I'll get out my deer rifle and shoot at them," a man said.

"Naw, they won't bomb this far. But San Francisco or Los Angeles is liable to be hit."

"I wouldn't live in California for no amount of money."

"Somebody seen a Jap in Des Moines yesterday and they run him into a park and beat him up before the police come got him."

"I'm going to buy me a new car before the price goes up."

Many kids seemed not to have gone to school. They ran up and down the street shooting each other, their mouths sounding like machine guns.

People came in to check their mailboxes after the mail was put up by Joyner and Ralph. But they did it distractedly, their minds on other things.

"Hey Joyner, look out for saboteurs," one called.

A man backed into the scaffold as he closed his mailbox. "What is this damn thing doing here still?" he said, then looked up and saw Gardner working.

"What you doing up there buddy?" he said. "The president is going to address Congress in thirty minutes."

Gardner kept working on the combine. For the first time he thought he might be getting it right. The wheel loomed up against the sky and touched the outline of the cloud. It turned like a great ferris wheel in the carnival of work and the men were turning with it, pitching straw, lifting sacks of grain, spinning the wheels of tractors and trucks. The sky was one long curving wheel of clouds and blue implying the pageant of the seasons and the orbit of the planet around the sun. For the first time in weeks he was beginning to feel good about the mural.

"Hey you up there," a woman called. He looked over the edge of the platform. "All WPA projects are being canceled. I heard it on the radio."

People came and went all morning looking up at him on the scaffold as though surprised to see him there.

"Don't splatter none of that paint on me," a man called to him.

"He only paints with red paint," another said.

"I always said old Franklin Delano would get us in a war," a woman said.

"No, Franklin don't want waa and Eleanor don't want waa," the man with her said, and they both laughed.

A euphoria had swept through the town, through the county, an invisible gas poured in from Indiana making everyone high and pleased with their tipsiness. There was a kind of élan Gardner had often dreamed about, a spirit bringing people together as a bad storm will or a fire. It was a feeling of common enterprise, of community, that no amount of organizing and speeches and guitar playing had ever been able to accomplish.

Sweat dripped down on Gardner's glasses. He had almost gotten the combine drawn in. In the afternoon he would paint it bright red, with the paddles white as Don Quixote's windmills and the wheat heads leaning gold with ripeness.

"Hey four eyes," a boy shouted up at him as he wiped his glasses.

"I bet he's a spy," another boy said.

"I'm closing up for lunch," Joyner called. "You coming?" Joyner would never leave him in the post office during his ninety minute lunch break. He always chased Gardner out before he locked up.

I'd better go back to the boarding house and call Johnson, Gardner thought. Find out if this talk about the WPA is real. All he wanted was a few more days to finish the combine, even if he couldn't fill in all the space on the wall with people and highways and villages on the horizon.

When Gardner heard the news on Sunday afternoon he was writing a letter to his girlfriend Sheila. She was still an art student in Chicago. As soon as she finished in May they were going to get married, if he was kept on by the WPA. Johnson had the option of picking him for another mural in the region or dropping him, and Gardner felt it all depended on how well he did the machinery in the present mural.

"The future is with machines," Johnson had said to him several times. "Machines are our friends, machines are the allies of the common people. Only machines will get rid of poverty and discrimination." Johnson had worked as assistant to Rivera on the big murals at Detroit and he was always looking for a second Rivera among the artists he hired. If Gardner could do the combine as heroic helpmeet to the common man, he was sure Johnson would keep him on, and he and Sheila could marry. Maybe Johnson would hire Sheila for the project also.

"The word combine is important," he wrote to Sheila. "Not only does the machine combine several functions different men used to do, cutting, gathering, threshing, bagging. It connects man and earth, present and future, steel and muscle. The combine ties a bond of energy . . ." It sounded too grand, even for a letter to Sheila. He was about to start over again when the landlady, Mrs. Chester, ran up the stairs. "Listen to that, listen to that," she was saying. "Just listen."

Gardner left his sentence unfinished and ran back down the stairs with Mrs. Chester. They stood by the big radio in the living room and listened to the frantic announcer. By then people were calling the radio station for more information.

"Please don't call us," the announcer said. "When we have more details we will give them to you on the air."

The other boarders gathered around the set too, those who had gone to church that morning and were still in their Sunday clothes after going out for dinner. They were returning from movies and from visits with friends.

"It's a stunt," someone said. "Like the invasion from Mars thing."

"No this is real. That's Paul Alvin the news announcer."

"You'll see. It'll turn out to be a hoax like the thing in New Jersey that had everybody scared to death."

Gardner had to get out of the house. The street was deserted except for a few people running from house to house, or getting in their cars and driving away. He passed a man sitting in his Ford roadster, his ear to the radio on the dash. Phones were ringing in the houses up and down the street. The tinsel and plastic Santa Clauses on the telephone poles looked somehow pathetic. Christmas lights in windows winked like lit scattered marbles.

Gardner walked by the post office and out by the feedstore

near the railroad tracks. There was a farm machinery business further on at the edge of town, but only tractors and corn pickers sat in the yard.

He had spent Sunday morning sketching the combine, then after lunch sat down to write Sheila. When he got back to the boarding house Gardner slipped through the parlor without being noticed and climbed back up to his room to rewrite the letter.

I had better call Johnson, he thought again, after he had eaten the soup and sandwich Mrs. Chester placed before him. Was he imagining it, that everyone at the table was looking at him accusingly? It was certainly his imagination, but he decided not to call from the boarding house where everybody at the lunch table could hear him. He would go down to the pay phone in the basement of the courthouse. Webster had at best a half dozen pay phones in the downtown area. The very busyness of the courthouse would ensure he would not be bothered.

An army recruiter had set up a table in the basement of the courthouse and lines of young men stretched out into the street. Gardner had to squeeze past them to get in the door.

"Hey, he's breaking in line," someone called.

"I'm not breaking in line," Gardner said.

"He wants to fight Hitler all by hisself."

It took some elbowing to work his way to the booth. But once inside he was pleased to find he had several nickels in his pocket, along with two dimes and a quarter. The operator had to ring Johnson's office three times before anyone answered. It was Johnson's secretary.

"Is Johnson there?" Gardner said.

"Who wants him?" The secretary giggled, as though someone was making faces at her as she talked.

"This is Gardner in Webster."

"Well, Gardner in Webster, Mr. Johnson is here and he isn't."

"Can I talk with him?" There was laughter in the background.

"He has joined the Air Corps and they are giving him a farewell party."

"Will he come to the phone? Let me congratulate him." There was a pause and some murmuring, as Johnson came on the line.

"Gardner, old buddy," he said. From the pitch of his voice it was obvious he had been drinking.

"Is it true, Mr. Johnson, that the WPA artists program is being discontinued?"

"Course it's true. Our country needs us."

"And present projects won't be completed?"

"There's a form, H-W-5, you can fill out, asking to stay on for up to two months to complete current projects. I can have Geraldine send you a form."

"And I can't stay without applying for the special extension?"

"That's right. There's a war on you know."

"I know."

"It's been nice working with you Gardner. See you over Tokyo." The line went dead.

By the time Gardner returned to the post office at one-thirty he was more confused than before. Had his job already been closed out? Was he now painting on his own time? Without the special H-W-5 form and an official extension was he in effect already fired? A group of young men gathered in front of the post office, waiting for a bus that would carry them to the nearest induction center. One's jacket had been folded up and was being thrown like a basketball over the owner's head as he grabbed and missed. Joyner called to Gardner as he came in the door. The afternoons were the long, tedious time in the post office. The mail had been put in boxes, the rural carrier was off on his route, and most of the town folk had already come in for the mail.

"Gardner, I want to talk to you," Joyner said. The last person Gardner wanted to talk to just now was Joyner. He needed to get back to work. He wanted to finish as much of the mural as he could before he had to leave.

"I've had a lot of complaints about the scaffold," Joyner said. "It's been in my way for two months, and your picture don't look any closer to being finished."

"It's mostly done," Gardner said. "Once I get the combine painted I can quickly fill in the blue sky." But even as he said it he knew it sounded weak to argue with an old fart like Joyner. Better ignore him the way everybody else did.

"I want you out of here," Joyner said.

Gardner hung his jacket on the crossbraces of the scaffold. He needed to get started if he was to fill in the outline he had made of the combine that morning. He had to decide just which red to use on the housing of the machine.

"The Federal Government gave me a contract," Gardner said.

"The Federal Government is cancelling all WPA projects. You heard that."

"There will be two months to finish current projects," Gardner said. He needn't tell Old Joyner about the H-W-5 form. He put the ladder up against the frame and began to climb.

"I have news for you," Joyner said, raising his voice. "We need this space here for a booth to sell war bonds. Every post office will have a space where war bonds are sold."

"You can put it somewhere else," he shouted down to Joyner.

It was warm up near the ceiling, and cozy. He sat down on the planks just under the outline of the combine and began to mix reds. He needed to get a shade that showed the machine had weathered some but wasn't rusty. All paint developed a frosting and faded if it was exposed to the sun and elements. The way he had drawn the combine it looked like a shoulder heaving out of the earth pushing the paddlewheel.

Gardner squirted two worms of pigment together on the

board and began mixing them with his knife. One was darker red and one had orange in it. The colors stayed separate in streaks until he stirred them vigorously. The streaks became hairs of color then melted and merged into each other. He turned the blob of paint over, the way you might turn an egg, to see if the colors were blended on the bottom. Never had he felt so confident of his ability to judge color, to predict what shade the dried mixture would have.

On the street a parade of some sort was going by. People were stopped on the sidewalk. When he stooped down on the platform to look, Gardner saw it was a group of veterans from the World War who were marching. There was a drum and someone played snatches on a trombone. Some of the men had on old uniforms, or pieces of old uniforms, a gunbelt, a jacket, an officer's cap. Some wore a sash over their civilian clothes. A few had medals and ribbons pinned to their business suits.

Old Joyner left his cage and stood by the window watching the troops go by. The veterans were followed by the high school band, with majorettes twirling along the sides of the street. Everybody's face seemed flushed with the excitement and cold air. Behind the band marched a lot of high school boys, and then older men with armbands. One here and there carried a hunting rifle over his shoulder. A group of police marched in ranks, and behind them came a firetruck with its lights flashing. In an open car rode the mayor, and the county commissioners followed in another car. There were more flags than Gardner had ever seen before in Webster, as if they had been saved from Fourth of July celebrations and taken out of closets and attics, out of storerooms and cedar chests and basements. Many people along the sidewalk carried little flags, and elementary school boys marched with flags.

When the parade had passed, Joyner turned back from the window and looked up at him. "I'm going to call in some carpenters to take your mess down," he said.

"You'll be interfering with official government work," Gardner said.

"I never wanted any mural," Joyner said. "And now the war has changed all contracts. You know that."

"The post office doesn't belong to you," Gardner said. "It belongs to the public."

"The public don't want any mural either."

"The mural is about done," Gardner said. And it would be, if he just had a few more days, or even one day of uninterrupted work to finish the combine and fill in the sky.

"I'm going to let the sheriff evict you," Joyner said.

"He has no authority over a Federal project."

"He can arrest you for trespassing."

Gardner needed to call Johnson again, to get a clarification of his status with the agency as of this afternoon. If he left the project unfinished he could be breaking his contract, and never be able to work again, after the war was over. But he was afraid to leave the post office even for a few minutes, for Joyner might call in somebody to dismantle his scaffold. As long as he was up there working surely they would not touch the platform.

Rather than take the chance of leaving the scaffold Gardner decided to work through the afternoon without coming down. Usually he came down in midafternoon to get some coffee and go to the bathroom.

Gardner put a touch of red paint on the wall and held the electric lamp close to the wet spot to make it dry. He wanted to be sure the color dried as he intended, with just the right amount of buffness. On top of the combine he would get the gleam of the harvest sun, but that could be painted on later.

Somebody opened the door of the post office and a draft of winter air swept in. Gardner could smell the town in that gust, not only the car exhaust and smoke from chimneys, and fumes from the bakery, but also the smell of rotting cornfields beyond the town.

When he was a boy Gardner tried to imagine the relationships between specific things out in the woods and fields, a rock, a particular tree, a spring hidden in the cedars, with the great world in general, the government, the mass of people, things in books, in history. And he wondered which was truer for him, the smell of cowstalls where he milked, or the discussions of milk and dairy products and a proper diet in his health book.

Gardner remembered the exact date, when he was in art school, when he realized that he needed both kinds of perceptions to be who he was. He could draw and paint the isolated, tattered cornstalks, the hidden alcove in the pines, but in doing so he had to be conscious of the world in general, of people of all kinds, even the course of history. He could not have one without the other.

Gardner was so busy concentrating on the combine, smoothing out the reds he had mixed, that he did not hear the voice calling him from below.

"Hey you up there," it was saying. "Hey buddy."

He leaned over the edge of the planks. A man in a dark suit and holding a briefcase stood by the stamp window.

"You talking to me?" Gardner said.

"No I'm talking to God."

"I'm busy," Gardner said.

"I'm busy too," the man said. "I'm Cyrus Downes, postal inspector. And I'm here to tell you your scaffold is coming down. We're putting up war bond exhibits in every post office in the district tomorrow."

Joyner stood behind the grille nodding as if to say I told you so.

"This painting is not finished and it's a Federal project," Gardner said.

"Not any more, not as of today," the man said.

"I haven't seen any orders from my office to stop," Gardner said.

"I'm giving you your orders now, buddy," Downes said. "This scaffold must be down by tomorrow morning, if not sooner . . ." He gave Gardner a long hard look, and left, banging the door.

"You see, it's out of my hands," Joyner said.

Gardner's only hope was to temporize that afternoon while he tried to finish the combine. They would never let him return to the mural. But if he got the combine right it would be there at least through the war. They would not go to the expense of repainting post offices while the war was on.

"Let me finish this section and I'll take down the scaffold tomorrow morning," he called to Joyner.

"Take it down now," Joyner said.

"There's no need to take it down before quitting time," Gardner said. He turned back to the wall and began spreading more red on the brushed plaster. He had almost finished with the housing, and could get the paddlewheel and some heads of wheat, and maybe the cloud above and some sky if they let him work steady until five. He spread the paint, going over the largest area with a wide brush, a house painter's brush he had gotten at the hardware store. He could use a wide brush for the blue sky also.

A man with a wide brim hat and a holster on his belt called up to him. It was Sheriff McFee.

"Hey Gardner," the sheriff said.

"Yes sir." Politeness was his best tactic.

"Joyner says he has asked you to leave, and you refuse to vacate the premises."

"This is a Federal project and I have no orders for cancelling it."

"All WPA work is now closing," the sheriff said. "You know that. There's a war on."

"I have to finish working today to draw my pay."

"Don't be a sap, Gardner. It's my duty to evict you."

"You have no authority to evict anybody who is working on a Federal project on Federal property. Joyner knows that. Only a Federal marshall can evict from this property. Isn't that right, Joyner?"

"Then I'll get a Federal marshall," Joyner said.

Gardner mixed his yellows and white for the paddlewheel,

making the paddles look like arms swimming through the wheat.

A group of drunk recruits came into the post office. Their bus to the induction center hadn't arrived, and they had been killing time by going from bar to bar along the street. Several times they had been given free drinks.

"Hey, 'fessor," one of the recruits shouted up at him. Gardner didn't look down or answer. He was afraid one of them would try to climb up if he acknowledged them.

"Hey, 'fessor, why ain't you in the army?"

The recruit took hold of the ladder and shook it against the platform. "There's a war on professor."

Several of the boys gathered around the posts of the scaffold and shook the frame. They took hold of the crossbars and shook them like branches of an apple tree.

"Stop that," Gardner hollered down. He held onto the palette board and braced a hand against the ceiling. He was afraid he would touch the wet paint and smear it. He had to think of some way to appeal to the drunken boys.

"Don't shake this down," he said. "I've got to finish this job so I can join up tomorrow."

"Join up now," one said. "Yeah, join up now and have a drink," another said.

"You boys go on now," Joyner said, coming out of his cage. "Just go on now." He acted as though he were shooing chickens out of a flowerbed.

"Hey old fart," one of the recruits said.

"Let's set Old Joyner on the scaffold," another said.

They gathered around Joyner as though to pick him up. Gardner thought he was going to have to jump down on top of them, for they were almost certain to knock down the scaffold. He gripped the paint board in his left hand.

"Stop that," a booming voice said. A man in a brown suit with a Stetson hat stood in the doorway.

"I'm Johns the U.S. Marshall," he said. "You boys are going to miss your bus."

"I don't see no bus," one of the recruits said.

"How can you see it in here? I just saw it coming down by the high school. It will leave you if you're not out there waiting for it."

The recruits let Joyner go and began edging to the door. There was a war waiting for them and they did not want to miss it.

"Better hurry up," the marshall said. When they were gone he looked at Joyner, and up at Gardner on the platform still gripping his brush and the palette. "OK, now what's the situation?" he said.

"This scaffold has got to go," Joyner said, his voice weak from the exertion of the scuffle. "We need this lobby for a war bond exhibit."

Gardner almost said he had signed a contract with the Federal government and had to finish the mural. But he saw that was useless. "Just give me an hour and a half to finish this section," he said, looking at the clock. "Give me to five and after that I'll be gone. I'm going to join myself tomorrow or the next day."

"Who's going to take this mess down?" Joyner said. "Somebody has got to clean it out."

The marshall pulled out his pocket watch and looked at it, then looked out the window at the recruits lining up and jostling each other. "OK, you've got till five," he said.

Joyner stamped back into his cage, shaking his head.

Gardner got his tubes of blues and grays from the paint box. He held up his right hand to see if it was steady. The fingers were still enough to hold a telescope.

"In painting clouds you get the roundness, the bulges, with shadow, with gray receding back to white, the lit edges," his teacher at the Institute had said. "A cloud should seem so real the viewer feels it floating out of the wall into the room. You can only do that with highlights and shadow. You can only have shadow if you know where the light is coming from."

Never had Gardner worked so hard. He knew the light in

the mural was a mid-afternoon light in the harvest season, not an early morning light, and not a golden sundown light. It was a light of work and reality, of hope, alertness. The cloud drifted above the combine and the wheat and the men as lovely and ambiguous as the future. He did not have time to glance at the clock again. All his years of practice went into his strokes. The cloud seemed almost lit from below, by the work and by the harvest and by the viewer looking up at the wall. In two years, maybe in ten, long after the war was over, people would look up and see the combine advancing over the curve of the earth and the clouds drifting free above it.

As he worked, Gardner's plans sorted themselves out in his mind. He would go back to his room and pack his things and take the bus to Chicago that night. If there wasn't a bus tonight he would go the next morning. He would see Sheila and ask her to marry him, and he would enlist as soon as they would take him.

When Gardner finished filling in the blue around the cloud it was two minutes till five. He was damp with sweat, and his arm and shoulder felt trembly with exertion. He packed his tubes and brushes in the paint box and climbed down the ladder. The brushes could be washed after he got back to the boarding house. There would be plenty of time if he did not catch the night bus. Old Joyner was shuffling around the back, probably counting change and stamps, recording the day's transactions. Gardner did not call to him as he gathered up his drawings and put on his jacket.

When Gardner slipped out the post office door he saw a crowd gathered on the sidewalk where three or four army buses were being loaded. There were cheers when a bus pulled out, and girls were kissing their boyfriends goodbye. Mothers and aunts were weeping, and fathers slapped their sons on the back and gave them steady, tearless looks of encouragement. No one noticed Gardner with his paint-smudged hands and face as he headed toward the boarding house.

REYNOLDS PRICE

~~~~~~~~~~~~~~~~~

Serious Need

I was thirty-six years old, with all my original teeth in place, most of my hair, and my best job yet — furniture sales on Oak Park Road, the rich-lady trade with occasional strays from the poor East End. Now that our girl Robin was twelve, Louise, my wife, had gone back to nursing at the county clinic. She worked the day shift; so that wasn't it, not my main reason, not loneliness. And by Lou's lights, which are strong and fair, she was nothing less than a good woman my age who tried hard, wore time well, and hoped for more. I wasn't too badly destroyed myself, according to her and the mirrors I passed. So I didn't crawl out, wrecked and hungry, to chase fresh tail on the cheap side of town. But honest to Christ I saw my chance after three and a half of what suddenly felt like starved decades that had stalled on a dime. I knew it on sight — a maybe last chance to please my mind, which had spent so long pleasing everybody else that was kin to me or that had two dollars for a sofa down payment.

She came in the store on Saturday afternoon that spring with her mother — a heavyset woman and a tall girl. I thought

I had a hazy notion of who they were, a low-rent family from up by the box mill, most of them weasel-eyed and too mean to cross. The mother had one of those flat raw faces that looks like it's been hit broadside with a board this instant — none of which meant you'd want to fool with her; she had prizefighter arms and wrists.

Both of them stayed near the front door awhile, testing a rocker. Then they headed for me; and before I got my grin rigged up, I saw I was wrong and remembered their name. They were Vaughans; the mother was Irma Vaughan — she'd been in my same class at school, though she quit at fourteen. I remembered the day; she sobbed as she left, three months pregnant (the child was a boy and was now in prison, armed robbery of a laundry).

I said "Miss Irma, you look fresh as dew on a baby's hand." I had no idea what I meant; words just come to me.

Her face got worse and she stopped in her tracks. "Do I know you?"

"You chased me down one Valentine's Day, when the world was young, and kissed my ear."

For a second I thought she'd haul back and strike, but she hunted around my face and found me. "Jock? Jocky Pittman? I ought to knowed!"

After we laughed and shared a few memories, she said "Here, Jock, you've bettered yourself — good job like this, that old crooked smile. See what I done, my pride and joy." Big as she was, Irma skipped a step back and made a neat curtsy toward the girl. Then she said "Eileen, this is one smart man. He can do long division like a runaway car. You listen to him."

Eileen looked a lot like Ava Gardner in schoolgirl pictures (Ava grew up half an hour south of us). Like a female creature in serious need that you find back in the deepest woods on a bed of ivy — a head of black curls, dark doe eyes that lift at the ends, and a mouth that can't help almost smiling, night and day. Almost, not quite, not yet anyhow.

I estimated she was near fifteen. So I held my hand out and

said "Here, Irma, you're not old enough to have a girl eighteen."

Irma said "So right. She's sixteen and what?" She turned to Eileen.

Eileen met my eyes straight on and said "Sixteen and four months this Wednesday noon." She met my hand with her own soft skin; those eyes found mine and stayed right on me like I had something she'd roamed the world for and had nearly lost hope of.

With all my faults, I know my mind. Ask me the hardest question you got, I'll answer you true before you catch your next full breath. I met those steady hazy eyes, volt for volt; and told myself *Oh Jocky you're home.* She felt that right, that custom-made, with two feet of cool air solid between us.

Not for long. Not cool, not two feet apart. That evening my wife and I were trying to watch some TV family story, as true to life but sad to see as a world-belt wrestling match in mud; and Lou said "Jock, you're dreaming upright. Go take you a nap. I'll make us some fudge."

Robin was off at a friend's for the weekend; the house was quiet enough for a snooze. But I said I was fine, just a touch dog-eared.

Louise could sniff my mind through granite. She came up grinning, took my face in her hands, studied my eyes at point-blank range and said "I hope you're dreaming of me in there."

Both my eyes went on and shut of their own free will and stayed shut awhile. For a change Louise didn't start on one of her Interpol hunts for the secret locked in me, but just the feel of her firm hands stayed on my skin, and in two seconds I knew that I'd find Eileen Vaughan someway before midnight, or else I'd keep driving till the rainbow ended in a pot of lead washers.

She was on her porch in an old-time swing with one dim light bulb straight overhead; and she faced the road, though I guessed I was too dark to recognize. I didn't want to drive unusually slow, but I saw enough to know I was dead right, back in the store. A socket to hold this one girl here had been cut deep inside my heart before I was born and was waiting warm.

Her dress was the color of natural violets exposed to black light, that rich and curious anyhow. The rest of the house looked dark behind her (I vaguely knew that there were no more children). Irma was likely playing bingo at her crazy church, the hollering kind. But I drove past to see who might be parked out back. Then I recalled that Irma's husband had died some years ago. Like so many drunks, for some weird reason, he lay down to sleep on the train tracks at night.

And by the time I'd gone a ways onward, turned and pulled to the shoulder out front, I told myself *Eileen Vaughan's young enough to be your first daughter. You don't know who's got hooks in her or even who she's hoping for now. Go lay your feeble mind on the tracks. It'll be a lot quicker and will hurt just you.*

But what Eileen said when she saw me was "I guessed it would be you before you turned." Not said like she was the earth's big magnet that drew me in but like the next nice fact of the evening – lightning bugs, the sweet crape myrtles, and Jocky Pittman.

Dark as it was, her eyes got to me, even stronger now. I said "Miss Vaughan, my actual name is Jackson Pittman. Nobody yet ever called me that – will you be the first?" I reached from the ground up toward her swing and gave her the great ball of deep-red myrtle I'd picked in the dark.

She disappeared down in it awhile. Then her eyes looked out. "Mr. Jackson, reach inside that door and switch off the light. Let's swing in the cool."

The fine and terrible thing is this. It is in the power of one young woman still in her teens to cooperate with your orphan mind; and inside a week, she can have you feeling like you're surrounded by kind ancestors, crown to toe, all waiting to do your smallest wish with tender hands. I've already said I had a good wife that tried the best she understood, and a thoroughly satisfactory child. I hadn't exactly been beat by fate;

but like a big part of the married men I knew in Nam, many nights of my life, and a good many days, I felt as hollow as a junked stovepipe. That is, till Eileen Vaughan took me that same mild night, saying she warmed the way I did, on sight at the store that same afternoon, which felt like two lifetimes ago.

From there it went like a gasoline fire. If I could give you one snapshot of her face and mine, close together, you could spell it all out in however much detail you needed. We burned that high in every cell; we taught each other ways and means that even the angels barely know, though for six fast weeks we never moved a step past the three-mile limit from the midst of town. At first, to be sure, it was all at night, on past her house in the heart of a thicket behind the mill.

But by the third week we were wild enough to meet by day, every chance we got. On three afternoons she babysat her brother's kids (his trash wife had skipped); but otherwise she'd get out of school and walk a straight line to the old cemetery, where I'd be waiting by my paternal grandfather's plot — he lies among three exhausted wives and nine children, having out-lived them all.

On weekdays nobody passed through there except black boys heading to swim in the creek; and they didn't know either me or her, though after a month, when boys passed too near the car more than once, Eileen sat up, buttoned her blouse, and said "Mr. Jackson, if this is your best, I'll thank you and leave. Don't look for me here, not after today."

I asked what she meant, *If this was my best*. Turned out, she meant the swimming kids. She thought they might be seeing her skin. I'd lived long enough to estimate she had almost as fine a skin as God had produced; and while she was not con-ceited a bit, every move she made showed how steady she meant to treat herself with respect. "Nobody else has" she said that day.

I asked who she meant.

"Every goddamned man and boy in space." She was still

half smiling, but I knew she was mad by the crouch in her eyes.

I laughed and said "I don't think Eaton's quite the same thing as space."

But she knew her mind like I knew my own. She said "So long and best of luck," then got out slowly and aimed through trees toward her mother's house, a long mile off. When she vanished she looked like my last hope.

I let her leave, though, and said out loud in my thick skull *Thanks, kind Lord. You cleared my path.*

He hadn't of course. Or I strowed mess and blocked it again by that weekend — my old path here, a dependable worker, husband, and father. Eileen had left the car on a Tuesday. By that Sunday evening, bright and dry, I was truly starved out. So I crept on toward her house again. It cost me almost all I had to climb those sagging steps and risk a knock. I felt like some untold crossbreed of the world's worst junkie and a child molester of the saddest stripe. The porch light was on and burned my mind.

But knock I did, a single blow, and nobody answered. I waited a long time, in plain sight of slow cars passing behind me, knowing my name. Then I knocked once more and finally begged out plain through the wood, "Eileen, I'm pleading with you. See me." In another few seconds, I heard bare feet.

She'd been asleep. First time I saw her confused like that, a hurt child with a pale blank mouth. It cut me deep as anything yet; I felt like the cause. But then she surprised me.

She said "Big *stranger*" but she still hadn't smiled.

In twenty more minutes we were back in the cemetery, parked by my graves. Eileen wanted to talk about school — how it was nothing she could use in the future; how she planned to quit at the end of this year, then make enough money to own her own soul and go to a secretary school in Raleigh. She saw herself in a clean single room in a nice widow's house with a private door key and kitchen privileges in case she wanted, every week or so, a soft-boiled egg or a slice of dry toast. Everything else good would follow from that.

I listened and nodded long as I could. But once she paused I politely asked her to leave the car with me — till then we'd stayed shut up inside.

She waited to think it carefully through but she finally nodded.

So I came round, opened her door, led her over to Granddad's plot, and read her the tall old moldy stones.

To be sure, she was bored as any teenager faced with death; but she tried to listen. I think she guessed I was up to something entirely new; at first she let me run it my way, just listening and nodding. I told myself the night before that if I could take her that near my kin and still feel like I needed her bones beside me for good — her skin and bones — then I'd tell her plain and ask for her life.

I was reading my own grandmother's stone — HER CHILDREN RISE AND CALL HER BLESSED — when Eileen came up quiet behind me and played an age-old playground trick. She bumped the backs of my knees with hers, and I came near to kneeling on Gran. First I was shamed to be ambushed and sacrilegious (I never knowingly walk on a grave), but all I could hear was high clear laughter.

I had never heard Eileen laugh till then; we'd been so dead-down earnest and grim. But when I finally stood and turned and saw her leaning on a baby's stone, lost in her fun, I still had to wait. I was stunned again. Nothing I'd seen from here to Asia, awake or dreaming, offered what looked like that full an answer to every question my life could ask. Till then I'd known I lacked a good deal; but seeing her there, in possible reach, I suddenly knew my two big hands were empty, and had been all my life. I wondered why; excellent women had tried to fill them — my mother, Lou, and even young Robin. I'd somehow declined every offer they'd made.

Now here was the fourth. I understood no offer was free, least of all from the hands of a girl with eyes like these dark eyes, which no Marine division could stem. If I reached out now and finally took, I estimated I'd feel and cause unmanageable pain. But before I thought another word, my mind made an actual sound like a tight box lid that shuts with a click. I held my ground six yards away; and I said "Sweet child, run off with me."

I didn't think Eileen heard my words. Her laugh calmed though, and she wiped her eyes. Then she leaned out slowly and set her lips on the family name, cut deep in the stone. When she faced me, even her smile was gone. She said "You got us a full tank of gas?"

I couldn't speak. But I nodded hard, she came on toward me; and my life bent like a thick iron bar way back in the forge.

$\mathcal{L}$ O U I S $\mathcal{D}$. $\mathcal{R}$ U B I N , J R .

~~~~~~~~~~~~~~~~

The St. Anthony Chorale

When I went to Staunton to work on the newspaper there I had the feeling, which I never afterwards quite lost, that I was moving to a far-off place, remote and different from what I had known. It is quite possible that if I had first gone there in any other season than wintertime it might not have seemed that way. As it happened, though, when the bus from Lynchburg turned off the highway east of the mountains to begin its climb over the Blue Ridge it was soon traveling along a steeply graded road with ice and snow everywhere about, and I had the sense that I was engaged in traversing a high wall, a barrier that shut off the Valley of Virginia from the rest of the world. But it was not only the mountains and the winter; I saw later that it was also the way that I was at the time.

I was twenty-three years old then, and this was a little more than a year after the war ended. I had gone for a job interview in Lynchburg, and from there I took the bus for another interview in Staunton – pronounced, I reminded myself so as to be sure not to make a mistake, as if it were spelled Stanton, with no *u* in it. Once the bus left the main highway and turned westward the ascent was steady, and soon there came hairpin turns and sharp climbs. From the window I could look down along the slopes of mountains and down ravines for long distances, and see only snowy hillsides and snow-covered trees.

It was a gray day and the clouds were low and heavy, a grayish white against the sky, so that it was difficult at a distance to tell just where the horizon ended and the clouds began. I wondered whether the deserts of Africa were any more desolate in appearance. The bus was a long time making its way over the summit and descending the western slope of the mountains, and even after it reached the floor of the valley and turned toward Lexington and Staunton there were mountains in sight east and west, and snow in every direction.

The impression of the city of Staunton that I took that day was that it was a raw, windy place, somewhat as I imagined towns might be like in the Far West. The wind was blowing very sharply, and though by then it was no longer snowing, fine grains of powdered snow from the mounds heaped along the sidewalks were flying about in the air. The sky had cleared a little, so that there were patches of blue. The buildings and stores of the city seemed old, as if built before the turn of the century or earlier. I saw very few trees along the street. Everything appeared open and exposed to the wind from off the mountains.

The newspaper office, which I found without difficulty, was the kind of old wooden building that I thought of as belonging to Civil War times. It had a show window, just like a store, with the words *Staunton News-Leader – Staunton Evening Leader* in black-shaded gold script on the plate glass, and above the second story a false front with scrolled woodwork and cornices. By comparison with the newspaper that I had worked on in New Jersey, and with others of my acquaintance, it was a very small plant, with business office, newsroom, composing room, pressroom all located on the ground floor.

Even so, I accepted the job when the publisher offered it to me. I had not been told whether or not there would be an opening for me in Lynchburg as a reporter on the considerably larger newspaper there. The job in Staunton was as city editor, with a $50 weekly salary — $12 more than I had been earning in New Jersey before my engagement had been broken and I had quit and come back home. To be made a city editor, after no more than six months of full-time newspaper work, was an elevation in status. True, there was only a single reporter on the staff, and the city editor handled all the telegraph, local and sports news, made up the pages, and even edited the church news. Nonetheless it could be considered a promotion, and after all that had happened I was in no condition of mind to pass up anything that might enhance my estimate of my own worth.

The Sunday before I left New Jersey for the South I had gone up to Newburgh to see my uncle. He was my father's older brother and originally from South Carolina, too. He lived by himself in a hotel room, and had a collection of phonograph records. He had begun his career as a newspaper reporter and now wrote radio scripts. He lived in a place like Newburgh, he said, because he detested living in New York City but had to be near enough to it to confer with the network on his script writing. Each morning, before beginning the day's stint at the typewriter, he would play music on his phonograph for an hour. In particular he liked the symphonies of Johannes Brahms.

What we usually did when I went up to visit him was to talk and listen to music. He had never met my fiancée, and did not offer an opinion about whether the cancellation of our plans to be married was a good thing or not. He merely listened. Talking to him about what happened made me feel less panicky, even though I was unable to bring myself to speak of the humiliation I felt. I made out as if the breaking of the engagement had been a mutual decision, but I think he suspected what had happened. When it was time for me to return to New Jersey he rode the ferryboat with me across the river to Poughkeepsie, and we walked out along the station platform to await my train. When the train had pulled into the station and I was stepping aboard the coach, he said, "Don't worry, bud, it'll all come out in the wash."

After I agreed to take the job in Staunton I went back to Richmond on the bus to collect my belongings. My parents were pleased. They had understood why I had given up my job in the North, but would have preferred that I move directly from it to another. As for myself, I too had begun dreading the possibility that I might have to ask them for help, as if I were still a child. When I had gone up to work in New Jersey I had felt that at last I was going to be earning my own living and otherwise becoming, for the first time in my life, a successful young man, practical and self-sufficient, able to make my own way. And for almost six months, despite my small salary, I had been able to convince myself that it was so – until my plans had collapsed and I had lost any reason for being up there.

The next morning I departed for Staunton, not on the bus but riding on a train, in a comfortable coach with a reclining seat. I had lunch in the dining car. Up ahead the locomotive whistled musically for the crossings. As I watched the piedmont Virginia countryside pass by the window, I thought that it was a considerable improvement over the previous train trip I had made, when I had come home to Richmond from New Jersey. The train that night had been late in leaving Washington and then had been delayed for several hours because of a wreck on the line just south of Fredericksburg. I had to sit for a long time at night in an old, overheated coach with uncomfortable, hard plush seats, trying to read but more often staring out into the darkness, thinking how I was going back to where I came from, and not even able to return there without trouble. My hopes for success as a newspaper reporter in New

Jersey and then, as I had confidently expected, in New York City itself were gone. So, too, the notion that I might quickly be able to emulate my uncle and move from newspaper writing into, if not radio scripts, perhaps plays, or, as seemed more appropriate to my interests, poems and stories. Instead I was back in the South, far away from where plays were produced and books published, and I had accomplished nothing. It had been after three in the morning before the train finally arrived in Richmond, and I had taken a taxi home and then had to beat on the front door for a long time before my father at last heard me and came down to let me in. "Well," he had said.

But now, en route to Staunton – pronounced without the *u*, I kept reminding myself – the immediate future at least seemed no longer so uncertain, for I was riding aboard a fast train westward to the mountains, to be the city editor of a daily newspaper, however small.

In Staunton, the place I found to stay was on the top floor of an old three-story house which had been divided up into rooms for rent. The room was large, with windows on two sides, a double bed, a desk, an easy chair, and a wash basin. Compared with the tiny room I had rented in New Jersey for the same price, it was far more satisfactory. It was located just at the eastern edge of the business district, a block south of the campus of a women's college, and about five blocks from the newspaper office, up a steep hill. The city of Staunton was very hilly and had considerably more trees along the streets than I had thought when I first saw it. The snow had melted a little when I arrived to stay, but it was still along the sidewalks and on the lawns and the rooftops. The people at the newspaper said that we would be likely to get several more heavy snows, for it was only February and the weather did not customarily break until about the first week in March.

However, in my new job the weather would be of comparatively little importance to me, for from the time I began work, in the late afternoon, until I left the office after 1 A.M., almost the only time I ventured outside the building was when I went out to eat dinner. I came to work about 4 P.M., checked the night Associated Press budget to see what was expected over the teletype that evening, learned from the woman who was the paper's only reporter what she would have in the way of local news, then began laying out the front page and editing copy. As the evening's news from the outside world began arriving on the teletype, I edited it up and wrote headlines. The teletype copy was in all-capital letters, and it was necessary to mark it for capital and lower case for setting on the linotype. About six o'clock I went out to dinner. On the way I usually stopped at a newsstand to buy a magazine or a paperback book to read at dinner. An hour later I was back at work, editing copy steadily. Sometimes I took news over the telephone from a correspondent, and sometimes the reporter had an evening City Council meeting or another such late story, but usually everything was on hand by ten o'clock, except for breaking news on the AP teletype. If I had a story to send out over the AP, I scheduled it on the wire, and when the bells rang to signal me to begin sending, I punched it out on the teletype keyboard.

When most of the copy had been set into type and I had edited and placed headlines on all the news that was to go into the paper, I went into the composing room and saw to the page layout, making cuts and changing about type to fit. There were only two or three pages of fresh type, which was all that the plant's four linotype machines could handle in an evening. Much of the type we carried was picked up from the afternoon paper, with the headlines reset into the morning paper's typographical style and the time references changed. By midnight we were usually ready to pull a proof of the front page, and after I checked it over for errors I went to work editing up some of the assortment of copy that was mailed in by rural correspondents in outlying areas, which would be set into type early the next day. The edition came off the press about one o'clock in the morning, and I was free to leave once I had finished editing up all the correspondents' copy and a few filler stories.

Several blocks away, not far from the railroad station, there was an all-night restaurant, and when I finished work I went there for what in effect was my supper. Since I knew no one, I sat by myself at the counter, reading the paper or a magazine while I waited for my order to be filled. After eating I walked up the long hill to my room. By then it was close to 2 A.M., but I was far from feeling sleepy yet, so I read for a while, and listened to the radio. Because of the altitude I could pick up stations in the Midwest much more clearly than those to the east or the south. From two to three in the morning I listened as I read to a classical music program on a Chicago station called the Starlight Concert. By three o'clock I was usually sleepy enough to turn off my reading lamp and go to sleep.

The truth is that during all of this time, from the very night I had come back to Richmond from the North, throughout the several weeks of job hunting, and now in the first weeks of my new job, I was waiting for a letter. Exactly what its contents were to be I should have been unable to say, even though I wrote drafts of it to myself in my mind from time to time. It was from the girl to whom I had been engaged to be married, and what it was supposed to announce was that everything was not irrevocably over between us.

It was not that I did not possess all the proof to the contrary that should have been needed to convince me. During the weeks after I left New Jersey I had come to realize in retrospect that the breaking of the engagement had not been a sudden decision, but planned out well in advance. I saw too that her parents, both of whom I had liked very much, had undoubtedly been in on the secret, and the three of them had plotted how and when it was to be done. In my naïveté I had failed to read signs that were being flashed at me. No doubt her parents, who I was sure liked me, had been chagrined at my inability to realize what was taking place. The thought of that was so humiliating that I could not bear to think about it.

Yet despite the fact that such realization was intermittently

The St. Anthony Chorale 221

coming to me, I was managing to keep from dwelling upon it most of the time, shoving it back into the periphery of my consciousness, as it were, by assuring myself that it did not matter, that one day soon the letter would arrive that would change everything. There need not be an outright confession of error and remorse, a plea to resume as before, to have the ring returned to her, to plan the wedding. What would suffice was a letter which took up as if nothing had happened, implicitly assumed a continuing relationship, expressed pleasure and interest in my new job, even hinted perhaps of a desire to come for a visit sometime to see me in my new surroundings.

Because of the late hours I was now working, when I woke up in the morning it was seldom earlier than eleven o'clock. I went out to a restaurant to get my breakfast while others were eating lunch. Then I stopped in at the newspaper office to see whether there was any mail for me. Afterwards there were three hours or so remaining before time to begin work. Usually I went back to my room, since there was no place else for me to go. I hoped that there would be mail, for then I could answer it. If not, usually I read until time to begin work. The city library was located near my room, and several days a week I stopped in there to find new books, usually taking three and four at a time to my room. What I liked most were archeology and Civil War history. The library was housed in the former residence of Stonewall Jackson's cartographer, the famous Jed Hotchkiss, and there were many books about the war.

During my first weeks in the new job I was busy learning what was involved in getting out the newspaper. Not even in the afternoon, in my room, did I often think to feel bored or lonely. My first Sunday in town, when there was no paper to get out that evening, I had felt the time hanging heavy for a little while, but I wrote letters. I rather liked being there by myself in my room, listening to the New York Philharmonic concert on the radio, with the snow falling steadily beyond the windowpane. I could hear the truck traffic on the Valley Pike, which ran just below my window, laboring up the hill, and the road maintenance crews scraping the snow and spreading sand and salt on the icy grade. Later on I heard the westbound Chesapeake and Ohio train whistling on its way through town. After dinner I wrote a letter to my uncle. He had responded to my account of my new job with the observation that it would be good training, though his guess was that after a time I would find it tiresome to be doing only a routine of desk work each day. I told him that while he might well be right, for now at least I found the editing quite interesting. I did not add that what I liked most of all was just that routine, and that the more hours a day it demanded of me, the more grateful I was for it.

The day when the letter arrived was at the very end of February. It came in response to one that I had finally written, on a pretext having to do with the return of a book I had borrowed from a library some time ago and left behind me in New Jersey. It was one of several letters waiting in my mailbox at the office, and my first, reflexive response was to shove it quickly to the bottom of the stack of envelopes I was holding, as if by postponing the reading of it, even for a few minutes, I might also postpone its meaning as well. For at that instant I was quite certain of what it would say, and I realized too that I had known all along. After a moment I tore open the envelope and hastily scanned the words, written in the familiar penmanship, on a double sheet of notepaper.

What was said was little more than a repetition of what had been said to my face a month earlier, together with the comment that my own letter had seemed to be written in anger, and that she was happy to see that I was indeed angry, which I had every right to be, she said. "The little bitch!" I said aloud, and looked around me to assure myself that no one had heard me speak. "The little bitch," I repeated under my breath. For not only had I not written in anger, but I saw that by pretending that I had been angry she was assuaging any feelings of guilt she might have had at having hurt me. What I had accomplished by writing was to provide her with an opportunity to enjoy feeling distressed at having to decline my love. I thrust the letter into my pocket and left the office. "The damn spoiled little bitch!" I said aloud as I walked up Coalter Street, after first looking to see that no one was within hearing distance. "Now I really *am* mad. Mad as hell!"

Yet as I was saying these things, I knew I was deceiving myself not at all. The truth was that I should have liked to be angry, to resent the way I had been put aside, as one might put aside a novel when one finished enjoying it, or, more appropriately, I thought, as a child might put aside a set of finger paints once the novelty of being able to make pretty configurations with one's fingers had worn off. But I could not make myself feel anger — only a sense of humiliation.

I felt grateful that the barrier of the mountains existed, protecting me from further involvement. The condition to which I should aspire, I felt, was an emotional and moral numbness, a complete freezing of emotional engagement, so as to make myself impervious. If I could cultivate an attitude of unconcern and indifference to my present circumstance, then ultimately I might be able to bring my memory to a similar invulnerability.

And for a while it seemed to be working. I found that if I went to the office a little earlier than usual, and if I worked a little later after the paper had gone to press, I could stretch my working hours so that they filled most of my waking hours, leaving only a brief period between the time I arose in the very late morning and went out to get breakfast, and the time I began the night's work, when my thoughts were not occupied by the requirements of my job. And after I had put the paper to bed and gone by for a sandwich at the all-night restaurant, I was sufficiently tired so that when I went to my room I could read about the Civil War or the exploration of the Upper Nile and listen to music on the radio until almost dawn without feeling restless and lonely. After a few days I came to know something close to actual contentment at the way I was managing. I even decided that there would be no need for me to go home to Richmond on weekends. I would simply stay in my room and read. For the first time since I had come back South, I felt that I was close to being master of my emotions. I did not require anyone else's company.

How long I might have continued in this way if the winter had held on, I cannot say. But there came a day when the ice and snow were gone, the streets and lawns were wet from the melting, and the temperature was suddenly up in the sixties. Almost overnight the Valley changed from a stronghold of frozen rock into a swiftly thawing garden. Everything around me now began turning toward color and warmth. To the west of my room, and visible from my window, was a low mountain called Salley Grey, which had loomed over the little winter city in barren woods and stark granite. So perfectly had it seemed to match the frame of mind to which I aspired that I would sit and look at it for long intervals, as if through focusing my thoughts upon it I might acquire its hardness. But now the bare crest was giving way to a faint but unmistakable green, and the trees along the slopes, which had seemed so sterile and rigid, were fringing into a blurred growth that softened and obscured the harsh outlines of the hillside. And late at night, when I finished my work and went by the all-night restaurant, I discovered to my dismay that the darkness, which had seemed so chilled and barren that I was glad to retreat to my room where I could read and listen to music, had now acquired a depth and resonance that I found threatening to my feeling of immunity.

Yet the night proved to be as much my ally as my enemy. For it was, after all, very late when I finished at the newspaper and had eaten my supper, I had been at work for ten hours and more, so that I was not obligated to reflect that under more fortunate circumstances I should have been enjoying the company of a girl — if I had a girl. Rather, by the time I was done with work it was an hour when I could only have expected to be alone anyway, so that I did not need to be ashamed at my solitary condition or believe that if only I were more attractive and desirable than I was I would not be left to myself.

Thus on a Saturday night in March, after the paper had been printed and I had stopped by the restaurant, I found the night so warm and inviting that instead of proceeding home to my room I decided to walk down to the railroad station two blocks away. It was, after all, no longer Saturday night at all but very early on Sunday morning, so that I need not feel, as I had so often done, that there was something wrong because I did not have a date.

The station was deserted except for a clerk in the ticket office of the lighted but unoccupied waiting room. I walked out along the platform to the west of the station, where the rock cliff that lay just beyond the double track slanted off. To the west I could hear a train whistle blowing. It must be a freight train, I decided. I would wait and watch it come through town before I went back to my room. I took up a seat on an empty baggage cart. Except for the whistle of the train, the town was still; I could hear an occasional automobile go by along Beverley Street three blocks away, but that was all.

Listening to the train drawing nearer, until eventually I could begin to hear the iron wheels reverberating along the rails, I felt a note of satisfaction in my solitariness that made the night seem not merely amiable but even harmonious, as if I were a part of it. To be seated there by myself in the darkness, past two in the morning, with no one else nearby and very few of the inhabitants of the community that lay around me even awake, seemed entirely appropriate. I felt a measure of pride in my separateness, a sense of resolution in being as I was, alone in the nighttime in a mountain town where I knew almost nobody and was known to few. The road that had brought me there, I thought, had been deceptive and erratic. It had not been remotely what I had imagined or intended for myself. Yet here I was, on a faintly warm night in the very early spring (or the tail end of winter, according to the calendar), with the city asleep around me and the C&O freight train blowing for the crossings as it neared town.

Finally the night freight came banging into the city, the locomotive headlight probing through the darkness like a baton, until as it drew close the light thrust into view, in swift counterpoint, objects I had not hitherto made out: a row of boxcars on a siding, semaphores, telegraph poles, switch blocks, a warehouse alongside the tracks. It played upon the jagged rock wall of the cliffside across the way, breaking it into a mosaic of planes and recesses. The locomotives — there were two of them, their drive wheels performing in unison — rolled powerfully up and past, and I could see for a moment the firemen and engineers in their cabs, high above the tracks, illuminated by the red glow of the open firebox doors. Then a freight car, and another, and another; one after the other clanged past, chains rattling and the flanged wheels singing as they cruised along, their song punctuated with a chorus of creaks and bangs and bumps as the cars held to the rails, in cadenced processional, a hundred cars and more, until at last the sound lightened and the caboose swung past.

As I turned to watch it go I saw a trainman standing on the rear platform, lantern in hand, with the red and green lamps above him. He waved to me and I waved back, and I watched as the caboose receded rapidly past the columns of the station platform and into the darkness, the signal lights solemnly glowing, and then around the bend of the rock cliff and out of sight. And all I could hear was the movement of the wheels in the distance, growing fainter as the train cleared the city limits and headed eastward. Further and further away, off to the east, the whistle sounded ever more distantly for the crossings. I sat on in the darkness, all by myself again, in no hurry to leave, listening pleasantly.

"The sleeping city," I said to myself, half aloud. I might write a poem entitled that. And only myself awake to listen. Lyrical whistle of the freight train, miles to the east and receding eastward. But then I heard another and, as it seemed, answering whistle, dirge-like and much fainter. The freight train could not possibly have moved so far away so rapidly. It must be the westbound passenger train, which came through the city each morning at about three o'clock. I looked at my watch in the darkness. It was indeed after three. If I waited for the passenger train to come and go, it would be almost four before I got back to my room and to bed. And what of that? What was to hinder my staying here for as long as I wished, till broad daylight if I chose? Tomorrow I could sleep even later than usual. Besides, tomorrow was Sunday — more properly, it had now been Sunday for more than three hours. I might do whatever I wanted; there was no one to object. Since I worked when others slept, the night was fairly my own.

I could now hear two trains whistling; there was no doubt of it. They were both far away, but one was coming toward Staunton. There was a noise behind me, not far from where I sat. I turned and saw a man engaged in loading some sacks of outbound mail onto a cart. When he was done he began pulling it up the concrete station platform. The train whistle was closer now, and presently I could hear the monotone of the wheels on the rails. Far down the platform, almost past the station, a man and a woman were standing, with suitcases alongside. That was where the pullmans would be stopping.

Now the passenger train came gliding into the station, the headlamp abruptly materializing from around the rocky bend. The locomotive moved up and past me, immense and stern, its high drive wheels performing their revolutions very slowly. It pulled to a stop a hundred yards ahead. Opposite me on the rails was a darkened coach. I watched down the track as the porters swung down with their yellow footstools. Even at that hour there were some passengers debarking. The man and woman I had seen waiting now stepped aboard, with the pullman porter following them, carrying their luggage; the arriving travelers walked off toward the station.

The train did not stay long. After only a few minutes I heard the conductor calling "All aboard!" and saw him signaling with his flashlight to the engineer up ahead. The air brakes went off with a hot iron hiss. The locomotive coughed twice in staccato explosion, and the train began easing forward into a slow, sustained rolling. I watched as the day coaches went by, then the dining car, cold and dark and the windows fogged, each to a swifter rhythm than its predecessor. Then the pullmans: City of Ashland, Collis P. Huntington, Balcony Falls, Gauley Bridge. The last pullman swept past in clattering haste. The red and green lamps receded westward. I listened until they were well out of sight. Soon the locomotive was blowing for grade crossings to the west of town. It would not be long before the train would have cleared the valley and begun climbing into the Alleghenies. As for the freight train, it was out of earshot now, and doubtless thundering along the grades of the Blue Ridge, bound for Charlottesville and the Northeast.

I walked home in the dark, feeling tired now and quite pleased with myself. It was well on toward four o'clock in the morning, I had seen two trains arrive and depart, and now I was all alone again on the deserted streets of the mountain town. I felt that I had accomplished something, had asserted my sensibility. I was persuaded, too, that whatever my present inconsequence, I was inevitable. On just what grounds this assurance was to be based, and for what, I could not have said. Yet the certainty, as I thought it, made me walk faster and breathe hard as I climbed up the hill toward my rented room, all by myself, at four in the morning, acting out a silent melodrama of prideful fulfillment.

The next day, however, after I had gone out almost at noon to eat breakfast at the hotel restaurant, I felt no such assurance. My confidence, my optimism of the evening before now seemed not merely misplaced but pathetically absurd. For in the light of a warmish Sunday in mid-March I saw myself in a different perspective, as a self-important young man with neither talent nor assurance, who had thus far failed at everything he had ever undertaken to do. I worked at a nighttime job that made it almost impossible to meet other people and make friends and have dates with girls. And what was worse, I had been glad of it, because it enabled me to hide from myself the knowledge of my ineptitude and unattractiveness. Now, because it was Sunday and I possessed no such refuge for the ten or twelve hours before I could fall asleep again, I felt trapped and in panic.

I remembered how, the previous evening when the freight train had been calling in the night as if to me alone, I had fancied that I was going to write a poem about the sleeping city. What vanity! For I knew very well that on all occasions when I had attempted to write anything, I had been quite unable to produce three lines that were not empty, pompous, and flat. Whenever I actually sat down before my typewriter and tried to begin anything other than a routine newspaper article, all my confidence, and all the ideas I had in mind, swiftly went stale.

I read the Sunday *New York Times* in my room, then tried reading a book for a while, but could not escape my gloom. I decided to go out for a walk. Perhaps the spring weather would divert me. On Sundays only there was an eastbound local passenger train that came through town about two o'clock. I would go down to the station and watch it.

As I headed eastward on Beverley Street I saw several couples, my age or younger, strolling along, looking at the displays in the store windows, chatting happily. There were two couples who were holding hands. Students from the local women's college and their dates, I decided. A year ago and I had done as much.

I passed the Stonewall Jackson Hotel. Would I end up like my uncle, living in a hotel room somewhere? He didn't seem to mind. I envied him his spartan invulnerability, his hermit-like ability to live by himself and not care about anything except his work.

I walked on toward the depot. Waiting near the tracks were

a young man and several girls who seemed to be a little older than college age; they did not look like students. I walked past them, near enough to be able to hear what they were saying. They were talking with each other in French, and laughing at each other's pronunciation. They must be teachers at the college, I thought.

I should have liked very much to get to know people like that. I would have delighted in using my French, as they were doing. But I had no excuse for venturing into their conversation. As if waiting for the train, I stood not too far distant, observing them from the corner of my eye. If only I had some reason, some plausible excuse, for joining them. I knew that someone more sure of himself, more sophisticated and less self-conscious, would need no occasion but would simply go up to where they waited and strike up a conversation.

The train came drifting into the station. I had been so preoccupied that I had paid it no heed. One of the girls was apparently going away on a trip, or else returning somewhere after a visit to the others; the man was carrying her suitcase. I watched them as they said good-bye. Then after the girl who was leaving had gone inside the coach and found a seat by a window overlooking the platform, they were waving. "Bon-Voyage!," one of the girls on the platform kept calling, mouthing her words very deliberately so that her friend on the train might read her lips.

If I were to go aboard, I thought, I might take the seat next to the girl and strike up a conversation. And why should I not do so? I might ride as far as Charlottesville and then take the evening train back to Staunton. I was free; I had nothing to prevent me from getting aboard and going along on the journey eastward. The thought frightened me, and instead I merely looked on as the railroad conductor signaled to the engineer, the vestibule doors slammed shut, the airbrakes went off, and the train moved from the station.

The young man and the two remaining girls who had escorted the traveler to the station waved good-bye, then walked off toward town. As they went by, one of the girls glanced at me for an instant. Hastily I averted my eyes, and so as not to seem to be following them, I walked a block eastward along the station platform and then took a side street back toward my rented room.

When I reached my room I turned on the radio. The New York Philharmonic Sunday concert was just beginning. Dmitri Mitropoulos was conducting the *Symphonie Pathétique*, which I disliked. Yet I did not switch it off. As if to torture myself, to make my afternoon complete, I lay on my bed, face downward, and listened to the oh so melancholy music.

They had been conversing in French. How very cultured, how very toney! And I, eavesdropping, watching them from a few yards away, had been standing there like a gawky fool and wanting to join them. The sensitive soul indeed. How very Romantic! the lonely young man in the mountains! The thought of my pathetic posturing made me wince.

A few months ago on a Sunday afternoon, and her father and I would probably have been playing chess and listening to this self-same concert. That *he* had been in on the plan! I writhed at the thought. During all that time, for at least a month and very probably two or three, she had her mind made up to send me packing, and had only been awaiting the Proper Moment. But in my invincible vanity I had proved so obtuse as not to see what should have been plain. So there had been the need to make it obvious, overt. And in discussing it, they had pitied me! The poor, naïve young man from down South . . .

"Damn!" I said aloud, over the melancholy music. "Damn!" Who in hell was she, who were they, to pity me?

It was true. Who *were* they? For while it was undeniable that I was lonely and missed very much having a girl, it need not be *her*. I could see that now.

I leaped up from the bed and walked across the room to the east window. The Sunday afternoon traffic was moving along Route 11. I thought, by God, I will write her a letter and tell her exactly what I think of her spoiled, stinking self. I went over to my typewriter, placed a sheet of paper in the machine. I stared at it a minute, then ripped it out. Hold on now, I told myself, just because you see daylight you are not out of the woods just yet. It would be exactly what she would want – another sequel to the little game of Falling Out of Love. I had had all I wanted of games. I crumpled the sheet of paper into a ball, threw it across the room at the wastepaper basket. It hit the wall, bounced in.

It must have been the people at the train station. I thought of how I should enjoy cramming their French conversation and their silly chatter down their cultivated throats. But that was not what I was angry about, was it? No, I had wanted to join them. My anger was for myself. Yet how could I expect to be other than what I was?

I lay in bed, and gradually became aware that the *Symphonie Pathétique* was concluded, and the commentator, Deems Taylor, was talking about the next number to be played by the orchestra. His mellifluous, too urbane voice droned on. Johannes Brahms had long put off writing a fully symphonic work, and it was not until he was forty-three years old that he completed his first symphony. The *Variations on a Theme by Haydn*, though originally composed for two pianos, was really a trial run, so to speak, whereby Brahms had for the first time used the full resources of an orchestra to develop an extended symphonic creation. The theme he had chosen, said Deems Taylor, was a choral work by Haydn, the *St. Anthony Chorale*.

Then, without warning, all unprepared as I was to meet it, there came the most cadenced, masterfully gentle music, calm and reassuring, that I had ever heard. In unhurried progression, tranquil and controlled, yet by no means without strength or resonance, the theme spoke out confidently, sustained and borne alone by the horns and violins. I had always liked Brahms, but this composition possessed a sweetness and harmoniousness that seemed to soften and transform everything around me – the air, the room, the time of day. The music formed itself into an assertion, an acknowledgment of purpose, but without either panic or desperation. It climbed steadily forward, building to a more urgent reiteration, but only enough to make its point, without any clamor or abandonment of its dignity and congruence. It closed on three drawn-out, unhurried chords. ST. ANTHONY, I thought, as if punching out the letters on a teletype keyboard, STANTON. Without the *you* in it.

The variations that Johannes Brahms had made on the theme by Haydn continued, and I listened on. But because I was young and had almost until that moment been in love, as I lay on my bed and the music played I did not think to wonder why it was that the pleasure I drew from the music was so like that which I took from the trains. Neither did it occur to me, being neither traveler nor musician but only a newspaperman temporarily resident in a mountain town in Virginia, to consider the odd coincidence in names, or even to ask who St. Anthony was. That truth, if such it proved to be, would come. For now, for Sunday afternoon, I was content to lie and listen to the music.

DONALD SECREAST

~~~~~~~~~~~~~~~~~~

Summer Help

Wanda Dey sat in the culled Louis XVI banquet chair, a gift from the man who had dropped it from the loading platform; she was eating a banana for her breakfast. Beside her, sitting in another banquet chair, Marleen Craig was drinking a cup of canteen coffee, telling Wanda the rumor about Old Man Chalfant's son. As Marleen talked, she kept sliding her eyes toward the door that led to the canteen. It was almost time for the seven o'clock whistle, and Marleen had to time her exit from Wanda's workroom so she could get back to the machine room before Mayhew got back from the boiler room, where he lingered every morning to smoke and talk about trolling. Mayhew insisted that Marleen have at least three headboard patterns traced out and ready to be cut by the time he turned on the band saw. Wanda was glad she didn't have to work with a man like Mayhew.

"But his boy really hates the factory," Marleen said through her upper lip, her lower lip pressed against the Vendomatic coffee cup.

"And I bet he can't stand the money it makes for Old Man

Chalfant." Wanda twirled the peel of the banana draping over her wrist and fingers like a deflated bouquet.

"From what I hear, he's not the kind of boy who'd think the two are connected. He's an artist."

"So are a lot of people." Wanda was aware of the striping brushes in her smock pocket and the pleasant odor of enamel paint coming from the center of the room where she was working on a gigantic hutch, painting Chinese ladies on the panels of the lower doors.

Marleen stood up. She was about forty-five but still had a nice figure. She wore the tight pants to prove it. Wanda suspected that her bright auburn hair was not completely honest. Once every two weeks, Marleen's hair had a pungent chemical smell, and it was not a smell that came from the furniture factory. Still, Marleen was a reliable source of information. All the men in the factory talked to her. "I'm just surprised she don't pick up more than gossip," Hutson, Wanda's husband, had remarked after last year's Christmas party.

"Well, he starts to work today." Marleen crumpled her cup as the factory whistle pierced the heavy air of the room. As soon as the whistle cut off, the snarl of the exhaust fans being switched on momentarily obliterated all human voices and the sounds of scuffling chairs in the canteen. Off to the left, one of the finishing room men had turned on the compressed-air pump, and it rattled like a skull inside a bass drum. The floor trembled slightly, indicating that the endlessly long conveyor belt, the chain, was now clacking through the factory, insinuating its rhythm into all the motions of the people who worked around it. Out in the rough end, the sound of a cutoff saw screeching through the first piece of raw lumber of the day reminded Marleen of Mayhew.

"The Old Man and the boy have some kind of deal going is all I know," Marleen said on her way to the door. "Otherwise, he'd never got the boy to step foot in this place."

Wanda was able to relax once Marleen left her workroom. She liked to be alone with her work first thing in the morning.

Of course, by nine o'clock break, she was ready to talk to somebody – Marleen, sometimes, but she really felt more comfortable with Rachel from the cabinet room. Wanda had been working at Chalfant Furniture for five years now, and she still found Hutson's original advice accurate. He had warned her to avoid the men from the lumberyard and the men from the rough end. "Most of them've not been too long out of the woods. And you're liable to get fleas or ticks off of them. Or something worse." He'd also warned her about the men from the finishing room. "Most of them have brain damage," he said, only half jokingly. "I swear. For eight or ten hours a day, they breathe the shellac, the stain, the varnish. Even with the little masks they wear, some of the chemicals gets through and busts brain cells like they was little balloons. Besides," he added, "they're the nastiest people to walk the earth."

Wanda knew that Hutson was protective, but what he'd said about the finishing room workers was true, especially for the men at the end of the spray booth chain who had to rub off all the excess finish. One little man who never seemed to leave the factory was known to everyone only as the Rat because of his color – a dull mahogany from his hair, over his clothes, down to his pointed shoes. His low forehead and large nose added to the resemblance. He never spoke to anyone, but about three minutes before break time, lunchtime, and quitting time, he'd wiggle out from between the large packing boxes and sniff the air as if he could tell time with his nose.

Wanda had just opened her bottles of paint and was in the process of tearing open a package of new striping brushes when the door from the canteen opened. The personnel manager, Huntly Vanderveldt, walked into her workroom, followed by a tall man wearing a seersucker suit. At first, Wanda assumed the tall man was a salesmen that Vanderveldt was taking to the shipping room. However, instead of walking across to the door that led to the shipping room where the furniture was crated up and loaded on trucks or boxcars, Vanderveldt stopped just inside the door.

"Wanda, you're not in the middle of something, are you?"

"Just getting ready to be." Wanda turned to face him. Vanderveldt was from the front office, but Wanda liked him. In a way, he was the one most responsible for getting her out of the machine room and settling her in as a furniture striper. But because he was from the front office, he didn't come into the factory unless something was wrong. All Wanda could think of was that she'd used the wrong pattern on one of the custommade commodes that they rushed through last week. Usually, she could take her time and do the job right, but lately some new hotshot salesman was getting quantity orders on custom pieces. She braced herself for Vanderveldt's quiet criticism, his reminding her about the importance of her work because it was done on their highest quality pieces and not easily corrected – the whole piece had to be taken apart, sanded down, and completely refinished. But she hadn't made such a mistake in three years.

Rather than criticize her, Vanderveldt said, "Well, you're doing wonderful work, Wanda. I certainly like what you're doing with that hutch." During his pause, while he walked closer to the hutch to admire her work, Wanda glimpsed the tall man leaning over to the left and then back to the right as if he too were inspecting her painting. "You're almost as rushed this week as you were last week, aren't you?" Vanderveldt stooped to be on an even level with the Chinese ladies, each of whom held an armful of cherry blossoms or dogwood blossoms, Wanda wasn't sure which; she just made them white.

"It's just starting to crank up," she answered.

"Well, when I found out what kind of orders Gray Westfall was calling in – and for custom stock – I knew you'd be standing on your head over here. No problem getting the pieces made: just speed up the chain. But no chain runs through here."

"Sometimes when they crank it up," Wanda said, "it feels like it's trying to work its way through."

"I know what you mean. I can feel it vibrate all the way up to the front office. Last week, though, I told Fonsielle that what makes that furniture custom furniture is Wanda Dey. Without her pictures and striping, it's just so much expensive wood screwed and glued together."

Wanda looked down into her lap where she had dumped the six striping brushes, whose long sable bristles were the shape of tiny foxtails. Often, she had thought exactly what Vanderveldt was saying, but to have one of the bosses say it out loud in front of a tall man in a seersucker suit was more than she could hear and keep looking him in the eye.

"Well, Mr. Vanderveldt, you know it's more than just a job with me."

"I certainly do." Vanderveldt stood up. "And that's why I think you deserve special consideration." He turned to the tall man and said, "Zavier, come over here and let me introduce you to the best striper we've ever had at Chalfant Furniture Factory."

The tall man approached, and for the first time Wanda noticed that he wasn't wearing a tie. He wasn't even wearing a dress shirt with his suit. He was wearing a turquoise T-shirt with crimson lettering, but Wanda couldn't make out the words because the seersucker jacket covered most of them. He was also wearing sandals of woven leather, Mexican looking. In the buttonhole of his jacket was a dandelion blossom.

"Wanda Dey," Vanderveldt said, a hint of formality creeping into his voice – enough to pull Wanda off her stool and turn her around to face the tall man. "I want you to meet Zavier Chalfant. He's going to be with us for a couple of months, and knowing your interest in art, I thought you might enjoy having his help while he's here because Zavier is already a serious artist."

All the time Vanderveldt was making this introduction, Zavier Chalfant was letting his gaze rest lightly on Wanda. Most boys – and that's what Zavier was, after all, a boy of about twenty-one – were very embarrassed their first day on the job. Zavier, in contrast, seemed more amused than embarrassed by what Vanderveldt was saying. His thick blond hair covered the collar of his jacket but was clean and expertly cut so he looked more like a knight than a hippie. His face was perfectly balanced above and below his cheekbones. The delicacy of his chin, however, prevented his jaw from seeming too long. He had green eyes, which he would occasionally force open wider than they were meant to be. Wanda noticed him do it the first time when Vanderveldt began his introduction, a second time when he mentioned how long Zavier was going to be working, and a third time when he made the remark about being a serious artist. Although Wanda didn't know what he meant by the wide eyes, the rest of Zavier's face was so friendly that she couldn't help but smile at him. She decided that his face looked like a Viking's face; she'd always been partial to Vikings. Of course, Zavier was too thin to be a Viking all the way down, but he had the face of an adventurer. Of an artist.

"So for a couple of months, with Zavier to help you," Vanderveldt was saying, "it'll be kind of like a vacation for you. Then come August, it'll be time for you to take your real vacation. Where are you and Hutson going this year?"

Wanda turned from Zavier. "Oh, we're still fighting about that. I want to go to Florida, you know, so I can paint some sunsets, but he wants to go to the mountains."

"If things work out for Zavier," Vanderveldt said, grasping the boy's elbow, "he'll be spending August in Paris."

This time, when Vanderveldt said Paris, Zavier not only widened his eyes, he also tilted his head back slightly. "Provided I can come to work here every morning for two months and get through the day without needing a transfusion or shock treatments."

Vanderveldt laughed. "Well, Zavier, you're going to be keeping company with one of the best people in the whole plant. Why, I wouldn't be surprised if Wanda got you to liking this place so much you just forgot about going to Paris."

Zavier's eyes got wide once more. "Well, she's certainly

lovely enough to do that." He smiled. "But my girlfriend is also counting on this trip, and I'm sure she'd have something to say about my deciding to stay in Boehm to finish out the summer painting furniture."

"Okay, then." Vanderveldt sidestepped toward the canteen door. "I've got some people to interview. If any problems come up, Zavier, drop by the office. But I'm sure Wanda can tell you anything you need to know. Once you get in the routine, you'll find yourself having a good time, I bet. Just keep telling yourself you're earning that ticket to Paris."

"You bet, coach." Zavier's nose flared along with his eyes.

With an ease that bordered on stealth, Vanderveldt slipped out of the room, leaving Wanda with the tall Viking and a blade of panic sliding up her throat. This is Old Man Chalfant's own boy, she thought to herself. She had never been comfortable with the bosses, the big bosses, and now here she was with the owner's son.

"Have you done any striping before?" Wanda brushed her upper lip with one of the new brushes.

"No." Zavier tossed his hands up and hunched his shoulders. "I'm completely ignorant. I *am* a fast learner, though." He squatted in front of the hutch. "You know, this isn't bad work at all." He gave her a sideways nod of approval.

"I've been doing it long enough." Wanda already felt comfortable with the boy.

"But you've had some lessons." He picked up a jar of gold enamel paint and smelled it. "I can tell."

"I've taken all the art courses they offer at the community college."

"That's a good place to start," Zavier replied. "Can I try finishing this lady? She's supposed to match the one you've got on the other panel, isn't she?"

Wanda handed him a brush. She didn't know what else to do. She wanted to tell him about how to mix the gold with the white in order to get the right flesh tone, but before she could get the correct proportions out of her mouth, he'd already applied the gold, then started daubing on the white, actually mixing the colors on the wood — and getting them to match.

"How can you mix like that right on the wood?" Wanda stooped beside him.

"Color is my specialty." Zavier deftly added the highlights to the woman's face and hands. "It's everything." He finished the flesh parts in a matter of minutes. He took another brush from Wanda and in six or seven strokes had filled in the woman's robe. Without seeming to look closely, he added the colors to the dogwood blossoms.

"I've never seen anybody work so fast." Wanda stepped back to her stool, where she sat down and studied the picture with her chin propped in her palms.

"Well, I was going by what you'd already done," Zavier said, wiping a brush. "My speed is simply a testimony to your ability." His eyes widened beyond their normal size. "We complement each other, I think."

"I bet you've had some lessons yourself."

"Lots and lots." Zavier stood up and studied a far corner of the workroom. "I've been taking lessons since I sent off one of those Draw Me pictures. Before then, I'd watch Jon Gnagy every Wednesday night. I even took a few classes at the community college when I was in high school. Now there's college — "

"I'd like to see your paintings. I've never met anyone who took it so seriously. I mean, I take it seriously, but you're making a career out of it."

"That's very good," Zavier said. "You've picked up in about fifteen minutes what my father has failed to grasp in twenty-one years."

"I'd still like to see your paintings." Wanda wasn't certain if the trouble between Old Man Chalfant and his son was any of her business. She had the feeling that Zavier Chalfant could show her real art. Marleen might be interested in the Chalfant family struggles, but Wanda wanted to be an artist.

As they waited for two men from the shipping room to remove the hutch, Zavier talked to Wanda about color. "You've got to know what direction a particular color will take when it's mixed with, say, white. And you've got to know its velocity, too."

"What do you paint?" Wanda felt herself lost in his color theory.

Before he could answer, two men from the finishing room dragged in another hutch. "Use the same pattern on this one that you did on the last one," the foreman said as they left the room. He gave a long look at Zavier and shook his head as he closed the door. Wanda could understand how the men in the factory might disapprove of Zavier; he didn't really belong there.

"I paint surfaces," Zavier replied.

"You don't paint pictures?" Wanda tried to hide her discomfort.

Zavier paused before answering. He was running his fingers over the lightly varnished surface of the hutch. "I think it's a shame to put pictures on this wood. Don't you?"

"But the pictures are what make it custom crafted." Wanda began looking for the wax pencil she used to trace the pattern on the wood.

"Oh, yeah. It has to have that distinctive Chalfant Furniture Factory touch."

As Wanda traced the first Chinese lady onto the door panel, without even an offer of help from Zavier, she asked, "If you don't paint pictures, what do you paint?"

Zavier picked up the other pattern and handed it to her. Carefully, she lined it up and began tracing again.

"See, Wanda," he explained, leaning back against a large cardboard box containing a discontinued style of dresser, "I've spent the last few years working with colors. Color is a caption for reality. Shape is haphazard; color is pure, musical." He picked up a striping brush. Before Wanda had finished tracing the second Chinese lady, Zavier had gotten a good start on the first lady's face. "Have you ever noticed it's the edges of things that fade first? Color hates edges. When I realized this, I knew I had to stop painting shapes." He said "shapes" as if it had bristles that punctured his tongue.

For the rest of the morning, Wanda and Zavier fell into a routine: she would trace the patterns, and Zavier would paint the two Chinese ladies. At nine o'clock, when the break whistle blew, Zavier settled down in the Louis XVI chair and pulled a magazine out of his jacket pocket. He didn't seem interested in getting to know the other people in the factory.

"You're not bashful, are you, Zavier?"

"Not a bit," Zavier replied. "But you're all the company I need for the short time I'm going to be here." He gave Wanda one of his wide-eyed looks. "On your way back, would you bring me a Pepsi?" He handed her the money.

As soon as she got into the canteen, Wanda saw Marleen waving her to a seat beside her. Rachel was already sitting across from Marleen, and Wanda felt a little disappointed when she saw that Rachel looked as curious and excited as Marleen.

"As soon as I saw Vanderveldt leading that tall boy through the machine room," Marleen said, "I knew he could fit in just one place – in the striping room with Wanda."

"Is he as good-looking as Marleen says?" Rachel was a pale woman with blond hair and blond eyelashes. Her husband was a preacher and expected Rachel to be a model for the other women in the factory, but she sometimes forgot herself.

"You'd better get all this straightened out with Hutson just as soon as you can." Marleen stirred her coffee.

Wanda sat next to Rachel. She liked to sit so she could keep both eyes on Marleen. For the next ten minutes, she told them all she had learned about Zavier Chalfant. She wasn't surprised to see both women as confused by Zavier's ideas about color as she was. Neither of the other two women had taken any kind of art course. However, Mrs. Mills, who taught the art classes at the community college, never mentioned color's dislike for shapes. When the whistle blew, Marleen wanted to go introduce herself, but Wanda advised her to give the boy more time to get used to the factory.

"I think he's kind of bashful." Wanda moved to the drink machine.

"Or he might be a snob," Marleen replied. "I can't figure out why he didn't go to work in the design room, or maybe over in advertising, if he's such an artist." Her speculations were cut short when she saw Mayhew draining off the last ounce of his Sun-Drop. "Well, I've got to get back to my own art." She stood up and adjusted the seams of her pants.

Quietly, Rachel followed Wanda back to the striping room. Rachel worked in the cabinet room, which was located an equal distance from the canteen whether she circled through the machine room or through the finishing room. As a rule, she preferred to circle through the machine room because she didn't like the smell of the finishing room. Wanda knew why Rachel was following her, but she didn't mind – better Rachel than Marleen.

Zavier was in the same position that he occupied when Wanda left the room. As soon as he saw Wanda and Rachel enter, he jumped to his feet and made a low bow. The dandelion in his lapel was looking limp and overcome. "Wanda, you've brought company." His eyes were wide. "And my Pepsi too."

"Zavier, this is Rachel Prevette. She works over in the cabinet room."

Rachel smiled, calm in the wake of Wanda's introduction. After all, she was a preacher's wife and used to meeting strangers. "I just wanted to come by and invite you to services at my husband's church, Zavier."

"Which church is that?" Zavier asked.

"The Gospel Wind Church of Daily Salvation."

"Up past the prison camp, isn't it?"

"About five miles." Rachel was flattered that the son of Old Man Chalfant would know her husband's church.

"It used to be a grocery store, didn't it?" Zavier took a deep drink from his Pepsi. "I bought a Sunbeam Bread sign from them just after the store closed. It was an interesting little building when it was a grocery store." Zavier munched ice from his drink. "I would never have thought about turning it into a church. Tell your husband I admire his imagination."

"I will." Rachel made her way for the door that led to the finishing room. "Don't work too hard." She turned toward Wanda and raised her eyebrows while giving a quick jerk of her head toward Zavier.

Wanda could have guessed that Rachel wouldn't know how to take Zavier. While she had been talking to her and Marleen in the canteen, she had realized just how much of an artist Zavier was. And he was nice. Rachel didn't know how a serious painter related to people. That was all. Surely, part of the problem, Wanda reasoned, was that Zavier was a genius. He had to be — the way he mixed paint, the way he talked about color as if it were something alive and moving. And the way he dressed. This was a side of art that Wanda had only heard about from television, certainly not from Mrs. Mills.

As they started back to work, Zavier took off his jacket. The factory hoards its heat. "Did you notice that your flower's wilting?" Wanda asked.

"I'm interested in that process, the process of wilting. Process is the closest we can get to color in terms of action — as in the process of travel."

"And you're painting it?"

"I'm painting the process," Zavier corrected. "Give color a chance to escape shape, and you have an ocean. Color is the source of all life on this planet."

Wanda noticed that the writing on his turquoise T-shirt said *Klee Is for Mee*. She wanted to ask him what it meant, but she decided she'd wait until later. There was already too much she didn't understand, and she felt she'd reached her limit, at least until after lunch. Besides, Zavier seemed to have gone into a trance, filling in the colors of the Chinese lady's dress.

The two men from the finishing room noticed the increased

pace and started bringing in the hutches much faster than usual. This kept Wanda and Zavier busy, too busy to talk. They fell into a rhythm that demanded only the periphery of their attention. Wanda was already trying to figure out how she was going to explain Zavier to her husband. She was also trying to decide if Zavier was the kind of person who might give her lessons. She didn't care about all that color-is-life business. She wanted her pictures to look nicer. All the sketches she did left her dissatisfied. Especially when she tried to do pictures of people she knew, she could feel her limitations as an artist. Every time she did a drawing of Hutson, he came out looking like a caveman — and it wasn't entirely his fault. His head was shaped a little like a block, and his hair did come down too far on his forehead, but his jaw really was solid and wide — stable.

When sitting in the cab of his Mack truck, he did sometimes look ferocious. He drove for Boehm Glass and Mirror Company. At first he'd worked there making frames, back before he and Wanda got married. Then, when he found out that truck drivers made more money than frame makers, he'd learned to drive trucks. Still, he made frames for all the pictures that Wanda painted or drew. He also liked everything that Wanda produced, even the pictures of his square, shaggy head.

At lunch, Zavier disappeared, probably to eat with his father in the Old Man's air-conditioned office, Wanda decided. Apparently, Marleen and Rachel had been discussing the boy at length. Wanda could tell from the way Rachel was dedicating herself to her Vendomatic chili and franks that she had told Marleen everything Zavier said to her during her brief visit.

"Well," Marleen said, raising her voice and letting her eyes sweep around the room, "any man who gets his thrills from dried-up grocery stores certainly ain't going to like me."

Most of the men in the canteen looked at her and smiled, their mouths full of sandwiches or pork and beans. Wanda knew every person in the factory had to have his place, even if the person was the factory's owner. Marleen was in the process of putting Zavier in his place. Wanda thought for a moment about saying something nice about Zavier, but that would give the people in the canteen the wrong idea. Besides, she realized it was possible that Zavier didn't feel a normal need, one she might feel, to be liked by the people who worked for his father. A serious artist probably wouldn't.

"Why's he not eating lunch?" Marleen asked. "Is he afraid Vendomatic might poison him?"

"He had somewhere else to eat." Wanda sprinkled pepper on her egg salad sandwich. "Probably with Old Man Chalfant. They *are* related, you know."

"If that's his idea of fun, I can see where he gets his fondness for creaky old buildings. I bet you didn't ask him why he wound up in the factory instead of design or advertising."

"We've been busy."

"Well, Mayhew thinks the boy might have problems." Marleen dropped her voice and shifted her eyes from Rachel to Wanda, back and forth, as if trying to weave some sort of insinuation between them.

"I can see that." Rachel tore open a package of crackers with her teeth.

"He's just a serious painter." Wanda spoke only to Marleen but knew that Mayhew would hear about it in the next hour.

"You're a serious painter, too," Marleen replied. "But you're here eating lunch where you belong, and you don't spend the weekends admiring twisted-up little buildings."

"No," Wanda agreed, "but he's different — "

"He's a fruit." Marleen slanted her hand through the air and shook her head.

After lunch, Zavier came through the canteen just as everyone was leaving. He was taller than the crowd he moved through, and he looked over everyone's head. Wanda noticed that he was looking at her, his eyes wide. He didn't seem to notice how everyone was measuring him from head to foot as if they were about to try jumping over him.

Marleen was standing beside Wanda. Rachel, as soon as Zavier started walking toward them, left through the door that led to the machine room.

"You must be Marleen." Zavier stopped at the table where they were straightening their chairs.

"Must be because I am." Despite her suspicions, Marleen was cautiously pleasant. She liked to be recognized.

"When Huntly led me through this morning, I saw you drawing . . . what was it . . . patterns for tabletops?"

"Headboards." A layer of Marleen's caution dissolved.

"And I said to Huntly, 'Why do we waste such beautiful women by hiding them back here behind all these machines? A woman like that ought to be a model.'"

Marleen looked at Wanda and said, "That Mayhew is the dumbest baboon in this factory."

"Then I asked Huntly what your name was. I hope you don't mind. But you see, I have some friends who paint – "

"I hear you paint too." Marleen stood up as straight as she could.

"Nothing you'd recognize as painting," Zavier said quickly and almost humbly. "But these other friends of mine are always looking for models. In a town like Boehm, it's hard to find someone with the classic proportions."

"You mean I've got classic proportions?" Marleen put her arm through Zavier's arm.

"Up one side and down the other." Zavier patted her hand. He looked at Wanda once more with his eyes wide.

"When I was younger, I thought I'd like to be a model, but then I found out you had to go to Atlanta or New York, and while I like to go to the beach two or three times a year, I don't really care for such long trips."

"Well, most of my friends are out of town for the summer, but when they get back, I'll talk to them. Tell them I have found the model of their dreams. The last I heard, they were paying about twenty dollars an hour – "

"Tell 'em they'd get their money's worth." Marleen patted Zavier on his stomach. "Meanwhile, you can find me at band saw number three being abused by Mayhew." As she was walking toward the door, she turned in such a way that all of her moving parts shifted from right to left in a lush arc. "By the way, Wanda and I were wondering why you didn't go to work in design or advertising."

"I wanted to," Zavier replied, "but I know too many guys over there, and my father was afraid I wouldn't get anything done."

"If you get too bored, you can always find me drawing headboards out there in the machine room. Just tell 'em you're looking for Marleen."

"I'll keep that in mind. But from the looks of things, Wanda is going to make sure my father gets his money's worth out of me."

"She can be a drudge," Marleen agreed.

Back in the striping room, Zavier talked about his lunch with his friends in the design room. But Wanda could only half listen because she was trying to figure out if she really was a drudge. She was thirty-six and had yet to win any of the local community art contests – not the industrial fair contest, not the Women's Club annual art contest, not the Community Arts Council contest. Maybe, she thought, it's not that my drawing is bad so much as it's dull. This thought made her feel more determined about asking Zavier for lessons. Even if she didn't understand what he said about color, she could surely understand suggestions about drawing.

All afternoon, she tried to ask him for drawing lessons, but as soon as she mentioned anything about art, Zavier would begin talking about color and how it must be left alone in order to grow, like a fungus in a dark room. For about thirty minutes, he explained a theory he had that all color started in the mushroom and ended up in the ocean. "That's why most mushrooms have so little color. They've given it all to the world around them."

Finally, just before the three-thirty whistle, Wanda asked, "Have you ever given art lessons? I don't mean fancy lessons, just drawing and maybe some painting."

"I'll tell you what, Wanda," Zavier said, "once we get to be better friends, we'll sneak in some drawing lessons right under my father's factory nose. I have to know a person pretty well, though, because giving lessons is a very personal thing for me."

This all made sense to Wanda. Perhaps, she thought, that was why Mrs. Mills never helped her that much. She didn't take time to be friends with her students. But here was a rich and serious artist who wanted to wait until the friendship was established. This was the way one artist should treat another artist, Wanda concluded, as she drove home.

When Wanda pulled into her driveway, she saw that Hutson was already home, raking the stones in their front yard. One of the courses she had taken at the community college had been a ceramics and cement course in which she had learned to make her own yard ornaments. By the time she finished the course, she had so many cement and ceramic animals in the yard that Hutson couldn't mow the grass. He resolved the problem by hauling several tons of river rock down from the Gorge. All of the stones were round, varying in color from dark brown to pink. It took a while for the neighborhood to get used to Wanda's yard, but the previous spring it had won an honorable mention in the Women's Club Yard of the Year contest.

As they were eating supper, Wanda told Hutson about Zavier. Hutson always listened carefully when she talked to him. They'd been married for ten years, and he still acted as if he considered himself lucky that she accepted his proposal. Hutson, despite his love of television and big trucks, was an unpredictable man. Wanda assumed that on his long trips he must do an awful lot of thinking; he had a CB, but he seldom used it. What Wanda really appreciated about Hutson was how he never lost his excitement about her being an artist. Anything she did was acceptable to him because she was an artist.

"Does he look like Old Man Chalfant?" Hutson asked after Wanda finished talking about her day with Zavier.

"He's taller . . . and he has blond hair."

"The Old Man had blond hair. A long time ago." Hutson poured himself another glass of tea. "Blonds lose their hair quicker. Light hair can't hold roots." He avoided looking at Wanda.

"Then Zavier'll probably be bald as his father by the time he's thirty."

"I guess in two months he can't do too much damage to the factory." Hutson poured honey on top of two biscuits he'd broken open on his plate.

"Then he'll be in Paris." Wanda began to clean the table.

"Personally, I'd rather be in the Great Smoky Mountains."

"Or at the beach?" Wanda turned to face Hutson.

"But don't you want to spend our vacation up where I proposed to you? That was ten years ago, come September." Now Hutson was gazing intently at Wanda. He had honey in the corners of his mouth. "You remember that, don't you?"

Wanda leaned against the sink and laughed. Each year, Hutson reminded her of his proposal. They had gone up to Linville Gorge to see the Brown Mountain lights. As they stood on the overlook, Hutson had busied himself with his binoculars. Wanda noticed that to her left was a fresh pile of dog manure. She had stepped next to the brown pile and slid a bright red maple leaf over it. "Hut," she challenged, "I bet I can pick up this red leaf before you can." Before she had finished speaking, Hutson had swooped down beside her, grabbing the leaf. While he was still down on one knee, he'd grabbed her hand with both of his and begged her to marry him. She was laughing too hard at first to answer him, but had managed finally to gasp out a yes. Hutson started to kiss her, but she wouldn't let him until they'd found a place to wash their hands.

"We could start up at Asheville," Hutson was saying, his voice lowered in an attempt to be persuasive. "And head toward Virginia, trout fishing all the way, bass fishing all the way. And there are some campgrounds that have trails where you can hike."

"But if we go to the ocean, we can go out on one of them big boats and you could fish from it, fish for something big, so big they'll have to strap you in a chair to keep from getting pulled in by it."

"If they have to strap me in to fish for it, I don't have any business hooking it in the first place."

"And there's the ocean, Hut. All that color running loose like it was trying to come alive." Still leaning back against the sink, Wanda tilted her head back as if enjoying a salt spray. Her brown hair almost dipped into the dishwater.

"Sounds like a monster movie to me."

Wanda could hear in his voice that he was full of appreciation for her pose.

"By August, I might even be ready to try a painting of you in your bathing suit." Wanda looked at her husband through the frame of her two hands, touching thumb to thumb.

For the next three weeks, Wanda worked every day with Zavier. He continued to talk about color in the same difficult way, but he never mentioned any drawing lessons. Wanda assumed they weren't good enough friends. At break time, Zavier would stay in the striping room, and at lunch he would eat with his friends in the design department. He continued to wear the decaying dandelion in his jacket. On payday, he took his brown envelope out of the foreman's hand just like everybody else. At least twice a week, Wanda mentioned that she would like to see some of Zavier's work.

Finally, in the first week of July, Zavier banged into the striping room, carrying a large, battered portfolio under one arm and a frame covered by a cloth sack under his other arm. "To celebrate my last month in the factory, I've brought a few of my old old old pieces." He settled his burdens down in a corner. "Despite the anachronistic, the obsolete, quality of the work, I think these are works you'll be able to best appreciate."

For the rest of the day, every spare minute that Wanda could get, she spent looking at drawings that Zavier pulled from the portfolio. At the end of the day, all that was left to see was the framed picture. A few minutes before the three-thirty whistle, Zavier removed the cover and turned the picture toward Wanda. All day long she had been marveling at Zavier's talent. Several times she'd told him he was a genius. At lunch, Marleen had come to look at the pictures, and she also declared that he was a genius. She wanted to know when his friends were going to get back to town. Zavier promised her that he himself would use her for a model before he went to Paris and take the picture with him to sell over there to a count.

Wanda let out a small gasp when she saw the picture in the frame. It was done in pen and ink, a picture of a young woman standing on a hill, but she was somehow part of the landscape. Her dress was part of the hill where she was standing. And her hair, thick tresses being styled by the wind, curled over her head to become branches of the tree against which she was leaning. The branches, in turn, reached up to form a moon and clouds. But what really held Wanda's attention was the face of the girl. It resembled her own.

"Is that me?"

"I knew you'd ask that." Zavier's eyes went wide. "Look at the date." Zavier pointed to the right-hand corner below the initials z.c.

"Nineteen seventy-six," Wanda read.

"I was fifteen at the time. I was deep in my romantic period then. I happened to be thumbing through an old high school annual that belonged to my aunt — a *Boehm Beacon, 1964* —"

"I was a senior that year." Wanda took a step closer to the picture of the girl.

"And you had the most romantic wide round forehead, and the most romantic diminutive nose, and the most romantic spheroidical chin — by far the Girl Most Likely to Be Descended from Edgar Allan Poe." Zavier widened his eyes.

"It's beautiful." Wanda touched the face that she had eighteen years before.

"For what it is, it is," Zavier agreed. "It won the Women's Club Art Contest Best of Show in 1977. But now, what's even more interesting to me than the picture is the frame. My mother was afraid somebody at the Women's Club might steal my masterpiece, so she bought this special frame — had it made to order. See, it locks." Zavier pointed to a small round hole. "But the big joke is that about a month after I won the contest, my mother lost the key. I'd have burned the picture years ago if I could have gotten it out of this beautiful frame."

"Would you sell the picture and the frame?"

Zavier's eyes grew very wide. "I don't sell art. Even bad art shouldn't be sold, especially bad art that is likely to embarrass me in the future. No, I couldn't sell this picture because years from now, an unscrupulous person might use it to blackmail me. It will have to sit, as it does now, in the darkest corner of my darkest closet." Biting his lower lip, Zavier began putting the linen cover back over the picture. He tied the strings with sharp irritated flicks of his wrists.

"I'd certainly like to be able to draw like that." Wanda wondered how long it took to become Zavier's friend.

"If you were my friend, you wouldn't talk like that." Zavier didn't look up from the strings.

For the remaining weeks of July, Wanda didn't bother Zavier about art lessons. He didn't seem to notice how much he had hurt her feelings. He continued to talk about color as if it were something he could make stand up on its hind legs — as if it were something *with* hind legs. Wanda continued to feel she was just outside Zavier's conversation, that if he would only lean five inches closer to her ear when he was talking about how this red was a heavy breather or how that blue had a ringing in its ears, she might understand what he meant. But he always kept the same distance between them.

Marleen had felt the distance too. Her reaction was to hold it against the boy. "He's a promiser," she declared one day in the parking lot. "He's more full of shit than a goat with a plug in its ass." She spit out her gum to emphasize her point.

"Well." Wanda turned her head away from Marleen to look up between the lumber hacks into the slack afternoon sky. "I can see his point. Art is kind of like a promise."

"A fart is kind of like a promise too, and I don't like being in a small room with either one."

Since that conversation, Marleen had made a point of eating lunch with Mayhew, and Wanda would eat her lunch sitting in her Louis XVI banquet chair. She had started trying to read the magazine that Zavier would leave lying around after his nine o'clock reading: *Art in America*. She read names like Arnulf Rainer, Cy Twombly, Ruth Snyder, Jan Commandeur, Andy Warhol, Anselm Kiefer, Jerry Concha, but as soon as she put the magazine down, she forgot them. She tried to work her way through articles about Pollock, de Kooning, Kline, Olitski, and Van Buren, but they made no sense at all, less sense than Zavier's talk about color. The fact that she came closer to understanding Zavier than she did to understanding the magazines convinced her even further that Zavier was a genius.

On Zavier's last day of work, he came in dressed as usual, even down to the remnants of the dandelion in his lapel hole. However, he was also wearing a light gray beret. All day long, he paced about the striping room. When he paused to paint in the faces and dresses of the Chinese ladies, he would sing to himself and to Wanda when he caught her staring at him. Wanda was irritated, but she didn't know if it was because he was leaving without giving her the lessons or because she hadn't qualified as his friend.

"I can tell you're upset that today is my last day." He paint-ed a mustache on one of the Chinese ladies. When Wanda gasped, he wiped it off. "I'm having a going-away party to-morrow night. A large blast to launch me properly on Sunday. We're going to have fireworks – "

"Sunday!"

"It was the soonest flight I could get. I've been booked since June. The first day I walked in here and saw you, I knew it was ordained, that I'd be able to get through the whole two months. So, in a way, this party is a tribute to your success as well as mine."

"If it was such a success, if I was such a success, why didn't you ever give me any art lessons?"

"Wanda, Wanda, Wanda." Zavier opened his eyes too wide. "This trip has had me tied in knots. I'm so disorganized. It has taken all my spare time to get myself ready. But I promise you; when I get back, first thing I plan to do is give you some lessons."

"Because I qualify as a friend now?" Wanda thought that being a serious artist's friend was getting pretty close to being a serious artist oneself.

"The best. That's why you have to promise to come to my party tomorrow night – and bring your husband. We're going to have beer and all kinds of other refreshments. You'll get to meet some more serious artists. None of them as serious as me, of course, because if they were more serious than me, they'd have to be living in Russia, in Siberia, in a cave, with only wolf paws to eat."

To Wanda's surprise, Hutson was not as hard to persuade as she thought he would be. She had been taking her irritation out on him lately, and when she did that, he always responded by being stubborn. In one week, she knew they would be head-ed for the glittering shores of Panama City. Even if Zavier was gone, she hoped she still might be able to track down some loose colors just joining the ocean. So far, the best she could do was to imagine a flock of pelicans slowly dissolving into the water, leaving a gray and white stain that would eventually turn green.

The main reason Hutson wanted to go to the party was to see the picture of the girl that looked like Wanda. She had told him about the drawing, and for the past few weeks, he suggested several times that he talk to Zavier about buying the picture. "I could get it out of that frame," he assured her, twisting his empty beer can in two. When Hutson was in this kind of mood, all Wanda could do was pretend to agree with him. She'd promise to ask Zavier about selling the picture, and Hutson would be soothed. The next morning, he would avoid the subject of the picture and quietly take his split beer cans out to the trash can. Wanda always left the cans on the nightstand by his side of the bed.

Zavier lived on the outskirts of town in a small stone house with a red tile roof. "It was the most French-looking place I could find," he explained as he led them inside. They got to the party around eight o'clock. Hutson had insisted on eating at the Western Sizzler because he hated trying to fill up on potato chips. When Zavier answered the door, the first thing he did was hand Hutson a beer. "Some people don't like to shake hands with a stranger, so I find it safer just to hand out beers," Zavier explained. Wanda could tell that Hutson approved of the practice.

The house was crowded with people, all trying to talk over the music spewing from speakers in every corner of every room. Hutson dealt with the communication problem by keeping his beer to his mouth. Every few minutes, he would disappear to get a fresh can. He refused to stoop to the hypocrisy of carrying around an empty beer can. After thirty minutes, Wanda knew she was going to be driving them home when the party ended. She didn't mind. He had come because she wanted to be here. Her main concern was that he would be able to find a soft place to fall asleep. And she also wanted to know where that place was.

After an hour, he disappeared and didn't come back. Wanda

knew this was her cue to find where he was hibernating. It couldn't be a place where he'd be in people's way, like on a kitchen table or in the bathroom. However, she knew she had misjudged his drinking when she saw him huddled in a dark corner with Zavier. Somehow, he had managed to talk the artist into letting him see the picture of the girl. He was leaning over the picture with his hands propped on his knees. He was swaying slightly, but he was completely absorbed in the picture.

"And you're sure you won't sell it?" he was asking Zavier when Wanda walked up.

"I'd be too embarrassed to sell it even if I could." Zavier patted Hutson on the back. "Besides, it's locked up in that frame. And the frame was a present from my mother. So I guess both the frame and the picture will always be with me. Actually, I'm too fond of the frame for its own aesthetic worth to let it go. It's a work of art."

"It sure is." Hutson ran his fingers over the polished surface. He helped Zavier put the cover over the picture.

"Tomorrow, all of it goes in storage," Zavier said. "It'll be a relief to have the excesses of my youth locked up for a few years."

Eventually, Hutson wandered off, looking for a place to get off his feet.

"Beer always works from the bottom up on him," Wanda said to a girl standing beside her. The girl glanced in Hutson's direction. Her stare made Wanda painfully aware of how out of place her husband was. As he wobbled among the casual but elegant artists, he looked like a coconut rolling through a room of crystal vases. Wanda drifted from one group to the next, never quite understanding what they were talking about. Once she tried to wedge herself in closer to a woman who was talking about stereotypic responses to pastels, but a very thin boy turned and said, "Behave yourself."

She would have left then, but she saw Zavier sitting with his girlfriend and five other people. He motioned for her to come over. They were circled around a large water pipe. Wanda didn't know what to do once she got to the smokers.

"Sit here." Zavier moved to his right and patted the space beside him. "You don't know any of these people," he said ceremoniously. "And actually, you're better off not knowing them — except for my traveling companion, Tobynne Neustadt." He pointed the mouthpiece of the pipe toward the girl sitting on his left.

What Wanda first noticed was that she had the same Viking features as Zavier. Her eyes were the blue of the fifty-point circle on an archery target, and even though she was sitting, the girl was obviously tall, perhaps not quite as slim as Zavier but just as satisfied with her body. Wanda glanced back in the direction where Hutson had disappeared. By now, he was asleep, waiting to go home where she would have to undress him. She felt a need to go check on him, but Zavier handed her the mouthpiece. "Get wild," he advised. "Have visions; escape shapes." His eyes were narrow, as if he wanted Wanda to scrutinize the truth he was sharing with her.

Wanda had smoked before. Hutson would sometimes pick up hitchhikers, and they would occasionally express their gratitude by giving him a joint. She hadn't felt much when she tried the twisted little cigarettes. Mostly, she had been bored because Hutson had started talking about his tractor-trailer. He told her how it felt driving through snow, rain, wind, and sand. He went into prolonged detail about how the weather sounded. Then he talked about what tire pressure did to handling, what suspension systems did to handling. From there, he described how a truck should be loaded, because that affected handling too.

Wanda took a deep draw. She realized if smoking could get Hutson to talk so much about what he deeply loved, maybe these artists would start talking about art. Or if they talked about color instead, maybe with the right buzz she would be able to move closer to them, to understand them, to be like them enough to follow what they meant. The mouthpiece went around leisurely four or five times. Mostly, Tobynne talked about how much trouble she had packing, but Wanda didn't mind. She had begun to feel like one of her ceramic animals, one of the frogs. She felt green, the green of Zavier's eyes. Maybe, she thought to herself, this is where he gets all his talk about color.

Sometime later, Zavier propped himself up on his knees and announced, "Before I leave Boehm, I want to make one contribution to the culture of my hometown. But this must be a group effort. There might be danger. So all of those who would join me in this adventure into vengeful art must gird up his or her loins — those of you who still have them — and assemble out in Tobynne's van." All the circle followed Zavier outside. Wanda went along because, as they were getting to their feet, Zavier had whispered in her ear, "You should come, because after I'm gone you'll be the only one to carry on. I've spent this whole summer training you. Don't let me down."

On their way out, Wanda asked Zavier to check on Hutson. She pointed out the general direction he had taken. When he came back, Zavier told her that her husband was stretched out on the couch.

"He won't be in the way, will he?" she asked.

"Naaaah." Zavier checked his watch. "Pretty soon, everybody's going outside to look at the fireworks. And we're going to be out making Boehm a little bit safer for whatever sensitive children might be walking the streets."

Wanda was sitting in the back of the van on the floor. She couldn't see where they were going, and she could hear only part of what Zavier was saying. She kept hearing words like atrocious, insipid, and vulgar. Once, she caught a glimpse of Zavier laughing, his teeth shining in the glare of an oncoming car. Then all of them started singing a song in French. Wanda tried to hum the melody. Soon Zavier hushed them, turned off the van's lights and engine, and coasted for a hundred or so yards.

She recognized the rocks in her yard as soon as she climbed out of the van.

"I don't know who lives here," Zavier was saying, "but it looks like all of Walt Disney's abortions are buried here."

Everyone laughed. Wanda leaned against the side of the van and kept her head down. The voices around her, soft and shimmering as they were, floated in the air like jellyfish, stinging Wanda whenever one bumped against her. She was glad she and Hutson had a post office box instead of a regular mailbox with their name on it.

"What we must do is load up as many of these ghastly effigies as possible; we must stop this cement cancer before it spreads through the entire town. There are pregnant women to consider." Zavier crept with exaggerated care to a cement donkey and tried to lift it. He straightened up and motioned for Tobynne to come and help him.

For the next twenty minutes, they loaded the animals into the van. Wanda worked harder than anyone, never looking up from the cement figures she dragged from her yard. She wanted to get away and back to Hutson as soon as possible. She tried not to think of what the yard would look like in the morning. All she wanted was the evening to be finished.

"Keep working like this," Zavier said as he helped her slide a fawn into the van, "and you'll be ready to go to Paris in a year or two yourself. Enthusiasm is the heart of color."

When the yard was empty, Zavier and his friends squeezed into the sagging van. "Wanda, since you're the smallest, you sit up front on the floorboards. You can lean back against Tobynne's legs." Zavier cranked up the van and rumbled toward the part of Boehm that dramatically surrendered to fields and forest. "We must dispose of these heathen artifacts in such a way that they will not torment my people again – nor be a temptation unto them."

He backed the van so close to the edge of the granite quarry that even Tobynne yelled for him to stop. Fifty feet below, moonlight streaked the dark water, so still it seemed solid.

Wanda was glad, in a way, that Zavier had picked the granite quarry. If there were any official tragic places in Boehm, the quarry had to be one of them. People came here to dispose of their guilt. Stolen cars, after they were stripped, were pushed off this cliff; two people had jumped from it; and now they were tossing in her ceramic and cement animals with a strange dignity. Each time a statue was thrown – or rolled off the cliff – everyone in the group watched its slow gyrations until it hit the water and disappeared with a hungry *plunk*, like a fist hitting a canvas bag.

On the drive back, Wanda ignored the conversation. Her arms ached from the lifting. Her fingers were raw. Back at Zavier's house, the fireworks were tormenting the sky. Wanda could see the party crowd silhouetted on the hill.

"Listen to that color!" Zavier collected several beers from the refrigerator. "Now make sure he takes you to the ocean, Wanda. Let the tide of tints carry you to true art."

"Will you help me carry Hutson to the car?" she asked.

Hutson was partially conscious, but he moved too stiffly to cover the tricky ground between the couch and their car.

"Are you going to tell him about your adventure tonight?" Zavier propped Hutson in the passenger's seat and leaned him toward Wanda.

"If he asks me" – Wanda cranked the engine – "I'll tell him."

She had such a hard time getting Hutson out of the car that she managed to avoid looking at her empty yard. Because she couldn't get him to sit on the bed, Wanda let him slide to the floor with his back against the foot of the bed.

As she was removing his shirt, he woke up. "Are you mad?" he asked.

Before answering, Wanda pulled his sleeveless T-shirt over his head, ruffling his thick hair as if it were feathers.

"You know I don't get mad about you getting like this." She took off his watch.

"I'm not talking about this." Hutson placed his hands flat on his chest.

Wanda had pulled his pants down to his knees when she noticed the long white cylinder tied to his right leg. "What have you got in your pants?"

"That's what you'll be mad about." Hutson's eyelids drooped. "That tall bastard had no right to it. Put in storage . . . shit. It's your picture — it's you, know what I mean? It's yours. His going-away present to you. Only he don't know it."

Wanda unrolled the cylinder. It was the picture that had been locked in the frame. "How did you get it out?"

"I just waited till everybody went outside. I heard people talking about the fireworks." Hutson pulled himself up to the foot of the bed, then squirmed to his regular sleeping position. "Then I took the frame apart, got the picture out, and put the frame back together. It was like old times. Then I put the cover back over the frame and stuck it back in the closet. After I got the picture in my pants, I had a few more beers."

"You took the frame apart?" Wanda sat down beside Hutson and turned his face toward hers.

"Yep. Where do you think them things are made? Boehm Glass and Mirror Company. When I think about how many of them fucking frames I riveted together, them little toy rivets that you can pull out with your teeth, it makes me sick." Hutson closed his eyes. "Or maybe it's the beer."

"Well, try to get better before we head for the mountains. We can't have you throwing up on the bears."

Wanda pulled the sheet over him. She switched off the light. Once her eyes adjusted, she could make out the shape of her husband. As she watched the soft rising and falling of his chest, she slowly became aware of her own shape, how it was composed without edges and how her heart was beating — a wise sound that had nothing to do with color.

~~~~~~~~~~~~~~~~~~~~~~~~~~~~~~~~~~~

The Bubba Stories

Even now when I think of my brother Bubba, he appears instantly just as he was then, rising up before me in the very flesh, grinning that one-sided grin, pushing his cowlick back out of his tawny eyes, thumbs hooked in the loops of his wheat jeans, Bass weejuns held together with electrical tape, leaning against his little green MGB. John Leland Christian III – Bubba – in the days of his glory, Dartmouth College, c. 1965. Brilliant, Phi Beta Kappa his junior year. The essence of cool. The essence not only of cool but of *bad*, for Bubba was a legendary wild man in those days; and while certain facts in his legend varied, this constant remained: Bubba would do anything. *Anything.*

I was a little bit in love with him myself.

I made Bubba up in the spring of 1963 in order to increase my popularity with my girlfriends at a small women's college in Virginia. I was a little bit in love with them, too. But at first I was ill at ease among them: a thistle in the rose garden, a mule at the racetrack, Cinderella at the fancy dress ball. Take your pick – I was into images then. More than anything else in the world, I wanted to be a writer. I didn't want to *learn to write*, of course. I just wanted to *be a writer*, and I often pictured myself poised at the foggy edge of a cliff someplace in the south of France, wearing a cape, drawing furiously on a long cigarette, hollow-cheeked and haunted, trying to make up my mind between two men. Both of them wanted me desperately.

But in fact I was Charlene Christian, a chunky size 12, plucked up from a peanut farm near South Hill, Virginia, and set down in those exquisite halls through the intervention of my senior English teacher, Mrs. Bella Hood, the judge's wife, who had graduated from the school herself. I had a full scholarship. I would be the first person in my whole family ever to graduate from college unless you counted my Aunt Dee, who got her certificate from the beauty college in Richmond. I was not going to count Aunt Dee. I was not even going to *mention* her in later years, or anybody else in my family. I intended to grow beyond them. I intended to become a famous hollow-cheeked author, with mysterious origins.

But this is the truth. I grew up in McKenney, Va., which consisted of nothing more than a crossroads with my father's store in the middle of it. I used to climb up on the tin roof of our house and turn slowly all around, scanning the horizon, looking for . . . what? I found nothing of any interest, just flat brown peanut fields that stretched out in every direction as far as I could see, with a farmhouse here and there. I knew who lived in every house. I knew everything about them and about their families, what kind of car they drove and where they went to church, and they knew everything about us.

Not that there was much to know. My father, Hassell Christian, would give you the shirt off his back, and everybody knew it. At the store, he'd extend credit indefinitely to people down on their luck, and he let some families live in his tenant houses for free. Our own house adjoined the store.

My mother's younger brother Sam, who lived with us, was what they then called a Mongoloid. Some of the kids at school referred to him as a "Mongolian idiot." Now the preferred term is Down syndrome. My uncle Sam was sweet, small, and no trouble at all. I played cards with him endlessly, all the summers of my childhood — Go Fish, rummy, Old Maid, Hearts, blackjack. Sam loved cards and sunshine and his cat, Blackie. He liked to sit on a quilt in the sun, playing cards with me. He liked to sit on the front porch with Blackie and watch the cars go by. He loved it when I told him stories.

My mother, who was high-strung, was always fussing around after Sam, making him pick up paper napkins and turn off the TV and put his shoes in a line. My mother had three separate nervous breakdowns before I went away to college. My father always said we had to "treat her with kid gloves." In fact, when I think about it now, I am surprised that my mother was ever able to hold herself together long enough to conceive a child at all, or come to term. After me, there were two miscarriages, and then, I was told, they "quit trying." I was never sure what this meant, exactly. But certainly I could never imagine my parents having a sexual relationship in the first place — he was too fat and gruff, she was too fluttery and crazy. The whole idea was gross.

Whenever my mother had a nervous breakdown, my grandmother, Memaw, would come over from next door to stay with Sam full time, and I would be sent to South Hill to stay with my Aunt Dee and my little cousins. I loved my Aunt Dee, as different from Mama as day from night. Aunt Dee wore her yellow hair in a beehive and smoked Pall Mall cigarettes. After work she'd come in the door, kick off her shoes, put a record on the record player, and dance all over the living room to "Ooh-Poo-Pa-Doo." She said it "got the kinks out." She taught us all to do the shag, even little Tammy.

I was always sorry when my dad appeared in his truck, ready to take me back home.

When I think of home now, the image which comes most

clearly to mind is my whole family lined up in the flickering darkness of our living room, watching TV. We never missed the Ed Sullivan Show, Bonanza, the Andy Griffith Show, or Candid Camera – Sam's favorite. Sam used to laugh and laugh when they'd say, "Smile! You're on Candid Camera!" It was the only time my family ever did anything together. I can just see us now in the light from that black and white Zenith TV, lined up on the couch (me, Sam, Memaw), with Daddy and Mama in the recliner and the antique wing chair, respectively, facing the television. We always turned off all the lights in order to watch TV, and sat quietly, and didn't eat anything.

No wonder I got a boyfriend with a car as soon as possible, to get out of there. Don Fetterman had a soft brown crewcut and wide brown eyes and reminded me, in the nicest possible way, of the cows which he and his family raised. Don was president of the 4-H Club and the Tri-Hi-Y Club. I was vice president of the Tri-Hi-Y Club (how we met) and president of the Glee Club. We were both picked as "Most Likely to Succeed."

We rubbed our bodies together at innumerable dances in the high school gym while they played "our" song – "The Twelfth of Never" – but we never, never went all the way. Don wouldn't. He believed we should save ourselves for marriage. I, on the other hand, having read by this time a great many novels, was just dying to lose my virginity so that I would mysteriously begin to "live," so that my life would finally *start*. I knew for sure that I would never become a great writer until I could rid myself of this awful burden. But Don Fetterman stuck to his guns, refusing to cooperate. Instead, for graduation, he gave me a pearl "pre-engagement" ring, which I knew for a fact had cost $139.00 at Snows Jewelers in South Hill, where I worked after school and on weekends. This was a lot of money for Don Fetterman to spend.

Although I didn't love him, by then he thought I did; and after I got the ring, I didn't have the nerve to tell him the truth. So I kept it, and kissed Don good-bye for hours and hours the night before he went off to join the Marines. My tears were real at this point, but after he left I relegated him firmly to the past. Ditto my whole family. Once I got to college, I was determined to become a new person.

Luckily my freshman roommate turned out to be a kind of prototype, the very epitome of a popular girl. The surprise was that she was *nice*, too. Dixie Claiborne came from Memphis, where she was to make her debut that Christmas at the Swan Ball. She had long, perfect blond hair, innumerable cashmere sweater sets, and real pearls. She had lots of friends already, other girls who had gone to St. Cecilia's with her (at first it seemed to me a good two-thirds of all the girls at school had gone to Saint Something-or-other). They had a happy ease in the world and a strangely uniform appearance which I immediately began to copy – spending my whole semester's money, saved up from my job at the jewelers, on several A-line skirts, McMullen blouses, and a pair of red Pappagallo shoes. Dixie had about a thousand cable-knit sweaters, which she was happy to lend me. In addition to all the right clothes, Dixie came equipped with the right boyfriend, already a sophomore at Washington and Lee University, the boys' school just over the mountain. His name was Trey (William Hill Dunn III). Trey would be just so glad, Dixie said, smiling, to get us all dates for the Phi Gam mixer. "All of us" included our whole suite – Dixie and me in the front room overlooking the old quadrangle with its massive willow oaks, Melissa and Donnie across the hall, and Lily in the single just beyond our little study room.

Trey fixed us up with several Phi Gams apiece, but nothing really clicked; and in November, Melissa, Donnie, Lily, and I signed up to go to a freshman mixer at UVA. As our bus approached the university's famous serpentine wall, we went into a flurry of teasing our hair and checking our makeup. Looking into my compact, I pursed my lips in a way I'd been practicing. Unfortunately I had a pimple near my nose, but I'd turned it into a beauty spot by covering it up with eyebrow pencil. I hoped to look like Sandra Dee.

Freshman year, everybody went to mixers, where freshman boys generally as ill at ease as we were, stood nervously about in the social rooms of their fraternity houses, wearing navy-blue blazers, ties, and chinos. Nobody really knew how to date in this rigid system so unlike high school — and certainly so unlike prep school, where many of these boys had been locked away for the past four years. If they could have gotten their own dates, they would have. But they couldn't. They didn't know anybody either. They pulled at their ties and looked at the floor. They seemed to me generally gorgeous, entirely unlike Don Fetterman with his feathery crew cut and his 4-H jacket, now at Camp Lejeune. But I still wrote to Don, informative, stilted little notes about my classes and the weather. His letters in return were lively and real, full of military life ("the food sucks") and vague sweet plans for our future — a future which did not exist, as far as I was concerned, and yet these letters gave me a secret thrill. My role as Don Fetterman's girl was the most exciting role I'd had yet; and I couldn't quite bring myself to give it up, even as I attempted to transform myself into another person altogether.

"Okay," the upperclassman-in-charge announced casually, and the St. Anthony's Hall pledges wandered over in our direction.

"Hey," the cutest one said to a girl.

"Hey," she said back.

The routine never varied. In a matter of minutes, the four most aggressive guys would walk off with the four prettiest girls, and the rest of us would panic. On this particular occasion the social room at St. Anthony's Hall was cleared in a matter of minutes, leaving me with a tall, gangly, bucktoothed boy whose face was as pocked as the moon. Still, he had a kind of shabby elegance I already recognized. He was from Mississippi.

"What do you want to do?" he asked me.

I had not expected to be consulted. I glanced around the social room, which looked like a war zone. I didn't know where my friends were.

"What do *you* want to do?" I asked.

His name (his *first* name) was Rutherford. He grinned at me. "Let's get drunk," he said, and my heart leaped up as I realized that my burden might be lifted in this way. We walked across the beautiful old campus to an open court where three or four fraternities had a combo started up already, wild-eyed electrified Negroes going through all kinds of gyrations on the bandstand. It was Doug Clark and the Hot Nuts. The music was so loud, the beat so strong, that you couldn't listen to it and stand still. The Hot Nuts were singing an interminable song; everybody seemed to know the chorus, which went "Nuts, hot nuts, get 'em from the peanut man. Nuts, hot nuts, get 'em any way you can." We started dancing. I always worried about this – all I'd ever done before college, in the way of dancing, was the shag with my Aunt Dee and a long, formless *clutch* with Don Fetterman, but Rutherford was so wild it didn't matter.

People made a circle around us and started clapping. Nobody looked at me. All eyes were on Rutherford, whose dancing reminded me of the way chickens back home flopped around after Daddy cut their heads off. At first I was embarrassed. But then I caught on – Rutherford was a real *character*. I kept up with him as best I could, and then I got tickled and started laughing so hard I could barely dance. *This is fun*, I realized suddenly. This is what I'm *supposed* to be doing. This is college.

About an hour later we heard the news, which was delivered to us by a tweed-jacketed professor who walked up on stage, bringing the music to a ragged, grinding halt. He grabbed the microphone. "Ladies and gentlemen," he said thickly – and I remember thinking how odd this form of address seemed – "Ladies and gentlemen, the President has been shot."

The whole scene started to churn, as if we were in a kaleidoscope – the blue day, the green grass, the stately columned buildings. People were running and sobbing. Rutherford's hand under my elbow steered me back to his fraternity house, where everyone was clustered around several TV's, talking too loud. All the weekend festivities had been canceled. We were to return to school immediately. Rutherford seemed relieved by this prospect, having fallen silent – perhaps because he'd quit drinking, or because conversation alone wasn't worth the effort it took if nothing else (sex) might be forthcoming. He gave me a perfunctory kiss on the cheek and turned to go.

I was about to board the bus when somebody grabbed me, hard, from behind. I whirled around. It was Lily, red-cheeked and glassy-eyed, her blond hair springing out wildly above her blue sweater. Her hot-pink lipstick was smeared. Lily's pretty, pointed face looked vivid and alive. A dark-haired boy stood close behind her, his arm around her waist.

"Listen," Lily hissed at me. "Sign me in, will you?"

"What?" I had heard her, but I couldn't believe it.

"*Sign me in.*" Lily squeezed my shoulder. I could smell her perfume. Then she was gone.

I sat in a back seat by myself and cried all the way back to school.

I caught on fast that as far as college boys were concerned, girls fell into either the Whore or the Saint category. All girls knew that if they gave in and *did it*, then boys wouldn't respect them, and word would get around, and they would never get a husband. The whole point of college was to get a husband.

I had not known anything about this system before I got there. It put a serious obstacle in my path toward becoming a great writer.

Lily, who had clearly given up her burden long since, fell into the Whore category. But the odd thing about it was that she didn't seem to mind, and she swore she didn't want a husband anyway. "Honey, a husband is the *last* thing on my list!"

Lily'd say, giggling. Lily was the smartest one of us all, even though she went to great lengths to hide this fact. Later, in 1966, Lily and the head of the philosophy department, Dr. Wiener, would stage the only demonstration ever held on our campus; they walked slowly around the blooming quadrangle carrying signs that read *Get Out of Vietnam* while the rest of us, well-oiled and sunning on the rooftops, clutched our bikini tops and peered down curiously at the two of them.

If Lily was the smartest, Melissa was clearly the dumbest, the nicest, and the least interested in school. Melissa came from Charleston, S.C., and spoke so slowly that I was always tempted to leap in and finish her sentences for her. All she wanted to do was marry her boyfriend, now at the University of South Carolina, and have babies. Donnie, Melissa's room-mate, was a big, freckled, friendly girl from Texas. We didn't have any idea how rich she was until her mother flew up and bought a cabin at nearby Goshen Lake so Donnie and her friends would have a place to "relax."

By spring, Dixie was the only one of us who was actually pinned. It seemed to me that she was not only pinned but almost married, in a funny way, with tons and tons of chil-dren – Trey, her boyfriend; and me; and all the other girls in our suite; and all the other Phi Gams, Trey's fraternity broth-ers at Washington and Lee. Dixie had a little book in which she made a list of things to do each day, and throughout the day she checked them off one by one. She always got all of them done. At the end of first semester she had a 4.0 average; Trey had a .4. Dixie just smiled. Totally, explicably, she loved him.

By then most of the freshman girls who weren't going with somebody had several horror stories to tell about blind dates at UVA or W&L fraternities – boys who "dropped trou," or threw up in their dates' purses. I had only one horror story, but I never told it, since the most horrible element in it was me.

This is what happened. It was "Spring Fling" at the Phi Gam house, and Trey had gotten me a date with a red-headed boy named Eddy Turner. By then I was getting desperate. I'd made a C in my first semester of creative writing, while Lily had made an A. Plus, I'd gained 8 pounds. Both love and literature seemed to be slipping out of my sights. And I was drinking too much — we'd been drinking Yucca Flats, a horrible green punch made in a washtub with grain alcohol, all afternoon on the night I ended up in bed with Eddy Turner.

The bed was his, on the second floor of the Phi Gam house — not the most private setting for romance. I could scarcely see Eddy by the streetlight coming in through the single high window. Faintly, below, I could hear music, and the whole house shook slightly with the dancing. I thought of Hemingway's famous description of sex from *For Whom the Bell Tolls*, which I'd typed out neatly on an index card: "The earth moved under the sleeping bag." The whole Phi Gam house was moving under me. After wrestling with my panty girdle for what seemed like hours, Eddy finally tossed it in the corner and got on top of me immediately. Drunk as I was, I wanted him to. I wanted him to *do it*. But I didn't think it would hurt so much, and suddenly I wished he would kiss me or say something. He didn't. He was done and lying on his back beside me when suddenly the door to the room burst open and the lights came on. I sat up, grasping for the sheet which I couldn't find. My breasts are large, and they had always embarrassed me. Until that night, Don Fetterman was the only boy who had ever seen them. It was a whole group of Phi Gams, roaming from room to room. Luckily I was blinded by the lights, so I couldn't tell exactly who they were.

"Smile!" they yelled. "You're on Candid Camera!" Then they laughed hysterically, slammed the door, and were gone, leaving us in darkness once again. But I was sobbing into Eddy's pillow because what they said reminded me of Sam, whose face would not leave my mind then for hours while I cried and cried and cried and sobered up. I didn't tell Eddy what I was crying about, nor did he ask. He sat in a chair and smoked cigarettes while he waited for me to stop crying. Finally I did. Eddy and I didn't date after that, but we were buddies in the way I was buddies with the whole Phi Gam house due to my particular status as Dixie's roommate. I was like a sister, giving advice to the lovelorn, administering Cokes and aspirin on Sunday mornings, typing papers.

It was not the role I'd had in mind, but it was better than nothing, affording me at least a certain status among the girls at school; and the Phi Gams always saw to it that I attended all the big parties, usually with somebody whose girlfriend couldn't make it. Often, when the weekend was winding down, I could be found down in the Phi Gam basement alone, playing "Tragedy," my favorite song, over and over on the jukebox.

> Blown by the wind
> Kissed by the snow
> All that's left
> Is the dark below.
> Gone from me,
> Oh, oh.
> Trag-e-dy.

It always brought me right to the edge of tears, because I hadn't ever known any tragedy myself, or love, or drama. *Wouldn't anything ever happen to me?*

Meanwhile, my friends' lives were like soap opera — Lily's period was two weeks late, which scared us all, and then Dixie went on the pill. Melissa and her boyfriend split up (she lost 7 pounds, he slammed his hand into a wall) and then made up again.

Melissa was telling us about it, in her maddening slow way, one day in May when we were all out at Donnie's lake cabin, sunning. "It's not the same, though," Melissa said. "He just gets *too mad.* I don't know what it is; he scares me."

"Dump him," Lily said, applying baby oil with iodine in it, our suntan lotion of choice.

"But I *love* him," Melissa wailed, and Lily snorted.

"Well," Dixie began diplomatically, but suddenly I sat up.

"Maybe he's just got a wild streak," I said. "Maybe he just can't control himself. That's always been Bubba's problem." Suddenly the little lake before us took on a deeper, more intense hue. I noticed the rotting pier, the old fisherman up at the point, Lily's painted toenails. I noticed *everything*.

"Who's Bubba?" Donnie asked me.

Dixie eyed me expectantly, thinking I meant one of the Phi Gams, since several of them had that nickname.

"My brother," I said. I took a deep breath.

"*What?* You never said you had a *brother!*" Dixie's pretty face looked really puzzled now.

Everybody sat up and looked at me.

"Well, I do," I said. "He's two years older than me, and he stayed with my father when my parents split up. So I've never lived with him. In fact I don't know him real well at all. This is very painful for me to talk about. We were inseparable when we were little," I added, hearing my song in the back of my mind. "*Oh, oh . . . trag-e-dy!*"

"Oh, Charlene, I'm so sorry! I had no idea!" Dixie was hugging me, slick hot skin and all.

I started crying. "He was a real problem child," I said, "and now he's just so wild. I don't know what's going to become of him."

"How long has it been since you've seen him?" Melissa asked.

"About two years," I said. "Our parents won't have anything at all to do with each other. They *hate* each other, and especially since Mama got remarried. They won't let us get together, not even for a day; it's just awful."

"So how did you get to see him two years ago?" Lily asked. They had all drawn closer, clustering around me.

"He ran away from school," I said, "and came to my high

school, and got me right out of class. I remember it was biology lab," I said. "I was dissecting a frog."

"Then what?"

"We spent the day together," I said. "We got some food and went out to this quarry and ate, and just drove around. We talked and talked," I said. "And you know what? I felt just as close to him then as I did when we were babies. Just like all those years had never passed at all. It was great," I said.

"Then he went back to school – or what?"

"No." I choked back a sob. "It was almost dark, and he was taking me back to my house, and then he was planning to head on down to Florida, he said, when all of a sudden these blue lights came up behind us, and it was the police."

"The *police*?" Dixie looked really alarmed then. She was such a good girl.

"Well, it was a stolen car, of course," I explained. "They nailed him. If he hadn't stopped in to see me, he might have gotten away with it," I said, "if he'd just headed straight to Florida. But he came to see me. Mama and Daddy wouldn't even bail him out. They let him go straight to prison."

"Oh Charlene, *no wonder* you never talk about your family!" Dixie was in tears now.

"But he was a model prisoner," I went on. I felt exhilarated. "In fact they gave all the prisoners this test, and he scored the highest that anybody in the whole history of the prison had *ever* scored, so they let him take these special classes, and he did so well that he got out a whole year early, and now he's in college."

"Where?"

I thought fast. "Dartmouth," I said wildly. I knew it had to be a Northern school, since Dixie and Melissa seemed to know everybody in the South. But neither of them, as far as I could recall, had ever mentioned Dartmouth.

"He's got a full scholarship," I added. "But he's so wild, I don't know if he'll be able to keep it or not." Donnie got up and went in and came back with cold Cokes for us all, and we stayed out at Goshen Lake until the sun set, and I told them all about Bubba.

He was a KA, the wildest KA of them all. Last winter, I said, he got drunk and passed out in the snow on the way back to his fraternity house; by the time a janitor found him the following morning, his cheek was frozen solid to the road. It took two guys from maintenance, with electrical torches, to melt the snow around Bubba's face and get him loose. And now the whole fraternity was on probation because of this really gross thing he'd made the pledges do. "What really gross thing?" they asked. "Oh, you don't want to know," I said. "You really don't."

"I *really do*," Lily insisted, pushing her sunburnt face into mine. "Come on. After Trey, nothing could be that bad." Even Dixie grinned.

"Okay," I said, launching into a hazing episode which required the KA pledges to run up three flights of stairs, holding alum in their mouths. On each landing they had to dodge past these two big football players. If they swallowed the alum during the struggle, well, alum makes you vomit immediately, so you can imagine . . . they could imagine. But the worst part was that when one pledge wouldn't go past the second landing, the football players threw him down the stairs, and he broke his back.

"That's just *disgusting*," Donnie drawled. "Nobody would ever do that in Texas."

But on the other hand, I said quickly, Bubba was the most talented poet in the whole school, having won the Iris Nutley Leach Award for Poetry two years in a row. I pulled the name "Iris Nutley Leach" right out of the darkening air. I astonished myself. And girls were just crazy about Bubba, I added. In fact this girl from Washington tried to kill herself after they broke up, and then she had to be institutionalized for a year, at Shepherd-Pratt in Baltimore. I knew all about Shepherd-Pratt because my mother had gone there.

"But he doesn't have a girlfriend right now," I said. Everyone sighed, and a warm breeze came up over the pines and ruffled our little lake. By then Bubba was as real to me as the Peanuts towel I sat on, as the warm, gritty dirt between my toes.

During the next year or so, Bubba would knock up a girl and then nobly help her get an abortion (Donnie offered to contribute); he would make Phi Beta Kappa; he would be arrested for assault; he would wreck his MGB; he would start writing folk songs. My creativity knew no bounds when it came to Bubba, but I was a dismal failure in my first writing class where my teacher, Mr. Lefcowicz, kept giving me B's and C's and telling me, "Write what you know."

I didn't want to write what I knew, of course. I had no intention of writing a word about my own family or those peanut fields. Who would want to read about *that*? I had wanted to write in order to *get away* from my own life. I couldn't give up that tormented woman on the cliff in the south of France. I intended to write about glamorous heroines with exciting lives; one of my first – and worst – stories involved a stewardess in Hawaii. I had never been to Hawaii, of course. At that time, I had never even been on a plane. The plot, which was very complicated, had something to do with international espionage. I remember how kindly my young teacher smiled at me when he handed my story back. He asked me to stay for a minute after class. "Charlene," he said, "I want you to write something true next time."

Instead, I decided to give up on plot and concentrate on theme, intending to pull some heartstrings. It was nearly Christmas, and this time we had to read our stories aloud to the whole group. But right before that class, Mr. Lefcowicz, who had already read them, pulled me aside and told me that I didn't have to read my story out loud if I didn't want to.

"Of course I want to," I said.

We took our seats.

My story took place in a large unnamed city on Christmas Eve. In this story, a whole happy family was trimming their

Christmas tree, singing carols, and drinking hot chocolate while it snowed outside. I think I had "softly falling flakes." Each person in the family got to open one present – selected from the huge pile of gifts beneath the glittering tree – before bed. Then they all went to sleep, and a "pregnant silence" descended. At three o'clock a fire broke out, and the whole house burned to the ground, and they all burned up, dying horrible deaths which I described individually – conscious, as I read aloud, of some movement and sound among my listeners. But I didn't dare look up as I approached the story's ironic end: "When the fire trucks arrived, the only sign of life to be found was a blackened music box in the smoking ashes, softly playing 'Silent Night.'" By the end of my story, one girl had put her head down on her desk; another was having a coughing fit. Mr. Lefcowicz was staring intently out the window at the wintry day, his back to us. Then he made a sudden show of looking at his watch. "Whoops! Class dismissed!" he cried, grabbing up his bookbag. He rushed from the room like the White Rabbit, already late.

But I was not that stupid.

As I walked across the cold, wet quadrangle toward our dormitory, I understood perfectly well that my story was terrible, laughable. I wanted to die. The gray sky, the dripping, leafless trees, fit my mood perfectly, and I suddenly remembered Mr. Lefcowicz saying, in an earlier class, that we must never manipulate nature to express our characters' emotions. "Ha," I muttered scornfully to the heavy sky.

The very next day I joined the staff of our campus newspaper. I became its editor in the middle of my sophomore year – a job nobody else wanted, a job I really enjoyed. I had found a niche, a role, and although it was not what I had envisioned for myself, it was okay. Thus I became the following things: editor of the newspaper; member of Athena, the secret honor society; roommate of Dixie, the May Queen; friend of Phi Gams; and – especially – sister of Bubba, whose legend loomed ever larger. But I avoided both dates and creative writing classes for the next two years, finding Mr. Lefcowicz's stale advice, "Write what you know," more impossible with each visit home.

The summer between my sophomore and junior years was the hardest. The first night I was home, I realized that something was wrong with Mama when I woke up to hear water splashing in the downstairs bathroom. I got up and went to investigate. There she was, wearing a lacy pink peignoir and her old gardening shoes, scrubbing the green tile tub.

"Oh, hi, Charlene!" she said brightly, and went on scrubbing, humming tunelessly to herself. A mop and bucket stood in the corner. I said good night and went back to my bedroom, where I looked at the clock: it was 3:30 A.M.

The next day Mama burst into tears when Sam spilled a glass of iced tea, and the day after that Daddy took her over to Petersburg and put her in the hospital. Memaw came in to stay with Sam during the day while I worked in the jewelers at South Hill, my old job.

I'd come home at suppertime each afternoon to find Sam in his chair on the front porch, holding Blackie, waiting for me. He seemed to have gotten smaller somehow – and for the first time, I realized that Sam, so much a part of my childhood, was not growing up along with me. In fact he would *never* grow up, and I thought about that a lot on those summer evenings as I swung gently in the porch swing, back and forth through the sultry air, suspended.

In August I went to Memphis for a week to visit Dixie, whose house turned out to be like Tara in *Gone With the Wind*, only bigger, and whose mother turned out to drink sherry all day long. I came back to find Mama out of the hospital already, much improved by shock treatments, and another surprise – a baby-blue Chevrolet convertible, used but great-looking, in the driveway. My father handed me the keys.

"Here, honey," he said, and then he hugged me tight, smelling of sweat and tobacco. "We're so proud of you," he said. He had traded a man a combine or something for the car.

So I drove back to school in style, and my junior year went smoothly until Donnie announced that her sister Susannah, now at Pine Mountain Junior College, was going up to Dartmouth for Winter Carnival, to visit a boy she'd met that summer. Susannah just *couldn't wait* to look up Bubba.

Unfortunately, this was not possible, as I got a phone call that night saying that Bubba had been kicked out of school for leading a demonstration against the war. Lily, who had become much more political herself by that time, jumped up from her desk and grabbed my hand.

"Oh, no!" she shrieked. "He'll be drafted!" and the sudden alarm that filled our study room was palpable – as real as the mounting body count each night on TV – as we stared, Lily and Dixie and Donnie and I, white-faced at each other.

"Whatever will he do now?" Donnie was wringing her hands.

"I don't know," I said desperately. "I just don't know." I went to my room – a single, this term – and thought about it. It was clear that he would have to do something, something to take him far, far away.

But Bubba's problem was soon to be suspended by Melissa's. She was pregnant, really pregnant, and in spite of all the arguments we could come up with, she wanted to get married and have the baby. She wanted to have *lots* of babies, and one day live in the big house on the Battery which her boyfriend would inherit, and this is exactly what she's done. Her life has been predictable and productive. So violent in his college days, Melissa's husband turned out to be a model of stability in later life. And their first child, Anna, kept him out of the draft.

As she got in her mother's car to leave, Melissa squeezed my hand and said, "Keep me posted about Bubba, and don't worry so much. I'm sure everything will work out all right."

It didn't.

Bubba burned his draft card not a month later and headed for Canada, where he lived in a commune. I didn't hear from him for a long time after that, all tangled up as I was by then in my affair with Dr. Pierce.

Dr. Pierce was a fierce, bleak, melancholy man who looked like a bird of prey. Not surprisingly, he was a Beckett scholar. He taught the seminar in contemporary literature which I took in the spring of my junior year. We read Joseph Heller, Kurt Vonnegut, Flannery O'Connor, John Barth, and Thomas Pynchon, among others. Flannery O'Connor would become my favorite, and I would do my senior thesis on her work, feeling a secret and strong kinship, by then, with her dire view. But this was later, after my affair with Dr. Pierce was over.

At first, I didn't know what to make of him. I hated his northern accent, his lugubrious, glistening dark eyes, his all-encompassing pessimism. He told us that contemporary literature was absurd because the world was absurd. He told us that the language in these books was weird and fractured because true communication is impossible in the world today. Dr. Pierce told us all this in a sad, cynical tone full of infinite world-weariness, which I found both repellent and attractive.

Finally I decided to go in and talk to him. I am still not sure why I did this — I was making good grades in his course, I understood everything. But one blustery, unsettling March afternoon I found myself sitting outside his office. He was a popular teacher, rumored to be always ready to listen to his students' problems. I don't know what I meant to talk to him about. The hour grew late. Shadows lengthened in the hall. I smoked four or five cigarettes while other students, ahead of me, went in and came out. Then Dr. Pierce came and stood in the door. He took off his glasses and rubbed his eyes. He looked tired, but not nearly as old as he looked in class, where he always wore a tie. Now he wore jeans and an old blue work-shirt, and I could see the dark hair at his neck.

"Ah," he said in that way of his which rendered all his remarks oddly significant, although I could never figure out why. "Ah! Miss Christian, is it not?"

He knew it was. I felt uncomfortable, like he was mocking me. He made a gesture; I preceded him into his office and sat down.

"Now," he said, staring at me. I looked away, out the window at the skittish, blowing day, at the girls who passed by on the walkway, giggling and trying to hold their skirts down. "*Miss Christian,*" Dr. Pierce said. Maybe he'd said it before. Finally I looked at him.

"I presume you had some reason for this visit," he said sardonically.

To my horror, I started crying. Not little ladylike sniffles, either, but huge groaning sobs. Dr. Pierce thrust a box of Kleenex in my direction, then sat drumming his fingers on his desk. I kept on crying. Finally I realized what he was drumming: the *William Tell Overture.* I got tickled. Soon I was crying and laughing at the same time. I was still astonished at myself.

"Blow your nose," Dr. Pierce said.

I did.

"That's better," he said. He got up and closed his office door although there was really no need to do so, since the hall outside was empty now. Dr. Pierce sat back down and leaned across his desk toward me. "What is it?" he asked intently.

But I still didn't know what it was. I said so, and apologized. "One thing though," I said, "I'd like to complain about the choice of books on our reading list."

"Aha!" Dr. Pierce said. He leaned back in his chair and made his fingers into a kind of tent. "You liked Eudora Welty," he said. This was true; I nodded. "You liked *Lie Down in Darkness,*" he said. I nodded again.

"But I just *hate* this other stuff!" I burst out. "I just hated *The End of the Road,* I hated it! It's so depressing."

He nodded rapidly. "You think literature should make you feel good?" he asked.

"It used to," I said. Then I was crying again. I stood up. "I'm so sorry," I said.

Dr. Pierce stood up too and walked around his desk and came to stand close to me. The light in his office was soft, gray, furry. Dr. Pierce took both my hands in his. "Oh, Miss Christian," he said. "My very dear, very young Miss Christian, I know what you mean." And I could tell, by the pain and weariness in his voice, that this was true. I could see Dr. Pierce suddenly as a much younger man, as a boy, with a light in his eyes and a different feeling about the world. I reached up and put my hands in his curly hair and pulled his face down to mine and kissed him fiercely, a way I had never kissed anybody. I couldn't even imagine myself doing this, yet I did it naturally. Dr. Pierce kissed me back. We kissed for a long time while it grew finally dark outside, and then he locked the door and turned back to me. He sighed deeply – almost a groan – a sound, I felt, of regret, then unbuttoned my shirt. We made love on the rug on his office floor. Immediately we were caught up in a kind of fever that lasted for several months – times like these in his office after hours, or in the backseat of my car parked by the lake, or in cheap motels when I'd signed out to go home.

Nobody suspected a thing. I was as good at keeping secrets as I was at making up lies. Plus, I was a campus leader, and Dr. Pierce was a married man.

He tried to end it that June. I was headed home, and he was headed up to New York where he had some kind of fellowship to do research at the Morgan Library.

"Charlene – " Dr. Pierce said. We were in public, out on the quadrangle right after graduation. His wife walked down the hill at some distance behind us, with other faculty wives. Dr. Pierce's voice was hoarse, the way it got when he was in torment (which he so often was, which was one of the most attractive things about him. Years later, I'd realize this). "Let us make a clean break," he sort of mumbled. "Right now. It cannot go on, and we both know it."

We had reached the parking lot in front of the chapel by then; the sunlight reflected off all the cars was dazzling.

Dr. Pierce stuck out his hand in an oddly formal gesture. "Have a good summer, Charlene," he said, "and good-bye."

Dr. Pierce had chosen his moment well. He knew I wouldn't make a scene in front of all these people. But I refused to take his hand, rushing off madly through the parked cars to my own, gunning it out of there and out to the lake where I parked on the bluff above Donnie's cabin, in the exact spot where he and I had been together so many times. I sat at the wheel and looked out at the lake, now full of children on some kind of school outing. Their shrill screams and laughter drifted up to me thinly, like the sounds of birds in the trees around my car. I remember I leaned back on the seat and stared straight up at the sun through the trees — just at the top of the tent of green, where light filtered in bursts like stars.

But I couldn't give him up, not yet, not ever.

I resolved to surprise Dr. Pierce in New York, and that's exactly what I did, telling my parents I'd gone on a trip to Virginia Beach with friends. I got his summer address from the registrar's office. I drove up through Richmond and Washington, a seven-hour drive. It was a crazy and even a dangerous thing to do, since I had never been to New York. But finally I ended up in front of the brownstone in the Village where Dr. Pierce and his wife were subletting an apartment. It was mid-afternoon and hot; I had not imagined New York to be so hot, hotter even than McKenney, Va. I was still in a fever, I think. I knocked on the door, without even thinking what I would do if his wife answered. But nobody answered. Nobody was home. Somehow this possibility had not occurred to me. I felt suddenly, totally exhausted. I leaned against the wall, and then slid down it, until I was actually sitting on the floor in the hall. I pulled off my pantyhose and stuffed them into my purse. They were too hot. I was too hot. I wore a kelly-green linen dress; somehow I'd thought I needed to be all dressed up to go to New York. I don't even remember falling asleep, but I was awakened by Dr. Pierce shaking my shoulder and saying my name.

Whatever can be said of Dr. Pierce, he was not a jerk. He told me firmly that our relationship was over, and just as firmly that I should not be driving around New York City at night by myself, not in the shape I was in.

By the time his wife came home with groceries, I was lying on the studio bed, feeling a little better. He told her I was having a breakdown, which seemed suddenly true. Dr. Pierce and I looked at the news on TV while she made spaghetti. After dinner she lit a joint and handed it to me. It was the first time anybody had ever offered me marijuana. I shook my head. I thought I was crazy enough already. Dr. Pierce's wife was nice, though. She was pale with long, long blond hair, which she had worn in a braid at school, or up on top of her head. Now it fell over her shoulders like water. I realized that she was not much – certainly not ten years – older than I was, and I wondered if she, too, had been his student. But I was exhausted. I fell asleep on the studio couch in front of a fan, which drowned out the sound of their voices as they cleaned up from dinner.

I woke up very early the next morning. I wrote the Pierces a thank-you note on an index card which I found in Dr. Pierce's briefcase and left it propped conspicuously against the toaster. The door to their bedroom stood open, but I did not look in.

Out on the street I was horrified to find that I had gotten a parking ticket and that my convertible top had been slashed – gratuitously, too, since there was nothing in the car to steal. Somehow this upset me more than anything else about my trip to New York, more than Dr. Pierce's rejection – or his renunciation, as I preferred to consider it – which is how I did consider it, often, during that summer at home while I had the rest of my nervous breakdown.

My parents were very kind. They thought it all had to do with Don Fetterman, who was missing in action in Vietnam, and maybe it did, sort of. I was "nervous" and cried a lot. Finally my Aunt Dee got tired of me mooning around, as she called it. She frosted my hair and took me to Myrtle Beach, where it proved impossible to continue the nervous breakdown. The last night of this trip Aunt Dee and I double-dated with some realtors she'd met by the pool.

Aunt Dee and I got back to McKenney just in time for me to pack and drive to school, where I was one of the seniors in charge of freshman orientation. Daddy had gotten the top fixed on my car; I was a blond; and I'd lost 25 pounds.

The campus seemed somehow smaller to me as I drove through the imposing gates. My footsteps echoed as I carried my bags up to the third floor of Old North, where Dixie and I would have the coveted "turret room." I was the first one back in the whole dorm, but as I continued to haul things in from my car, other seniors began arriving. We hugged and squealed, following a script as old as the college. At least three girls stopped in mid-hug to push me back, scrutinize me carefully, and exclaim that they wouldn't have recognized me. I didn't know what they meant.

Sweaty and exhausted after carrying everything up to our room, I decided to shower before dinner. I was standing naked in our room, toweling my hair dry, when the dinner bell began to ring. Its somber tone sounded somehow elegiac to me in that moment. On impulse, I began rummaging around in one of my boxes, until I finally found the mirror I was looking for. I went to stand at the window while the last of the lingering chimes died on the August air.

I held the mirror out at arm's length and looked at myself. I had cheekbones. I had hipbones. I could see my ribs. My eyes were darker, larger in my face. My wild damp hair was as blond as Lily's. I looked completely different.

Clearly, *something had finally happened to me.*

That weekend Dixie, Donnie, Lily, and I went out to Don-

nie's cabin to drink beer and catch up on the summer. We telephoned Melissa, now eight months pregnant, who claimed to
be blissfully happy and said she was making curtains.

Lily snorted. She got up and put Simon and Garfunkel on
the stereo, and got us all another beer. Donnie lit candles and
switched off the overhead light. Dixie waved her hand, making
the big diamond sparkle in the candlelight. Trey, now in law
school at Vanderbilt, had given it to her in July. Dixie was already planning her wedding. We would all be bridesmaids, of
course. (That marriage, oddly, would last for only a few years,
and Dixie would divorce once more before she went to law
school herself.) Donnie told us all about her mother's new
boyfriend. We gossiped on as the hour grew late and bugs
slammed suicidally into the porch light. The moon came up
big and bright. I kept playing "The Sound of Silence" over
and over; it matched my mood, my new conception of myself
("In my dreams I walk alone, over streets of cobblestone. . . ."
I also liked "I Am a Rock; I Am an Island").

Finally Lily announced that she was in love, *really in love* this
time, with a young poet she'd met that summer on Cape Cod,
where she'd been waitressing. We waited while she lit a cigarette. "We lived together for two months," Lily said, "in his
room at the Inn, where we could look out and see the water."
We all just stared at her. None of us had ever lived with anybody, or known anyone who had. Lily looked around at us.
"It was wonderful," she said. "It was heaven. But it was not
what you might think," she added enigmatically, "living with
a man."

For some reason I started crying.

There was a long silence, and the needle on the record started scratching. Donnie got up and cut it off. They were all
looking at me.

"And what about you, Charlene?" Lily said softly. "What
happened to you this summer, anyway?"

It was a moment which I had rehearsed again and again in

my mind. I would tell them all about my affair with Dr. Pierce, and how I had gone to New York to find him, and how he had renounced me because his wife was pregnant. I had just added this part. But I was crying too hard to speak. "It was awful," I said finally, and Dixie came over and hugged me. "What was awful?" she said, but I couldn't even speak; my mind filled suddenly, oddly, with Don Fetterman as he'd looked in high school, presiding over the Tri-Hi-Y Club. He held the gavel firmly in his hands; he could call any group to order.

"Come on," Dixie said, "tell us."

The candles were guttering; the moon made a path across the lake. I took a deep breath.

"Bubba is dead," I said.

"Oh, God! Oh no!" A kind of pandemonium ensued, which I don't remember much about, although I remember the details of my brother's death vividly. Bubba drowned in a lake in Canada, attempting to save a friend's child that had fallen overboard. The child died, too. Bubba was buried there, on the wild shore of that northern lake, and his only funeral was what his friends said as they spoke around the grave one by one. His best friend had written to me, describing the whole thing.

"Charlene, Charlene, why didn't you tell us sooner?" Donnie asked.

I just shook my head. "I couldn't," I said.

Later that fall I finally wrote a good story — about my family, back in McKenney — and then another, and then another. I won a scholarship to graduate school at Columbia University in New York, where I still live with my husband on the West Side, freelancing for several magazines and writing fiction.

It was here, only a few weeks ago, that I last saw Lily, now a prominent feminist scholar. She was in town for the MLA convention. We went to a little bistro near my apartment for lunch, lingering over wine far into the late December afternoon while my husband babysat. Lily was in the middle of a divorce. "You know," she said at one point, twirling her tulip wineglass, "I have often thought that the one great tragedy of my life was never getting to meet your brother. Somehow I always felt that he and I were just meant for each other." We sat in the restaurant for a long time, at the window where we could see the passersby hurrying along the sidewalk in the dismal sleet outside, each one so preoccupied, so caught up in his own story. We sat there all afternoon.

The Fishing Lake

She was crossing the edge of the field, along the ridge, walking with a longer, more assured step now; she knew just about where he was. She knew because she had seen the jeep parked just off the road, where it got too soggy to risk and too narrow to go through without a limb batting you between the eyes, and she stopped the car about a stone's throw back from there. Something told her all along he would be at the lake. She cleared the ridge, and there he was just below her, down at the pier, tying up the boat. He didn't look up. She eased herself sidewise down the wet, loamy bank that released the heavy smell of spring with every step, and she was within a few feet of him before he said, still not looking up, "There ought to be a better boat down here. I spent half the time bailing. There used to be another boat."

"I think that's the same one," she said. "It's just that things get run down so in a little while. I bet the Negroes come and use it; there's no way to keep them from it."

"It's got a lock on it."

"Well, you know, they may just sit in it to fish. Either that or let the children play in it."

He had found the mooring chain now; it grated through the metal hook in the prow and he snapped the lock shut and stepped out on the pier.

"Did you catch anything?"

He leaned down and pulled up a meager string – two catfish, a perch, one tiny goggle-eye. "The lake needs draining and clearing the worst kind. All around the bend there's the worst kind of silt and slime. The stink is going to get worse." He paused. "Or maybe you'd say that I'm the stinker."

"I didn't say that. I didn't say anything about it."

He stood with his back to her, hands hooked on his thighs, like somebody in the backfield waiting for the kickoff, and his hair, still streaked with color – sunburned, yellow and light brown – made him seem a much younger man than he would look whenever he decided to turn around. "I would tell you that I'm going to quit it," he said, "but you know and I know that that just ain't true. I ain't ever going to quit it."

"It wasn't so much getting drunk. . . . I just thought that coming home to visit Mama this way you might have put the brakes on a little bit."

"I intended to. I honestly did."

"And then, if you had to pick somebody out, why on earth did you pick out Eunice Lisles?"

"Who would you have approved of?" he asked. He looked off toward the sunset; it was delicate and pale above the tender, homemade line of her late uncle's fishing lake, which needed draining, had a leaking boat and a rickety pier.

"Well, nobody," she said. "What a damn-fool question. I meant, by the cool, sober light of day, surely you can see that Eunice Lisles – "

"I didn't exactly pick her out," he said. "For all I know, she picked me out." He lit a cigarette, striking the kitchen match on the seat of his trousers. He began to transfer the tackle box, the roach box, the worm can, and the minnow bucket from the boat to the pier. He next took the pole out of the boat and began to wind off the tackle. "Where we made our big mistake is ever saying we'd go out. We came to Mississippi to see your mother, we should have stayed with your mother."

"Well, I mean if it gets to where we can't accept an invitation — "

"It hasn't got to where anything," he said irritably. "I'm exactly the same today as I was yesterday, or a year ago. I'm a day or a year older, I've got a hangover worse than usual. And I would appreciate never having to hear anything more about Eunice Lisles."

Her uncle had made a bench near the pier — a little added thought, so very like him. It was for the older ladies to sit on when they brought their grandchildren or nieces and nephews down to swim, and he had had a shelter built over it as well, to shade their heads from the sun, but that had been torn down, probably by Negroes using it for firewood. She remembered playing endlessly around the pier when one of her aunts or her grandfather or Uncle Albert himself brought her down there, and at twilight like this in the summer seeing the men with their Negro rowers come back, solemn and fast, almost processional, heading home from around both bends in the lake, shouting from boat to boat, "Whadyacatch? Hold up yo' string! Lemme *see* 'em, man!" The men would have been secret and quiet all afternoon, hidden in the rich, hot thicket quiet of the brush and stumps, the Negroes paddling softly, holding and backing and easing closer, with hardly a ripple of the dark water. Then, at supper up at Uncle Albert's, there would be the fish dipped in corn meal, spitting and frying in the iron skillets and spewing out the rich-smelling smoke, and platter after platter of them brought in to the table. You ate till you passed out in those days, and there wasn't any drinking to amount to anything — maybe somebody sneaking a swallow or two off out in the yard. Her husband always told her she was wrong about this, that she had been too young to know, but she was there and he wasn't, she said, and ought at least to know better than he did. What she really meant was that her family and their friends and relatives had been the finest people thereabouts, and were noted for their generosity and fair, open dealings, and would never dream of getting drunk all the time, in front of people. He might at least have remembered that this was her hometown.

She sat down carefully now on what was left of the bench her uncle had made. She opened her bag. "I brought you something." It was a slug of her sister-in-law's Bourbon she had poured into a medicine bottle, sneaking as though it were a major theft, and adding a bit of water to the whiskey bottle to bring the level up again, nearly to where it was. She knew that all the family had their opinions. In the house she had kept as quiet as death all day, and so had they. The feeling was that gossip was flying around everywhere, just past the front gate and the back gate, looping and swirling around them.

"That was nice of you. By God, it was." He began to move methodically, slowly, holding back, but his sense of relief gave him a surer touch, so the top of the tackle box came clanging down in a short time, and he came up beside her, taking the small bottle and unscrewing the top. "Ladies first." He offered it to her. She laughed; he could always make her laugh, even if she didn't want to. She shook her head, and the contents of the bottle simply evaporated down his throat. "That's better." He sat companionably beside her; they had to sit close together to get themselves both on the bench.

"I reckon you feel like you get to the end of your rope sometimes," he sympathized. "I think maybe you might."

She had too much of a hangover herself to want even to begin to go into detail about what she felt.

"I don't feel any different toward you," he went on. "In fact, every time you do something like today – go right through your family without batting an eye, steal their whiskey for me out from under their noses, and come down here to get your fussing done in private – I love you that much more. I down-right admire you."

She said, after a time, "You know, I just remembered, coming down here up past the sandpit that Uncle dug out to sand the lake with so we could swim without stepping ankle-deep in mud, there was this thing that happened. . . . I did it; I was responsible for it. I used to go there in the afternoons to get a suntan when we used to come and stay with Uncle Albert. And back then they had this wild dog – they thought for a long time it was a cooter, or some even said a bear – but it turned out to be a wild dog, who used to kill calves. So one day I was lying there sun-bathing and I looked up and there was the dog – that close to the house! It scared me half to death. I just froze. I went tight all over and would have screamed, but I couldn't. I remembered what they said about not getting nervous around animals because it only frightens them, so I didn't say anything and didn't move, I just watched. And after a while, just at the top of the hill where the earth had been busted open to get at the sand, the dog lay down and put its head on its paws – it must have been part bulldog – and watched me. I felt this peaceful feeling – extremely peaceful. It stayed there about an hour and then it went away and I went away. So I didn't mention it. I began to doubt if it had really seen me, because I heard somewhere that dogs' vision is not like humans', but I guessed it knew in its way that I was there. And the next time I went, it came again. I think this went on for about a week, and once I thought I would go close enough to pat its head. I had got so it was the last thing I'd ever be scared of, but when it had watched me climb to within just about from here to the end of the pier away from it, it drew back and got up and backed off. I kept on toward it, and it kept drawing back and it looked at me – well, in a personal sort of way. It was a sort of dirty white, because of a thin white coat with blue markings underneath. It was the ugliest thing I ever saw.

"Then it killed some more calves, and they had got people out to find it, and more showed up when the word got round, bringing their guns and all, and there was almost a dance on account of it, just because so many people were around. A dollar-pitching, a watermelon-cutting – I don't know what all. I was only about fifteen, and I told on it."

"*Told* on it?"

"Yes, I said that if they would go down to the sandpit at a certain time they would see it come out of the woods to the top of the hill on the side away from the house. And they went out and killed it."

"That's all?"

"That's all."

"And that's the worst thing you ever did?"

"I didn't say that. I mean, I felt the worst about it afterwards."

"You might have thought how those poor calves felt."

"I thought of that. It's not the same thing. The link was me. I betrayed him."

"You worry about this all the time?" He was teasing, somewhat.

"I hadn't thought of it in ten or maybe even fifteen years, until today, coming along the ridge just now. You can still see the sandpit."

At that moment, the bench Uncle Albert had built to make those long-dead ladies comfortable collapsed. They had been too heavy to sit on it, certainly, and shouldn't have tried. As though somebody had reached out of nowhere and jerked a chair from under them, just for a joke, it spilled them both apart, out on the pier.

They began to laugh. "Come out here next year," he said, in his flat-talking Georgia way, "there ain't going to be one splinter hanging on to one nail. Even the bailing can's got a hole rusted in it."

She kept on laughing, for it was funny and awful and absolutely true, and there was nothing to do about it.

$\mathcal{M}$ A X $\mathcal{S}$ T E E L E

~~~~~~~~~~~~~~~~~~~~~~~

The Hat of My Mother

My mother, if she were alive today, would be ninety years old, my father a hundred. In the forty years they were married, my mother spent only one night away from home without him and that was the day she was kidnapped.

To understand how a woman like her could be taken away, you would need to understand how deeply she believed in manners. Manners and courage, she felt, would take one safely through any situation. Once, for instance, during the Depression, a terrible-looking white man, tattooed and scarred, appeared at our back door and demanded food, good food, not any corn bread scraps and hominy, he wanted a full meal. My mother stood close to the screen door, locking it while holding his eyes steadily with hers and saying: "Why certainly, but you must come around to the dining room off the side porch, we never serve anyone in the kitchen."

She stood in the bay window of the dining room and

watched him pull on the door which had not been opened all summer. The porch roof had been leaking, and the tongue-and-groove porch floor had swollen and buckled. "Now," she said, firmly through the window, "I don't believe I know you, do I? I don't remember ever seeing your face or hearing your name before."

He allowed, in a Northern industrial accent, as how he didn't give a damn for the South and such formalities, that it was food and plenty of it he was after.

"Perhaps you have the wrong house," she said. "Maybe I should call the police. I'm sure they'd be glad to help you find your friends."

The sanity in her voice and the calmness in her eyes brought sanity to his face. He stepped back, blinked at the door, surveyed the porch, said he believed she was right, he didn't remember any side porch, but not to bother, the house he was looking for must be on the next block over. He stepped back down the steps and she walked quickly and locked the front door while watching him running across the lawn and down the gravel drive and through the grillwork gate beyond the boxwoods.

She had often hired worse-looking men to cut the grass, dig up the garden, or do any sort of outside work, and had never had any trouble with anyone except my father, who was not so sure that good manners were all the protection one needed in a Southern town which had grown so large he could no longer identify everyone in it by sight or hearsay. With the cigarette factory laying off, there were some mean-looking drifters arriving every day and angry they'd come so far to work when there was no work.

My mother, though, was supremely confident in her own home. Outside of it she became a different person: an actress who hid her natural shyness by a graceful, but not haughty, upward tilt of her chin and a way of walking usually reserved for aisles. Ladies, after a certain age, she felt should be seen at church, if they liked going to church, which she didn't, weddings if the bride was the daughter of a close relative or friend, and funerals of those few people one had known twenty years or longer. Funerals and weddings of prominent people were to be avoided. "If you wouldn't be among the first twenty-five asked, you don't belong there." In such cases she "sent": flowers, food, and any handmade object. But the present should represent a sacrifice of time, or money, or thought. New clothes were to be worn several times at home before being worn in public. In that way they did not seem "new" and one could be quite at ease and natural in them. In general she disliked anything that was for the purpose of impressing others or calling attention to oneself.

Her one exception was an indulgence in hats. Because of the special angle and tilt of her head and her rather handsome profile, she wore hats well. She bought few of them but they were expensive and they lasted ten and twenty and sometimes thirty years. Somewhere I have read that women always retain in their style some aspect of dress which was in fashion during the time of their first or greatest love. My mother and father were married in 1910 and she retained always, especially in her summer hats, something of the Gibson Girl aspect. Soon after the First World War she had bought an extremely becoming one, broad-brimmed and almost all flowers which, except for once or twice a year, stood with her two other hats in her hat closet.

In 1933 the hat was so old and so much a trademark that it was a joke in the family. The year before she had promised my father to replace it, and on one spring visit to town she had tried to buy a new one and had not found another one well-made enough to have trimmed. When she returned that day to put on her ancient hat she could not find it, and Mr. Ramsey and all the salespeople were embarrassing her by the fuss they were making in their search for it. She had slipped out of the store and there in the window was her twelve-year-old hat where the new window dresser was featuring it in a display.

The following year, the year she was kidnapped, she promised my father again that she would replace it. Mr. Ramsey had told her there was a lady in town who would know how to trim one properly if she could find one the shape she liked.

My mother shopped twice a year at the oldest stores. Once in August for school clothes for the younger children, and once at Mardi Gras to buy materials for the older girls' Easter clothes. Her shopping, even on those two occasions when she would venture downtown, was done largely over the telephone. For a week or so before each outing, she would telephone the few stores which she felt still carried items of quality and would ask to speak to the owner of the store or to one of the oldest salespeople. She would say: "Mrs. Henley, I am going to be coming in on Tuesday, and I wonder if you could have some wool challis to show me in a houndstooth or in a solid Cambridge grey." Or: "Mr. Hodges, this is Mrs. B. F. Russell. Last fall when I was in, you said you had ordered some French kid gloves such as you used to carry." Many of the things she ordered were imported and hard to find, but in the long run, because they lasted forever, not as expensive as "stylish, thrown-together-for-the-moment" clothes. We did not have many clothes and we hated them from the beginning because they would last and be handed down and down and down.

But that Tuesday morning in late March, her telephone shopping done, my mother opened the door for Mrs. Honeycutt, which we all thought was a fine name for a dressmaker. Mrs. Honeycutt whistled, very unladylike, through the gap in her front teeth, as she brought in her sewing machines, scissors, baskets and cushions and special chair. She set up shop in the alcove upstairs. We were allowed to go into the sewing attic and roll the dressmaker dummies down the long hall to her and to help her set up the ironing boards and sewing tables. My mother brought out button boxes and old dresses from which the laces and furs and buttons were to be removed. She would be leaving Mrs. Honeycutt with enough work to keep her busy this first day of a sewing week.

Before the Depression my father had always sent a car to take my mother to town; later she had called cabs; but today she was going by streetcar. Regardless of how she travelled to town, she always walked the two miles home. She shopped only at stores that still delivered and therefore never carried any packages.

It was always a moment of adventure when she finally walked across the porch, still giving instructions to the cook and to each of the children about what was to be accomplished and what left undone during her absence. This morning she was especially cheerful and promised to return with a new hat. She was very much against spending the money she had saved (in a basket in the hat closet) for a hat when we needed so many other things. But after all, she had been putting odd change there for more than six years and if that was what everyone wanted most she would do it. She wore a black cloche and carried the old flowered hat with her to find another as much like it as possible. She planned as usual to walk home.

Late that afternoon my father was sitting on the porch, pretending to read the paper, but looking up constantly to see if he could see her rounding the corner and coming into sight. There was a thunderstorm in the air and he was a little worried. The rain began and he ran immediately to the drive and drove off looking for her.

He came back after going only to the streetcar stop. "She'll have sense enough to get inside," he said. The storm lasted until dark and she was still not home. My father began walking through the house from room to room. And then he began telephoning every store he knew she might have been in. Some of them were closed already and he called the owners at their homes. Finally he learned that she had left Hodges and Swensons to find a French woman who lived in the old Mayberry Smith house and trimmed hats. My father could not find the number and so rushed off again to fetch my mother.

He came home alone. Between then and the time we were

sent to bed at nine he was in and out of the house, phoning, demanding that various proprietors reopen their stores to see if by chance she had been locked in a dressing room. He found the man who had sold her a hat and had sent her on her way to the French milliner. Before three-thirty that afternoon. Only two blocks from the store. Within those two blocks she had disappeared. My father, at one moment furious and the next dead-white, called the police. He then sent us off to our rooms. We were to be asleep when she got home. Just as if nothing had happened. That, he was saying in a miserable voice, was what she would want.

The next morning we were waked, as usual, at seven. My father was already up and dressed and walking about the house, grinning, talking, laughing. The dining room smelled of hot biscuits and ham. The cook was singing in the kitchen, and Mrs. Honeycutt was having breakfast on a tray in the sewing alcove. My mother, in the clothes she had worn to town the day before, was sitting at her desk, counting little piles of change, and sorting bills, and sipping her early morning tea.

One by one, as we came down, we asked if she had really been kidnapped, if my father had found her, when had she gotten home, how had she gotten home, had the police found her, and did she have a new hat? To all these questions my mother said: "I will tell you when we're all ready to sit down."

Seated, she at one end of the table, my father at the bay window end, two children on one side, three on the other, she said she would tell it once, and then she did not want to hear any more about it ever from any of us, and certainly she had better not ever hear of it from anyone outside the family. She looked each of us directly in the eye and we each nodded. It was understood: no one would speak of it again. She began by waiting for my father to quit smiling and then she began in a quick, reasonable voice, to recite her story:

I shopped awhile at Hodges and Swensons where the streetcar let me out and saw Mrs. Jones at Pride and Patton and then went on down to have the setting secured on my ring at Hellam's, and told them I'd be back after lunch to pick it up. And then I crossed over and did some shopping on the sunny side and spoke to Mrs. Latham and had lunch at a tea room in the Farmer's Bank Building, the small room where I used to do my banking, but apparently now men and women are all going to bank together.

After lunch I walked a bit, just noticing all the changes, how many of the beautiful old homes have been torn down and how many ugly little one story buildings are being put up with those ordinary plate glass fronts, and with doors stuck over to the side, and all the strange-looking people on the street, not a soul I knew by sight and remembering when I would at least be able to nod to someone on every block.

I had told Mr. Ramsey I would be in to look at hats between two-thirty and three and he was busy when I went in but didn't keep me sitting but a few minutes and then he started having his girls bring out hats and try them on, nothing I would have worn. I showed him my flowered hat, what I had in mind, and he laughed and said yes, yes, indeed he remembered it and so did the window dresser and he knew that was what I had been wanting and that was what he was saving to show me. Then with a great to-do he had one of the girls go back to the shipping department and bring in a box that hadn't yet been opened. He took it himself and cut the cord and unwrapped the parcel in such a way as to save the foreign-looking stamps and labels, and opened it up and brought it out from the tissue. Well!

Well, I wish you could have seen it, it really was beautiful, and I laughed and said Oh, Mr. Ramsey, it is lovely, but I'm twenty years too late for it. Maybe one of my daughters in a few years. And he said not at all not at all and wouldn't I try it on. I said just to see how it sits. Which of course was a mistake.

Mr. Ramsey has no sense of style. He tilted it down over

one eye and I looked a fool and a hundred years old. And I said, oh, no, Mr. Ramsey, it is lovely but it won't do. But then I set it flat on my head, the line cutting straight across my brow and there was nothing frivolous about it. It was quite distinguished. Almost severe in spite of all the flowers, which weren't, I'm glad to say, gaudy. Sweet flowers, violets, and rose buds and small white and yellow flowers, so close one couldn't see the straw, not even at the edge of the broad brim. I must say it was most distinctive and I knew I could never wear my old one again after seeing such a creation.

Mr. Ramsey said he thought it was really aristocratic look-ing and I said I could not help agreeing but still it was too young for me. And he just kept saying no, no, and the girls kept saying no, no in a way that convinced me, I could see the admiration in their eyes, and they called in another girl who said it could not be more becoming and by then I had an idea I would take it, if I could afford it.

"It was your money," my father said. "Saved for how long?"

I didn't think I had enough money even with all I had saved, and I really hadn't meant to spend but half of it on a hat. I could see the London label and Mr. Ramsey was talking about the French woman who lived on the next block down, in the Mayberry Smith house, who trimmed hats and who could take off a bow which really was excessive and maybe she could fill it in with one of the extra flowers, you know how they send extra flowers with those hats. And I thought what all we really needed, but how I had promised myself a hat and hadn't had one in a dozen years and so I said: all right, I'll take it if it can all be done today. He telephoned the French woman while I waited and she said she could do it that afternoon if I brought it in before four o'clock and I said in that case I'd take it along and he could send my old hat today with my other packages. It even depressed me to put back on that black cloche.

"Madame Rosay," my father said.

"What?" my mother asked as if he were calling her names.

"The French lady. Her name is Madame Rosay. That's who

Mr. Ramsey put me in touch with last night. When I talked to her she said you never got there."

"I didn't," my mother said.

She sipped some tea and buttered a corner of toast and looked at him as if for the first time in a year. They seldom looked directly at each other and when they did there was always a moment of silence in which the children felt left out of some secret. "I had no idea I would be so late. So really late. You must have been . . . in any case, I'm glad I wasn't here to see you."

He nodded as if she understood and had even seen him pacing the house, driving in and out the drive, and telephoning, telephoning.

"But I did keep trying to telephone home. Every chance when their backs were turned. But the line stayed busy. . . ."

"I was phoning everyone I knew and finally the police. . . ."

"It's all right," she said, glancing about the table at each of us. "No one need know he called the police except if one of you should tell and you've given me your promise. . . ."

"I don't see why you're so sensitive about your feelings when your own children went to bed not knowing whether you were alive or buried somewhere in a shallow grave by those yardmen you hire."

"Don't mention graves to me," my mother said, and then as if she were determined to be cheerful said, "It was really the only other hat I've ever seen that looked better on me and made me feel so young."

Then she went on: I started out of the store with it, thinking I'd not put it back in the box since I was only going a few doors down. At first I didn't notice there were a few drops of rain, and I was holding it in my hands like a cake, and I thought it's only a step and there are awnings halfway there. But then the drops seemed heavier and without looking I thought it was the Mayberry Smith house already and I would just duck out from under the awnings and straight up the steps to the porch and that's what I did.

A young girl, not more than fifteen, met me at the door the second I set foot on the porch and said, "Oh, you've come to see Grandmother." She took my hat and naturally I assumed I was at the right place and turned my hat over to her and she said, "It's beautiful," and then she said, "Won't you come in and speak to Mother." Very good, plain country manners. You know when we moved to town my mother said we'd never see lovely manners such as those we were leaving, but here this girl had just that nice, plain air about her and showing me into the parlor as if I were the grandest sort of company instead of someone coming to have a hat trimmed.

Well, I looked about and realized I was not in the Mayberry Smith house and then it took me only one minute to realize what was going on. The whole family was arranged in chairs and sofas along the walls, all dressed in the best black they could scrape together, and a woman about my age stood up, and all the men stood up, and the girl handed the woman my hat and said, "It's for Grandmother."

"Oh!" The woman said, choking up immediately. "How unusual. How perfectly beautiful. Won't you come and see her?"

Whether I wanted to or not, she took my elbow on one side, and a young man took me by the elbow on the other and they steered me through an archway to the coffin, and there lay a perfect stranger, a woman I'd never seen in my life. I wanted to turn and run, but then I thought, no, I'm not so busy that I can't spare a few minutes to be decent. There were one or two timid-looking relatives in that room, and the mother said: "Let's place it here," and they put my hat on the coffin. There were one or two pitiful sprays there, one of carnations with a sleazy satin bow, and one homemade one with early forsythia and a sort of white flower I haven't seen since I was a girl which would have been nice if they'd left off the rayon ribbons. And then my hat. Well, I thought, I'll sit long enough to show my respect and then when I leave I'll just go put the hat on and thank them. But then I touched my forehead and realized I had on my black cloche and then's when the tears came to my eyes. They saw the tears and started making a fuss over the hat, calling it a wreath, and trying to distract me out of politeness, and saying how it put the live flowers to shame and certainly Grandmother would be proud.

The woman my age introduced herself as Anita Dobson and then introduced all of them to me and I kept looking at the old lady in the coffin and wanting to cry, the situation I'd got myself in. But Mrs. Dobson was saying: "Where did you know her?"

I thought I'd say I used to stop and chat with her on the porch but the truth was I couldn't remember ever seeing anyone on any porch on that part of Main Street, and now I wasn't even sure which house I was in, who had ever lived here, it all seemed so turned around. And I thought, well, it never does any harm to mention church and so I said, "Church." After that there was no way out.

"I knew it," Anita said, "one of Mama's Sunday School girls."

I nodded and the tears must have been coming down my cheeks then because she offered me her handkerchief and I nodded no and took out mine and when she put her arm around me we stood there and had a good cry. Just a real good cry. Six years of savings gone.

"Oh," the young girl said, "you're the only one of them who has come and we were hoping at least one of them would."

And Mrs. Dobson said, "But it's been so many years since she was able to teach we didn't really think any of them would remember her."

I said, "I don't think I'll ever forget her." And I don't think I will.

While we sat there, waiting, I know now for the undertakers (the Mauldin Brothers, wouldn't you know they'd have the Mauldins) I learned that it was a Mrs. Ralph Carruthers who was dead and that she was eighty-four and they were, just as I suspected, from up-country, not far from my own grandmother's place, and that they hadn't lived in town long enough for the old lady to make any friends of her own and that not many of them knew many people here and that they hoped more would be at the church and that I certainly would come along to the church with them, wouldn't I?

I couldn't very well ask what church and by that time the hearse was there and the Mauldin brothers and men folks were rolling the coffin through the living room and before I had time to stand up and say "My hat," they were already going across the front porch with it, and down those side steps.

I thought, well, it wouldn't do me any harm to go to church every now and then, and I wouldn't be much farther from home than now no matter which church in town. There's not one I couldn't walk home from and I said, yes, I intended going to the church but that I had wanted to stop by and pay my respects first. They all were kissing me again and saying I must ride with the family, they had engaged two cars but they had other cars, cousins and such and in any case, they wanted me to sit in the front car with the family, and so there I marched out with them, straightening my gloves and dabbing at my eyes, as if I were one of them. They must never find out.

My mother glanced about the table at us and at my father who was grinning so proudly at her he looked drunk.

So, off we went! The hearse moving out and then us and cars stopping and the policemen directing us through the traffic lights, and everything else but us coming to a complete halt, and between the shoulders of the Mauldin sons I could see the hearse up ahead with the two sprays and my hat and it was one of the saddest thoughts in the world that a woman could die with no more recognition than that and I almost decided I wouldn't try to get the hat back at the end of the service.

First I thought, because we were going up Kirkpatrick Street that it would be at the A.R.P. Presbyterian Church, and then when they drove past that I thought, it's going to be the St. Paul's Methodist out on Betts Place, and when we drove on past Betts Place without turning I knew I would have to telephone your office and ask you to send for me. It had quit raining for a spell now and then I realized we were going faster than a funeral procession should, we were in the outskirts then, past all those used-car places, and it was open country on each side and I didn't know how to phrase it, but I finally said: "Oh, you're going to the *old* church."

Mrs. Dobson said yes. And the granddaughter said that that was where the old lady wanted to be buried from, where she'd married: "Ebeneezer." You know there's an Ebeneezer on every country road in South Carolina and I didn't have sense enough to be worried.

We drove and we drove and we drove. It seemed to me an hour at least and then the man in the hearse stopped, in the middle of open country, and signalled, and our driver went up and talked to him and came back and reported very respectfully he would stop in Tryon, North Carolina. He was having trouble with his windshield wipers and didn't want to be driving on mountain roads without them. Tryon! There was a phone in the garage. That's the first time I called. It was already after five o'clock and not an answer at your office and of course this line was busy.

So there was nothing to do but get back in and in a way I'm glad I did. (The service was planned for six o'clock and the Mauldin brothers apologized for driving so fast but all arrangements had been made for the church and we mustn't be late.) It was one of the finest sermons I've heard preached. They just don't preach like that anymore, I imagine. It was good, honest, country preaching. For awhile I thought he was going to be one of those men who would shout too much but he kept his voice just inside breaking. And I sat there with the family, and I'm glad because there weren't more than a handful of people in the church, each coming up with a little handful of homegrown flowers, in fruit jars wrapped in tinfoil, and all of them seeming a bit shy as they placed them next to my hat. It made me ashamed. What the preacher said made me ashamed of feeling so possessive and materialistic. (I kept thinking, even if I don't get it back at the graveside, it's been put to good use.) Vanity, vanity.

At the end of the service Mrs. Dobson said, "You will go to the graveyard with us." Well, naturally, I thought she meant the one right outside, or the new part across the road in the cedar grove, and I said, "Yes." I didn't have any way of leaving anyway. The rented family cars and the Mauldin brothers had gone back during the hour-long service and the men in the hearse were the only ones going on.

So we all crowded into one of the old cars parked there and still thinking we might just be going to the back of the cedar grove I didn't mind being crowded.

But the hearse pulled out and we pulled out, the rain still spattering, and headed straight toward the mountains. "Where is she to be buried?" I asked.

"At her home place. There's a family graveyard there," the granddaughter answered. Mrs. Dobson was crying again.

"Her home place," I wept. "Yes. She loved it so much."

Mrs. Dobson put her hand over mine and squeezed it but I still had no idea we were going all the way across the Tennessee state line till I saw a sign saying: "Rock City, Tennessee." I knew then I wouldn't be home before midnight and so I said I simply would need to stop and make a call and that's when I called the second time and the line was still busy here so I called Mrs. Honeycutt's sister.

"Why didn't you call one of the neighbors?"

"And have the whole neighborhood know I was way up in Tennessee without your father? It already dark. What could they have thought?"

"She didn't get the message to us until ten o'clock," my father said.

"By ten o'clock we already had the body in the living room of the Carrutherses' old house," my mother said. The grave was already open but they weren't going to bury her until sunrise. There was to be a sitting-up, but the men in the hearse said they were coming back and I asked if I could ride with them. I got in and we drove back to put a canvas over the open grave and in the headlights of the hearse I could see what those men had done. They'd planted all those little jars of flowers in the red mud piled up by the grave, and there at the head, in the pouring down rain, was my hat stuck up on one of those tacky little stands they use for wreaths.

"Why did you?" I asked the driver. He wanted to know what and I said, "Why did you put the flowers at the grave?"

"That's our job, lady," he said. "What we're paid to do."

He dropped a pebble in the grave and listened to it splash while I stared at the ruined flowers on the hat. (No one else had noticed my hat gone any more than I had, we were all so concerned about getting the body across the rotten porch and getting chairs arranged, and eating all the food the neighbors had brought.) I asked the driver if I could ride in back, knowing I'd feel safer back there than I would sitting up front with two strange men. The other man walked me under the umbrella to the back of the hearse, opened the door just as polite as you please, and said, before shutting the door, "Pleasant dreams, lady!"

"And did you have?" my father asked.

"It was one of the most comfortable rides I've ever had. I slept the entire way. The first thing I knew we were parked in front of the house and you were opening the door and it was almost morning. I want you to promise me one thing: when I die. . . ."

"For God's sake!" my father set his coffee cup down with a clatter, threw his napkin on the table, and stood, "Don't even talk about it. It was bad enough . . . waiting . . . seeing you brought home in a hearse. . . ."

I'd never seen tears in my father's eyes before and I'd never seen my mother leave a table without saying a word, but before he reached the bottom step she had her hand on his elbow. I cannot remember ever seeing them touch each other but that one morning as they walked up the stairs, his arm around her waist, her bare head on his shoulder.

~~~~~~~~~~~~~~~~~~~~~~~~~~~

Disasters

We were riding the South Shore in summer. Clattering through the swollen, slow city. It was not yet dark, but the
streetlights were on, angling whitish pools across empty periwinkle sidewalks. Framed stills slipping by, some artist's idea
of a movie, that slow sad twilight time that gives me a chill
(for myself I prefer a good love story, something to cry at).
Inside the coach the passengers said nothing; the rasp of the
wheels was the only sound. The air smelled of 2 A.M. cigarettes
at 8, and the enameled walls glared though the lights were soft
yellow. I was sleepy from beer. The stubby plush scratched;
our clothes were clammy with afternoon sweat.

"Nice day?" Jesse smiled at me, and I nodded. We were
quiet. The train rattled on. "Pretty locust," he said. Green fingers of alianthus slid past.

"It's a tree of heaven," I said. "Didn't you ever read *A Tree
Grows in Brooklyn?*" But he knew nothing of city trees, nothing of Drexel off Sixty-third, of three-flat buildings, of Mrs.
Sibulic and her apartment pigs, of green wood fences with
four-by-fours in diamond position, of hot summer evenings

with screenless windows and whirring fans, the blades dusty and greased, of street games and vacant lots, of the Good Humor Man or the Cubs, of WLS bouncing off buildings, of vacant tenements and torn windows, of brick walls seen from the El where someone long ago had written SUICIDE.

I closed my eyes. When I had come north from college on the Greyhound, a great gray cloud hung just ahead of the Kankakee River on Highway 41; inside this cloud I grew up. When asked where I am from, I always say Chicago, and in truth I was born there, lived there until my fifth year. Later, with a parade of boyfriends I went back, sipped espresso before midnight movies, drank crazy rum concoctions, danced till dead at the Gate of Horn, and later still, after Mister Kelly's and the Cafe Bellini burned down, we moved north (with the action) to Old Town and Second City. And now, with Jesse, another return, to find the action gone still north of that, Old Town just a bunch of boarded-up buildings and strip joints; so we wandered up Wells and sat on the steps of the Lincoln Park beach.

While we still lived in Chicago, my parents had friends who lived not far from Lincoln Park, and the friends had a daughter not much older than I. We visited them and all went to the zoo, but first the daughter showed me her block. The streets were wide, but I remember no traffic, just pale empty streets, the sun-washed color of stucco. At her corner a few stragglers hung at the lamp post. ". . . accident . . ." we heard, but the cars and ambulance were gone, nothing left in the vacant khaki sun. ". . . terrible . . ." we heard, "woman. . . ." They said her lips were still in the street; I imagine them red but bloodless, gracing the gutter with broken glass and the car's bent emblem. We were little girls in plaid cotton dresses, we hurried on, we didn't look. Still I think sometimes about those cut-out carmine lips in the street (ridiculous, we must have heard wrong), and I think if I'd seen them Chicago would somehow be forever my city. I grew up in Hammond, Indiana.

What do I remember? Oh, freight trains, tracks, heavy

winter skies. Yellow brick cocktail lounges dark through the doors, glass-block windows so thick no light could get through. Friends whose fathers stoked fires in the mills. Brown shingle houses with grimy trim, salt-rotted fenders crumpled on cars, dirt skimming the snow. The first Hammond supermarket, Model's, and a long-gone hamburger joint called Hopper's. State Line Avenue. I once saw a child walking down the Indiana side calling to another on the Illinois side. My dream was to walk down the center of State Line Avenue with one leg in Indiana, the other in Illinois. I moved away and forgot.

I opened my eyes. Chicago was somewhere behind us. The blue land was losing color, going blank, a flat dark marshland beaded with lights that couldn't begin to light it. The yellow coach lights reflected in the thin slick on Jesse's forehead. A few dark curls were damp, he looked handsome and hot, and I loved him and nudged closer to him.

"Were you asleep?" he asked.

"Sort of."

"Don't sleep through our stop. I might miss it."

"I couldn't miss it if I tried."

He smiled and touched my shoulder. "The all-too-familiar, huh? Well, I'll call the garage tomorrow and see how the car is coming."

"It won't be done."

"You don't know."

"It'll never be done," I cried. "We'll be stuck here forever! I'll have to spend the rest of my life in Hammond, Indiana! Oh, I'm so mad at that garage I could die!"

Jesse dropped his hand. "Don't be silly. They can't fix the car without parts."

"Well, if you can't get parts, what do you have it for?"

"Now you're being ridiculous," Jesse said coldly. "Why don't you be quiet? Everyone on the train is looking at us."

Expressionless gray eyes were staring over the back of the next seat, above them a wide baby-skin forehead and spikes of blonde hair. "Oh go jump in a lake." I scowled at the kid, and he was jerked down from our view. "I'm sorry, don't be mad at me."

"It's okay," Jesse said, looking out the black window, finger-smudged. "I know it's not easy to live with relatives, especially yours."

"What do you mean by that?" I asked, but he didn't answer, and we both stared at nothing through the window. "You know what I just thought of?" I asked after a while. "My uncle Angie. When I was little, we always ate Silvercup bread because my uncle Angie worked for the Silvercup Bakery, and, when your uncle worked someplace, you bought that product. We used to go to the Silvercup picnics where they served thousands of sandwiches made with Silvercup bread, and then, later, when my uncle got laid off, we changed breads."

"Oh." He rubbed his forehead. "An uncle named Angie?"

"Oh he was Italian, his name was Angelo, and we called him Angie. He married my father's sister, and they lived in the neighborhood where . . ."

"Is this our stop?" The train was slowing.

I squinted through the window at the dark cement building moving toward us, hung with huge eaves and naked light bulbs, a life-size replica of every toy train station you've seen, except dingy. "That's it."

We stood, holding ourselves by seat backs on the still-moving train, and lurched up the aisle. "Got everything?" he asked. I held out the postcard-sized bag bulging with a fifteen-cent leather shoestring bought at the Dead Cow Boutique (a poor joke, we'd agreed), one of the few shops left in Old Town. "What's there to have?"

"I guess I was thinking of luggage," he admitted as the car snapped to a stop and we jumped down. The station door was locked (every night at 6, the new-policy sign said). In the 60-watt lightpool on the station sidewalk we seemed more than a train trip from the dazzling city that had overwhelmed me at 4 A.M. on Rush Street six or eight years before. Things had moved around, I didn't know where the dazzle was now, everything I showed Jesse was shabby, he had only my word for it. He frowned. "Now what?"

"I guess we have to walk uptown to call a cab."

"Why not call your brother?"

I shook my head.

"Why not?"

"You don't understand. We've never been close."

"What does that have to do with it?"

"My family just doesn't do things for each other."

"So I've noticed." We started walking. "This had better not be far."

We walked past streetlights tatting the land cleared for renewal, crossed a bridge over some dark sludge. I wished we hadn't come. Even more, I wished his damn sports car, which had so impressed me and should have impressed my brother and the same faded, flaccid neighbors who remembered me as the weird one who went off to college, hadn't broken down. My brother shook his head. Foreign cars, give him a Chevy every time. And still more, I wished that Jesse hadn't looked so plainly baffled and beaten as he stared into the puzzle of corroded components. I could have smashed my brother's smile when Jesse mumbled vague pleas into the phone, and I could have smashed Jesse for phoning, for mumbling, for owning a dazzling machine that wouldn't work.

It was supposed to be a short stopover on our way to Jesse's parents in Iowa – they hadn't met their prospective daughter-in-law yet – but here we were, sliding into a second week of silent dinners with my brother and his wife at the chrome and yellow table he'd inherited from my parents when they'd retired to hopelessly dismal St. Petersburg, Florida, and sold him the house I grew up in, complete with the neon doughnut stuck to the kitchen ceiling that brutalized our faces at those same silent meals. My brother was tired; he worked all day. There was dirt beneath his nails that just wouldn't come out, and how was Jesse to know that in the Calumet Region you weren't a man unless you worked in a mill?

I pointed out where the old public library had been, a boxy stone building more stately than big, visited only when some book report was due. It was so like dozens of libraries I'd seen that I couldn't remember one special feature to tell Jesse. It had been replaced by garden apartments strung over asphalt so like all the garden apartments I'd seen that pointing them out seemed hardly worthwhile. "We couldn't have walked here ten years ago," I said. "This used to be a very bad neighborhood."

"Is it a good neighborhood now?"

"No, it's not any neighborhood. See those lights? That's downtown."

The store windows were bright and dead, the doors meshed and barred. The streets were in a wash of mercury vapor, greenish and empty, the scarlet traffic light blinking and clicking like a mindless mechanical strobe. I stepped into a booth, pulled the door half-closed, and balanced the book on the shelf.

"Do you have a dime?"

He shoveled through his pocket. "Maybe you'd like to go get a drink first. We could call a cab from a bar."

"Okay." I dropped the book and shoved the door open. The light went out.

"Where's the nearest bar?"

"Oh."

"What?"

"I was just thinking — when I was a kid Calumet City was famous — strip joints, gambling, bars, stag shows, and all — but they closed it down, and some of it burned, and there's nothing to it now, but it was just around the corner, a couple of blocks down State Street. You must have heard of Cal City, the strip."

"No. Besides, aren't we looking for a nice quiet bar?"

"Yeah, well I guess we'll find one if we walk down to State Line." We walked down State Street, past the bus station and the Goodwill. "There were so many things," I said.

"What things?"

"Oh, around here. Cal City, Chicago. I'll bet you heard of the Our Lady of the Angels fire."

"I might've."

"It happened on my birthday, I don't know, 1957, 1958. Right before afternoon recess the whole school went up in flames, all the kids were trapped. Oh some of them jumped out windows, but most of them were too scared, and some of them just suffocated at their desks. They found a whole class of dead children bent over their open books, it was in the paper with pictures, the prettiest little girl killed, they were all pretty, Italian, such beautiful dark hair and eyes. My Uncle Angie lived in that parish. His kids were older, of course, but they remember how the word went through their school that day, and some of their friends had to drop out and work to help pay hospital bills and funeral expenses. Almost a hundred died, mostly little children, a few nuns. It happened on my birthday, and I read the paper and saw the school pictures of the ones that died. It seemed like I knew them, and I was afraid to go to school, afraid that my school would burn, too, and I'd be killed."

"I think I remember reading about that. I remember a fire in a movie theater that killed hundreds of children."

"I don't remember that," I said, "just Our Lady of the Angels because it was so close to me."

Jesse stopped in front of a dark brick building with a long window slanting toward the yellow door. A pink fluorescent cocktail glass spilled multicolored bubbles like ball bearings. "Is this okay?"

"I guess so. I've never been here."

There were no tables. We sat at a scratched black bar, and I watched a dim version of myself swing my stool in half circles behind the bottles in the mirror. Two men drank quietly and alone, the same kind of beer. At the far end of the bar a couple held hands and whispered, they were middle-aged, and the woman was painted. I sipped a Brandy Alexander. "I was terrified when the Grimes girls were murdered."

"Friends of yours?"

"They lived in Chicago. It was in the paper. They went to an Elvis Presley movie and never came home. Their bodies were found a month later, stabbed with an ice pick."

"Can't we talk about something else?"

"They found a slip that belonged to one of the girls in the possession of a suspect. He said it was a joke, and I said, if that's a joke, what do they find when he's serious? I was in sixth grade. Funny, I don't remember whether he was ever tried and convicted."

He ordered two more drinks.

"The autopsy showed peanuts in their stomachs. They were killed right after the movie."

"You're beginning to get morbid."

"Wasn't it in the Iowa papers?"

"I don't remember if it was. I remember that guy who murdered all those people in Nebraska and took his girlfriend with him."

"Did it scare you?"

"I don't think so. What are we talking about this for, anyway?"

"These are my disasters, things I identify with."

"Why?"

"I just do."

One of the lone men walked over to the jukebox, leaned against it, gripping each side. He was wearing gray work pants, sagging cotton socks. He worked in the mills, I knew. Charlie Pride began to sing, but the man still hung at the jukebox. The couple slid off their stools and danced slowly, elaborately, in the narrow space between the bar and the wall. Jesse watched them.

"Right there, that was entertainment in Iowa, all there was to do summers. We only had one movie, and it was usually Walt Disney. On a big Saturday night maybe you'd drive to Des Moines and see a show."

"I wonder if this bar is run by the Syndicate." I leaned close and whispered. "One of my girlfriends went to one near here once, and the head of the Syndicate bought her a drink. He told her she had nice legs." I giggled. "She said he was probably looking at the barstool." I pointed to my empty glass, and Jesse ordered two more drinks. "You know what the boys used to say to us in junior high? 'Something-something, what a figure, two more legs and you'd look like Trigger.'" I laughed.

"It's 'man oh man,'" Jesse said. "Everyone knows that one."

The bartender was talking to the man who'd come back from the jukebox now. They were discussing baseball scores. The bartender had gone up to Wrigley Field to see a game in the spring, and he was recounting it inning by inning. The man from the mills listened without answering.

"Oh," I said. "I thought maybe it was just special to this area."

Jesse shook his head.

"When I was in college," I said, "my sophomore roommate was at the ice show at the Indianapolis Coliseum when they had that explosion under the stands. Linda wasn't hurt, but hundreds of people were, and over fifty were killed. She was on the opposite side – she saw the bodies flying and everything."

"Will you quit?"

"What?"

"We've been together eight weeks now; all of a sudden I come home with you, and all you can talk about are fires, accidents, murders."

"I'm sorry," I murmured. "Being here just reminds me of those special things. I don't think of them as morbid, but to someone else I suppose they are."

"They sure are," Jesse said. "Come on, finish your drink and call a cab."

We rode home in sleepy silence. The front door of my brother's house let a diamond of light out. In the darkness the block didn't seem so drab. I remembered summer evenings eight and ten years before, that same diamond of light left burning so I wouldn't wake up the house as I stumbled through the door. I remembered the nuzzling breath of the now faceless names of my lovers. I wasn't sad for them because I still loved them, but they had loved me, maybe, and maybe still did, and that thought was sad and sweet and beautiful; but Jesse spoiled it by knocking, and I pulled at his hand and whispered quick, "Do you love me?" My sister-in-law opened the door without speaking and went back to her place on the couch, next to my brother. They were watching TV.

Jesse and I sat in polite silence, our eyes fixed on the TV, our minds somewhere (the same place?) drifting. When the commercial came, my brother looked up and said, "Have a nice day?"

"Sure did," Jesse said. "Saw some of your old haunts."

"Not me," my brother said. "I never go up there."

"Me either," his wife said. "I can't get anyone to take me."

"We stopped off at a bar for a drink," Jesse said, "kind of a nice, quiet place. If we don't get the car back tomorrow, why don't we all go out, have a few beers?"

"Beer in the refrigerator," my brother said, "no need to go out for it."

The program resumed. Jesse and I excused ourselves and went to my old room. I was remembering Mrs. Sibulic and the two baby pigs she kept in her apartment because meat was expensive, until one of them bit her.

"Excuse me," Jesse said, "but your brother pisses the hell out of me."

I was remembering pictures of my mother, younger than I, by Buckingham Fountain, with a girlfriend on the steps of the Field Museum, Science and Industry, the Planetarium, the zoo. I was remembering my mother, who cried for Chicago when we left but never went back because no one would take her. And I was thinking of my mother doing nothing, as I knew that she would, in a fat pink cigar of a house while my father tinkered with cars in a driveway in St. Petersburg, Florida.

"You can't blame him," I said. "That's just my family."

"Well then your whole family pisses me off."

I was sitting on the bed, rubbing my fingers over the faded pink chenille I'd slept under for years and years. I was looking around at the icky blonde furniture that was so familiar, the cute pictures of kittens I'd framed from a magazine when I was seven, much too small for the wall above my dresser, the wall painted an imaginative pink instead of mint green as when I'd lived there, the only hint that my mother had been replaced as lady of the house, and I said, very casual like I'd never lived there at all, "I hate this house."

"He makes no effort," Jesse said. "No one in your family makes any effort at all. All wrapped up in their goddamn empty world, too damn selfish to show any interest in anything."

"If you're putting me down because I didn't have advantages . . ."

"I'm not putting you down," Jesse said in a huff. "I'm certainly not putting you down for that. But you're passive, like the rest of them; you don't make much effort either, living in memories or fantasies, I don't know which. You don't reach out to me, you don't try to know me."

"Do you really think that?"

"Yes, seeing you here, I do."

"Oh," I said and thought for a while, if it might be true, if I might be like that. I thought about my family coming from Chicago and not going back. I thought about my uncle Angie, I thought about the fire. I thought about the dead Grimes girls, I thought about fear. I thought about college, and I thought of the explosion. I thought about that faraway accident and the lips I never saw in the street. I thought about Jesse, and I wanted to know him.

I said: "Tell me the worst thing that ever happened to you," my face sad and limber, ready for grief.

ALICE ADAMS was born in Virginia and grew up in Chapel Hill, North Carolina, where she mostly went to school, before Radcliffe. By now she has lived a long time in California. Her recent books are *After You've Gone* (stories), *Carolina's Daughters* (novel), and *Mexico: Some Travels and Travelers There*. She still thinks of herself as living in Chapel Hill.

MAYA ANGELOU was born in St. Louis, spent the early part of her childhood in Stamps, Arkansas, and then moved with her family to San Francisco. In 1981 she was appointed to a lifetime position as the first Reynolds Professor of American Studies at Wake Forest University in Winston-Salem, North Carolina. In 1987 she was honored with the North Carolina Award in Literature. Her publications have appeared in *Life*, *Cosmopolitan*, *Essence*, *Harper's Bazaar*, and the *New York Times*. She has written film and television productions and made numerous appearances in both media. Angelou is the author of *I Know Why the Caged Bird Sings*; *Just Give Me a Cool Drink of Water 'Fore I Die*; *Gather Together in My Name*; *Oh Pray My Wings Are Gonna Fit Me Well*; *Singin' and Swingin' and Gettin' Merry Like Christmas*; *And Still I Rise*; *The Heart of a Woman*; *Shaker, Why Don't You Sing?*; *All God's Children Need Traveling Shoes*; and *Now Sheba Sings the Song*. *I Shall Not Be Moved*, her most recent book of poetry, was published in 1990.

DAPHNE ATHAS moved at age fifteen from Massachusetts to Chapel Hill, North Carolina, where she attended high school and graduated from the University. Her fourth novel, *Entering Ephesus*, about these years, was cited on *Time's* Ten Best Fiction list of 1971 and was reissued in a 20th Anniversary Classic Edition in 1991. Besides fiction she has written nonfiction, plays, poetry, and essays. Her article "Why There Are No Southern Writers" was named as outstanding nonfiction in the Pushcart Prize Collection of 1984. Her latest book, *Crumbs for the Bogeyman* (1991), is a collection of poetry, and she is presently working on a book of essays.

DORIS BETTS lives in Pittsboro, North Carolina, and teaches in the English department at the University of North Carolina at Chapel Hill. Her books include *Heading West*; *Beasts of the Southern Wild*; *The River to*

Pickle Beach; *The Astronomer and Other Stories*; *The Scarlet Thread*; *Tall Houses in Winter*; and *The Gentle Insurrection*.

LINDA BEATRICE BROWN like many modern writers divides her work between writing and teaching. She has published a prize-winning novel, *Rainbow 'Roun Mah Shoulder*, and many poems and articles. She has taught both as a full-time faculty member — currently at Guilford College — and as a guest lecturer or writer-in-residence at many schools and colleges throughout the state of North Carolina. At fourteen she began writing, publishing first in *Beyond the Blues*, a poetry anthology, when she was only nineteen. After completing high school in Akron, Ohio, she came to Bennett College in Greensboro, where she majored in French and English literature and graduated as valedictorian. She was then awarded a Woodrow Wilson Fellowship to pursue graduate studies at Case Western Reserve. She received her Ph.D. from Union Graduate School, focusing her studies on creative writing and African American literature. She has published poetry in scholarly magazines such as *Black Scholar* and children's magazines such as *Cricket* and is a writing consultant for the National Episcopal Church.

FRED CHAPPELL is a native of the mountains of western North Carolina and has utilized that background in most of the twenty books of fiction and poetry he has published. His latest fiction is a collection of short stories, *More Shapes Than One*; his latest poetry a volume of epigrams, *C*. He teaches English at the University of North Carolina at Greensboro.

ELIZABETH COX lives in Durham, North Carolina, where she teaches creative writing at Duke University. She has published novels, short stories, and poetry. Her first novel, *Familiar Ground*, was published in 1984. *The Ragged Way People Fall Out of Love*, her second novel, was published in 1991, and a paperback was issued in 1992. Her stories have appeared in magazines such as *fiction international*, *Antaeus*, *Crescent Review*, and her story "Land of Goshen" was cited for excellence by Pushcart Press and in *Best American Short Stories* (1981). She has received the North Carolina Arts Fellowship Award in Fiction and fellowships to both Yaddo and MacDowell writers' colonies. She is working on a new novel and a book of short stories.

CHARLES EDWARD EATON was born in Winston-Salem, served as Vice-Consul in Rio, taught creative writing at the University of North Carolina at Chapel Hill, and lived for a number of years in Connecticut. His most recent works are *New and Selected Stories, 1959–1989* and *A Guest on Mild Evenings* (1991), his eleventh collection of poetry and winner of the Roanoke-Chowan Award. He has also received an O. Henry Award and the North Carolina Award for Literature, among others. He now lives in Chapel Hill, North Carolina.

CLYDE EDGERTON was born in Bethesda, North Carolina, near Durham. He attended public schools and the University of North Carolina at Chapel Hill, where he received degrees in English education. He has published four novels – *Raney, Walking Across Egypt, The Floatplane Notebooks, Killer Diller* – and he has an untitled novel in press. In 1989 he was awarded a Guggenheim Fellowship and in 1991 he received a Lyndhurst Prize. He lives in Durham, North Carolina, with his wife, Susan Ketchin, and his daughter, Catherine.

KAYE GIBBONS was born in rural Nash County, North Carolina. She won the American Academy's Sue Kaufman Prize for the best first work of American fiction and the Ernest Hemingway Foundation's Citation for Fiction for her first novel, *Ellen Foster* (1987). Her second novel, *A Virtuous Woman* (1989), was a Literary Guild and Doubleday Book Club selection. The *San Francisco Chronicle* called it "a small masterpiece." She was recently awarded a PEN/Revson Foundation fellowship for *A Cure for Dreams*. Her books have been translated into French, German, Spanish, Swedish, Danish, and Italian.

ALLAN GURGANUS was born in 1947 in Rocky Mount, North Carolina, the son of teachers, farmers, merchants – minor but stubborn gentility. His first novel, *Oldest Living Confederate Widow Tells All*, won the American Academy's Sue Kaufman Prize for the best first work of American fiction. His collection of stories and novellas published as *White People* was awarded the Southern Book Award, the Los Angeles Times Book Prize, and was nominated for the PEN-Faulkner Prize. Gurganus has taught fiction writing at Stanford, Duke, and Sarah Lawrence. He continues to celebrate and chronicle his fictitious Falls, North Carolina, in a new novel, second in the Falls trilogy, begun with *Widow*. The new work,

The Erotic History of a Southern Baptist Church, is due to be published in 1994. Gurganus lives in Manhattan and in Chapel Hill, North Carolina.

RANDALL KENAN was born in Brooklyn, New York, but came to Chinquapin, North Carolina, at six weeks old and stayed there until he went on to the University of North Carolina at Chapel Hill in 1981. He received a degree in English there in 1985. He has been an assistant editor at Alfred A. Knopf, and teaches writing at Sarah Lawrence and Columbia University. He is the author of a novel, *A Visitation of Spirits*, and a collection of stories, *Let the Dead Bury Their Dead*.

JILL McCORKLE grew up in Lumberton, North Carolina and then went to the University of North Carolina at Chapel Hill. After graduation, she went to Hollins College in Virginia where she received a master's degree in the writing program. She is the author of four novels – *The Cheer Leader, July 7th, Tending to Virginia, Ferris Beach* – and one short story collection, *Crash Diet*. She has taught creative writing at University of North Carolina at Chapel Hill and Tufts University. She is married and has two children. Though she has lived away from her native Lumberton for many years and is about to make another big move to Massachusetts, McCorkle's fictional landscape remains close to her southeastern North Carolina roots where she finds a strong sense of place and the manner of speech that comes most naturally to her.

TIM McLAURIN, born in Fayetteville, North Carolina, is the author of two widely praised novels, *The Acorn Plan* and *Woodrow's Trumpet*, and a memoir, *Keeper of the Moon: A Southern Boyhood*. He has done stints as a Marine, a Peace Corps volunteer, and in between as Wild Man Mac, proprietor and star human attraction of a traveling snake show. He now lives in Chapel Hill, North Carolina, with his wife and their two children.

ROBERT MORGAN was born in Hendersonville and grew up on the family farm in Henderson County, North Carolina. Most of his work has been set in the Blue Ridge Mountains. *The Blue Valleys*, a volume of stories, was published in 1989, and *The Mountains Won't Remember Us and Other Stories* in 1992. He won the James G. Hanes Poetry Prize and the North Carolina Award in Literature in 1991, the year his *Green River: New and Selected*

Poems appeared. Since 1971 he has taught at Cornell University. His stories have been reprinted in *New Stories from the South* in 1991 and 1992.

REYNOLDS PRICE, except for four years at the University of Oxford, has lived in North Carolina since his birth in 1933 in Warren County, North Carolina. He has taught at Duke University since 1958. His work includes novels, short stories, poems, plays, essays, and translations. His novel *Kate Vaiden* won the National Book Critics Circle Award in 1986; his ninth novel, *Blue Calhoun*, appeared in 1992; his books have been translated into sixteen languages; and he is a member of the American Academy and Institute of Arts and Letters.

LOUIS D. RUBIN, JR. was born in Charleston, South Carolina, in 1923, grew up there, taught at Hollins College, Virginia, and joined the University of North Carolina at Chapel Hill in 1957, retiring as University Distinguished Professor of English in 1989. In 1982 he founded a publishing house, Algonquin Books of Chapel Hill, retiring as its publisher and editorial director in 1991. He is author and editor of some forty books, including two novels, *The Golden Weather* (1961) and *Surfaces of a Diamond* (1981). His most recent books are *The Mockingbird in the Gum Tree* (1991) and *Small Craft Advisory* (1991). "The St. Anthony Chorale" appeared originally in the *Southern Review* and was reprinted in *Best American Short Stories* for 1981.

DONALD SECREAST was raised in Lenoir, North Carolina, and, having matured in Boone, sees the world through eyes shaped by western North Carolina, where making a living is difficult but the scenery is transcendent, a combination that gives rise to a sort of proletariat mysticism. His first short story collection, *The Rat Becomes Light* (1991), will be followed by *White Trash, Red Velvet* (1993). Secreast has begun two other novels about North Carolina: one takes place in Lenoir and the other in Louisburg. His first novel, an unpublished fantasy/travel book, is about two North Carolina tourists in Peru who get involved with a plot to return the country to the rule of the Incas.

LEE SMITH was born in southwest Virginia but has lived in North Carolina for twenty years and considers it her home. She has written two collections of short stories, *Me and My Baby View the Eclipse* and *Cakewalk*, and eight novels, including *The Devil's Dream, Oral History, Family Linen,* and *Fair and Tender Ladies*. She is the recipient of the 1991 Robert Penn Warren Prize for Fiction and the John Dos Passos Award, among other honors. Currently a professor of English at North Carolina State University and a Fellow at the Center for Documentary Studies at Duke University, she has also taught at the Carolina Friends School and the University of North Carolina. She lives in Chapel Hill, North Carolina.

ELIZABETH SPENCER grew up in Mississippi but as a child North Carolina became her "other state." Her first connections with North Carolina began in the Mississippi summer, during "those pre–air conditioned days" when her mother escaped to Montreat, North Carolina. She currently teaches part-time in the English department at the University of North Carolina at Chapel Hill, another North Carolina connection that began with a month spent as writer-in-residence there in 1969. She is the author of nine novels – *The Night Travellers, The Salt Line, The Snare, No Place for an Angel, Knights and Dragons, The Light in the Piazza, The Voice at the Back Door, This Crooked Way,* and *Fire in the Morning*. Her short story collections are *Jack of Diamonds and Other Stories, Marilee, The Stories of Elizabeth Spencer,* and *Ship Island and Other Stories*.

MAX STEELE lives in Chapel Hill, North Carolina, and for many years directed the creative writing program at the University of North Carolina at Chapel Hill. A former editor of the *Paris Review*, his books include the short story collections *The Hat of My Mother* and *Where She Brushed Her Hair* and the novel *Debby*.

LEE ZACHARIAS is a native of Chicago but moved to North Carolina in 1975 and, except for one year in Princeton, has been there ever since. She is the author of *Helping Muriel Make it Through the Night* (short stories) and *Lessons* (a novel). She teaches at the University of North Carolina at Greensboro and was for ten years editor of the *Greensboro Review*.